SGUISES

CONTENTS

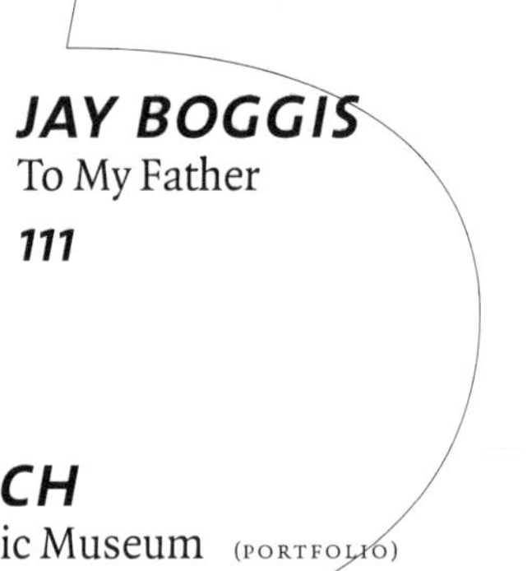

GRAND STREET

GRAND STREET

FRONT COVER Pierre Molinier, *L'Enfant Homme*, 1968/70.
BACK COVER Hannah Höch, *Mother: From an Ethnographic Museum*, 1930.

Grand Street (ISSN 0734-5496; ISBN 1-885490-09-7) is published quarterly by Grand Street Press (a project of the New York Foundation for the Arts, Inc., a not-for-profit corporation), 131 Varick Street, Room 906, New York, NY 10013. Tel: (212) 807-6548, Fax: (212) 807-6544. Contributions and gifts to Grand Street Press are tax-deductible to the extent allowed by law. This publication is made possible, in part, by grants from the National Endowment for the Arts and the New York State Council on the Arts.

Volume Fifteen, Number Two (*Grand Street* 58—Fall 1996).

Second-class postage paid at New York, NY and additional mailing offices. Postmaster: Please send address changes to Grand Street Subscription Service, Dept. GRS, P.O. Box 3000, Denville, NJ 07834. Subscriptions are $40 a year (four issues). Foreign subscriptions (including Canada) are $55 a year, payable in U.S. funds. Single-copy price is $12.95 ($18 in Canada). For subscription inquiries, please call (800) 807-6548.

Grand Street is printed by Hull Printing in Meriden, CT. It is distributed to the trade by D.A.P./Distributed Art Publishers, 636 Broadway, 12th floor, New York, NY 10012, Tel: (212) 473-5119, Fax: (212) 673-2887, and to newsstands only by B. DeBoer, Inc., 113 E. Centre Street, Nutley, NJ 07110 and Fine Print Distributors, 6448 Highway 290 E., Austin, TX 78723. *Grand Street* is distributed in Australia and New Zealand by Peribo Pty, Ltd., 58 Beaumont Road, Mount Kuring-Gai, NSW 2080, Tel: (2) 457-0011, and in the United Kingdom by Central Books, 99 Wallis Road, London E9 5LN, Tel: (181) 986-4854.

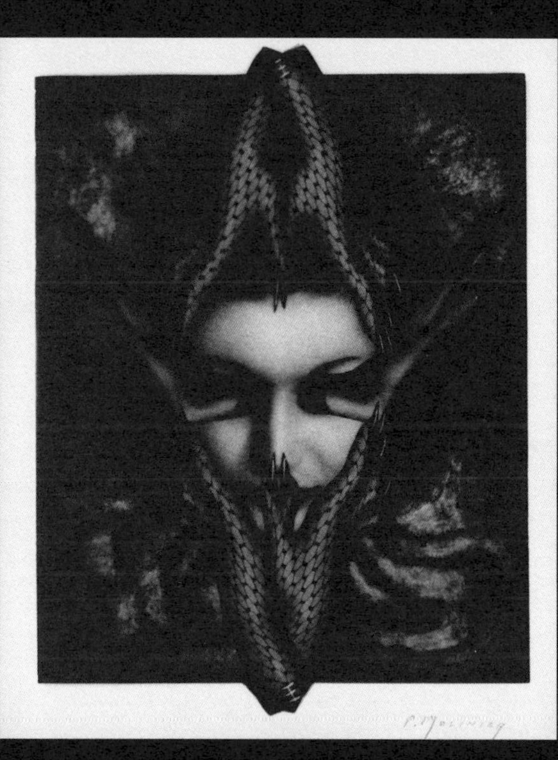

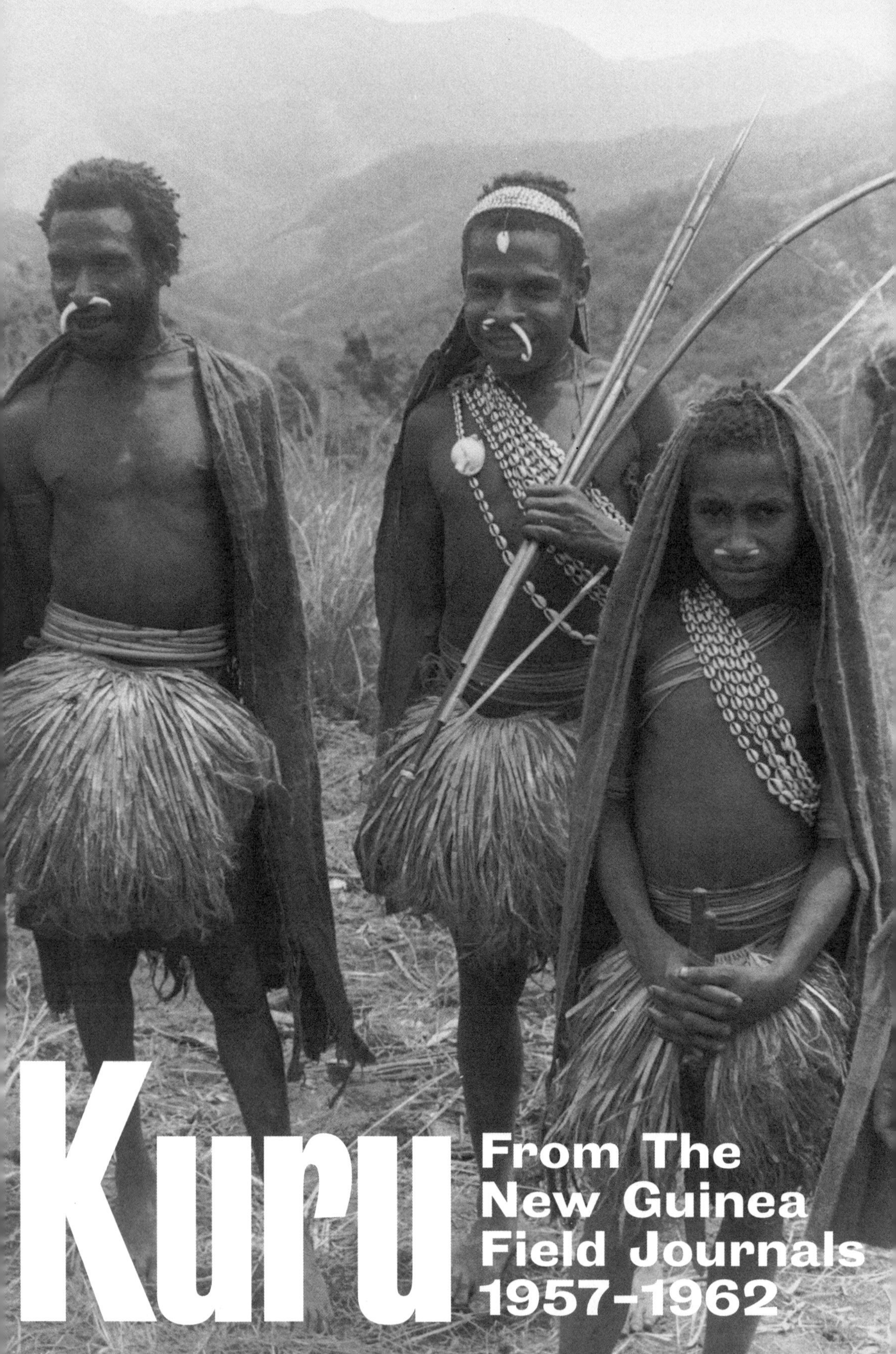

Kuru

From The New Guinea Field Journals 1957-1962

D. CARLETON GAJDUSEK

After having spent 1956 and part of 1957 conducting post-doctoral research in Melbourne, Australia, Carleton Gajdusek traveled to the island of New Guinea to continue a study of child development and disease patterns in primitive and isolated populations that he had begun with the Tarahumara Indians in Mexico, and with isolated ethnic populations in Iran, Afghanistan, the U.S.S.R., New Guinea, and Australia. In New Guinea, Gajdusek encountered reports of a devastating epidemic of a fatal neurodegenerative disease, known to the natives of New Guinea's Eastern Highlands as "kuru"—a native Fore word for "trembling" and "cold." Investigating this disease and conducting far-ranging epidemiological patrols would occupy much of Gajdusek's attention over the following decades. His work on kuru demonstrated slow virus infection of man for the first time, and led to his discovery that a similar infectious agent containing no DNA or RNA was the cause of worldwide Creutzfeldt-Jakob disease. These studies laid the basis for an understanding of such illnesses as SSPE (delayed and slow measles) and "mad-cow disease," as well as providing a necessary conceptual breakthrough in the understanding of AIDS. In 1976, Gajdusek was awarded the Nobel Prize in Physiology or Medicine.

During his visits to New Guinea, Gajdusek often made contact with communities of cultural and linguistic groups that had been previously visited only by neighboring hostile New Guineans. He conducted medical examinations of thousands of native children and adults, shipped numerous clinical and autopsy tissues to his laboratory in the U.S., and initiated investigation of many new, exotic tropical diseases. He also amassed a large ethnographic record of film, photography, sound recordings, and drawings, and kept a detailed journal of his findings and observations, from which most of the following excerpts are taken. (In some cases, unmarked minor abridgments have been made to these passages.)

LEFT Three members of the Kukukuku (Anga) group, atypically unarmed, watch the construction of Gajdusek's camp at Aurugosa.

1957

The Medical Journal of Australia, "Kuru: Clinical Study of a New Syndrome Resembling Paralysis Agitans in Natives of the Eastern Highlands of Australian New Guinea," by Vincent Zigas and D. C. Gajdusek

About five years ago, the region south and east of Mount Michael in the southern portion of the Eastern Highlands of the Australian Trust Territory of New Guinea was pacified by a series of contact patrols through the native villages of three linguistic groups, the Fore, the Keiagana, and the Kimi. Intertribal and intervillage warfare, ritual killings, sorcery, and cannibalism, which included the eating of all those who died, were discouraged; but even at present remnants of these practices survive.

The first recorded Caucasian contact received by the Fore people was the expedition in 1932 of Ted Eubanks, a gold prospector. A Lutheran Mission was set up in 1949 at Tarabo in the Keiagana Linguistic Area, and the Tarabo region was selected as the site for the first Governmental Patrol Post in the region, which was established by Patrol Officer J. R. MacArthur in 1952. In the diary of his patrol report on the opening of the new area south of Mount Michael, Mr. J. R. MacArthur reported as follows on Sunday, December 6, 1953:

> Proceeding SW across range, and down and across a small creek ascending to Amusi villages, nearing one of the dwellings, I observed a small girl sitting down beside a fire. She was shivering violently, and her head was jerking spasmodically from side to side. I was told that she was a victim of sorcery, and would continue this shivering unable to eat until death claimed her within a few weeks.

Succeeding patrol officers found the problem of kuru to be the most important medical problem in the region. Patrol Officer J. R. MacArthur and others all brought this strange disease to the attention of Dr. V. Zigas, then District Medical Officer at Goroka. Since that time, Dr. Zigas has taken every opportunity at his disposal to observe cases of kuru. In October 1956, he was able to spend a few weeks in the Okapa region, and during that time, he obtained blood serum specimens from 26 subjects of kuru and the brain from one patient dead of the illness; all this material was sent to the Walter and Eliza Hall Institute of Medical Research in Melbourne, Australia. No infectious agent was isolated from the brain.

OPPOSITE PAGE Two Awa warriors soon after first contact with Kuru Epidemiological Patrol, and a map of the kuru region of New Guinea.

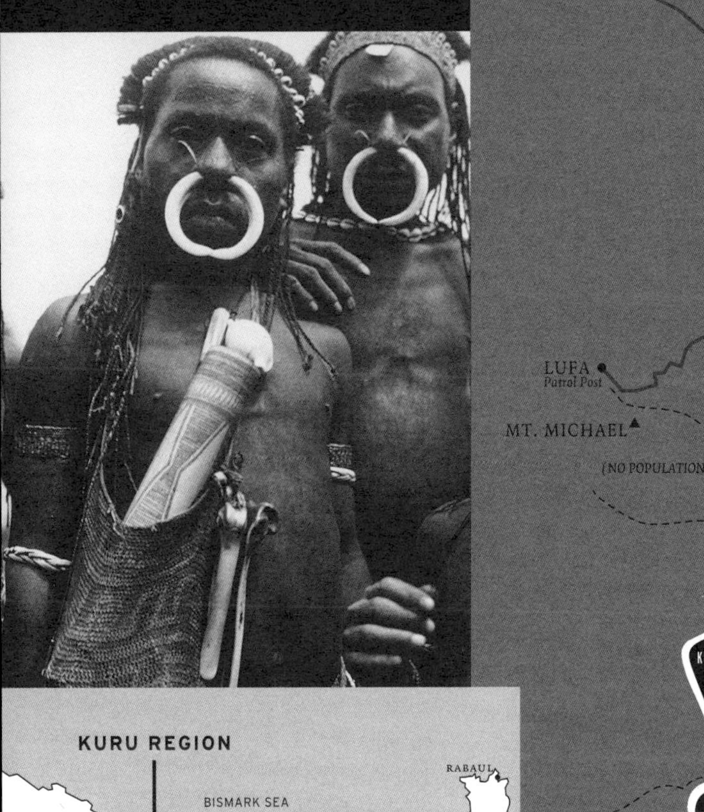

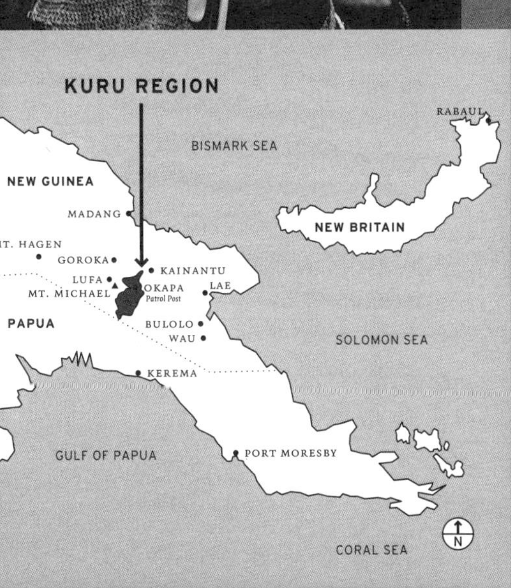
KURU REGION
RABAUL
BISMARK SEA
NEW GUINEA
MADANG
NEW BRITAIN
MT. HAGEN
GOROKA
KAINANTU
LUFA
MT. MICHAEL
OKAPA
Patrol Post
LAE
PAPUA
BULOLO
WAU
SOLOMON SEA
KEREMA
GULF OF PAPUA
PORT MORESBY
CORAL SEA
N

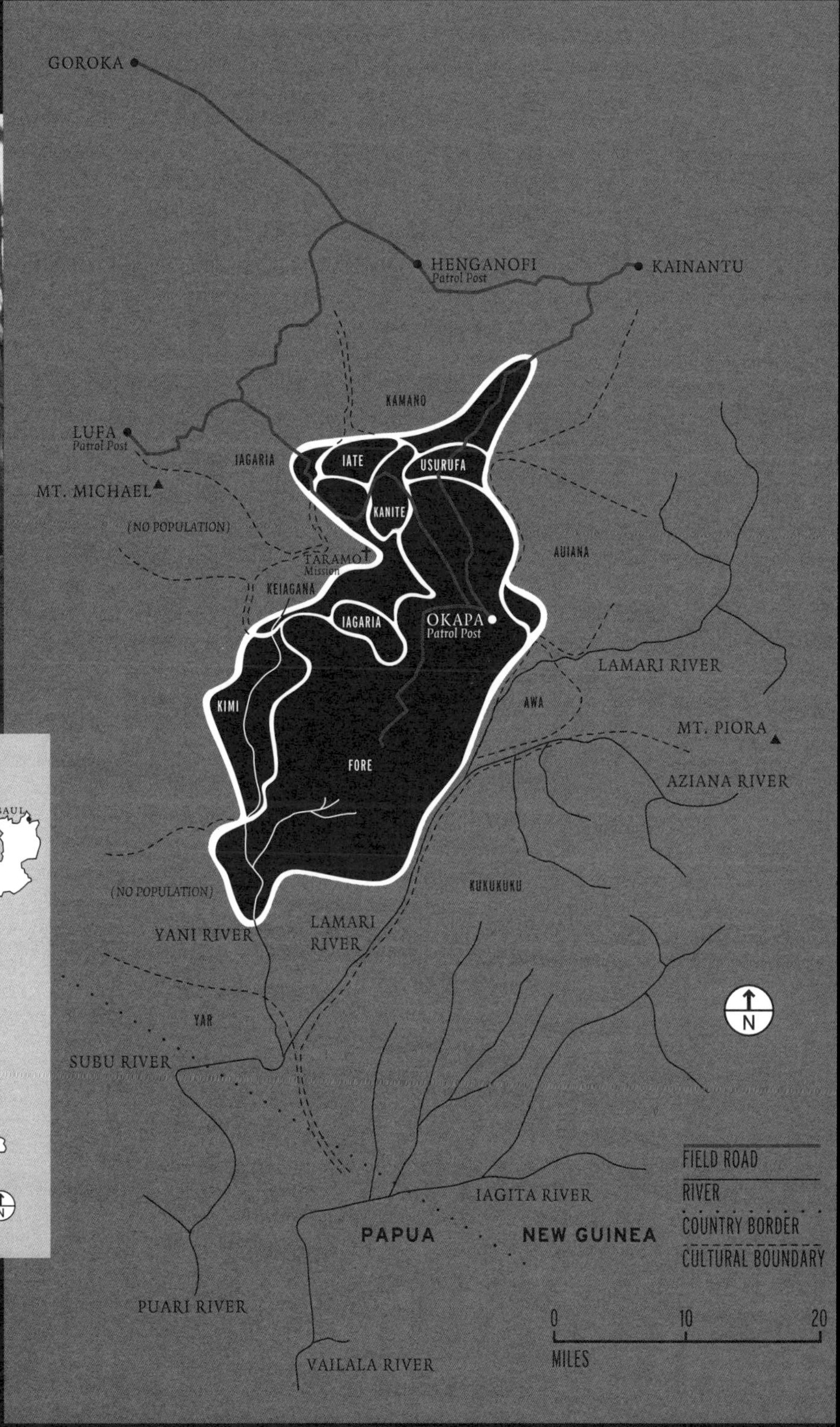

GOROKA
HENGANOFI
Patrol Post
KAINANTU
KAMANO
LUFA
Patrol Post
IAGARIA
IATE
USURUFA
MT. MICHAEL
KANITE
(NO POPULATION)
TARAMO
Mission
AUIANA
KEIAGANA
IAGARIA
OKAPA
Patrol Post
LAMARI RIVER
KIMI
AWA
MT. PIORA
FORE
AZIANA RIVER
KUKUKUKU
(NO POPULATION)
YANI RIVER
LAMARI
RIVER
YAR
N
SUBU RIVER
FIELD ROAD
RIVER
COUNTRY BORDER
CULTURAL BOUNDARY
IAGITA RIVER
PAPUA
NEW GUINEA
PUARI RIVER
0
10
20
MILES
VAILALA RIVER

Early in March 1957, Dr. Gajdusek joined Dr. Zigas in New Guinea, and the two inaugurated an intensive study of the disease at the Okapa Patrol Post, which is the administrative center of the area affected by kuru. The Kuru Research Center which was thus set up subsequently proved to be located very close to the geographic and population center of the kuru region.

MARCH 15: Okapa Patrol Post, Moke, New Guinea, letter to Joseph E. Smadel*

I am in one of the most remote, recently opened regions of New Guinea (in the Eastern Highlands), in the center of tribal groups of cannibals only contacted in the last ten years and controlled for five years, still spearing each other as of a few days ago, and only a few weeks ago cooking and feeding the children the body of a kuru case, the disease I am studying. This is a sorcery-induced disease, according to the local people; and that it has been the major disease problem of the region, as well as a social problem for the past five years, is certain. It is so astonishing an illness that clinical description can only be read with skepticism; and I was highly skeptical until two days ago, when I arrived and began to see the cases on every side. It is a mighty strange syndrome. To see whole groups of well-nourished healthy young adults dancing about, with tremors which look far more hysterical than organic, is a real sight. But to see them, however, regularly progress to neurological degeneration in three to six months (usually three) and to death is another matter and cannot be shrugged off. If psychological, we have the very best epidemic psychosis for study in the world; and the Institute of Mental Health should be most interested. If a heredofamilial disease, we have the highest incidence-concentrated "epidemic" ever seen; and the geneticists should be on the ball. If a post-encephalitic or toxic or allergic encephalitic epidemic of basal gangliar disease is here, then all of medicine should be interested.

* Chief of Microbiology at the Walter Reed Army Institute of Research, Washington, D.C.

APRIL 3: Moke, letter to Joseph E. Smadel

I am writing to you just after returning from a patrol down to the southern fringe of the South Fore region, and to the Lamari River and Kukukuku* and Awa linguistic areas. The patrol was directed to this little-known region to determine the southern extent of the kuru disease, which has so occupied me and is the subject again of this note.

Here in Moke, in a mat-floor hospital which was quickly built with native materials, in which we have a microscope,

* The Kukukuku people, a cultural and linguistic group occupying the Eastern Highlands region of New Guinea, are now known as the Anga people.

hemocytometer,* a host of lab reagents and equipment, and all the diagnosis instruments that such a "bush" hospital would be expected to possess, including ophthalmoscope and tuning forks, Dr. Zigas (the Kainantu physician and only M.D. in the Eastern Highlands), who discovered the disease, and I have set up a kuru investigative station. I am rapidly learning the language, getting fine and extensive accurate family histories, and a better controlled epidemiology than could ever be expected in less isolated, "civilized" communities.

With this in mind, I now write to assure you that my last letter was no ruse. This is no wild-goose chase, but a really big thing.

MAY 19: Kuru Research Center, Kainantu, letter to Ian Burnet and Gray Anderson**

Last week we had our first death in the Hospital of a kuru patient; and at 2 A.M. in rain and cold wind, a *dokta boi* [Native Medical Assistant] and I did a complete autopsy in our treatment/laboratory hut by lantern light, and then at first cockcrow got the body borne homeward with the mourning mother well rewarded with axes and salt and *laplaps*† (in which she appeared to take as much interest as in the death, to which, it must be said, she had long, long ago resigned herself). Thus, we got the "dastardly deed" done without awakening much local curiosity or attracting too much attention to our butchery. There were no gross pathological findings of interest.

* An instrument for counting blood cells.

** Ian Burnet, an Australian government official, and Dr. S. G. Anderson, a virologist at the Walter and Eliza Hall Institute of Medical Research, Melbourne.

† Waistcloths made of cotton or other trade fabric, worn by men.

SEPTEMBER 3: Paiti village, South Fore

For the past two years, I have kept a personal journal in a haphazard, irregular, and half-hearted fashion. It is with a constant desire to keep a journal but with such a tight schedule that I never do, that I have lived these past eighteen months, and I feel this omission has been something of a loss to me, loss of richness in the experiences, for journal-keeping tends to add condiment to them. Again, I make a start....

We have at last arrived at Paitisa after a six-hour hike from our Bush Camp No. 5. This eighth day of our trek through previously "unvisited" country was track-cutting all the way. Since we left the Oriei rest house, we have been over roads and country which no European has previously traveled. Agurio, a Kukukuku lad of 13-appearance and 16-development, sits beside me on the patrol boxes as I type under a *kunai*-covered* shelter just erected beside our *kunai* hut and overlooking the cloud-filled forested valleys of Haiti and Somai to the west. We had our new "kuru house" filled with Kuks and their lice for the two days

* A tall grass that covers vast tracts of the Highlands.

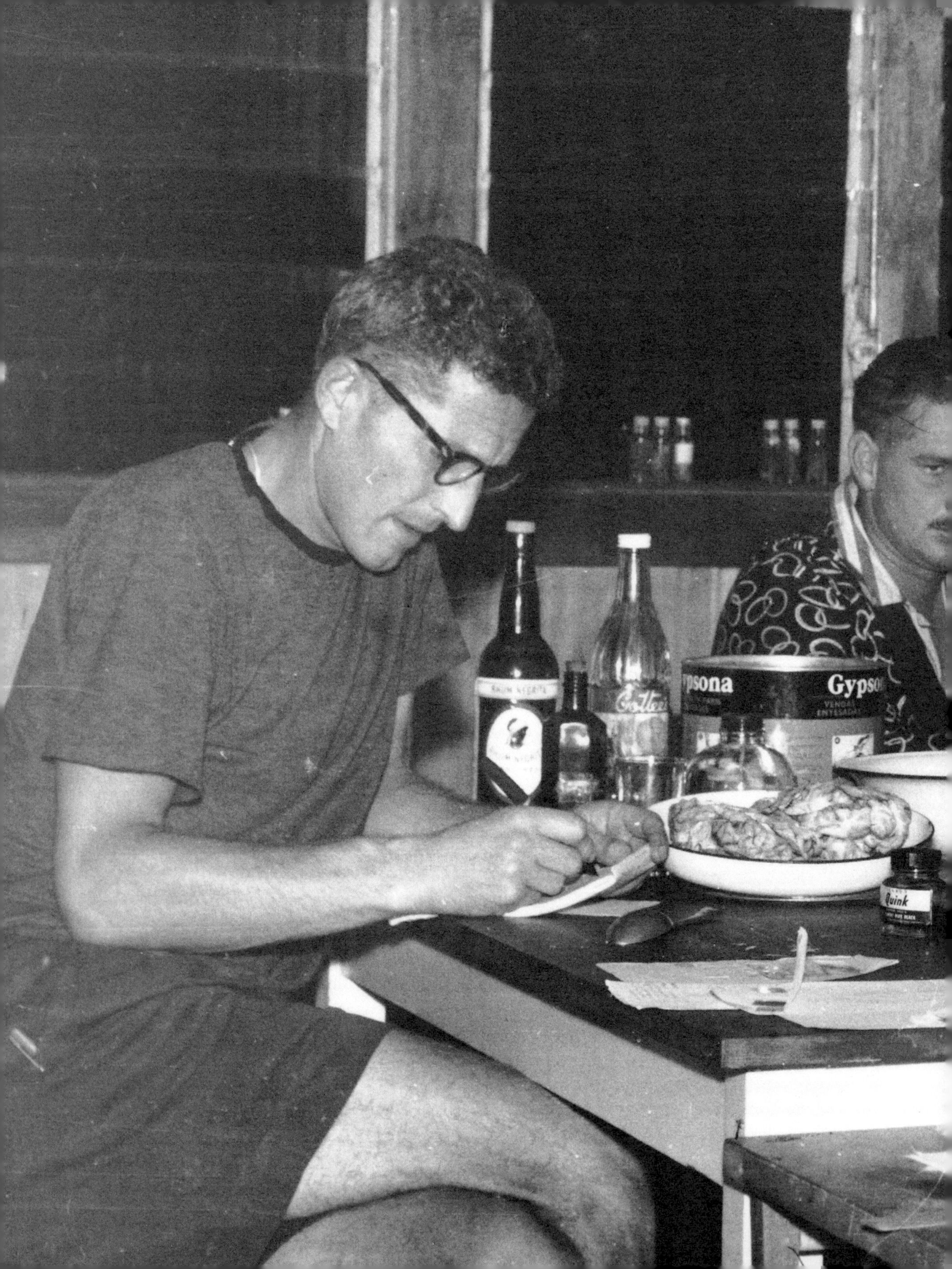
Gypsona
Quink

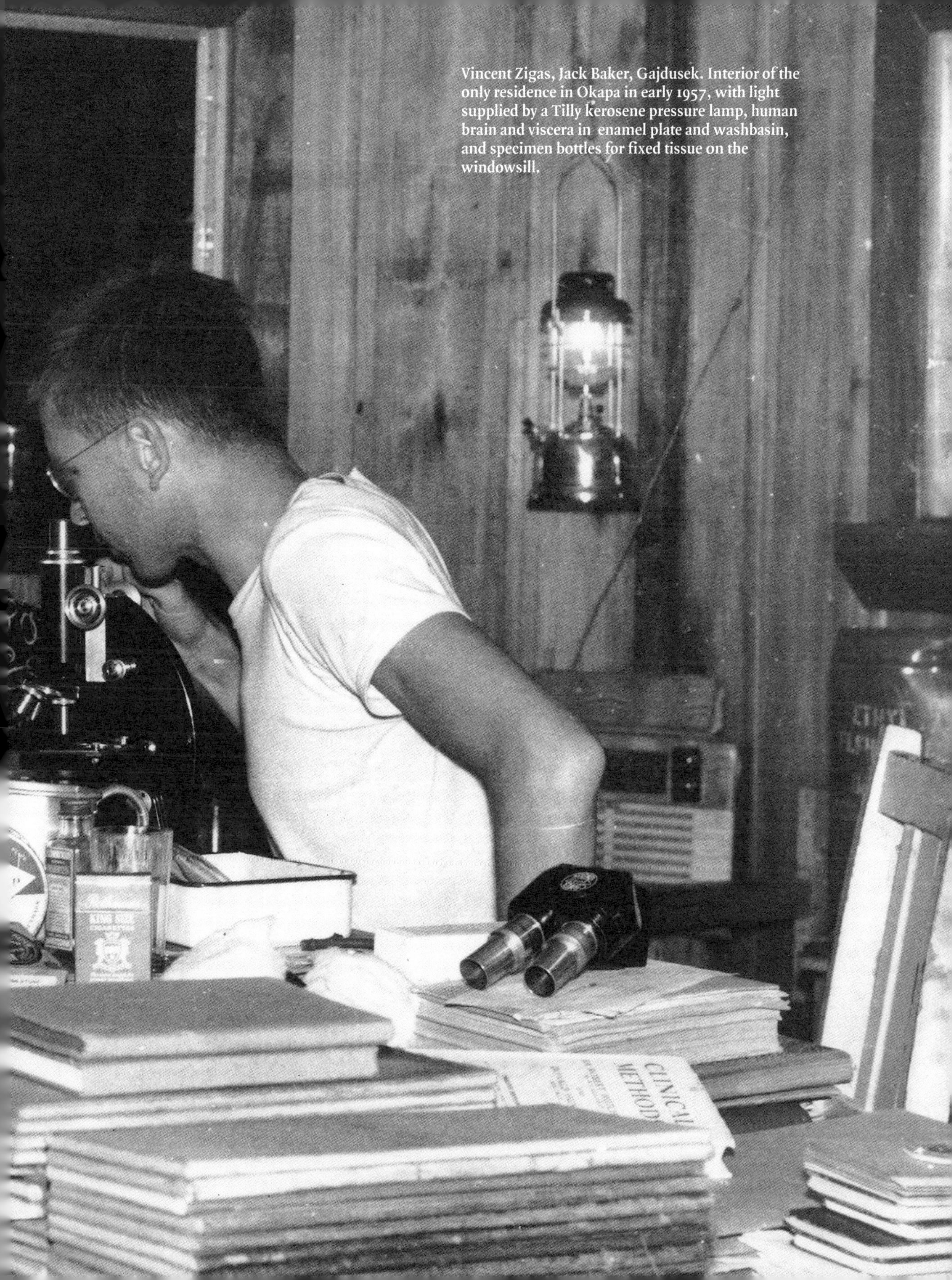

Vincent Zigas, Jack Baker, Gajdusek. Interior of the only residence in Okapa in early 1957, with light supplied by a Tilly kerosene pressure lamp, human brain and viscera in enamel plate and washbasin, and specimen bottles for fixed tissue on the windowsill.

before my departure on this patrol. I tried to win their favor with friendship and payment, payment being held part thereof hereabouts, I find, and won at least Agurio's firm following.

SEPTEMBER 6: Uvai Rest House, South Kimi
In pouring rain, although the afternoon was fine. The now quiet Yani, roaring south of here, where it becomes a bigger river, and roaring above here, over rocky rapids, was on our left the entire trip, until we crossed back to the western side on another vine-suspension bridge. We live well on Kimi foods, and at each place they have had a *mumu** prepared. When we are hungry, nothing could be more welcome than freshly *mumued kaukau* [sweet potato] and *pitpit* [edible cane grass]. Thus, we eat in style in spite of the "isolation."

In this entire 30,000 to 60,000 population center of Kimi, Keiagana, Fore, Yar, Iagaria, Auiana, Kukukuku, etc. linguistic groups, John** and I are, today, the only ones who have seen anything of the world other than the island of New Guinea. Few have seen the coast and most of those few are with us now. During these entire two weeks I have not missed "civilized" company any more than I did on the last eighteen-day patrol or during the month of patrolling with Melanesian natives in New Britain. These people are sufficient unto themselves; they have a complex and organized enough society to provide a cultural entirety devoid of contact with the outside world. Language and culture may close much of it to me, but I am at home with them.

I have abandoned my French and Russian authors; my correspondence, which has fallen to naught but the voluminous scientific exchange about kuru and our three kuru papers, has afforded me little time to follow world news, literature, or home events for these six months. I am a bit shocked when I consider how little all this bothers me and how little is my anxiety to leave. I know full well that I shall be walking the streets of Paris, Rome, London, New York, and Washington again and that from those places the New Guinea jungles and the "savages" are but remote museum pieces or subjects for arty cine films and literature, hardly the humans with whom I now live and sleep. To me they are, as were my friends of New Britain, among the warmest and closest friends I have had. I respect, admire, and love them, and know that once I part from them, I may never see them or hear from them again. I am in no hurry. Kuru work, at any rate for the first field stage, is nearly done and I must be on my way, long and devious though it may be.

---

* A method of steam-cooking over stones in a covered earth pit.

** John Berkin, a European Medical Assistant stationed at Kainantu.

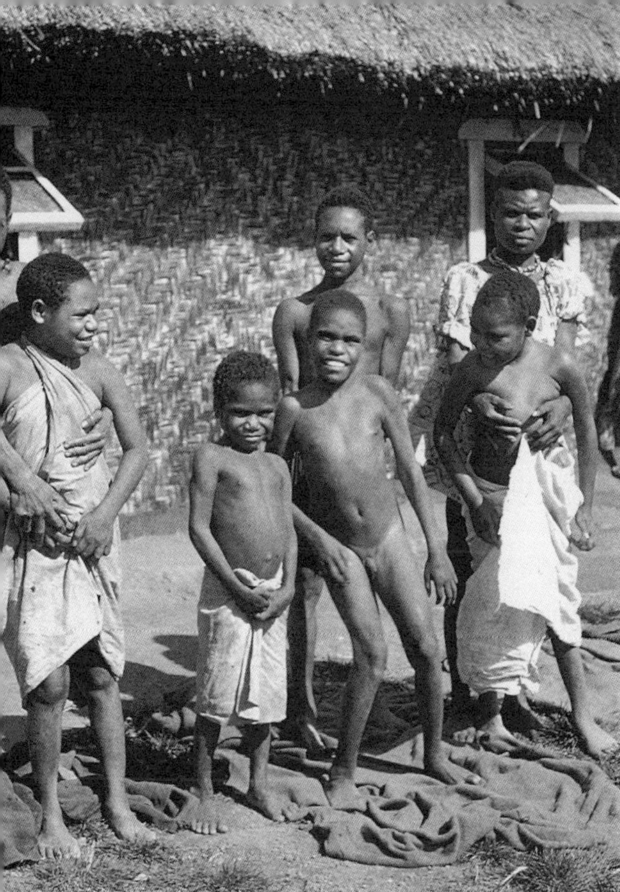

ABOVE Five children with kuru at the Kuru Hospital. An adolescent boy with very early kuru holds a boy who cannot stand without support. All five died within less than a year.

SEPTEMBER 9: Hegeteru, Kimi

I have spent my thirty-fourth birthday on patrol, walking an arduous six hours of stiff trail and I am astounded that, at this age, I am still doing such things. To me, everything beyond the twenties is "aged," and though I am well in the thirties myself, I consider it closer to senility than to youth.

OCTOBER 2: Auroga village, our first camp with the Kukukukus

We arose at 5 A.M. and by 6:15 our entire patrol was on the trail. We number some seventy-two carriers, six boys, eleven police, and a contingent of a dozen or more Mobutasa men and boys who have come with us. A group of Agamusei people came along as well. Thus our line was about a hundred strong.

At 10:15, we stopped at a small stream and prepared tea. Then we continued on through the forest and after about an hour emerged onto a short *kunai* slope on the summit, where we met four Kukukuku men carrying excellent bows and arrows, their bow strings tightly set. They said, through our Agamusei interpreter, that they were out hunting, but they were obviously sentries and had already been heard, shouting over the hillsides with a warning to the others of our approach, and had lit a fire in the hot noonday sun on the *kunai* summit. They were most friendly, however, not a bit afraid, and embraced us smiling, laughing, and exchanging shoulder pats. They examined our clothing as we examined theirs, without fear or anger, and told us to pass. We asked them to come along to their villages with us and they consented, voicing their independence, however, in a nonchalant statement that they would first have a smoke and sit down a while, and then later catch up with us. This they did; and soon they overtook and passed us on the trail. They had warned their villages ahead of our arrival by lighting large signal fires behind us after we went on.

We climbed until we reached a low, long, *kunai*-covered rectangular house and found many women and children who were a bit apprehensive, but the children all took my offered handshake and played with us while the women were encouraged to smile. Our reception was thus far obviously friendly and without undue apprehension from a people who had only twice before seen Western culture representatives on their lands.

OCTOBER 5: Auroga village, Camp No. 2, Kukukuku

I brought out paper and pencils and four Kuks made rather interesting pattern designs, all producing the same type of pattern, a "weaving" across the page from left to right with parallel bands of broken lines, often a regularly broken line of acute angles. No human or animal figures were produced. Every one of the artists had to be shown that the pencils were drawing instruments. However, they immediately grasped their purpose and attacked the drawing with pride and purpose, as individuals,

BELOW Gajdusek (left) examines a South Fore child victim of kuru while Vincent Zigas takes notes, at the Kuru Hospital, Okapa Patrol Post.

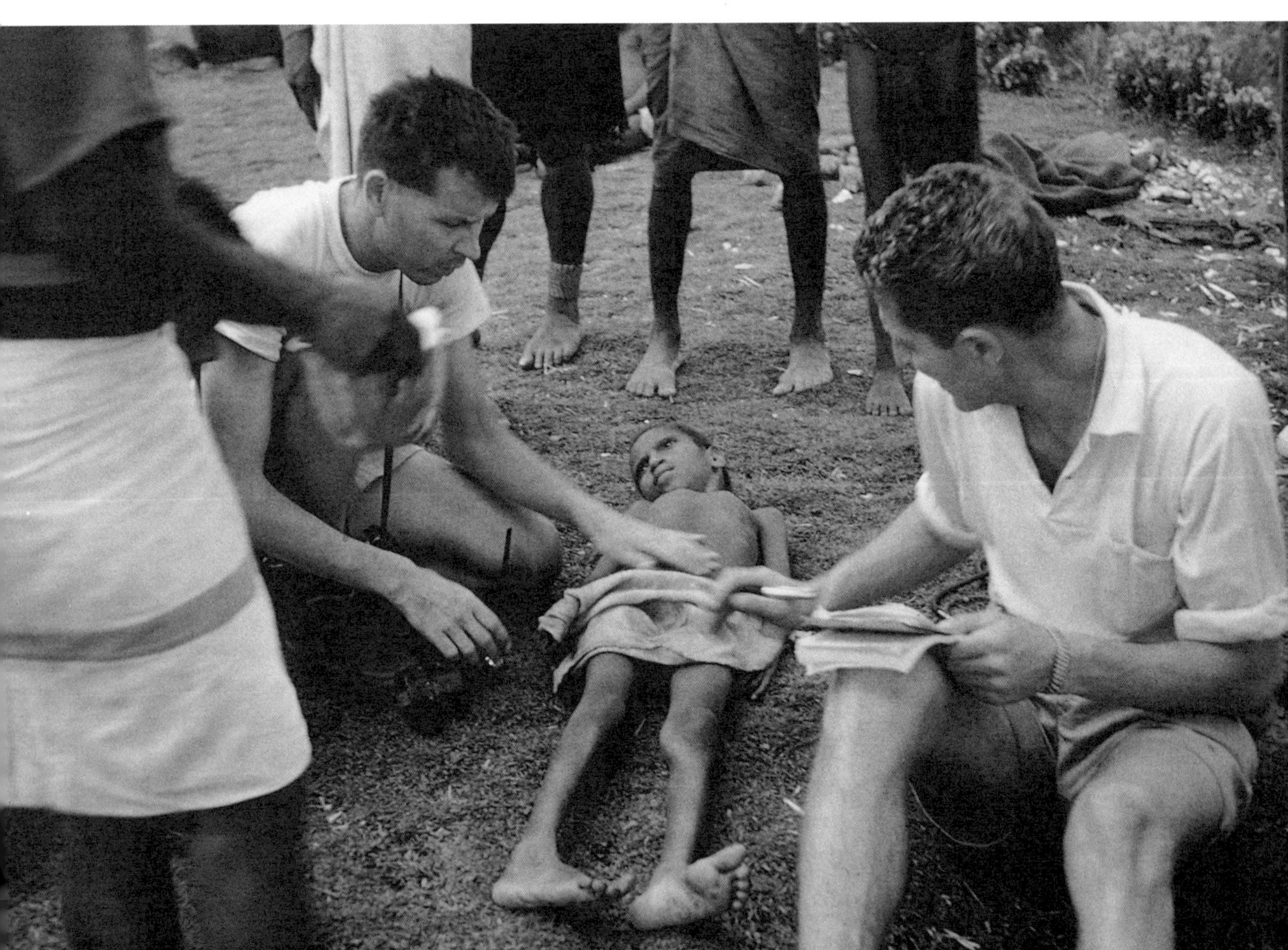

paying little attention to any production but their own. I hope to collect many more Kukukuku drawings. They are more rugged individuals than many other New Guinea natives and far more self-assertive and proud, confident, and even somewhat more arrogant than our Fore, Kimi, or Keiagana.

Although these Kuks are interested and intrigued by typewriter, radio, flashlight, cine camera, and all other manufactured devices, they soon digest their function and range of application and treat them with the nonchalance of old experienced hands. Thus, they hardly deign to look at the planes which fly overhead about twice a day, from Goroka to Moresby, we believe. We look at every one, even take out field glasses to study them. Field glasses intrigue the Kuks for the first few minutes, then they demand to use them, and after a few minutes of use they are satisfied that they fully understand them and are no longer even interested in them.

OCTOBER 15: Camp No. 8, Moraei Kukukuku

On the radio this evening, we hear further kuru news, that kuru is probably hereditary, and that it seems restricted to the Fore-Okapa region. Since all kuru data must stem from Vin[cent Zigas] or myself, we are mighty astounded at all these radio reports. To be left out of all the extensive publicity accounts of kuru, which keep appearing while the Administration blows its horn about kuru studies, kuru films, kuru projects, is a bit ego-deflating. However, in spite of the initial wound to pride and vanity, I would, in all honesty, rather have it so. I know full well that kuru study is all part of what Vin and I have planned and for which we have laid the foundation. If it contributes in any way to solving the problem, fine! If not, it is wasted effort and only embarrassing to have to talk about it.

NOVEMBER 8: Hotel Cecil, Lae

Lucy has received an atrocious clipping from the Sydney *Sunday Herald* on the "Laughing Death," a name with which tabloid journalists have dubbed kuru. Dr. Gunther* assures us that a several page article on kuru is about to appear in the tabloid *People* in Australia, and *Time* is shortly to carry two columns of a story on the disease. Vin assures me that the *Time* story will be okay for *Time*'s representative visited him, came to Okapa and saw patients, and wrote the story from Vin's information. I hope he is right. Thus far, southern newspapers have made a farce of the pathetic plight of the Fore and have usually presented a much garbled account of the kuru investigations. If only we might pursue our studies unpestered.

---

* Lucy Hamilton, a nutritionist with the Territory of Papua and New Guinea Public Health Department, and Dr. John Gunther, Assistant Administrator of the Territory of Papua and New Guinea.

1959

JULY 13: Kuru Research Center, Kainantu

Vin and I have a new Kuru Research Center going. Six kuru cases, all the typical stage II, clearly define our reentry into the clinical investigation of kuru. I have rushed Vin's lab into makeshift readiness so that we can now do the most simple tests, but it will be considerably more sophisticated before too long. The important thing is that we are original and that we advance in our thinking and approach, not stagnate in the same procedures. The work alone counts, and if collaborators fall by the wayside, I shall work by myself.

JULY 19: Laiagam Patrol Post

Tei and the other *dokta bois* tell me of the Maramuni people. They claim a large nut is collected and placed in a muddy pool where it ferments and rots and where all sorts of insects, larvae, and "snek" [snakes] come and die in the muddy, stinking ferment. Then the people sit around this pool and dish out handfuls of rotting mud, and they eat this uncooked. Supposedly it causes severe nausea and emesis and abdominal distention. It is a good story and I should like to know its origin, for it probably stems from some peculiar dietary custom.

As we sit around the campfire, Tei and the others tell me of all the strange, little-known people on their distant frontiers. Down at Lagaip, one eventually finds strange people called Ned who supposedly build large houses on stilts, shave their heads, pluck out their eyelashes, and use frightening face paints. They are particularly remarkable to my Enga-speaking informants because of their clean, blemish-free skin, devoid of scars, sores, ulcers, or yaws*. These tales are apt to be as much imagination as fact, but they do put me on the track to new peoples. Keith** verifies the story of the fermented nut, identifying the people as Penali. The nut, as it is consumed, is toxic and causes gastroenteritis and probably death to some children.

JULY 25: Panduaga (Pandiwaka on maps), 7,700 feet

At one site along the way, we met a group of people from Tari visiting *wontoks*† here, but one is a Lutheran native missionary, and the *kiap*‡ is *kros*. The uncontrolled area is closed to missionaries and "missionizing," and as around every such area soul savers stand like a pack of hungry wolves, panting for entrance. However, the Seventh Day Adventist trick of collecting candidates from remote, uncontrolled regions, and educating them as missionaries (and only

* An infectious tropical disease which causes ulcerated lesions.

** Keith Wilson, the Medical Officer of Wabag, Western Highlands.

† Members of their clan or language group.

‡ A Department of Native Affairs official.

that!), and then sending them back home, cannot legally be interfered with in any way. I hold nothing against the missions, other than their pathetic juvenilism, searching for souls, when there is so much more to do back home where they come from. A creed to replace the crumbling native magic and superstition is needed, however, and government workers fail totally to supply one. It is a pity that we have only the pathetic compromises of Christianity, and what is even worse, feuding groups of petty, dissenting sects, none of which has a really acceptable scheme of life for these people, but any one of which would be better than the feuding mess. What will be accomplished, without doubt, is a discrediting of them in the natives' minds, and it is to be hoped that some more enlightened creed than Communism will then take over. An optimistic hope, and one requiring, I fear, a new prophet or "savior."

I type here in our tent, wearing a woolen shirt and still shivering, and the rain pours without. The small, inadequate assemblage of local natives is far too few to represent a survey of the population, but they are required to sit miserably here in the rain, huddled under their pandanus frond rain capes, waiting for the rain to cease. Actually, it is those who have not come up with whom we are dissatisfied, and it is those who have come up who are being penalized by waiting in the cold and rain for the lineup and medical inspection. It is hard to see why they should feel at all pleased with these "inspections." They do not really appreciate what medical aid we bring, and for our curiosity as to what maladies may plague them, they have no interest or sympathy, I fear. Thus it is only sensible for them to remain huddled in their warm houses, rather than to roam the wet, rough trails, only to be inconvenienced and given work to do once here. It continues to pour... the natives are chanting a *singsing**, huddled under the trees and their rain capes.... I should love to know the words.

We have now had a break in the rain, the sun came out for an hour or so during which we lined up eighty-four local people. Of the children, one boy was missing the last joint of his fifth finger, as was one girl of similar age. This is said to be a practice carried out by the mother at birth of the infant. In order to release menstrual blood from the child, she amputates the terminal joint of the left fifth finger. The boy was also missing his left ear helix, which had been amputated when he was five or six years old because he had stolen someone's pig, so he said. In the Wabag area, women's noses are amputated for adultery, but this is the first childhood amputation as punishment that I have ever seen.

* A celebration or festival involving dancing, singing, and often feasting. Gajdusek has made extensive sound recordings of traditional *singsings*.

1960

MARCH 11: Kemiu-Kanite, Eastern Highlands
The boys ask me about religion tonight. Many of them have not *waswased* [been baptized] they tell me, and since of old they never went to church to go to heaven, the fate of their ancestors is suitable for them now. They do fear dead people, however, and they have heard that the dead may work illness. This, however, is an unusual story among the Fore and by no means a major component of their nosology.*

MARCH 17: Auiyana-Asepa *Haus Kiap*, center of Auiyana Linguistic Group**
I was very pleased and proud of the boys as they worked under pressure, with speed and efficiency, and without errors today. Most remarkable of the contingent was shivering and shaking Azibara, Tiu's younger brother, in late Stage I of kuru, but still able to have negotiated the long, difficult walk here from Agakamatasa and insistent on making this last patrol, the last patrol of his life, the last *walkabaut* with a tragic vengeance. What can I do? Refuse him? He does walk without aid, just. It seems insane to drag a late kuru victim into unknown, uncontrolled regions and on a difficult explorative patrol, but I cannot and will not refuse Azibara. It is as a "last wish." I admire him and am deeply grateful that my little attentions to him and his people have resulted in such an unusual show of allegiance and accord. I only hope I can justify it.

MARCH 27: Asara, Tairora Linguistic Group
Last night I finished part I of *Within a Budding Grove* of Proust's second book of his *Recherche*. Such intensity in such simple uneventful living is the full demonstration of the fact that action and adventure of the sort that fill my current days are hardly necessary for exciting existence and probably prevent any really deep penetration into the emotions and events that pass. Could I ever reconstruct all these days and nights of feeling, even in memory?

But the Proustian penetration in recall is a wonderful accompaniment on patrol in New Guinea. From the upper-class salon of Paris one moves to the Stone Age in a glance; I read about the Balbec Hotel society with nose-pierced boys sitting beside me on my canvas bed sleeve, feathers in their hair, bodies anointed with pig grease, a tight genital-anal band under their grass skirts, and boar's tusks through their nasal-septal holes. Some have additional holes in their nostril lobes through which bits of bamboo are inserted, but how rapidly all this will disappear! At Oraura, a rare piece of cloth, bit of mirror, or chain of trade beads were all the signs of civilization I saw.

* A system of classifying diseases.

** Shelters that were built along government patrol routes to house Patrol Officers and their entourages on exploratory, census, and medical expeditions.

A few axe blades and knives and tins could be noticed, but little else. At Himarata, we suddenly found all the armament and personal decoration lost. Braided hair, universal in young boys and youths at Oraura, is rarely seen there and *laplaps* almost equal grass skirts in frequency.

Azibara continues to stumble along with us and many do not notice that he is dying from kuru. We are certainly a strange patrol, yet a good one for the region, I believe. We carry no arms; we have an entourage of local native representatives of government; we have a crusade of children of many tongues, and a young, exemplary cargo line of marvelous *esprit du corps*; we bring medical aid and dispense it liberally, and we are paying well by local standards for the food we buy.

BELOW A seven-year-old Agakamatasa Fore boy with advanced kuru is caught during an athetoid, involuntary jerk precipitated by his attempt to remain standing.

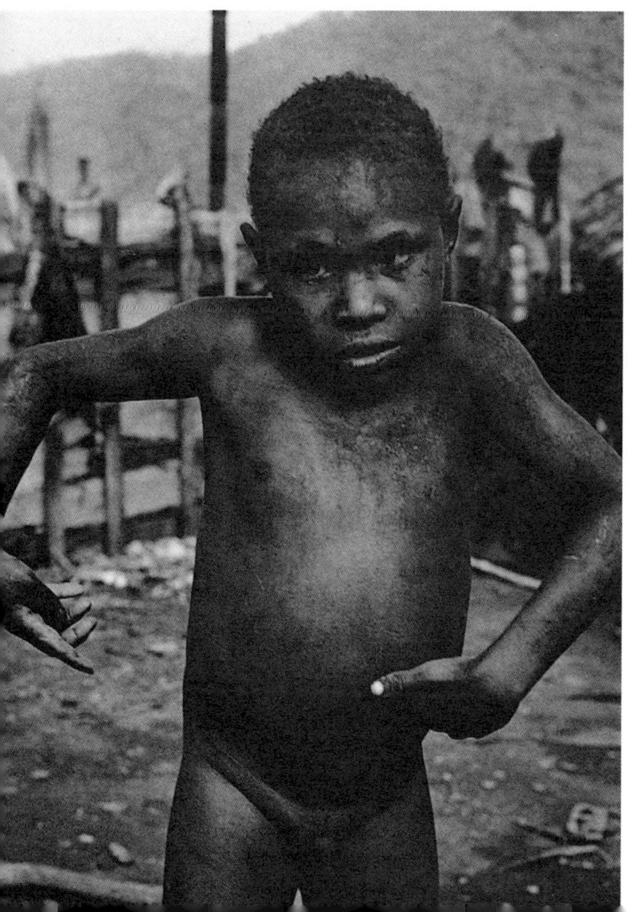

Medicine is a difficult matter here, but not greatly different than practice in Boston and New York. Everyone wants *shoots* and pills and they want these in return for saying they are *sik*. To get a further history and symptomatology from them is a long and tedious task and, to satisfy them, they must have as many pills as the next man. I have tried to avoid dispensing needlessly, but old men, dying of old age, and old women are the bane of work here; for, as we are treating children with yaws, they crowd around for *shoots* with their chronic complaints which are beyond the scope of efficacy of antibiotics. As psychotherapy and a necessary social procedure to secure the acute infectious cases for treatment, I must dispense some of this placebo medicine; but I hate to do so with true medications and I have no placebos, for they are much against my medical ethics. This non-Western culture, however, imposes problems on any ethic, and I am not beyond compromise. Now I only wish I had a great tin of several thousand peppermint tablets!

APRIL 3: Kuru Hospital, Kainantu

I find curriculum vitae requests from *American Men of Science* and *Who's Who in the Pacific Islands*, invitations to participate as discussant in the New York Academy of Science Conference on Culture, Society, and Health, and numerous other "honors"... and although there is a bit of pleasure and pride associated with my learning of these, it is more annoyance and disinterest that dominates my response: all this means so little, and creative work so much! It is the latter which I must accomplish and these laurels are but empty, meaningless honors, like rejoicing at finding one's name in a telephone book!

APRIL 6: Kainantu

Having failed to keep more notes than this, I find already that too much is lost to make up the gap or to ever record the experience which lingers with me in full force of moments, those moments of night *singsing*, bathing in the stream of a morning, sunning on the rocks of the river in the afternoon, resting exhausted on the summit of the divide. This notebook is such a small fragment of those giant days that it is disappointing to leaf through. Perhaps with the photographic record it may preserve a valid fragment of this strange universe.

APRIL 9: Ofafina (Famia), North Fore

Coastal labor from the kuru region has already been stopped, although a great many are out and Bennett* is still set on putting a big fence around the region. This is an insane idea. I am completely for encouraged migration and free egress from the area, but I shall not enter into any battle, for Bennett will lose it in time. Now the new Moke *kiap*, Wiltshire, is all excited about his "big fence" and very worried about autopsies, which he thinks should be abandoned, and disturbed about the "native situation" which is friendly and cooperative as it has always been. I do not propose to lay further coals on the fire of our differences. I am in a moment of inertia myself, and a bit discouraged as to just how much I shall achieve. The resistance to our work has so disturbed Vin, ruined his family life, and stifled his initiative as to have greatly curtailed our enterprise and I am, admittedly, tired. I hope that in the swing of the patrol I may get back into high gear.

APRIL 11: Okapa *Haus Kiap*, North Fore

Other oddities are bothering me. One case of kuru is in a woman who is definitely said to be of Arora (Auyana) mother and father. This is moving without the kuru region into the very low-incidence border zone. As I recall, one of the Garufi or Tirokavi cases is in a woman from further into the Kamano, again an "unlikely" source of the gene. Finally, and more conclusively, one of the Iate boys, who has died as a youngster of kuru is traced to a Lufa region parent who could hardly have the gene. There are thus many problems in our too simple genetic constructions accounting for kuru. The

* Dr. Bennett, a geneticist at the University of Adelaide.

further study of these is crucial. It is in such "exceptions" that we shall find the threads of evidence for the selective factors and the environmental variables at work. We still have much to learn, very, very much.

APRIL 15: Iresa, South Fore

Tomorrow we shall again climb to the heights as we cross the ridges to Awarosa, and if the weather is with us, we shall again behold the great Lamari valley which I love as perhaps no other spot on earth. If it is here that I have found myself and lived my most satisfying days, I have no excuses nor apologies to my fellow civilized men, for I am proud of the fact. There has been much of life and wisdom revealed to me on the hanging slopes of this immense drainage... and with Roosevelt High School, University of Rochester, Harvard Medical School, Cal Tech, the Boyce Thompson Institute, and Walter Reed, this has been one of "My Universities," and the one which Maxim Gorki would most appreciate!

It is only when one lives closely with these ethical, very moral, and emotionally sensitive people, who have a great respect for person and property, a rigorous yet "enlightened" sexual code, a keen and proud individuality coupled with a strong sense of family responsibility and community solidarity, that one realizes how little we have progressed in five millennia. One can instead easily see only their uncured yaws, their violence, and their warfare.

MAY 15: Hollandia, Netherlands New Guinea, letter to Joseph E. Smadel and Richard Masland*

The long living alone with natives with no language but theirs about me never bores me, but I do try to keep perspective and balance with some reading. Sophocles's plays have tempered my life with Kukukuku, Tairora, Fore, and Awa natives in the past month, and a few biochemistry books help preserve proportion. Yet life on the trail and in hamlets usually leaves little time for such reading or study. Watching children trained in warfare, babies crawling over corpses, youngsters undergoing nose-piercing, isolation, and other "initiations," and patterned homosexuality, juvenile heterosexuality, polygamy, and many another psychosexual pattern in action, the nonsense of much of our pseudoscientific speculations and philosophizing in medical journals is immediately apparent. Just what to do with the observations, how to make and record them, and what to conclude, however, are no simple problems and I will not be quick in solving them.

1961

DECEMBER 13: Kuru Research Center, Kainantu

In a haven within the Highlands, I sit alone at midnight, puttering about the laboratory

* Assistant Director at the National Institute of Neurological Diseases and Blindness, Bethesda, Maryland.

which is so much my home and refuge that I sit with the same comfort and pleasure as in my library or laboratory at home in the U.S. I feel more alone than ever, now that all the "old guard" have left the Eastern Highlands Kainantu-Okapa region. Vin is gone and about the laboratory I find shades and ghosts of him: urine lists in his hand, notes to me....

DECEMBER 25: Agakamatasa-Waieti, South Fore

With all the children of Agakamatasa crowded about all day, I sorely miss Azibara, Tiu's next-younger brother who developed kuru while on patrol with me. Today was, essentially, a pilgrimage to his grave. Azibara died about a year ago at Kesiri and his body was carried along the lower trail to Pomawanipinti beneath a banana tree. The whole grave and lower garden are beautifully planted with sugar canes, bananas, a decorative purple-red-leafed plant, and ornamental *tanket**.

As I climbed down the steep hillside after two hours of arduous hiking to visit the grave, I thought of my failure ever to pay anyone in my own culture a similar homage. I suspect that I have never adjusted to either the death of my grandparents or of my father, and rather than defile my memories and thoughts by socialized mourning practices and grave visits, I act as though these outer culturally-approved recognitions of the dead were nonexistent. I suspect that some day, later in life, I will find the value in these social institutions which I now see so clearly in primitive cultures and civilized societies alien to my own.

DECEMBER 26: Agakamatasa-Waieti

This morning started with a rush of conferences. As I was typing up notes, Igaga descended upon me, crowded into my house with an entourage of many of the senior men. It soon turned out that he and his group were seeking my commitment that my hint and mention that I might eventually build among them would actually be carried out. They want me here, not somewhere else, they state. I have had Wanevi and others explain that my work as a doctor permits me to be here but briefly on each occasion. Missionaries, teachers, and *kiaps* have more reason to be here for long periods and are able to stay. I might, some day, be able to scrape together funds to build a place here among them, simply because of my love for their region and people, and if I can, I will some day do so. I would gladly spend the money necessary to build a comfortable residence capable of also entertaining the daily, and often nightly, crowd of native visitors, and risk its maintenance on all the uncertainties of local disagreement, strife, jealousy, and change of attitude. If only once I could get others to see it, to stay in it, to give of themselves to these people, I would be

* A decorative large-leafed plant, sometimes used to make pubic coverings.

amply repaid for the venture! What they need and want is honest, direct contact with the civilized world, its men and women, not distant admonitions.

DECEMBER 29: Agakamatasa, South Fore

Report of an eclipse has apparently been circulated by the Port Moresby radio and as told to the natives by the *dokta bois*, *kuskuses* [secretaries], and *polis bois* [police assistants] has, here in the Fore region, been magnified to "Seven Days of Darkness" with everything from the loss of all gardens, continuous rain, persistent hail, earthquakes, and even the end of the world. I have explained to the boys what an eclipse is, and some of them already accept the fact that the world is round and rotating, and seem to know as much about it as the average American grammar-school boy, which is not saying much! However, most of them treat the rumors with a good deal of thought, worry, and misgiving.

1962

JANUARY 10: Anei'aiuti and Kwagangai hamlets of Muniri Group

In the later morning, I found the men of the surrounding hamlets sitting in serious conclave with the newlywed youths. The young boys took me down to see the affair, and said, as I understood them, that it was an argument or a fight. However, this was only their misunderstanding, not mine. The loud session was a haranguing by the older men to these youths, instructing them in sex and their function in marriage. The major discussions were directed by one of the older men to one youth at a time, sometimes to two. At one stage, one of the older men kept jabbing at the genitalia of one of the youths, then took his bamboo pipe and held it like a vagina over his pubis (never, of course, disturbing the *kanila* [grass skirt]), and from his movements of it there was no mistaking that he was referring to coitus. However, from the excited, angry tone of it all and his sudden fierce mimicking of discharging an arrow, it was obvious that he was warning the youth not to permit anyone else to touch his wife. Much of the instruction was to encourage sudden use of the bow and arrow to settle the issue of anyone approaching their wives.

JANUARY 14: Moraei-Morandugai Ground

A full dozen Moraei and Fore youths are beginning to read this week and all have caught on to what it is about. I suspect the sight of me reading, writing all day—the stimulus of plenty of paper and colored pencils available to everyone all day for drawing, and the constant fingering through the stack of books and magazines I brought here has produced an aura about the written word and writing which is so intense as to be bewitching. Even the newly-arrived Muniris are mystified by it and soon start on

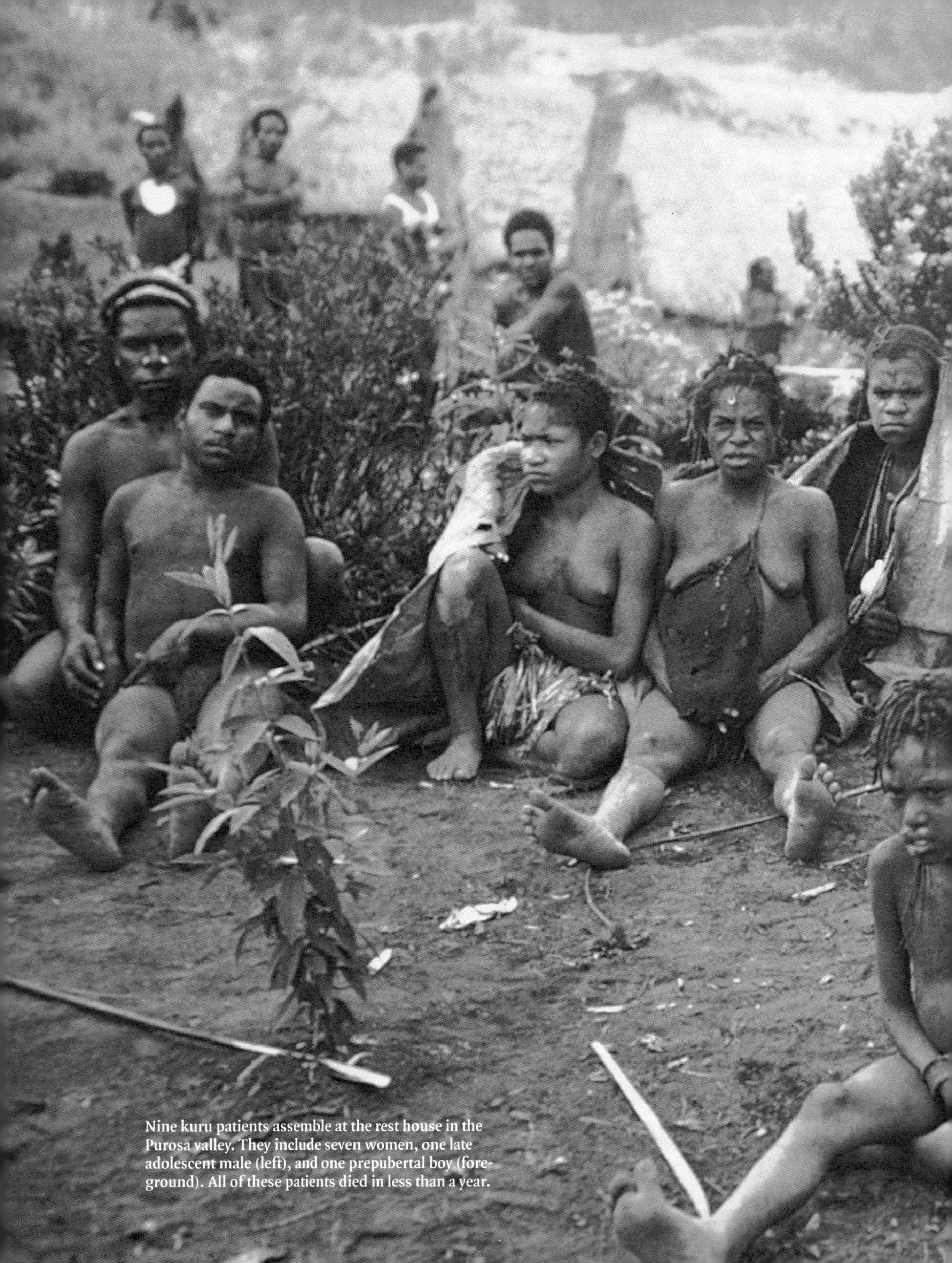

Nine kuru patients assemble at the rest house in the Purosa valley. They include seven women, one late adolescent male (left), and one prepubertal boy (foreground). All of these patients died in less than a year.

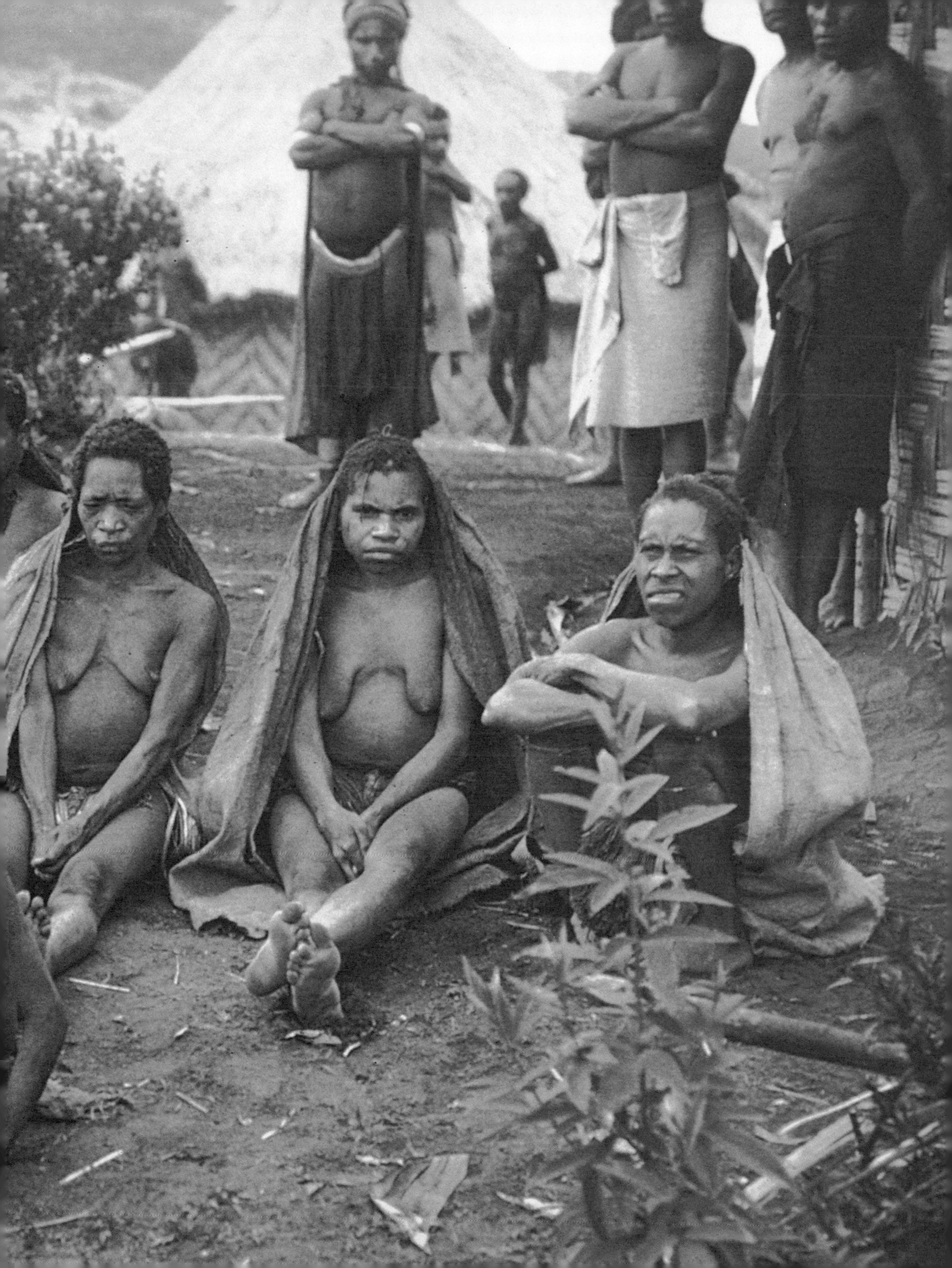

my makeshift, "Gajdusek"-system of teaching to read. I give them numbers 1, 2, 3, 4, 5, 6, 7, 8, 9, 10 all at once. Half an hour later, the full alphabet A, B, C, D, E, F ... X, Y, Z. Then, in the very same day, I write out A, E, I, O, U, and teach this phonetically, distinguishing the "name" from the "sound" of the letters.

With a dozen boys, Kuks and Fore, studying aloud, and without my suggestion or insistence, but with their demanding each and every one of them, a further lesson, help, an exercise sheet, correction of their "reading"... it is a most remarkable experience and one I had never anticipated. Thus I come to study the "primitive" and ruin it with my own sophistication! Damn it!

I have no illusions—few if any of them will learn to read—but that they have all irrevocably caught on to what reading is all about, what its mechanics are, and what it consists of is certain.

JANUARY 26: Agakamatasa-Waieti

As we were dressing the sores, wounds, ulcers, etc., which have accumulated here at Agakamatasa in my near-month of absence, I noticed a boy who looked almost fourteen years of age and who was still the image of a smaller boy of eleven or twelve I have had with me in previous years, but had not yet realized that he was missing: It was Kageinaro! I greeted him but was a bit surprised by his lack of vocal response, by his unusually dirty appearance, his shredded loincloth, and his rather restrained stance and lack of usual boyish response. I attributed it to his embarrassment. When I turned to Wanevi to ask why I had not seen Kageinaro earlier while I was here, Wanevi embarrassedly diverted his eyes and said, "Me tink e gat sik." And as though electrocuted, I suddenly realized that another of my boys had kuru. For a few seconds, I had failed to notice the classical stoic stance, quiet restraint of speech, which is restrained in embarrassment, for the patient thinks his voice will be a giveaway since it has begun to become dysarthric. Here was Kageinaro, the wiry, noisy, impish, always naughty, and constantly playing youngster of my last trips, now a fattening adolescent, restraining his speech, holding himself stiffly. I was spellbound, with the discouraging realization thrust so forcefully upon me that I was back in kuru country and that there is no life here without the ever-threatening death from kuru! Kageinaro, who has worked with me on kuru for several years, knows all about this as well as I, and, seeing himself now as we both looked upon Azibara but two years ago, is awkward. Thus, even engaged in peripheral studies, trying to avoid the clinical disease for a while, I have it thrust upon me in this too dramatic fashion.

JANUARY 31: Awarosa-Oriondumuti hamlet, South Fore

Late at night: I continue with Kageinaro huddled on the bamboo floor beside me in the blanket I have given him. The others are off sharing the hind-quarter of the huge pig Igaga gave to me, of which I had a good feast this evening. For the past three nights Kageinaro has slept in my house beside me, voided each morning, and saved all his daily voidings. Even at this late date I am learning more about kuru associating with him, and if kuru is contagious I certainly will have it, for had he leprosy I would have it in spite of its low contagiousness. Unfortunately, I fear, kuru is not going to be that simple!

FEBRUARY 6: Waieti, Agakamatasa, South Fore

This morning I was up before sunrise typing up the Slow Virus Infection abstract. I have submitted one paper on kuru in childhood and another on slow virus infections in which I shall develop the possibility of kuru-scrapie slow virus and temperate virus analogies and our current approach to the problem. In spite of the fact that kuru looks worse, if anything, right now, with eight current cases in the "lower" Miarasa hamlets—four young boys at one time!—and another eight in upper Miarasa, I am very much afraid that we may be very, very surprised eventually to find infection or toxin far from a discardable hypothesis, in spite of all my evidence to the contrary. Our approach therefore must continue to be that of hunting for toxic factors and infectious agents. Scrapie-like virus remains a very, very good possibility.

FEBRUARY 27: Purosa, South Fore

I have only today begun carefully studying the kuru cases of Purosa, which are many. Ivuti, a youngster of about seven years, is with us here, staying with me for the night on urine collections, and I have spent most of the afternoon examining, studying, and observing him. He is still perfectly oriented in time, place, and person, intelligent,

BELOW A young Fore boy in terminal stage of kuru, held by his father. Intravenous and tube feeding at the Kuru Hospital permitted him to live to this advanced stage of the disease, whereas at home he would have been smothered by relatives before his inability to swallow without aspiration of food or water caused him to starve and thirst to death.

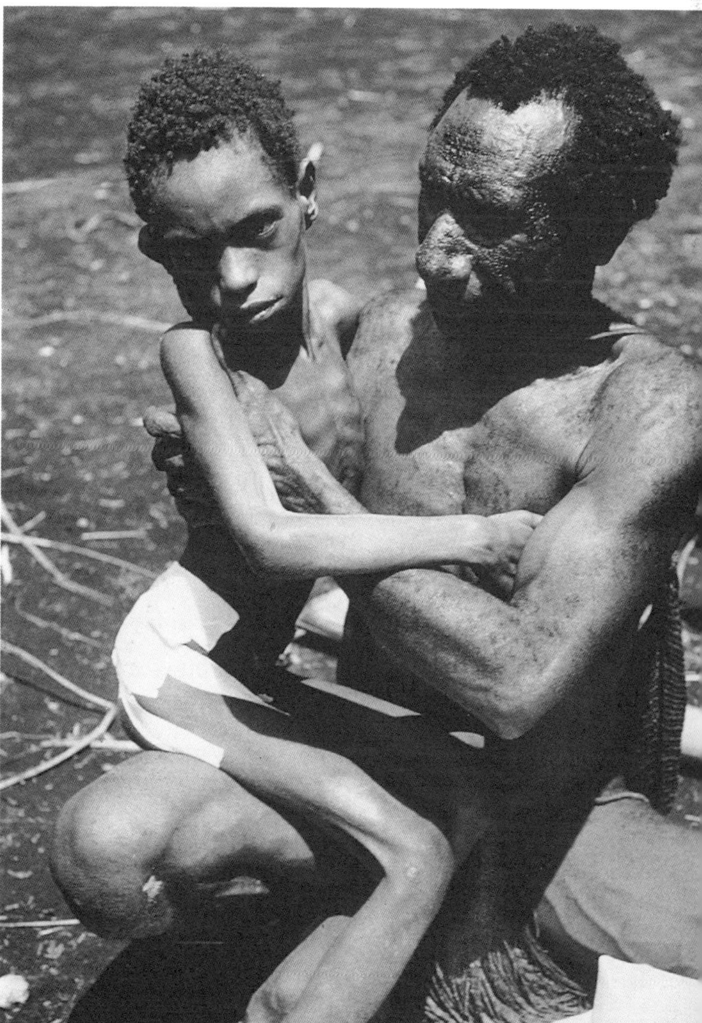

friendly, and shows the euphoria of most kurus, laughing sooner than anyone else, laughing inordinately, and on the slightest provocation. Now he is in the *haus kuk* [cooking house], where Anua and I have tried to make scones, using the recipe the two Lutheran sisters at Okapa wrote out. With Ivuti sitting with us and the crowd of native men and boys in the *haus kuk* to watch the fun and keep out of the rain, I had my hands full trying to be a physician and an observant investigator while covered with flour, powdered milk, and butter, and trying to get a blazing fire to heat our makeshift reflector oven of cut tins and tin foil. Ivuti took it all in, fell over in his laughter a few times, and was propped up again rather passively and as a matter of course by the bystanders more interested in the baking than in whether he rolled over into the fire. But just in this callous lack of concern—if that is what it is—and nonchalance lies the total absence of any sense of tragedy or catastrophe in his current plight, either by him or those about him ... and it is this that makes kuru so tolerable for everyone. Here is where I want to be if I ever get it!

The scones are quite edible.

MARCH 7: Umasa, South Fore

I found two active kuru cases, both mild, in adult women whom I examined and from whom I took blood specimens. However, here I encountered resistance to venepuncture for the first time, by the once cooperative *tultul* [assistant village official] who patrolled with me in 1958! He eloquently stated his case: he had helped us collect specimens, draw blood, and study and examine patients in 1957 and 1958, and since then, time and again; yet the victims died quickly, as quickly, perhaps quicker than before. Nothing was helping them, obviously, and perhaps it was harming their brief life expectancy! I accepted this remarkably cogent, beautifully stated argument, and made no attempts to take large volume specimens here or get family bleedings; however, I went to long efforts to explain that we were studying, and that whether further study would be needed for five years, ten years, or several generations, I could not predict. I explained that the "treatment" I am using on a few Purosa and Agakamatasa patients is not "curative" but "investigative," telling him at length what I meant by this.

Everyone, particularly all the older men, crowded about me as we stood at an open grave discussing all this philosophy of kuru research, and there followed rhetorical eloquent thanks for my explanation, understanding agreement, and an impressive statement of their plight. "Look, our village was much larger, our hamlets more numerous, and now bush is engulfing them. Houses stand vacant, our women are all dying, our men are disappearing, as are our children. Please understand us if we are a bit touchy and exasperated: we are in the hands of a wicked fate which is the work of ourselves alone!"

Then followed the usual discourse that kuru was caused by themselves alone, by wicked sorcerers who would not hear the pleas and admonitions of those who demanded and begged for subsidence of all this sorcery. All blame for sorcery the Fores take upon themselves, upon their very own men, for although enemy groups may cause their kuru, they are equally sure that their own men cause it in enemy groups, and some sorcerers may even cause kuru within their own group.

I stated, as I usually do, my skepticism and our "Western" approach to study, investigation, trial, and constant attempts to find the causes in our terms of microbes, toxins, poisons, or genes, and a means of preventing or curing the disease. Although neither of us budged a particle in our "beliefs," there was an appreciative understanding of both schools of thought, with the Intamatasa spokesman formally thanking me and my colleagues for our efforts and wishing us success and promising continued cooperation, although they know well that on their own part they must continue to fight for the abandonment of this sorcery....

In order to write this journal, to keep up field notes and case records, to prepare specimen lists and pack them for dispatch, and to get examinations and studies and interviews done, I have had to admonish the carriers and the boys about crowding around to interfere with my work. My threatening bursts of temper have left me embarrassed and chagrined with myself, but short of this, the situation would become hopeless, and I might as well abandon all attempts at work. In order to do the work I am doing, to lead the life I will lead, I must consciously and purposely make myself blind—or apparently blind—to the personal problems, the personal tragedies and needs of those about me. I do this also in the States, but I wonder whether the family, colleagues, and friends there really "understand" this any better than do these boys, and even if they should, it would be expecting far too much to ask them to accept it without malice or disappointment, as do these boys.

APRIL 20: Agakamatasa, South Fore

Kageinaro is dying, starving and thirsting to death in a hideous state. I sit here knowing I should be at his side, yet neglecting him as do his fellow villagers. Tubinaga and Yobiga have brought him into the old *wai* [men's house] where he has been without food or water for the past two days and where he has been secluded without being carried out for over two weeks. However, only about three weeks ago, he still walked with support to Wagorori to watch the work on the aid post which is now well under way. I went down to see him, found him wrapped in the blanket which I gave him in

January, lying on a pile of *kunai* straw in a boarded-up, pitch-dark cubicle of the *wai*. I asked to bring him out of doors and even Wanevi and Tubinaga were a bit reluctant. The removal of the boarded-up cubicle door brought in a dim light which produced in the wretched boy a painful photophobia and he was obviously in immense misery without being able to communicate any of it to us. We dragged him out of doors from his excrement-soiled lair, with a few groans of protest coming from him, and had to cover him with his filthy blanket in order to keep the bright sunlight from his eyes which he closed tightly. He could not close his parched lips and his thick sticky, saliva-covered teeth were revealed in a hideous grimace which he managed to cover with his arm and forearm in a manner suggesting that embarrassment still prevailed in this woeful state of extremis. On his legs and hips we found extensive sores and ulcers. I suggested giving him water—he was obviously thirsting to death—but everyone rejected this suggestion until I insisted. Kageinaro sucked avidly at the water poured over his mouth and teeth with his head held to one side to avoid aspiration and drowning and obviously wanted all the water he could get. We poured three cups over his mouth in this way and he may have managed to consume a cupful of water from this procedure. He then began to open his eyes and focus his attention on me, forlornly gazing in helpless misery at me. I spoke to him quite naturally and from his helpless gaze I knew he heard and understood. As I fought back tears and struggled for words, I heard Wanevi crying and looked up to see both him and Tubinaga crying over the pitiful sight of our friend and their kinsman. Wanevi soon dried his tears and controlled his sobs and helped me give Kageinaro more water, but choking spells, even from this cautious method, soon discouraged the boy in his sucking attempts. I shouted for soap from our camp

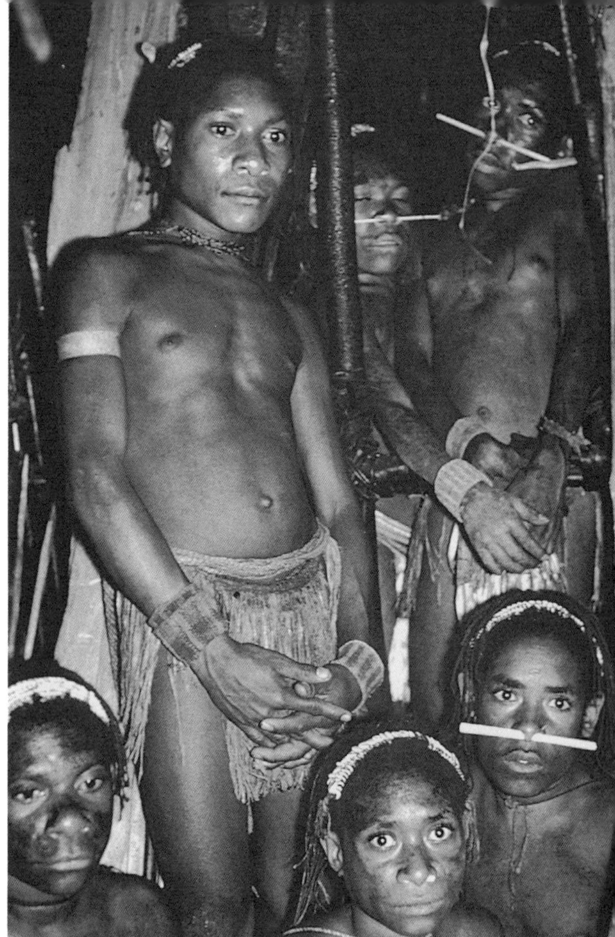

ABOVE Six adolescent Awa warriors in their young men's house. The braided waist and arm bands indicate their initiation grades.

and Wanevi and I washed Kageinaro. He shuddered and trembled but, as I occasionally caught his gaze, I knew he was grateful. He was a fastidious boy, loved soap, clean *laplaps*; washed often and objected to dirty native houses, preferring to stay with the Okapa missionaries than at home. As I write, he is thirsting, starving, suffering, and dying in the filthy cell of the *wai*, his sores bandaged and a clean *laplap* over him. I hope this produces more comfort than pain. He cannot live for long. I took two small blood specimens and found him trying to help in extending his tonically flexed elbow. As I write here at camp, having deserted him as has his whole world of *wontoks*, I feel depressed and dreadful. I told him I would be back in a few days; he groaned and struggled for some coordination in protest, I felt convinced that this was Kageinaro's last plea for help, a "take me with you, save me!" plea I could do nothing but ignore.

Playing with Kageinaro but a few months ago, in this house in which he lived, I little suspected this rapid decline to terminal extremis, and as I work here this evening while four boys draw pictures on paper placed upon our cargo boxes I recall uncomfortably that the last time I sat in this scene, Kageinaro shared it with me. I am torn by a desire to rush down to the *wai* to sit with Kageinaro—yet deterred by the same helpless repulsion that leads the Fore to abandon hope and sustenance at this final stage. He could be more comfortably nursed through these painful days, but this might prolong the pain from a few days to a few months! Azibara and now Kageinaro! Who next? It is a curse of such magnitude that I am ashamed of my feeble efforts and appalled by my own callousness. Wanevi standing there over me as I stooped to give water to Kageinaro, and crying in deep sobs, I cannot relegate this part of my life to a "less important" status, it is my life as it is theirs.

JUNE 20: Sailing up the coast of South New Guinea from the Digoel mouth to Cookbaai

It is not the century in which one can carve a destiny for a people, but were it, I would have my life changed. As it is, I can only be an observer, and trust that by being a bit more knowing and better informed than the others, I may be of eventual help to these people, unreal though they may be in the modern world. My emotional investment in New Guinea has been great. I shall not sell out.

Author's Note: No one born since cannibalism ceased in the late 1960s has died of kuru. Thus, kuru has now been entirely eradicated among New Guinea natives under the age of forty, with only a few long-incubation cases occurring each year.

KARA WALKER

A Dissection from the Bowel

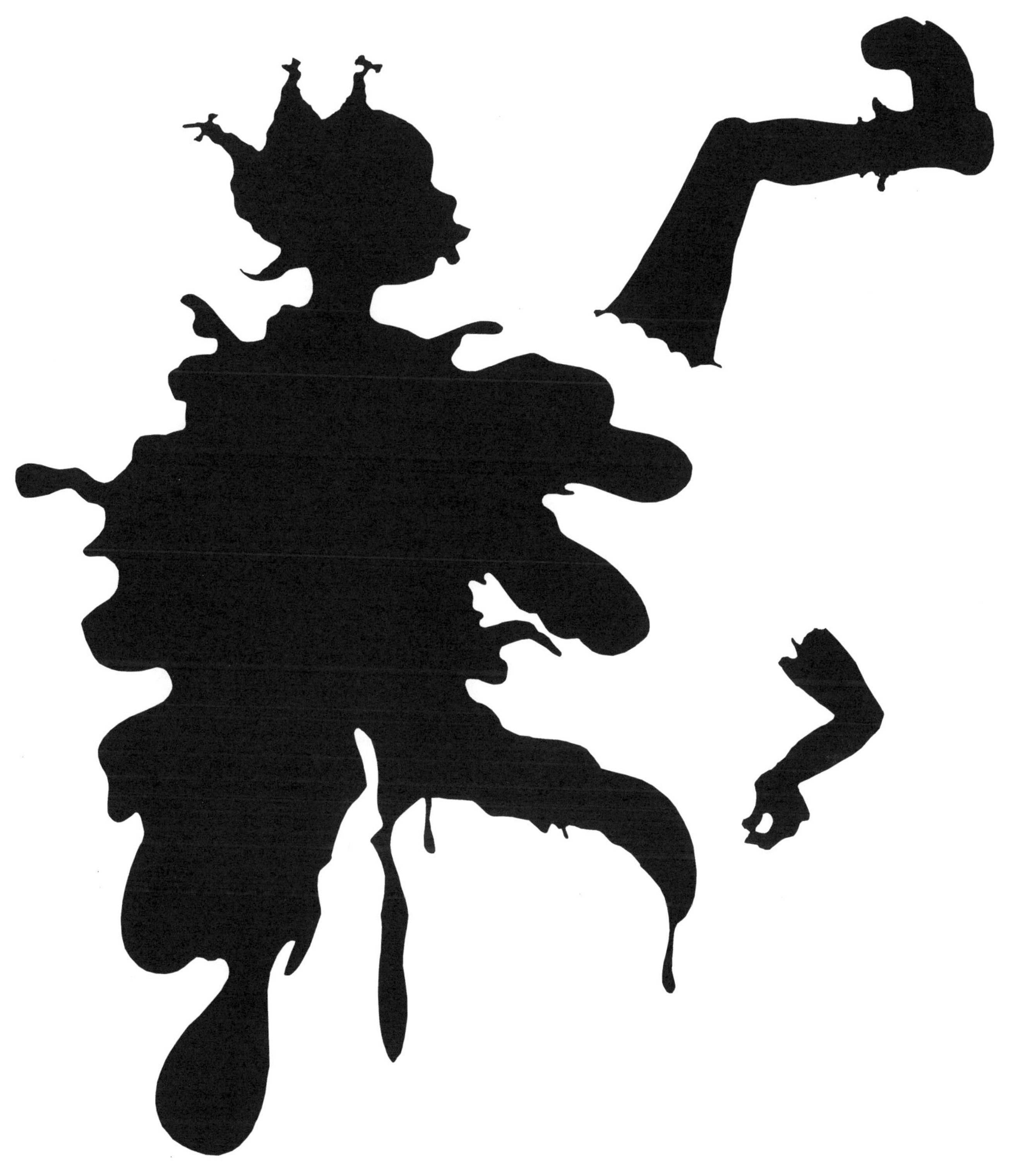

. . to the Bosom

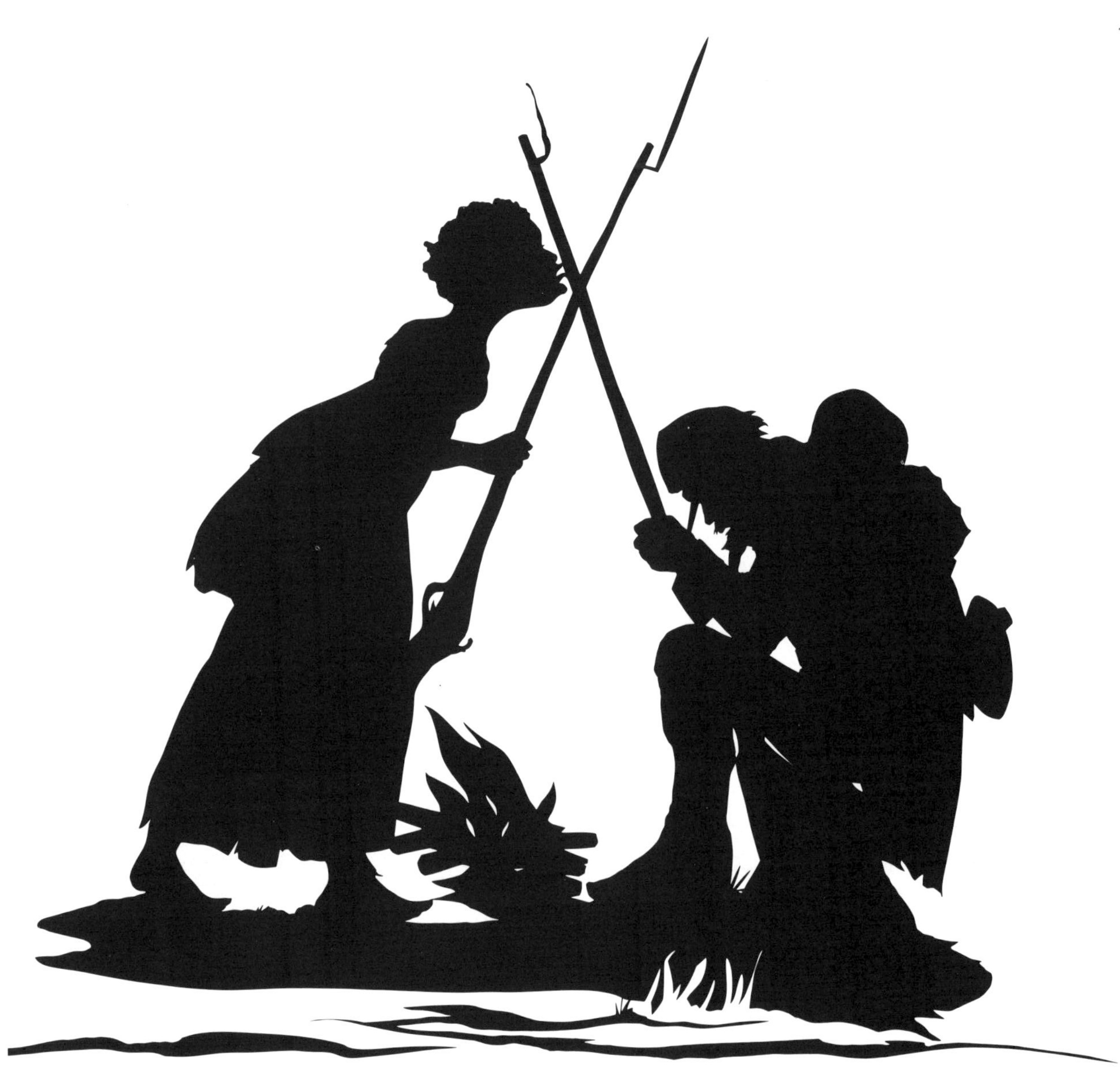

PRECEDING PAGE *Girl*, 1994.

BELOW AND OPPOSITE PAGE

The Battle of Atlanta: Being the Narrative of a Negress in the Flames of Desire (details), 1995.

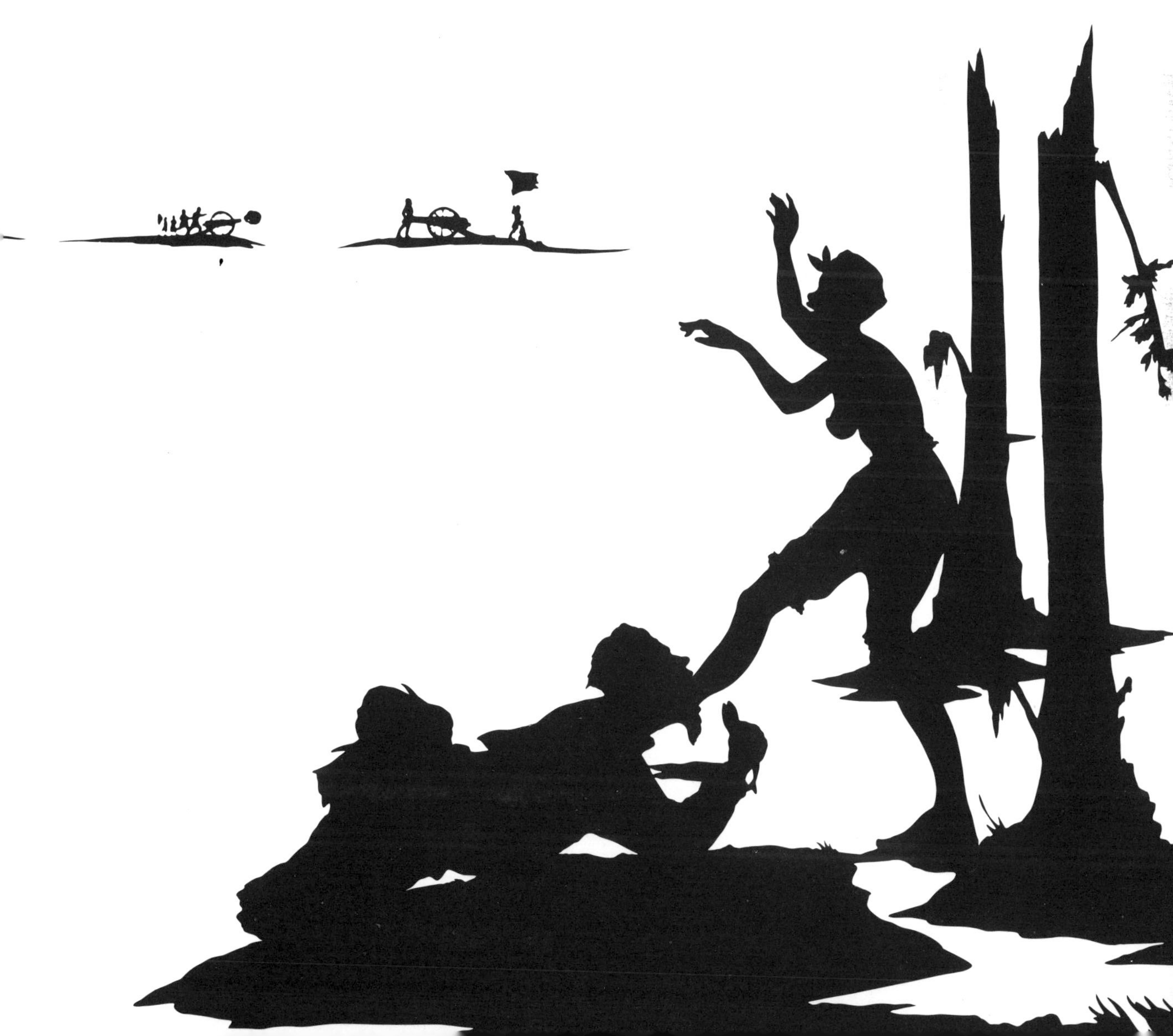

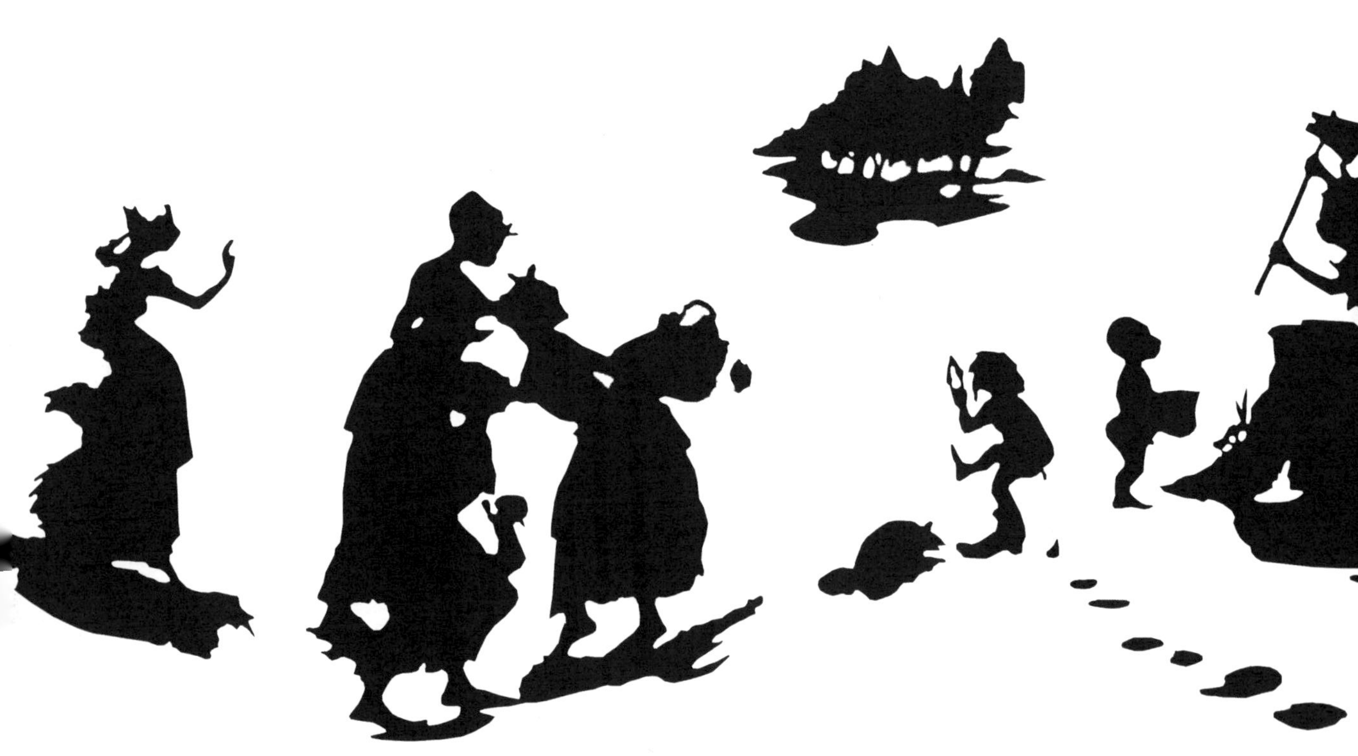

The End of Uncle Tom and the Grand Allegorical Tableau of Eva in Heaven, 1995.

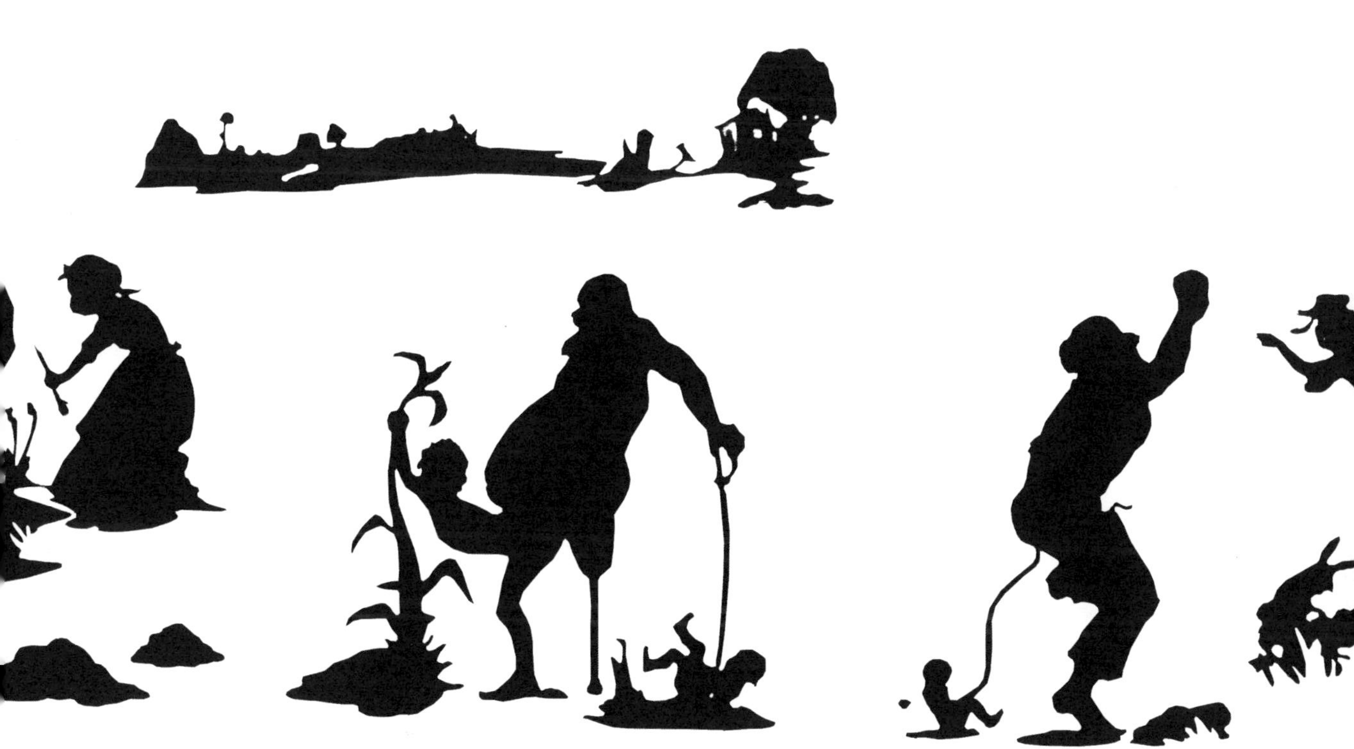

Gone: An Historical Romance of a Civil War as it Occurred between the Dusky Thighs of One Young Negress and Her Heart (detail), 1994.

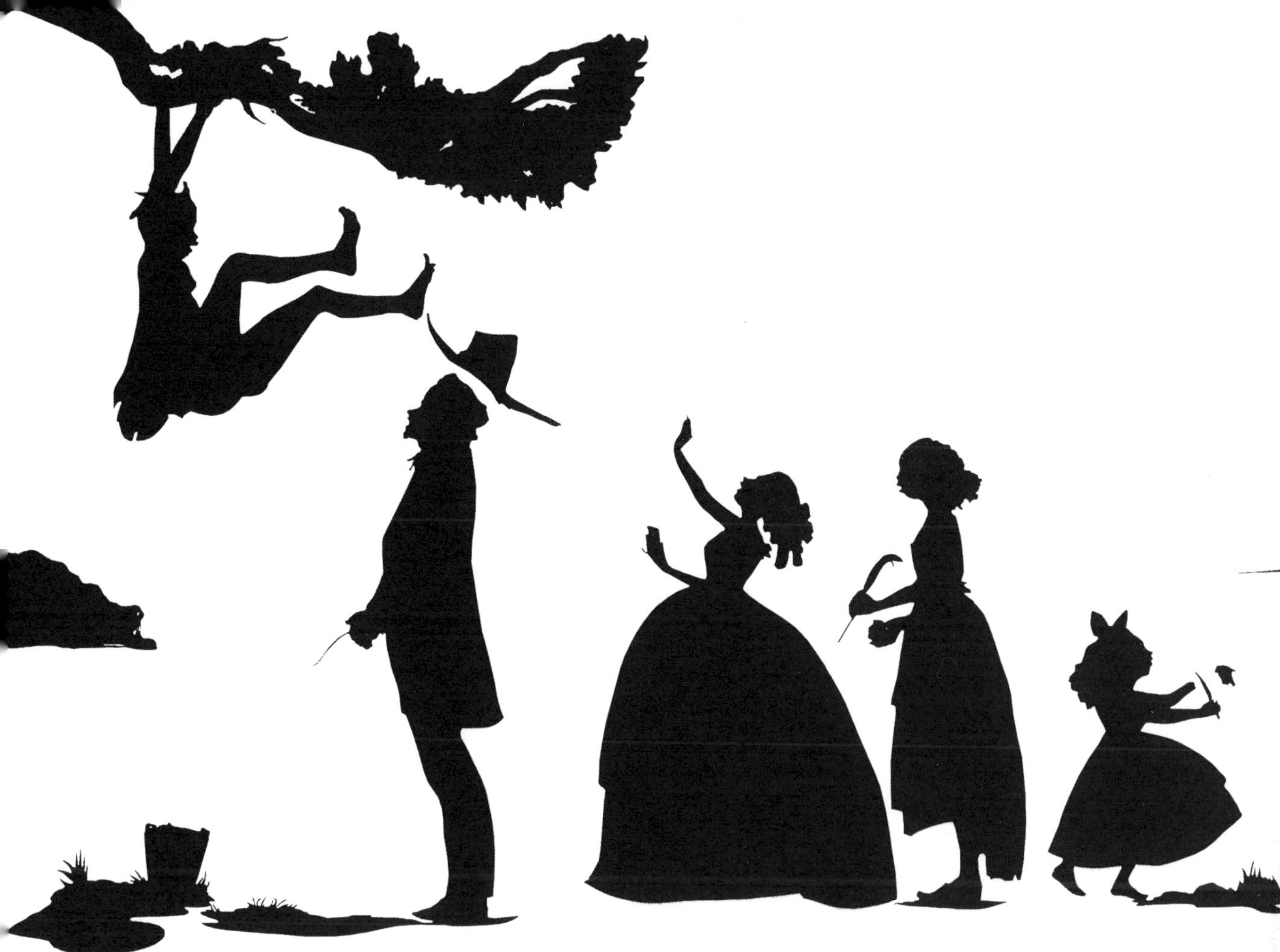

Look Away! Look Away! Look Away! (detail), 1995.

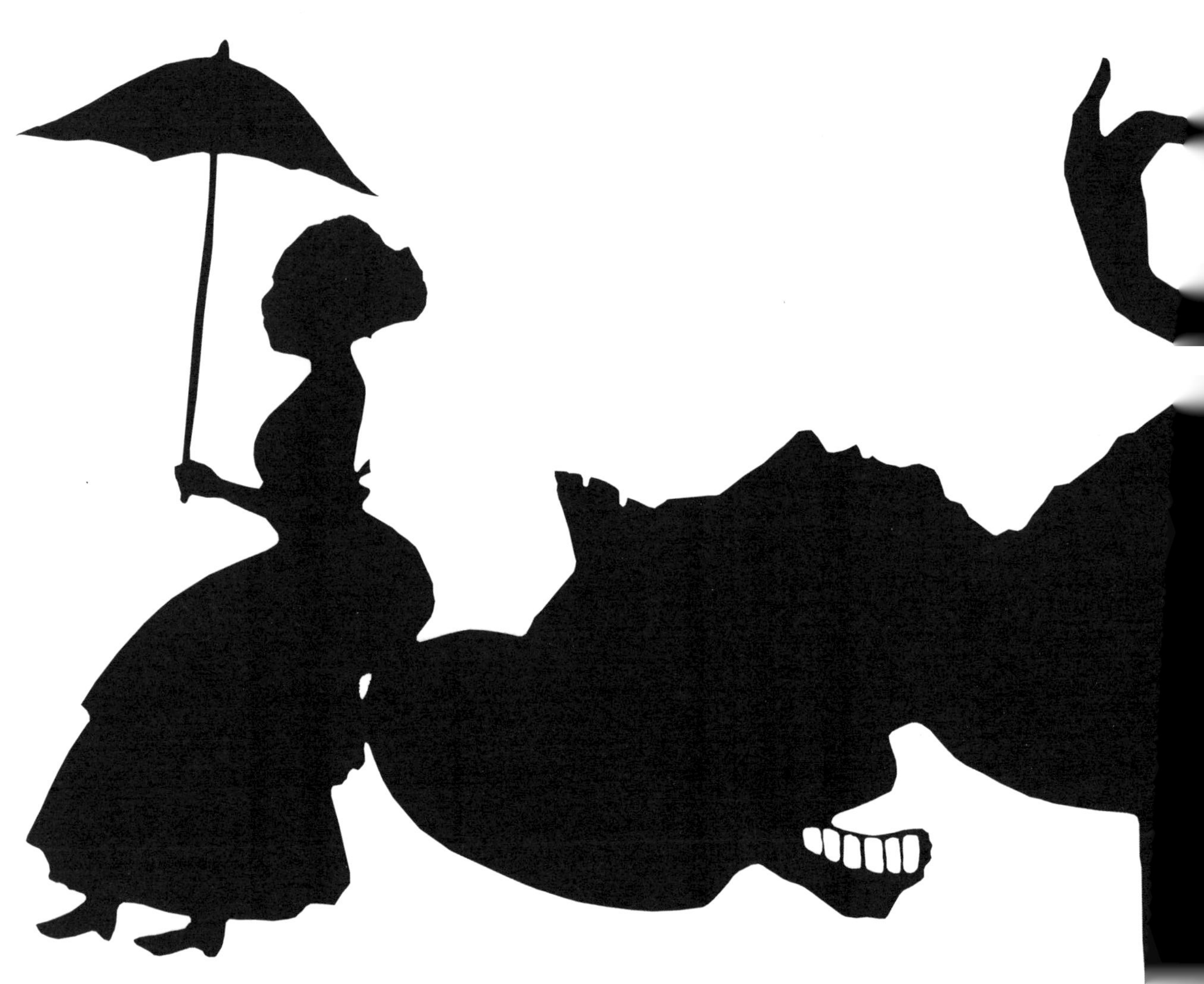

KARA WALKER

Kara Walker's unholy narratives find their roots in genre painting, the grotesque history of slavery and race relations in America, pornographic stories set in the ante-bellum South, civil war reenactments, and Harlequin romance novels. A series of bawdy pantomimes, they are the resurrection and mutation of submerged history, acted out on a kind of "inner plantation" where fiction has at least as much force as historical fact, and desire, ambivalence, and dependency are allowed to coexist with horror. This is a region of contradictions, where each figure can be master, slave, and abolitionist at once, simultaneously inhabiting and being inhabited by a multitude of others. Here, conflicting realities overlap and push at each other, destabilized by Walker's dark wit. Her animated Southern Belles, Uncle Remuses, Creole Beauties, Confederate Soldiers, Southern Crackers, and Pickaninny Children seem to spill directly from the inky realms of America's collective unconscious onto the wall. On moonlit lawns, under trees dripping Spanish moss, in tussocky swamps, and from pillared verandas, they gleefully pursue their lustful, violent, and curiously intimate relationships.

Both silhouettes and stereotypes, in Kara Walker's observation, blot out specific detail—while making sometimes unpalatable truths about perception, belief, and desire more obvious. Executed in the style of nineteenth-century silhouette portraits, her cut-paper wall murals, however, dissolve the stiffness of an old-fashioned art, just as the animated creatures who populate them vigorously deny, embrace, and subvert the natures given to them by their outlines. These figures are as fluid and entangled as their histories. In Walker's spirited response to abject art, it is no longer clear who has the upper hand. Her technique is a leveling device through which everyone becomes black: both kin and non-kin, each one the disguised, mysterious "other." Walker's work assumes a complex whole from which nothing can be easily eradicated or safely suppressed, and in which each action has an equal and unpredictable reaction. She knows that through humor we digest the indigestible, through myths and games we both reinforce and subvert accepted realities, and through desire we imbibe knowledge of the other. Our banished stereotypes have not disappeared: they have only been hidden. Here, they are released to write their own stories.

ANNE DORAN

Untitled, 1994.

THE LIGHTNING FIEL

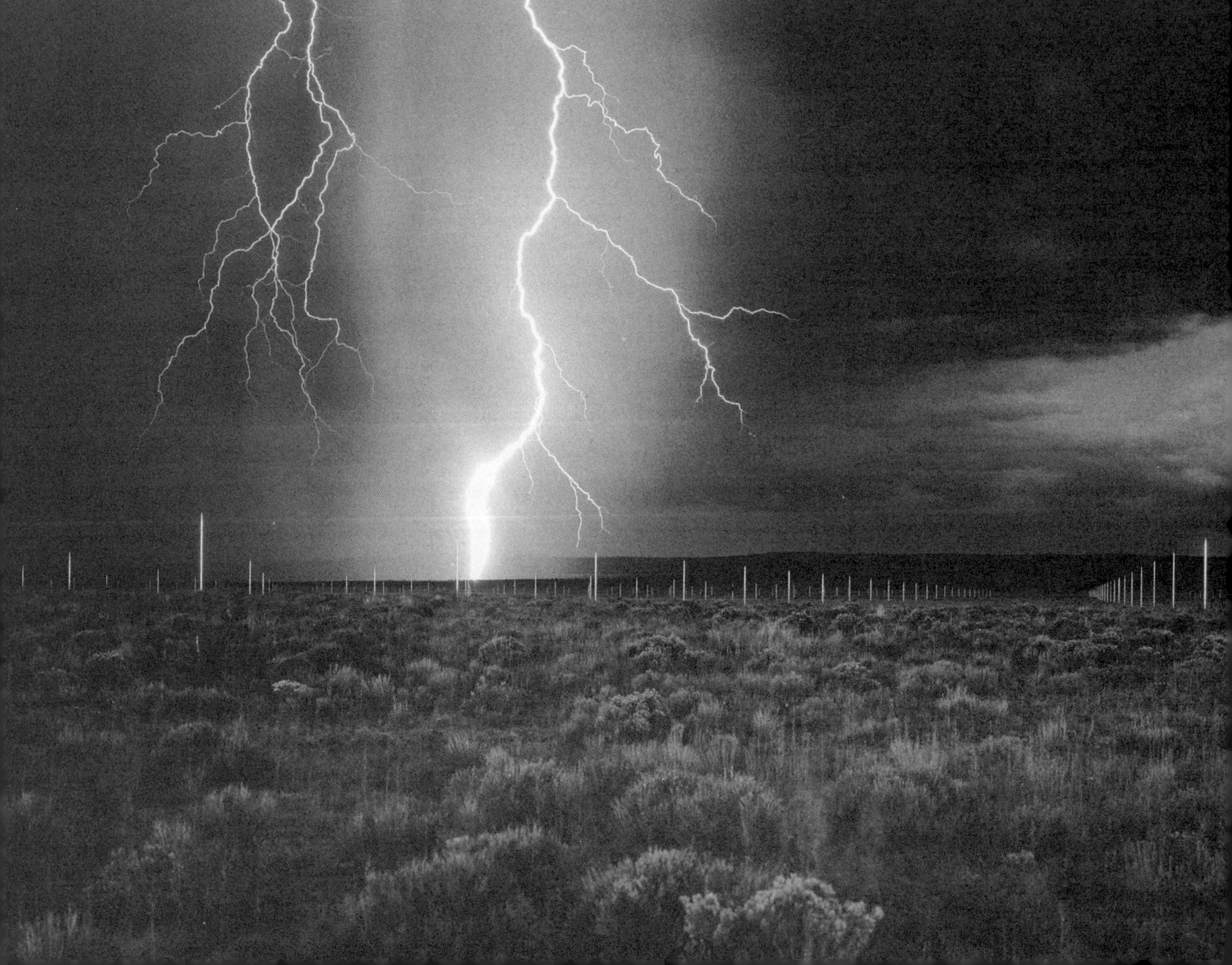

GEORGE EVANS

for PL & BJ

The title refers to The Lightning Field *(1974–77), by Walter De Maria, a monumental work of landscape art located in a remote desert basin ringed by distant mountains near Quemado, Mexico. It consists of 400 pointed, stainless-steel poles (lightning rods) two inches in diameter, standing at an average height of 20 feet, 7.5 inches, adjusted to the terrain so that the poles are of an equal height, so perfectly aligned that a sheet of glass the size of the field could rest safely upon their tips without cracking. They are arranged in a grid with 16 rows of 25 poles stretching east to west, and 25 rows of 16 poles stretching north to south. They stand 225 feet apart (311 on the diagonal), with the total east-west dimension of the piece running exactly one mile, and the north-south distance just over a kilometer. A requirement for viewing the work is that one remain on the site for a minimum of 24 hours. Visitors are driven in, then picked up at the end of the stay. There is a cabin for sleeping, and a supply of food and water.*

The invisible is real.
—Walter De Maria

1

It blends with the desert until you are almost in it or struck by sunlight
sparking on the rods.

You look but can't see it against brilliant sky, though once in focus it won't stop being seen, like subtle truths we bargain with and struggle to ignore.

Then it appears to have grown from earth, the quills of a subterranean, the spines of a whole field as a cactus. A model of infinity the desert doesn't need, but one which embodies time and light in an essence native to space, which makes it tolerable, though still a form of destruction, as much that is beauty is, and as all touched wildness must be.

The sun moves and the rods move, their colors shift. At noon they become invisible, upright sun blending them into land and sky, their glistening bodies prominent as it sinks, dyeing them while it drags away into dusk, clouds shifting in flamingo and purple folds. When it's gone, the rods turn white but begin to disappear again until the moon transforms them to silver rows that diminish in vanishing points, mystery lines in blackness illuminated by stars, the tips of other rods poking back from the dark.

2

Rocks are flying in far-off cities where men measure resolve with fire, their exchange of words reduced to weapons, free moments to exhaustion, free will to bread.

Lives absorbed in struggle, time parsed by argument and withered, children reamed and doused and orphaned.

South of here, a border crosses the desert, an invisible curtain dividing earth into landscape and scenery—the first a geography to survive, the second a possession to protect. A fence and barbed-wire intellect. A beginning and an end.

Along it, the tribes surge north. They see no threat in their own eyes, no reason in their hands to be stopped, no logic in splitting sand into one world or a next. They see only motion, and work, and living.

Here in the north, hunger is questioned by those who have eaten, weather by those who are warm, shelter by those who are home. We are high above the south, where truth is a form of suicide. It becomes the same among us, but slowly. We are free to have ideas, but there are no bad ones, only horrible enactments.

One shuts the mind to so much it destroys the purpose of sleep, creating worlds without sleep, worlds where the body shudders into rest but does not rest because the mind does not shut by looking away. Looking away is the same as looking, but more intense. The effort is greater, the afterimage takes longer to dissolve.

As in this field, the space confined by the rods stands out from the rest of the desert when you look away.

3

Outside, near the towns and cities, and in them, the desert is reduced to sewage troughs, undulating rolls of sand and clay converted to toilets by Rotarians and tract-house artists. Tertiary folds ruffling the highway shoulder bridged by roads are a tagger's heaven, a hiding place for drifted children near millennia to have sex, tempting death or sheathed, afterward spray-painting their dissent, lonely wishes to belong that pale to idiocy next to marks left by the ancients. But who can blame them. They are sincere. And they are lost.

The hard part is knowing that the poor flood north across the border to own what ruined them, and that being fixed on possessions peels the soul and pounds one senseless, but history isn't written by the conquered, nor direction set by those who've been stopped.

4

In late afternoon, a raven passed back and forth above the field, unable to perch on the pointed rods. Two friends and I stretched out and watched its shape against vaulted sky. Holding the air with the tip of a wing, it wheeled and crossed and recrossed.

Someone told me once that if the shadow of a passing bird (a hawk in particular, or a relative) touches your car while you're driving, your destinies will all connect, and in their nexus your life will be solved, solutions revealed. But it doesn't count if you swerve on the road after shadows—it has to be natural, the way driving through once-wilderness spewing fumes, crushing mice and rabbits, is natural. We were driving through mountains into eastern Washington when he said it. It was something he learned from a Nez Perce with whom he'd traveled the same road years before. Hawks were crossing in rapid succession scanning for road kill, and, we thought after he told the story, taunting us. But the birds were so numerous we knew we'd have to go out of our way to avoid being touched. Every few seconds red tails appeared above the windshield. We passed near a kestrel hung against the sky like a bird crucifix, brushed near the swoop of an osprey by water, and were rejected by sharp-shinned and Cooper's hawks, goshawks, bald and golden eagles, and a turkey vulture uninterested in our future. We crossed the mountains untouched. It reminded us that you cannot pursue your fate. Go where you are going; it will be there.

Opposite gravity, birds carry inexplicable forms, noises, objects, things we can never see, so why not fate I thought, on my back there in the desert, and in that world especially, why not a raven.

One by one we were swept by its shadow, and when I stood up, it happened: I saw through a blue range of mountains one might reach by foot in several days, and beyond them viewed our destinies connected in death. It was a practical fate.

Our bodies dissolved into salt, leaking into spaces made by creosote root, mixing into dry lake cracks and ruts, alkaline, basalt, precious metals, waste, our dust mixed in with radioactive sand, scattering a million places, catching the wind, going on, and I saw clearly it's not only to live that one exists, and that being optimistic or pessimistic about any of it is foolish. Our only purpose is to govern ourselves with one eye dreaming and one eye on the difficult balance at hand.

Afterward, we sat on the back porch drinking whiskey. Lizards bobbed.
Ants perfected their mounds.

The raven disappeared in a spot. I heard its wings chop the air for miles.

Watch the rods. Wait for lightning. Live.

5

Everything is selfish in the heart.

The emptiness one feels is the collapsing of time
from a seed that has sprouted the end of time, a seed
we have tended carelessly with meticulous inattention.

Everything is generous in the heart.

The emptiness one feels is that same flower, the heart,
which is too fond of life to wish it gone, but spends its days
worrying over what has not yet happened.

Everything and nothing is in the heart.

I watch an ant carry its planet—the insect Atlas—and if one thinks
humans are not immense, think of that one, the size of two poppy seeds,
and what, if it pays attention, despair could really mean.

6

In early evening weedstraw started blowing down gully and wash,
tumbleweed skeletons spit out in bristled arcs, the wind splintered with
memories swept up as it passed: the earth, its rocks, a flashing snake, and
histories in stone: a row of figures with arms linked millennia away,
feathered dreams on an outcrop: one whose head was fire, outlines of many
hands in place of statements, and precise marks for the motion of seasons
and stars.

As its power increased, the air was torn brown, the dips and swells of sand became bunkers at the edge of a dust-blurred village erased by ancient bombs. When it hit in force, swallowing all sound, elusive thirsts locked down in shelter and one would swear the world was empty.

Facing its force, I imagined the body of war: a head rushing from a ruined distance, its tail diminished in a brush of bitter calm. Back turned to it, I searched through its forward flow for the moment it hit and went on, as if abstract force has clear beginnings, as if it's possible to make sense of men and women and what they do.

I saw only the past being swept up in storm.

Still, the missing remain among us. The wind takes them, but also leaves them behind. They own nothing, yet remain. We can't see them, but we look, and would reach our hands into any fire to draw them back, knowing they are there.

Then we die. We become the missing, and the wind keeps blowing. The water we drink goes on, its molecules will pass through mouths in the future, just as water that rolled over dinosaur tongues is sipped in the capsules we shoot into space.

And in this field the wind will keep blowing, bearing the shapes of all bones.

7

On another day in the world, walking and careless for a minute, I stopped in Washington Square to listen to students debate the causes of war. They were shouting, screaming, but on the edge of a dance, the sexual tension between them much more interesting than a subject not worth words beyond chanting: money, money, money.

I thought: they'd be better off in bed together in any combination. They should have been at the ocean with gallons of wine, drunk on the speed of their bodies. Failing that, I wanted them to stop talking and take over, march the streets and take the banks, take city hall, the derricks of black blood, the military with its medals and weird suits. Take it, I wanted to shout, it's yours. It gives me an unreachable itch, I'm sick of it, sick of petty affairs that eat countries, sick of morning papers ruining days, radio voices poisoning coffee, TV eating brains. Take it. Anything would be better.

But I came to my senses. The students grew calm. One of them, a runt, held his pinkie aloft while drinking an expensive bottle of water. Another was whining. They were artfully dressed in black, polite, and the subject was television, not war.

What things are really about is always another matter.

The lines between subjects, the borders, are not even gray, they're the same as the ground they cross. And where they overlap is invisible because the world is bored with its problems.

One begins to think that whether or not things might come to a sudden end is not what bothers us, but what bothers us is that things might never end.

8

Then the wind was gone, and daylight. In the distance, lightning began to unfold elbow after elbow above mountains erased by dark.

We waited for its approach from thunder, imagining its veins ripping across the rods, waiting for the metal to attract and harness its mystery. But that night it would not happen. And it did not matter.

It's not just lightning but the place. Not the act alone, but its potential. The journey, not just the arrival. Not only the thrill, but the wait.

We are waiting for something, and though not always ready, we are always waiting, dying second by second, revived in each tick by what there is to learn and the urge to learn it. Disappearing at night into shadows like the rods into new terrain.

9

At dawn, the sun broke over a scarp lip, illuminating
the ears of a jackrabbit, its red veins attenuated
for an instant before it disappeared in scrub.

A momentary understanding of life.
Getting it, only to watch it vanish.

How difficult to live with the inequities
and contradictions wrought by humans,
but how necessary, and how stunning
because of them the momentary
things, the patterns of being,
the way beauty has
of turning up seconds
before it leaves.

I did not intend to come here and think about war
or death or fate, or even time, but the desert
is opposite what we inhabit, its geography
frail, its stripped-down body so obvious
it is clear in each second that life is
a brief matter worth every degree
of effort it is so at risk, worth
all pondering, and pain
when it comes
to that.

Along the highway and on the road in,
mormon teabushes glowed, winter fat
blurred into sagebrush and snakeweed,
white and golden dunes were clouds
behind heat devils, and such beauty
leads the mind to think not only of what
there is, but of what is gone, behind, over,

in the same way amputees feel missing limbs,
vestigial shadows with weight and motion—
the past is half the reason for beauty,
the other half being the future it bodes in promise.

I envy the ocotillo its flower flames,
and the stoop of the kestrel, smallest falcon,
creature that lives but a dozen years yet lives no less
than corrupted heads of state, and the cactus wren,
late sleeper, cooling its beak on the cholla, condensing
and reabsorbing its own liquids to go on, and woodrats
clumped beneath cholla, living for generations among the spines,
and the kangaroo rat with urine so dense it crystallizes hitting the air.

There is no waste in the undeveloped
parts of the desert, no unintended death,
no death by economics, no patriot death,
just simple death, an end to the effort,
an end to having lived by living.

I envy even the sand that was once awake in this place
where the heat is so intense the air so silent
you hear the blood in your veins, you
become the jackrabbit's ears, you
become the sun against rocks—
so thin, so deep a glaze.

10

The invisible is real.

But like an urchin test,
its simplicity is necessary,

not wanted.

ELÉNI SIKÉLIANÒS

CAMPO SANTO

—Non ai, voir, mère, non ai, non!

I learned to say no in the old language
studying at the Nightschool

of Electricity on Rocket Street
Before I got my eye put out

on a teeth of forests

No to the angels, no to electricity

No to pretending to read when the ear is open

the Pearl

of venery, this vertical blanking
about ten lines outside the TV's frame

no, no, for what is not No
hid by umber & alcove

QUAMASH

In the cave of St. Desire
I was saved from the clutch

of matter Before
we learned to eat

the death camas
in the deep woods off I repeat

this train
will not leave

the station, the night-
tortoise riding an iron
horse, & spit-

shining the floor

AU LAIT

Had we not betrayed the farmer
then the cow
might we

still live on Milk Street
with a bit of Mary's shirt next door
I don't want this

house in Cheapside
anymore. They are asking me
something from the accordion again.

I won't give in.

Marcel Duchamp & Rrose Sélavy

of or by

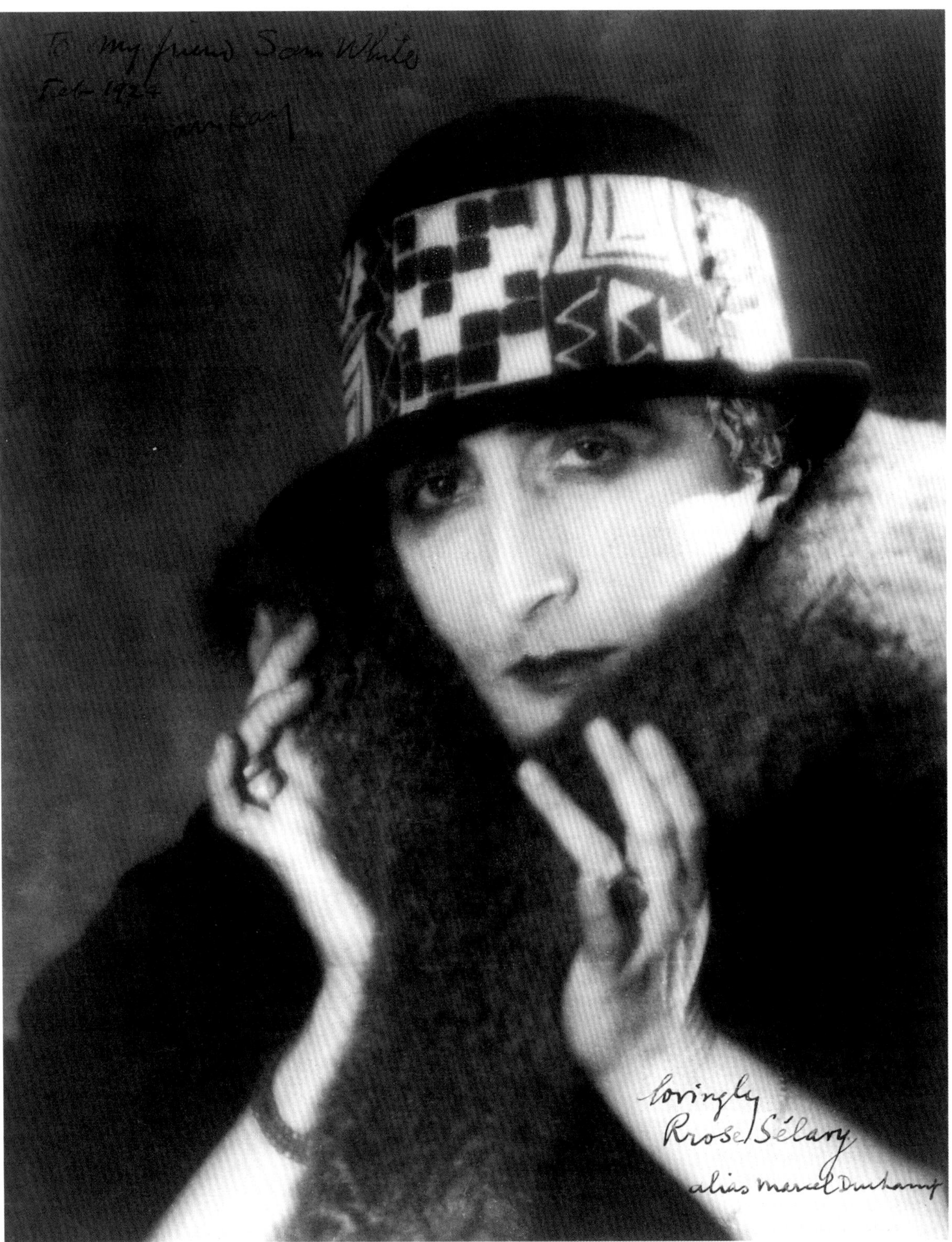
To my friend Sam White
Feb 1924
man Ray
lovingly
Rrose Sélavy
alias Marcel Duchamp

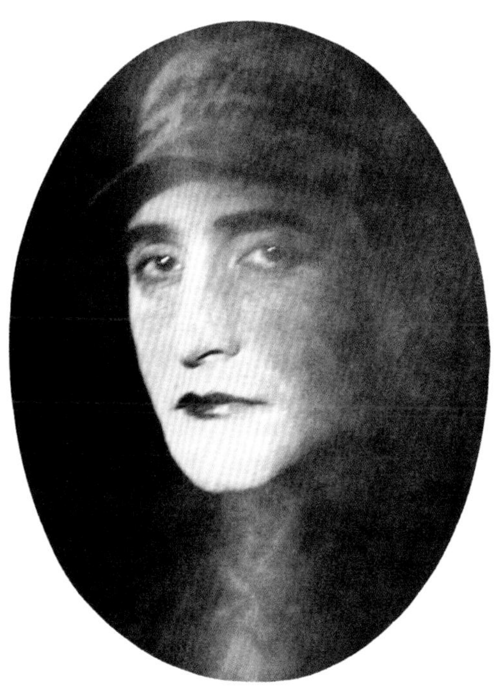

LEFT Man Ray, *Marcel Duchamp Dressed as Rrose Sélavy*, 1924.
RIGHT Man Ray, *Rrose Sélavy (looking to the right)*, 1921.
BELOW LEFT Man Ray, *Rrose Sélavy*, 1921.
BELOW RIGHT Man Ray, *Rrose Sélavy*, 1921.

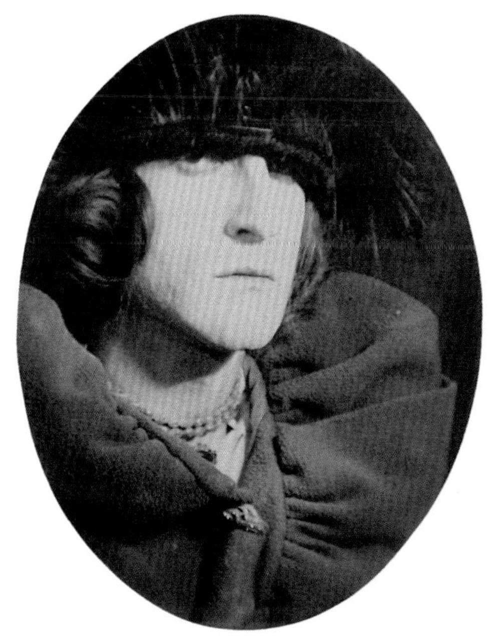

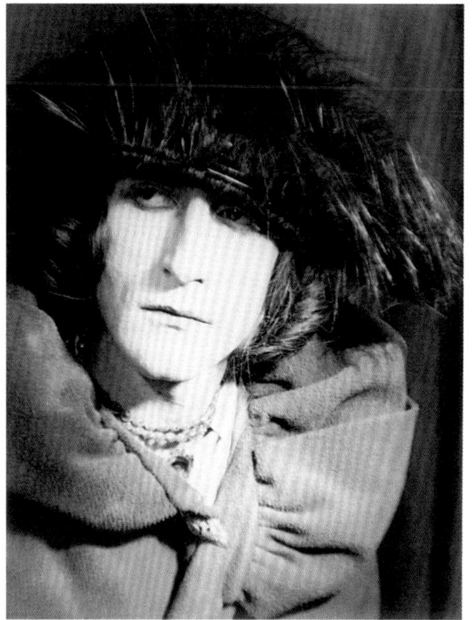

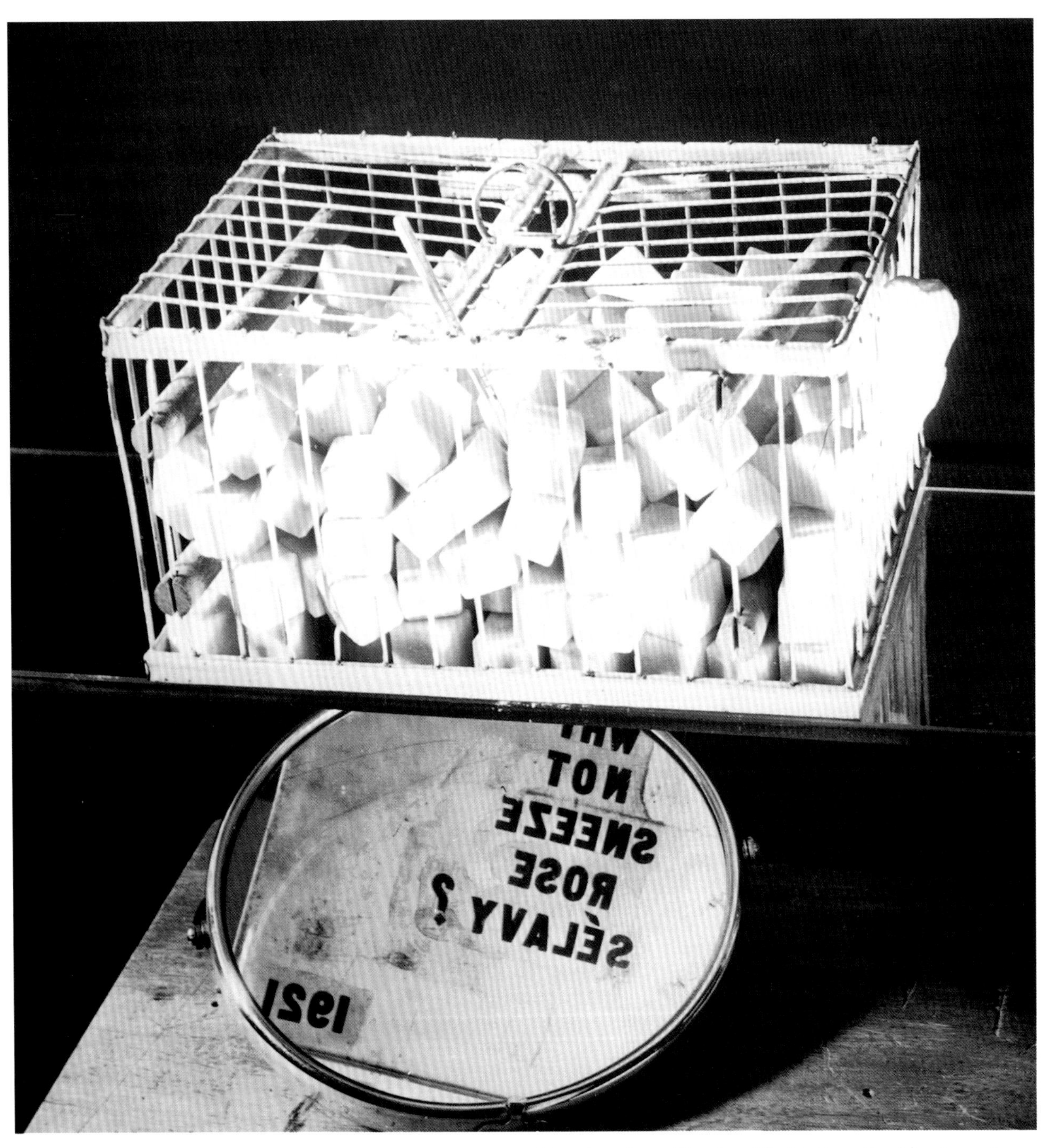

Marcel Duchamp/Man Ray, *Why Not Sneeze Rose Sélavy?*, 1921/1935.

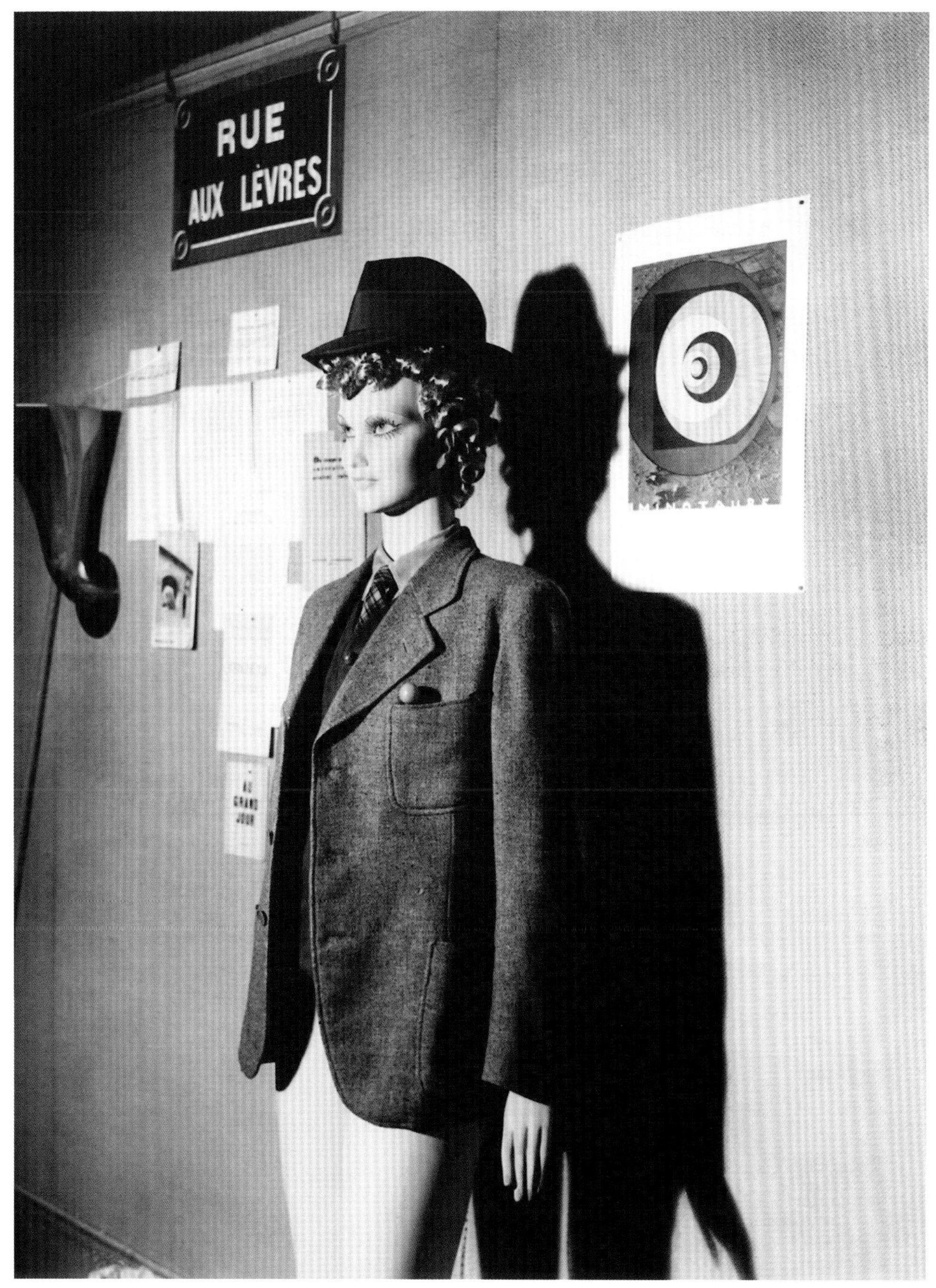

Marcel Duchamp/Man Ray, Mannequin exhibited at the *Exposition Internationale du Surréalisme*, 1938.

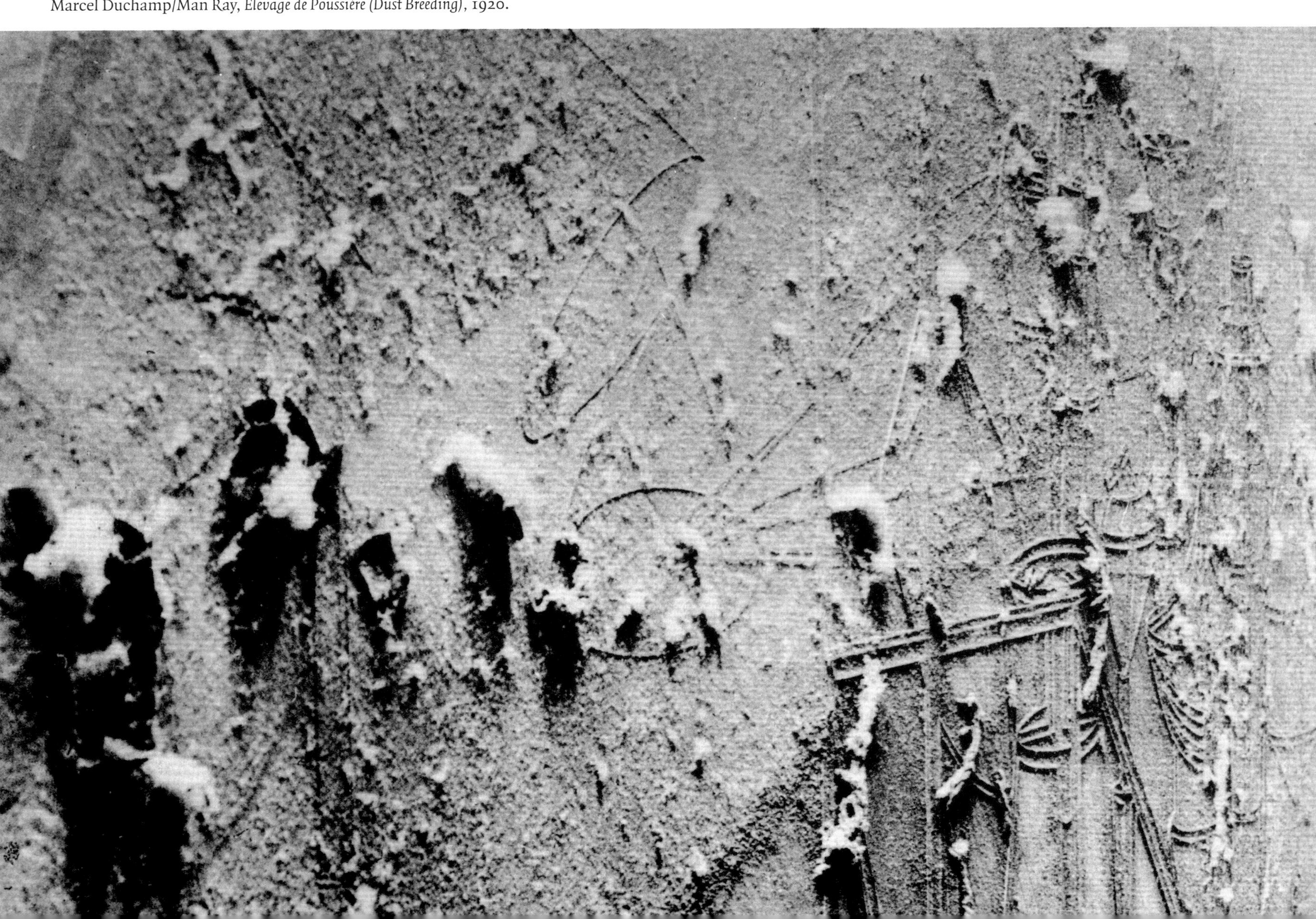

Marcel Duchamp/Man Ray, *Elevage de Poussière (Dust Breeding)*, 1920.

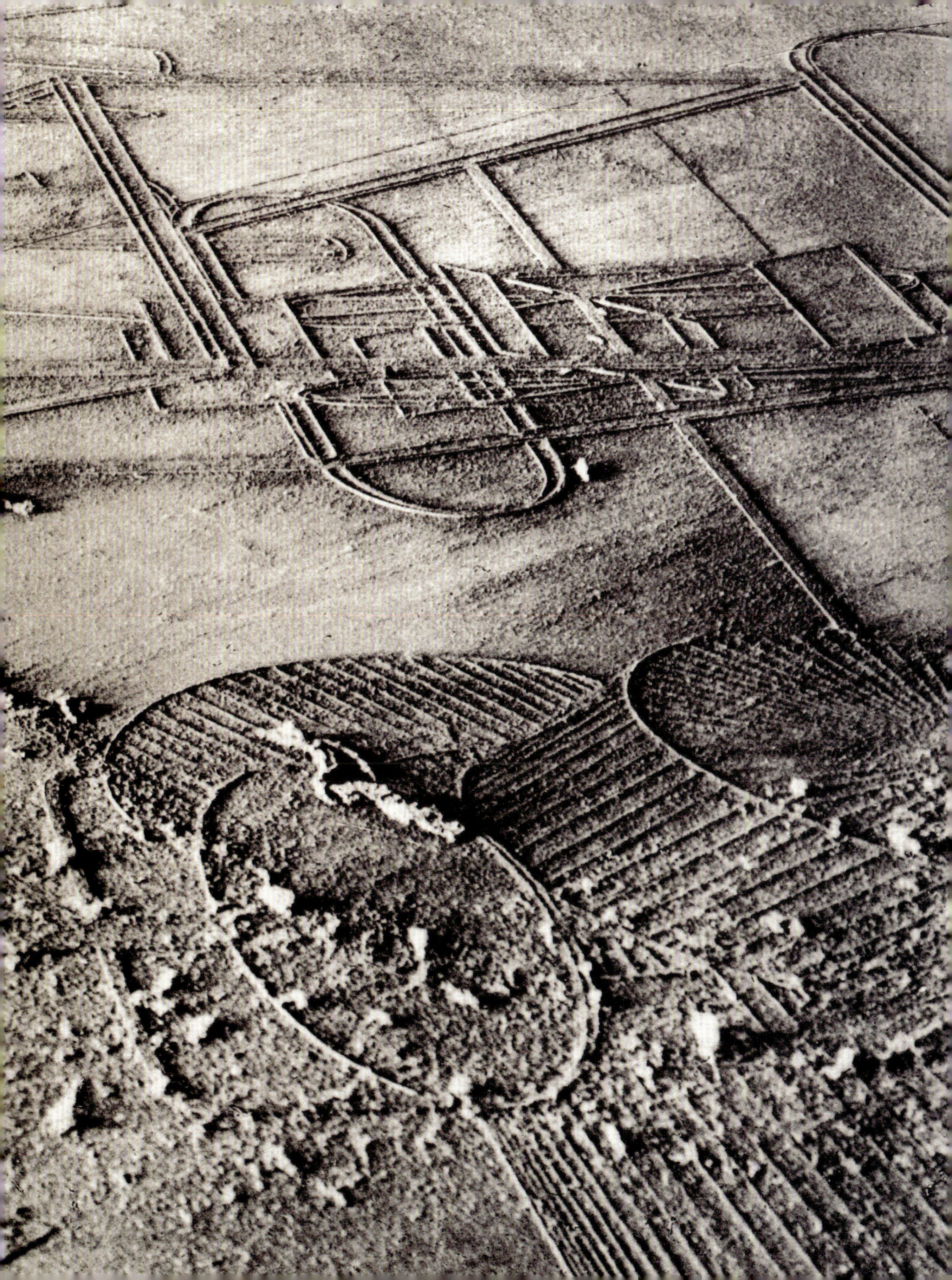

Marcel Duchamp, *Anemic Cinema*, 1926.

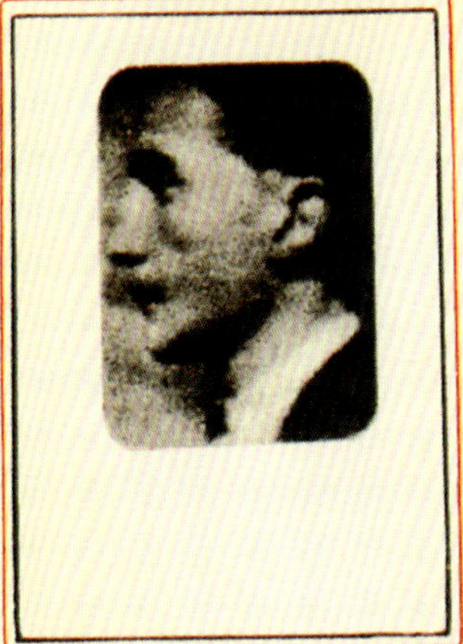
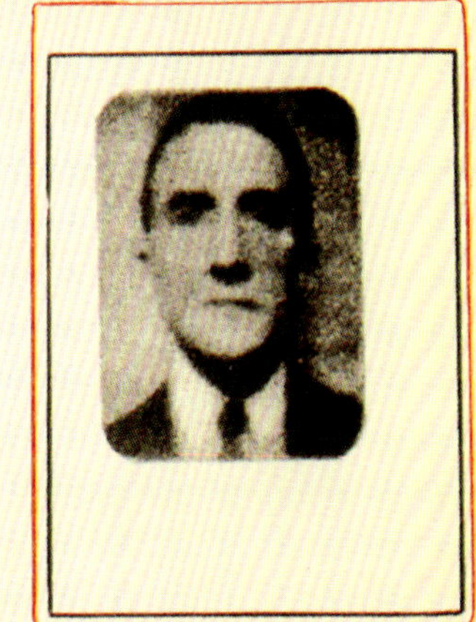

Marcel Duchamp, *Wanted/$2,000 Reward*, 1923.

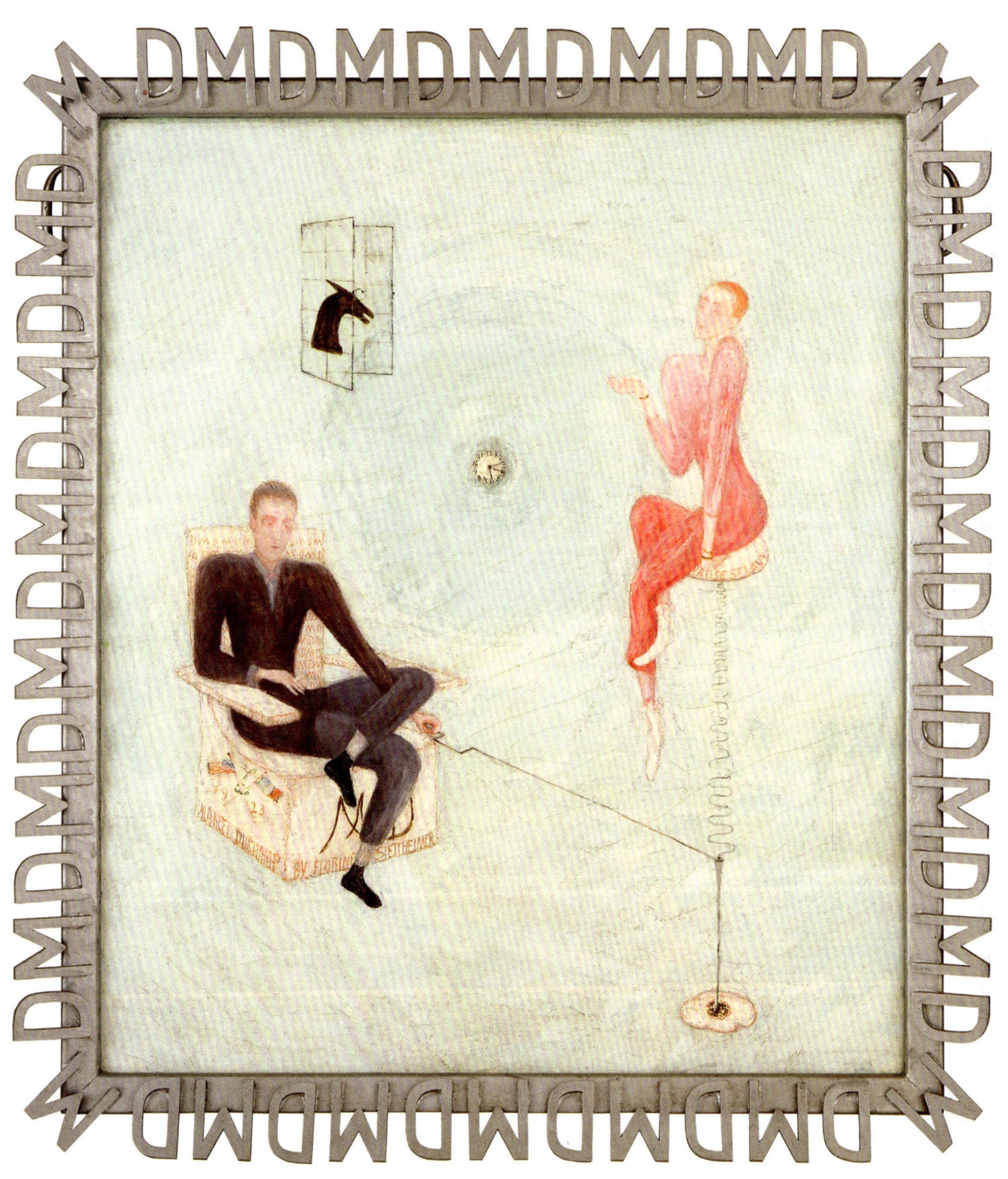

Florine Stettheimer, *Portrait of Marcel Duchamp*, 1923.

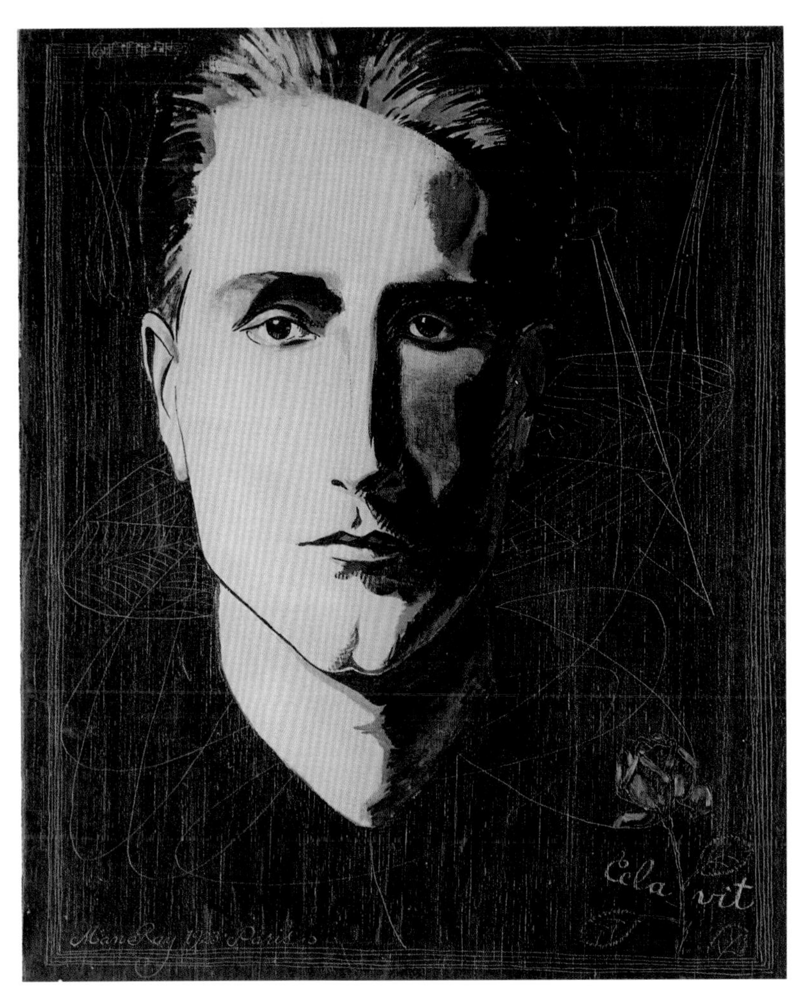

Man Ray, *Rrose Sélavy*, 1923.

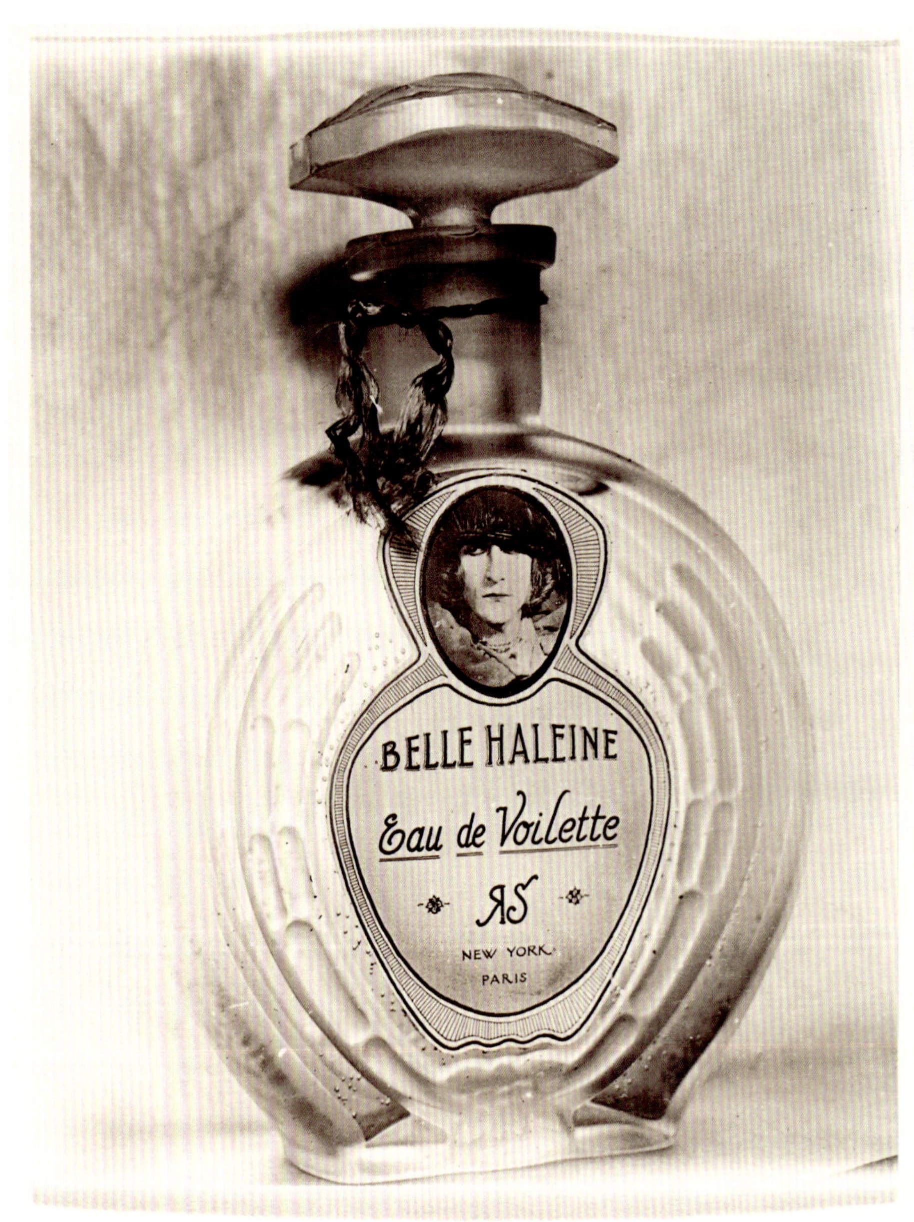

Marcel Duchamp/Man Ray, *Belle Haleine, Eau de Voilette (Beautiful Breath, Veil Water)*, 1921.

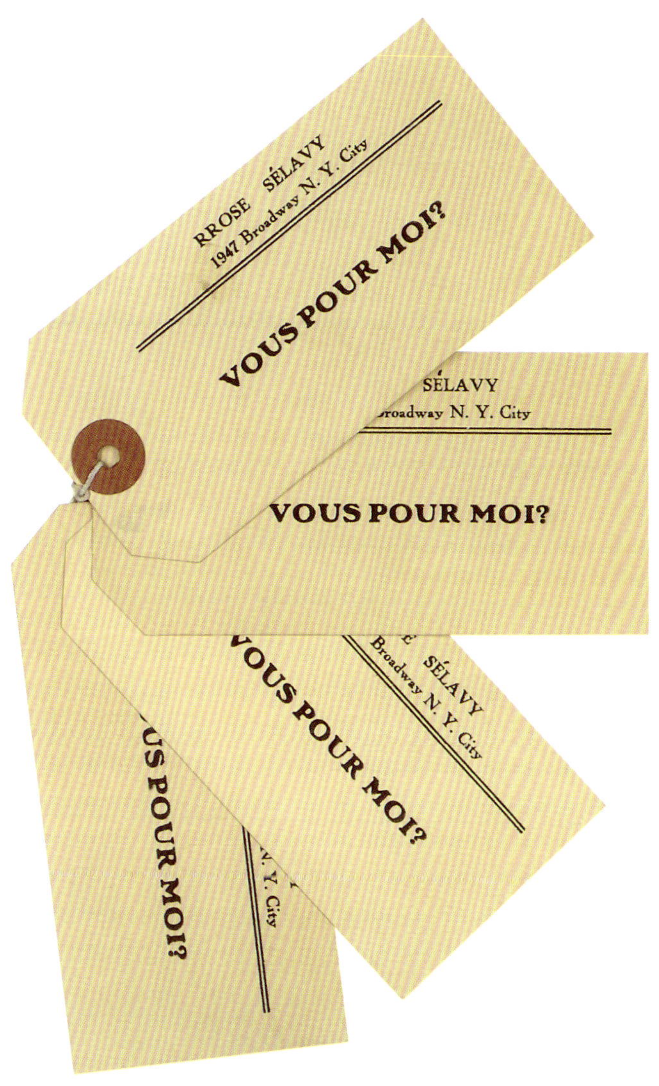

Marcel Duchamp, *Baggage Tags for Rrose Sélavy*, 1921.

Marcel Duchamp & Rrose Sélavy

nom juif? changement de sexe . . .

MARCEL DUCHAMP, *NOTES*

Rrose Sélavy's calling card announced her specialty as "precision oculism/whiskers and kicks in all genres." Born in New York in 1920 simply as Rose, she adopted the second "r" when she went to Paris in 1921. The new spelling described the proper French enunciation of her name, and contained both an aphorism (*eros c'est la vie*—or, eros is life) and a piece of advice (*arroser la vie*—or, live it up). Her euphonic name provided the mandate for a corpus of visual and verbal creations in which, André Breton observed, "words have finished playing. Words make love."

Rrose's penchant for lingual adventure harks back to her immediate forebearer, a goateed, mustachioed Mona Lisa bearing the inscription L.H.O.O.Q. (pronounced aloud in French, an "oculist" phrase meaning "she has a hot ass"). Her own debut occurred on the cover of *New York Dada*, in April 1921, as purveyor of "Belle Haleine—Eau de Voilette" ("Beautiful Breath—Veil Water"), a homely *parfumeuse* photographed by her friend Man Ray. Rrose and Man Ray arrived in Paris later that year, and French chic had its fortunate effect: Man's only other record of her shows a far more stylish Rrose, in alluring makeup, modern hat, and fancy fur.

Rrose's early work intertwined "assisted" readymade objects and punning titles that complemented the object in question. (The subtraction of "n" impelled her first creation, *Fresh Widow*, a miniature French window paned in black leather.) But soon Rrose's phrases liberated themselves from objects and became objects themselves. Usually French but occasionally English ("my niece is cold because my knees are cold"), they appeared in Dada and Surrealist books and journals on both sides of the Atlantic. Forming phrases replete with sexual innuendo, Rrose developed an erotics of language built on flipped syllables, alliterative liberties, and homophonic experiment. Unrelated to Dada non-sense, her rigorous equations split the difference between lavatory humor and high philosophy.

These prose creations are most spectacularly visible in the film *Anemic Cinema*, copyrighted in 1926 by Rrose Sélavy with a signature and a fingerprint in the film's last frame. The anagrammatic title describes a movie that goes around rather than forward, echoing the circularity of Rrose's syntax. The film records the alternating rotation of ten disks painted with swirling designs (early op art) and nine disks of spiraling Rrosian phrases. Spinning slowly around on camera, the texts and designs dilate and contract with amorous intensity.

Rrose's American roots gave her an entrepreneurial character, and she was a ready partner in new business ventures. She had a brief stint as a gambling official, endorsing as "president of the administrative council" a bond for investors in a scheme to win at Monte Carlo roulette (Marcel Duchamp cosigned as "administrator"). More often, her ventures tended toward the literary (an advertisement for the Monte Carlo bond aptly misnamed her Prose Sélavy). An astute art critic, she provided introductions to sale catalogues for works by both Picabia (1926) and Man Ray (1934). As graphic designer, she formulated anelegantly eccentric loose-leaf book for the collected essays of critic Henry McBride, *Some French Moderns Say McBride*.

Rrose's work as a publisher ranks among her greatest contributions to the culture of her time. In 1934, she sponsored the publication of ninety-four of Marcel Duchamp's notes for his *Large Glass*, assembled together as *The Green Box* (Edition Rrose Sélavy, 18 rue de la Paix, Paris). Here Rrose's "precision oculism" reached full flower: meticulous facsimiles reproduce the inks and papers of the individual notes, faithful to the originals in color, texture, and shape. They document both the content and the look of the thinking behind Duchamp's glass masterpiece.

Duchamp's next major undertaking, *De ou par Marcel Duchamp ou Rrose Sélavy*, was a monumental effort to catalogue and preserve, in miniature, a unique body of artistic accomplishment. After several years of preparation, the first versions of this *Box-in-Valise* (or *se-la-Vi*) appeared in 1941. Here the works of Rrose and Marcel come together in museological splendor, with careful unfoldings, liftings, and spreadings required to reveal the results of two decades of co-conspiracy. It is a museum both portable and erotic, intimate and handsome, perfect for this longtime pair of traveling companions.

ANN TEMKIN

MAN RAY
Marcel Duchamp Dressed as Rrose Sélavy, 1924.
Gelatin silver print, 8 1/2 x 6 13/16 in.
p. 58

MAN RAY
Rrose Sélavy (looking to the right), 1921.
Gelatin silver print, 5 3/4 x 4 5/16 in.
p. 59 (top)

MAN RAY
Rrose Sélavy, 1921.
Gelatin silver print, 6 7/8 x 4 15/16 in.
p. 59 (bottom left)

MAN RAY
Rrose Sélavy, 1921.
Gelatin silver print, 10 13/16 x 8 7/16 in.
p. 59 (bottom right)

MARCEL DUCHAMP
Why Not Sneeze Rose Sélavy?, 1921.
Assisted Readymade: painted metal, bird cage, thermometer, marble cubes, cuttlebone, 4 7/8 x 8 3/4 x 6 3/8 in. Photograph by Man Ray, 1935.
p. 60

MARCEL DUCHAMP
Mannequin, 1938.
A mannequin dressed in Duchamp's hat and coat, exhibited on the Rue Surréaliste of the *Exposition Internationale du Surréalisme* at the Galerie des Beaux-Arts, Paris, January 1938. Photograph by Man Ray, 1938.
p. 61

MARCEL DUCHAMP
Elevage de Poussière (Dust Breeding), 1920.
A photograph recording several months' accumulation of dust on the lower section of Duchamp's *Large Glass*. First published in 1922 in *Littérature*, with the caption, "Voici le domaine de Rrose Sélavy/Comme il est aride—comme il est fertile/Comme il est joyeux—comme il est triste." ("Here is the realm of Rrose Sélavy/How arid it is—how fertile it is/How joyous it is—how sad it is.") Photograph by Man Ray, 1920.
p. 62–63

MARCEL DUCHAMP
Anemic Cinema, 1926.
Seven-minute film, made in collaboration with Man Ray and Marc Allégret. (Still photograph from last two frames, with copyright and thumbprint.)
p. 64

MARCEL DUCHAMP
Wanted/$2,000 Reward, 1923.
Rectified Readymade: two photographs of Duchamp pasted on a joke "Wanted" poster, 19 1/2 x 14 in.
p. 65

FLORINE STETTHEIMER
Portrait of Marcel Duchamp, 1923.
Oil on canvas, 30 x 26 in.
p. 66

MAN RAY
Rrose Sélavy, 1923.
Oil on canvas, 23 1/4 x 19 1/2 in.
p. 67

MARCEL DUCHAMP
Belle Haleine, Eau de Voilette
(Beautiful Breath, Veil Water), 1921.
Assisted Readymade: perfume bottle with label, in oval box, 6 7/16 x 4 7/16 in. Photograph by Man Ray, 1921.
p. 68

MARCEL DUCHAMP
Baggage Tags for Rrose Sélavy, 1921.
Printed manila tags, dimensions variable.
p. 69

VITTORIO SERENI

PASSING THROUGH

Just one day, if that. A few hours.
A light never seen.
Flowers in August you'd never dream of.
Blood pooling on the fields,
oleanders not yet on the seaward side.
Hot, but who feels like swimming?
Windswept Tyrrhene Sunday.
Have I died and come back here?
Am I the only one left alive in the vivid stilled
blankness of a memory?

IMAGE

That evening the window held you
high above the street songs.
In the dark of restless years
that's how you'll stay—often
thunder tricks you into horrors
of a war far away.

Sometimes I still see you, when bells
toll beyond the rain, stooped
over fall's first burning brand.
O it was a face, a moment's flash,
on fields slashed and burnt
at Garessio, summertime, in Val d'Inferno.

Midnight on the hills, we came outside
called by that dim cry far away
from a veranda we couldn't see: *Santa,*
Santa mia.
In the distance, untroubled, some are smiling,
making their way across the whirling years
the river shrieks tonight
under the brightest full moon.

Translated from the Italian
by W. S. Di Piero

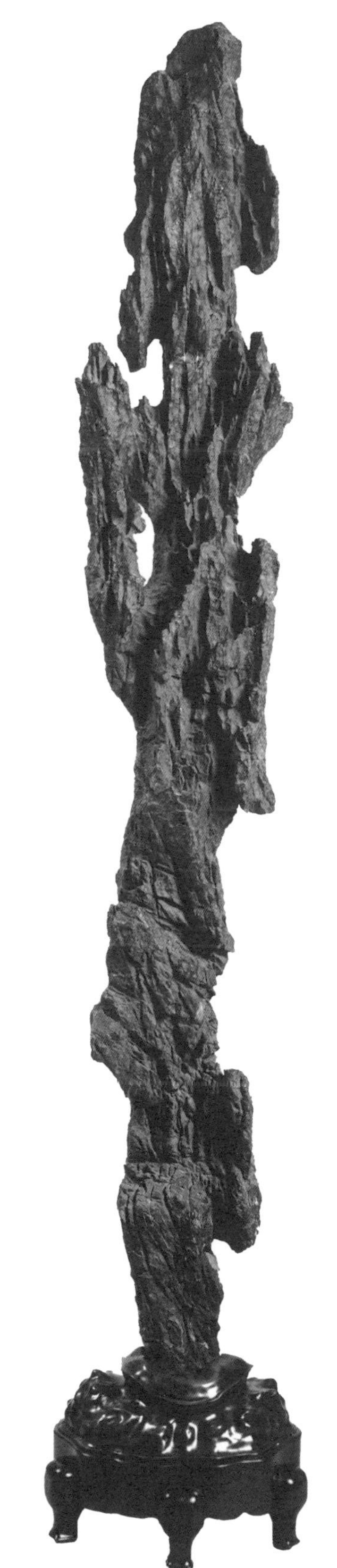

CREATIVITY AND NEUROSCIENCE

JEAN-PIERRE CHANGEUX

A visitor to the Taipei National Museum's imperial collections is immediately drawn to some rather unusual objects: the "oracular bones" of the Shang period (1523 to 1028 B.C.). These fragments of turtle shells are marked by strange, randomly distributed cracks that developed when glowing embers were inserted into cavities drilled into the shell's inner surface. Next to these fissures, texts written in the oldest known Chinese characters ascribe a meaning to each line: an answer (of good or bad omen) to a question posed by a soothsayer (concerning the success of a military venture or harvest, the course of a malady, or the meaning of a dream), and, logically enough, the ostensible "proof" of the prophecy.

This earliest of written evidence attests to one of the fundamental activities of the human brain: its tendency to ascribe meaning to a physical structure—in this case a collection of randomly distributed lines—for the purpose of imposing order on otherwise puzzling developments in the world. The human brain works in ways that are antithetical to the input/output model cyberneticists have long taken for granted. Rather, it continually projects onto the world spontaneous internal "mental representations," which it then tests against an intrinsically meaningless external reality. This development of mental forms implies that creativity is an essential predisposition of the human brain.

PREVIOUS PAGE Scholar's rock (tall rock in the form of an old man), Ming Dynasty.

Is it plausible to think that a conglomerate of nerve cells with axonal and dendritic extensions through which various electrical and chemical signals travel can be responsible for something as seemingly incomprehensible as creativity? There is no physical proof against it. The human brain consists of roughly 100 billion neurons, each of which interacts with numerous others through an average of 10,000 discontinuous connections known as synapses. Thus there are approximately 1,015 synapses in the human brain, or roughly 600 million synapses per cubic millimeter. The number of possible combinations of neurons is astronomical, roughly of the same order of magnitude as the number of positively charged particles in the universe. What's more, the efficiency of each synaptic connection is itself a function of experience. No numerical limit can legitimately be imposed on the possible functional combinations of the neuronal network. The connectivity of this network is neither totally random, like a gas, nor totally regular, like a crystal. It is organized, both locally specialized and globally integrated.

Finally, the structure of the brain, which remains stable from generation to generation, is the result of biological evolution, essentially genetic in nature, extending over hundreds of millions of years. As neurologist Hughlings Jackson said, this evolution is accompanied by "movement from the simpler to the more complex, that is, from a lower, well-organized center toward higher, less well-organized centers ... *that organize all of life.*" Over millions of years, the relative surface area of the parietotemporal lobes and especially of the prefrontal cortex increased, and hemispheric dominance grew as language, cognitive functions, and social life developed. The first tools were invented roughly two million years ago. The first paintings appeared on the walls of caves thirty thousand years ago. The conscious creative activity of the human brain then supplanted the "blind" organic activity of biological evolution. In other words, the higher one looks in the hierarchical structure of the nervous system, the greater the self-organization one finds and thus the greater the capacity to create, provided that the system remains "open" to its environment.

Within the brain, other, non-genetic forms of evolution also occur but on much shorter time scales. The connections between neurons and synapses are not entirely preestablished, as they are in a microprocessor. Cerebral connectivity develops gradually with a certain amount of random variability. Phases during which connections are made at a rapid pace are followed by phases of pruning and elimination under the control of spontaneous and stimulated network activity. The neurons acquire their functional "singularity" in identifiable periods of postnatal development, which are particularly long in man.

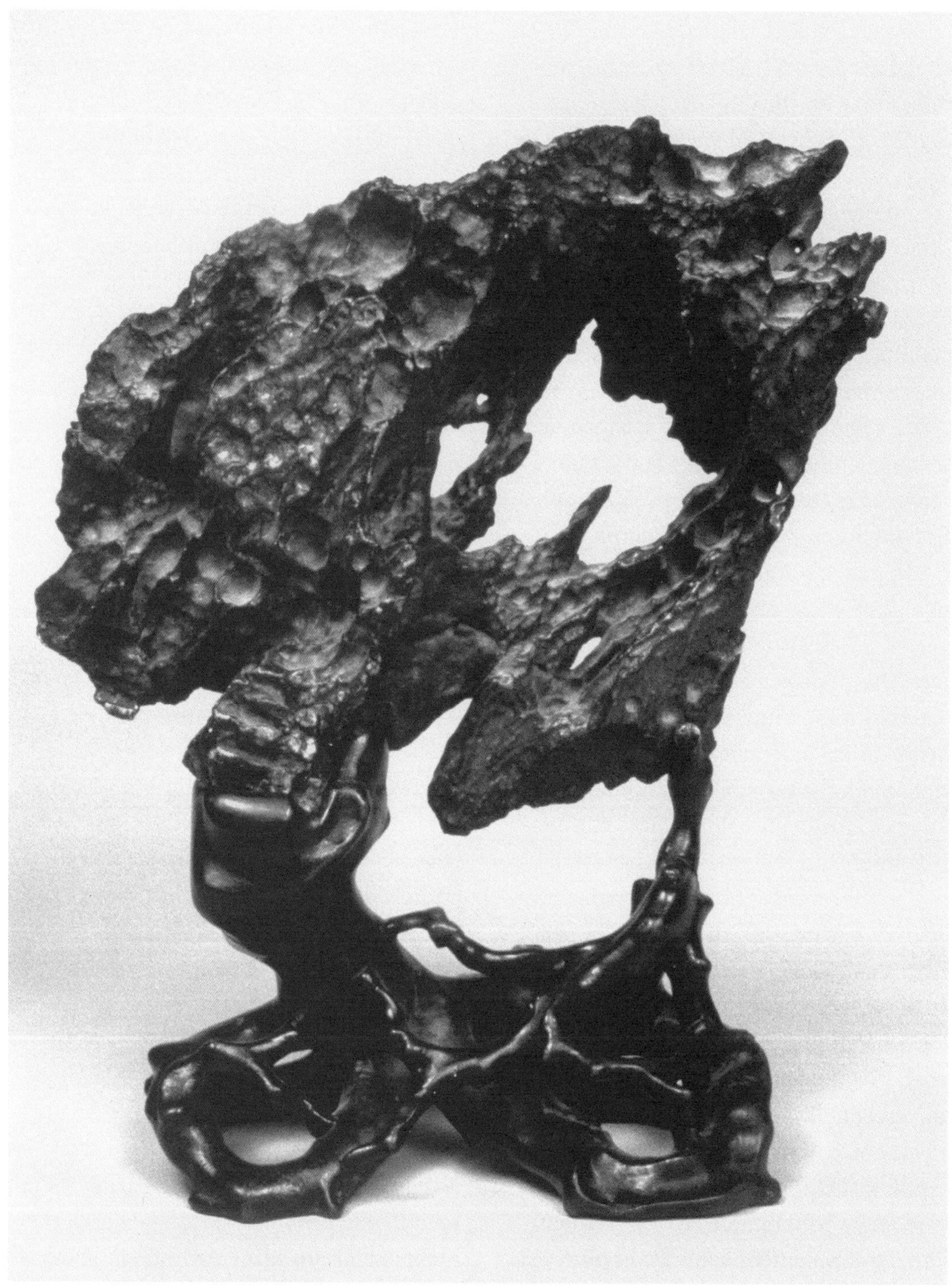

Scholar's rock (diagonally oriented rock with cave), Ming Dynasty.

During these periods, a child experiments with his physical and social environment; he acquires his mother tongue and absorbs the visual and sonic images, musical scales, symbolic systems, and rules of behavior intrinsic to his cultural milieu. This epigenesis through selective stabilization of synapses frees man from genetic determinism. It makes cultural evolution possible and gives creativity a historical dimension.

Describing her work as a sculptor, Louise Bourgeois writes: "When my ideas fail to cohere into convincing metaphors, I am beset by images. I see images everywhere." Similarly, the molecular biologist Jacques Monod once found himself "so lost in the imaginary process that [he] was identifying with a protein molecule."

The most widely accepted theory, first proposed in 1949 by the psychologist Donald Hebb, is that these images, or rather "mental objects," correspond to a private, internal state of the cerebral network defined by the temporal sequence of electrical and chemical neural processes affecting a topologically circumscribed population of neurons. Under this hypothesis, the "indicator function" that connects this physical cerebral state to its meaning would depend on the geography of the cerebral maps that are shaped by evolution and "stabilized" in early childhood.

The formation of visual representations is by far the most completely understood on a sensory level. In the lower temporal cortex one finds neurons activated by simple geometric shapes—inverted T's of the sort found in certain works of Paul Klee. There are also neurons that respond to hands or faces. Others respond to a head no matter what its angle of tilt, and thus to the concept "head." This process of abstraction continues as we "move up" the cortical hierarchy, however, to the anterior temporal cortex, where attributes such as the color, shape, movement, and depth of perceptual objects gradually coalesce to construct a unified image of the world. Here we find neurons which, after training, can individually distinguish ninety-seven fractal shapes of extraordinary geometric complexity. The ape turns out to be an excellent geometer.

Musicians should not feel left out of this chiefly visual cerebral world. Specialized areas of the cerebral cortex help to process sounds by identifying their frequency, source, melodic structure (contour, interval, and tonality), as well as their rhythm and meter. There is even a special system for perceiving environmental noise. John Cage very likely relied on this while composing certain of his pieces. Finally, it has been known since the surgeon and anthropologist Paul Broca's time that the representation of language depends on certain specific areas of the left hemisphere. Images obtained with brain scanners show activity in the temporal lobe during listening, in the occipital lobe during reading, in the Broca region during speech, and in the frontal lobe when words are conceived.

Despite the progressive reconstructions and recompositions that take place as we move up through the hierarchy of cortical regions, we are still a long way from pinpointing the "singing state" described by Paul Valéry, that "realm of musical language" where images, words, and rhythms come together in the process of creation, particularly poetic creation. But recent work on brain imaging seems to be bringing us closer. Researchers have compared the brain activity of French-speaking subjects in response to three types of stimuli: a story in Tamil, which they did not understand, a list of French words, which they did understand, and a carefully structured story in French. They found that the more comprehensible the narrative, the greater the number and the more extensive the surface area of the active regions of the left hemisphere.

When the story is fully understood, a new cortical region comes into play: the prefrontal cortex, which plays a role in the formation of mental syntheses, and in the organization of thoughts as intentions. It also participates in the construction of mental representations that relate to social interaction. The relative surface area of the prefrontal cortex increases dramatically from ape to man, and a lesion in this region gives rise to serious behavioral disturbances, which, depending on the location of the lesion, can affect attention, reasoning, and planning. The prefrontal cortex also plays a central role in the attribution of mental states to others, thereby contributing to empathy, a cerebral capacity that is of fundamental importance in the appreciation of the aesthetic qualities of a work of art as well as in moral judgment.

The concept of empathy brings us to another "continent" of the creative brain: the emotions. The limbic system, ancient, primitive, and, according to some observers, animal (because of its role in the vital function of survival), plays an essential role in assessing dangers and pleasures and thus in constituting the subject's affective and "corporeal landscape." It is associated with the systems of neurons in the brain stem that give rise to autostimulation in rats. With its abundant connections to the prefrontal cortex, the limbic system marks out possible courses of action with emotional or affective signposts. It links pleasure to reason in the creative mind.

In his defense of "genetic criticism" of the process of literary creation as illustrated by the manuscripts of French writers Gustave Flaubert and Francis Ponge, critic Almuth Grésillon points out that "the royal road, the inexorable march toward denouement, the teleology of the straight line, are opposed by metaphors indicating more sinuous paths: forks, ... bifurcations, blunders, explorations, deviations, detours, side paths, backtrackings, dead ends, accidents, false starts." For Claude Simon, "the writer progresses laboriously, *blindly feeling his way*, bogging down, starting over." Matisse compared the path of his pencil "to the actions of a man feeling his way in the dark."

No one has yet used a brain scanner to make an objective record of the successive stages of the creative process in the brain of an artist or scientist. For now the working hypothesis is that creativity unfolds in psychological time through a process of trial and error. This process involves both biological evolution and connectional epigenesis in a projective style of "mental Darwinism." The idea is that, during the "preparatory" or "incubation" phase, certain fragmentary images or preliminary mental representations—*pre-representations*—arise briefly and spontaneously in the brain. A combinatorial phase of "mental tinkering" then associates or dissociates objects in memory and actual perceptions until some "recombinant" form emerges victorious from the ensuing competition. This selection of a particular representation is what mathematician Jacques Hadamard calls "the moment of illumination." That representation usually then enters into an ongoing process of mathematical invention, biological modeling, or artistic creation. Sooner or later the work of the imagination triggers a mechanism of selection by evaluation, which in all likelihood involves the limbic system and its satellites. By "flooding" the synapses of the relevant complex of neurons with a defined neurotransmitter, the limbic system alters the efficiency of the connections and thereby establishes a physical trace in long-term memory.

The space within which this "struggle for life" among mental images takes place is, as one might expect, not easily characterized. This "conscious environment" or simulation of virtual actions allows for comparison between current perceptions of the external world, internal representations, and memories of previous experiences somatically marked with emotional value. Also contributing to these deliberations are internalized social rules as well as innate forms deriving from biological evolution, whose effects often escape the subject's conscious awareness. The physical contours of this conscious environment most likely include the frontal cortex, the limbic system, the brain stem, and other regions of the brain whose interconnections make the system feed back on itself.

The touchstones of any chemical definition of consciousness, psychotropic drugs such as mescaline are associated with certain categories of neurotransmitters. The Huichois Indians in Mexico ritually consumed mescaline in the course of their annual pilgrimages to Wirikuta in the north-central Mexican desert. They experienced hallucinations that involved colorful and remarkably symmetrical geometrical shapes. When they returned home, they embodied these fleeting visions into

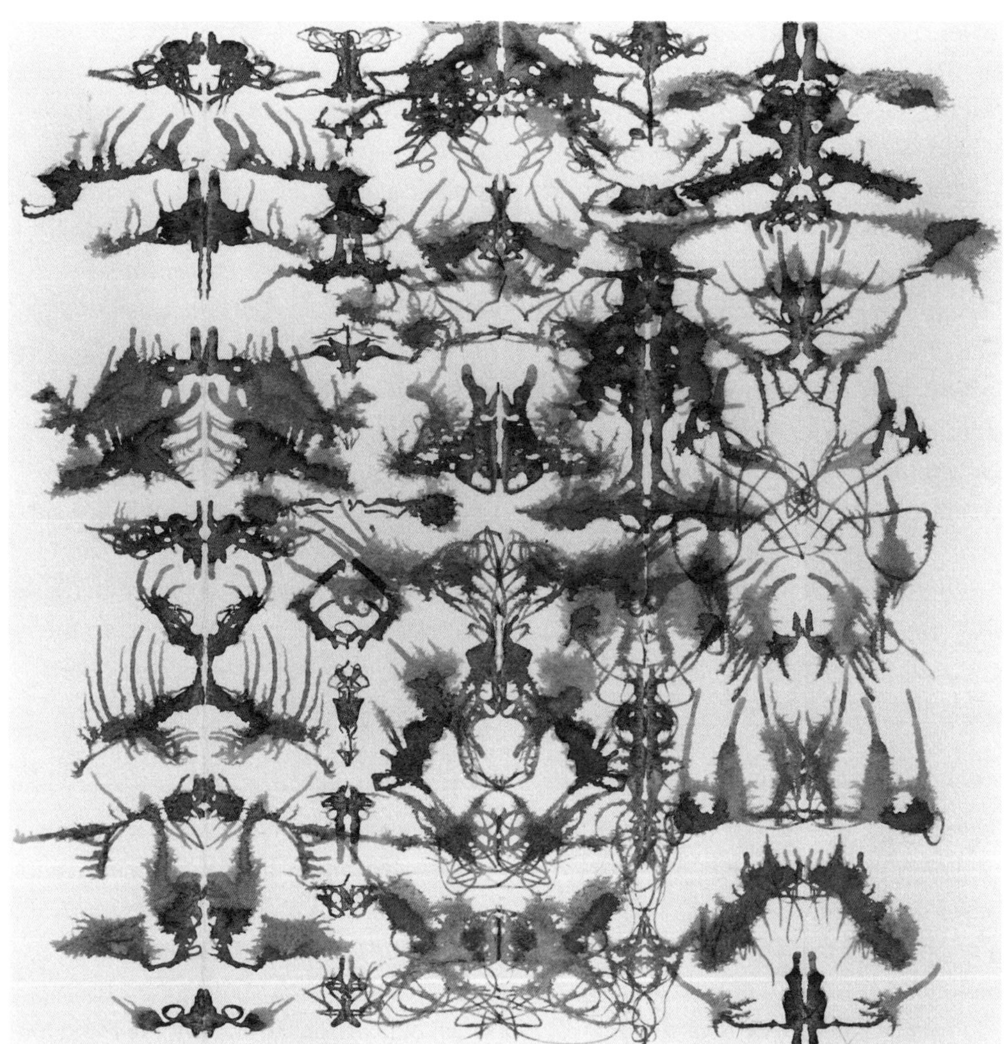

Bruce Conner, *Inkblot Drawing (C)*, 1975.

tapestries said to depict their journeys to the "other world." Do these regular colored images reflect the neural geometry of color zones in the visual cortex? Do the same receptors come into play when artists such as Kandinsky deliberately use similar figures, or when the musician Messiaen, who says that he "hears colors," composes?

In the "mental experience" of creative work, one finds both concurrent and sequential processes. It all begins with what Leonardo da Vinci called "vague forms," "random blots" upon which, according to poet and critic Yves Bonnefoy, "the imagination builds" to develop an original idea, a *concetto*, a rough sketch or all-important definition of a subject. This mental object is then passed through the filter of reason before being physically embodied on paper in a series of "external drawings," a graphical sketch or *disegno*. The movements of fingers and hand, often developed through lengthy apprenticeship, are guided by images stemming from an "interior survey" of the object. These movements ultimately control the artist's pen or brush. A cascade of activations of premotor and motor regions in the brain follows the tacit, internal evolution of the mental creation. An "evolving dialogue" develops between the brain of the creator and the emerging work, as "reasoning corrects the eye" through erasures and revisions to the work in progress.

Artistic and scientific creativity are embodied in the history of an individual, a history which is itself dependent on prior historical evolution. Every scientist, no matter how ingenious he believes himself to be, knows how much he owes to the culture in which he took his first steps, to the discoveries of his predecessors, to chance encounters with colleagues, to accidental observations, to references and new techniques picked up here and there. Within these fugitive networks of unforeseen interactions, in which happenstance and rationalization both play a part, "cognitive crystallizations" occur; the validation and ultimate acceptance of these crystallizations then become matters for open debate. Historians of science have deftly analyzed the difficulty of unraveling such a tangled skein.

The historical evolution of artistic and scientific representations is not as obscure or random as it might appear, however. It involves rigorous selections based on the rules ("mental tools") that creative individuals have always imposed on themselves, rules that evolve over time, through experience. "I like the rule that corrects the emotion," Braque observes. To which Louise Bourgeois adds: "My sculptures are algebraic equations with variables. Those equations must be tested."

A universally accepted rule in science and art is that there is value in novelty, that is, in that which is not yet known or which has not already been seen or heard. A very powerful cerebral mechanism is responsible for the detection of the new and unforeseen, a faculty that is essential for the survival of any organism. Pavlov and later Sokolov showed that an animal subjected to a new stimulus (a sound, for instance) turns his head in that direction, but if the stimulus is repeated, the animal eventually ceases to respond to it. It has been "desensitized." The moment the stimulus changes, however, the organism again directs its gaze and posture to the source. This powerful novelty-detection mechanism also contributes to the production of novelty. Michael Posner's brain-imaging work has shown that when a subject becomes familiar with a list of names after reading it several times, his cerebral activity gradually diminishes. But when a new list of names is read, the (cognitive) frontal cortex and the Wernicke region (involved in language) light up along the lateral face, as does the cingular (limbic) cortex along the median face. There can be little doubt that reading a poem by René Char, the score to a melody by Poulenc, or a scientific report by Louis Pasteur triggers an elevated blood flow in the brain of the reader which mirrors that in the brain of the creator.

Artists have always also exploited the "rules" that nature gives them. Mondrian uses lines, elementary forms, and colors that, as we have seen, reflect the fundamental neuronal mechanisms of visual perception. In Matisse's terms, the artist "organizes his sensations" in order to elicit those of the spectator (or listener). In music, Boulez has tried to achieve "modulations through superimposition," contrasts of timbre, perturbations, and accidents in "a world in which consonance and dissonance have been abolished."

The rules that creators forge to characterize their styles are not immutable. They evolve. Perspective in painting is an attempt to depict "truly," just as the tempered scale in music is an attempt to sound "right," although one actually deceives the eye and the other deceives the ear. Internalization of these rules requires a lengthy apprenticeship similar to the learning of a language, and what is once learned is not easily unlearned. Babies spontaneously prefer "satisfying" intervals such as the perfect fifth and cadences such as the tonic-dominant. Yet at six months both Western and Javanese babies can detect false notes in melodies based on both the Western major scale *and* the Javanese *pelog* scale, whereas adults recognize false notes only in the scale appropriate to the culture in which they grew up. This drop in performance, which can be understood as a "perceptual calibration" through selection of innate patterns, places sharp limits on the currently widespread notion that the human perceptual apparatus is infinitely malleable. Together with the theory of epigenesis through selective stabilization, this finding contradicts the assumption of composers

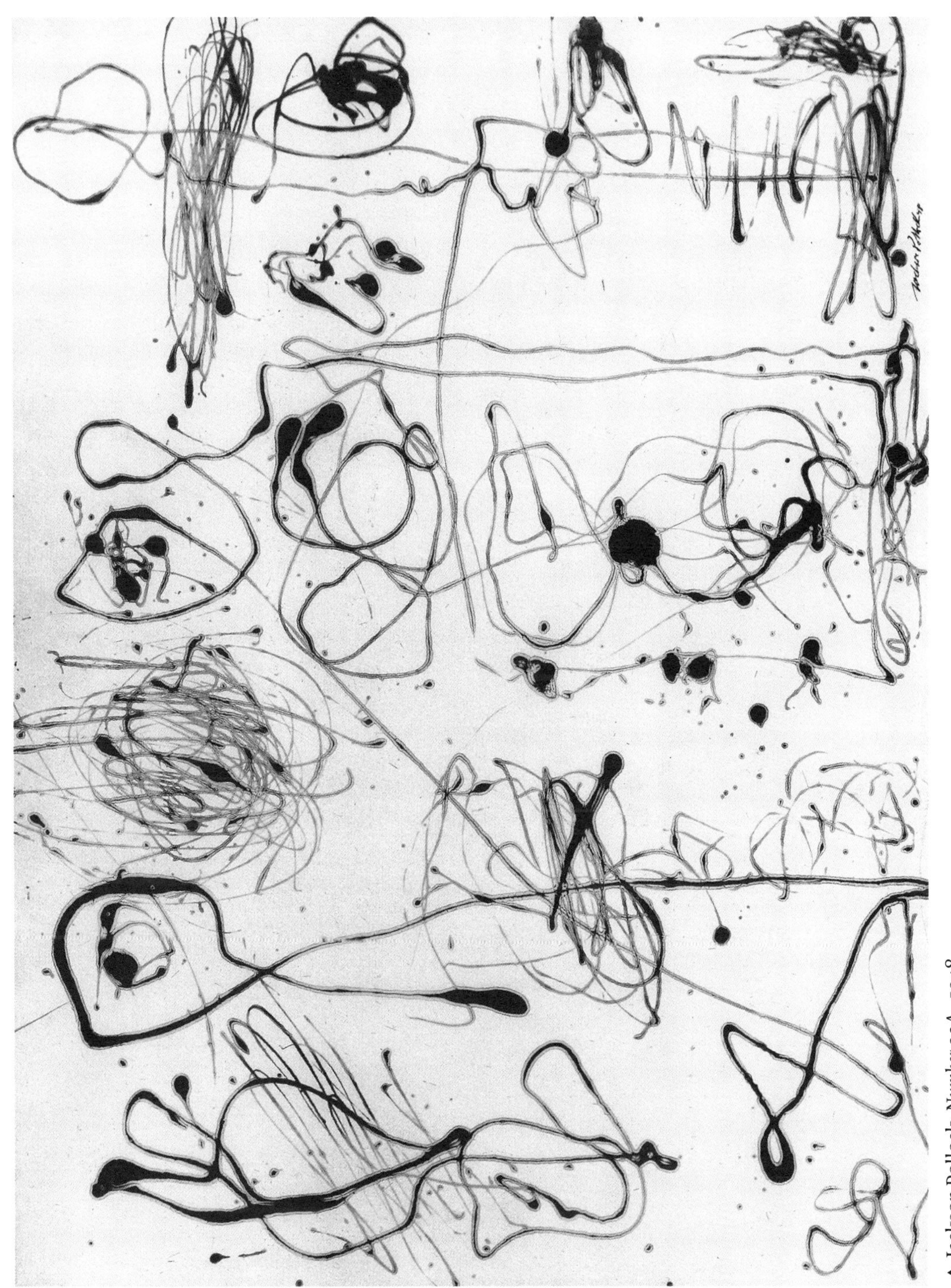

▲ Jackson Pollock, Number 22A, 1948.

like Boulez and Schönberg that adult listeners can acquire any imaginable musical structure as easily as they perceive and acquire the conventional structure as children. Limits are imposed by the innate dispositions or "neural forms" peculiar to the species and by the epigenetic selections resulting from the history of the individual and the culture.

Various contemporary artists have tried to return to the sources of creativity, to the cerebral mechanisms we have discussed—thereby giving rise to a sort of pictorial fiction, a backtracking through time, which leaves the spectator free to complete the creative process in a myriad of ways. The brain's random generation of mental representations is in a sense mirrored by the Surrealists' technique of "automatic writing," by Pollock's "dripping," by the "conscious clumsiness" of Cy Twombly's scrawls, by Dubuffet's "psychosites," and by Frank Stella's production of images that engender one another through endless deformation. All these are, in Jean Clair's words, "neuromotor pantomimes" of the creator's inner experience.

Translated from the French by Arthur Goldhammer

LISA JARNOT

FROM *SEA LYRICS*

Today I am rivets of sails in a log cabin where
Jack London lived in Alaska until they moved his
cabin here, where we collect the change to buy our
drinks and eat the free hors d'œuvres, where the
neighbors are somewhat pleased beside the
railroad trains, where the vague sense of the
Union Pacific is with opossums of freeways and
you, where we've assembled plastic birds all
morning, where the airplanes fill the plastic sky,
where the fish are brightly colored on the lawn,
where an underwater bird is pummeled on the
sidestreet, where we take hallucinogens and
wander through museums, where the people
construct the artificial ponds, where theosophists
arrive on all the hillsides, where I have been
bowling all morning, where we have been
airplanes and also the plastic small birds,
where this is the type of leisure that I am,
where these are the largest of fires, where the
highway trembles on the edge of the waterfront
square.

I am here inside the freezer where you left me, I am
the unobstructed silence of the avocado dawn, I am
the neighborhood of foreign things, I am the
telemarketer of evening, I have only donuts and
the doors are locked, I am as thick as the morning
down on Broadway, I am walking near the freeway
as it shakes, I am the overpass and shattered in the
midst of day, I am the last of the partially submerged
vehicles on the waterfront on Sunday
buying jam.

I have come from here to there on multicolored
subways through the multicolored lawns with wet
feet being webbed and nearly sober where the
baseball teams are frenzied and Peralta herds his
cows, where abutting all the artificialist lagoons are
moonlight and the sound of wheels, where the
palm trees are imagined, where the knotted
branches ring the edge of all the hillsides by the park,
where in the microcosms of the lunar tides I
fall outside the porch into tequila, I am at the
library with the health-food stores, I am upon the
roof to glare across the city where I am, I am
trembling like the traffic, I am on the backs of
motorcycles in the pull of tides in astrology and far
from Detroit.

Richard Pettibone

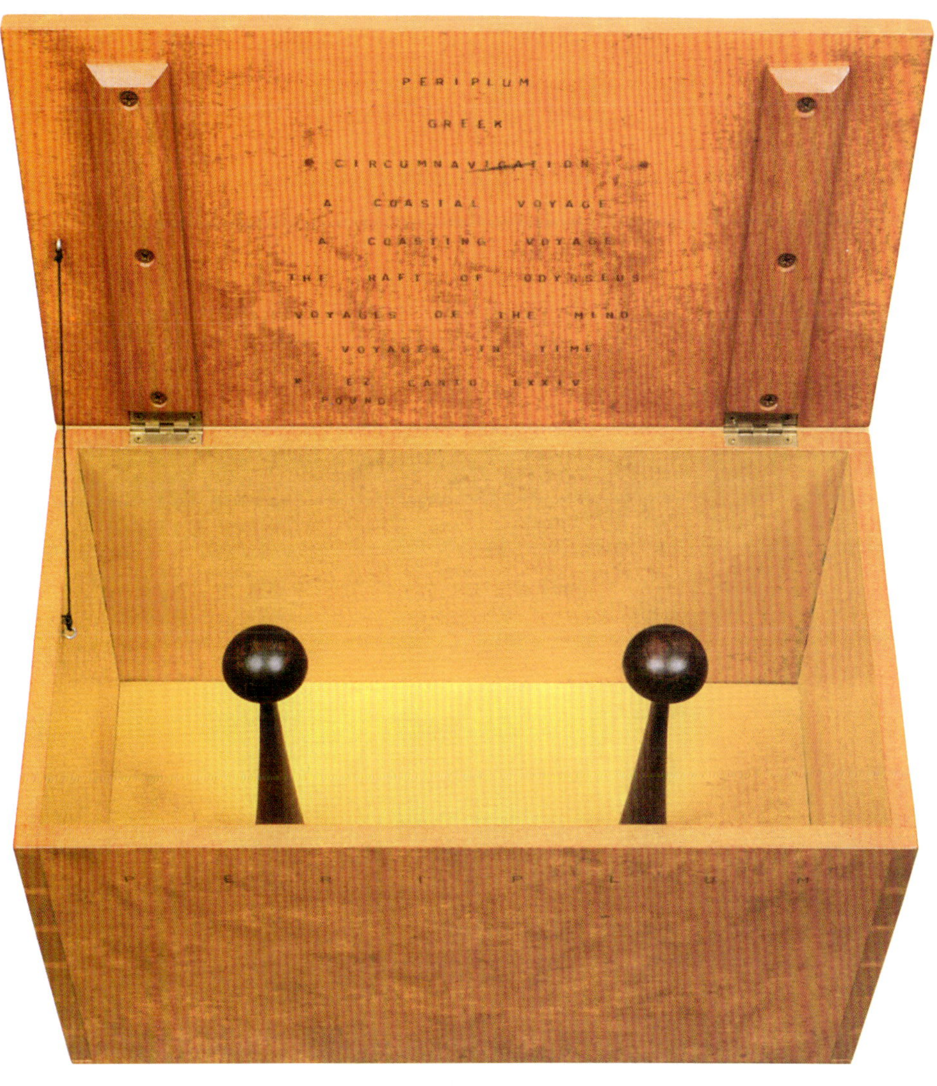

Periplum

PRECEDING PAGE *Box with Two Pegs,* 1993–1

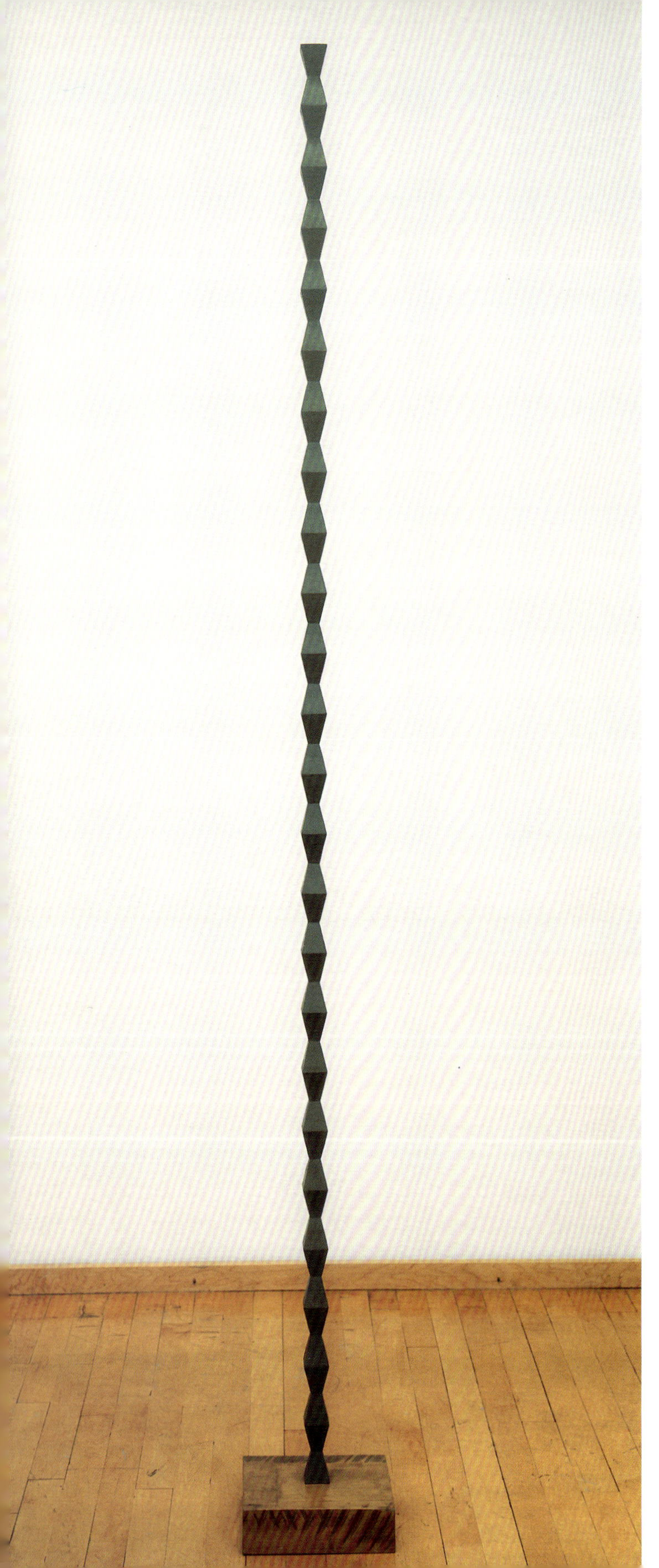

Constantin Brancusi, "Endless Column," 1918–1937, 1992.

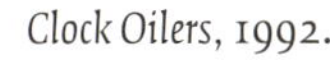

Clock Oilers, 1992.

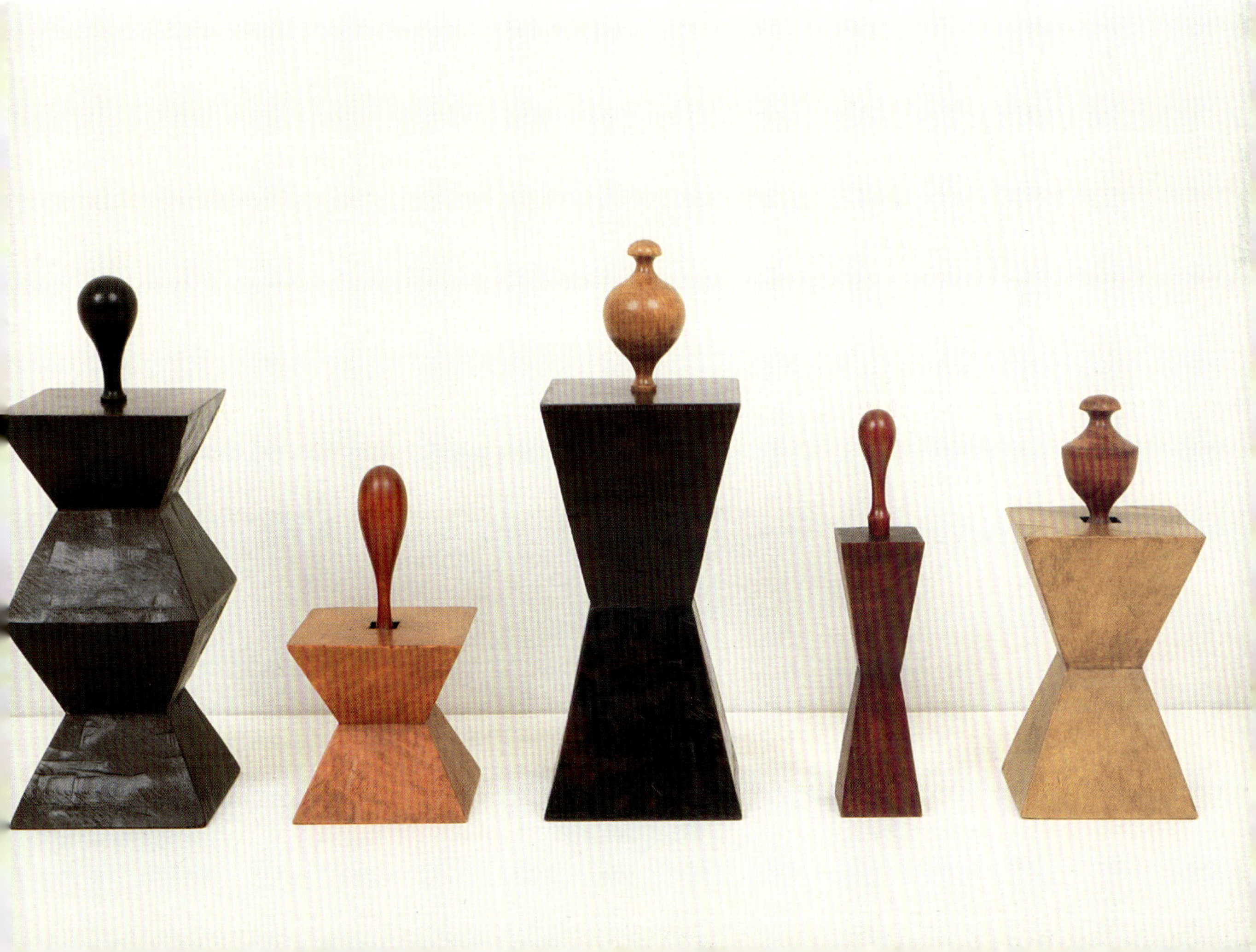

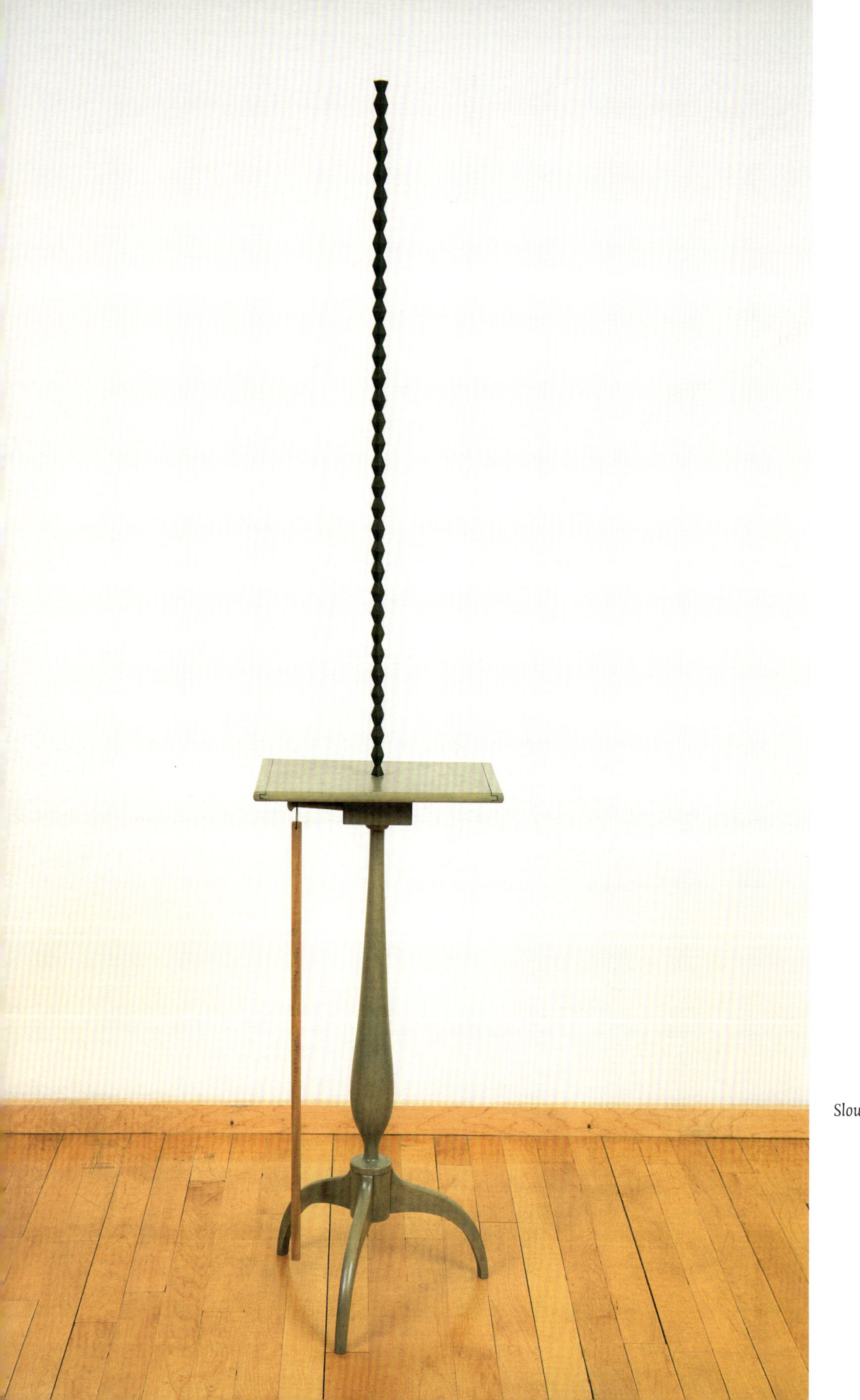

Slowness is Beauty, 1988–89.

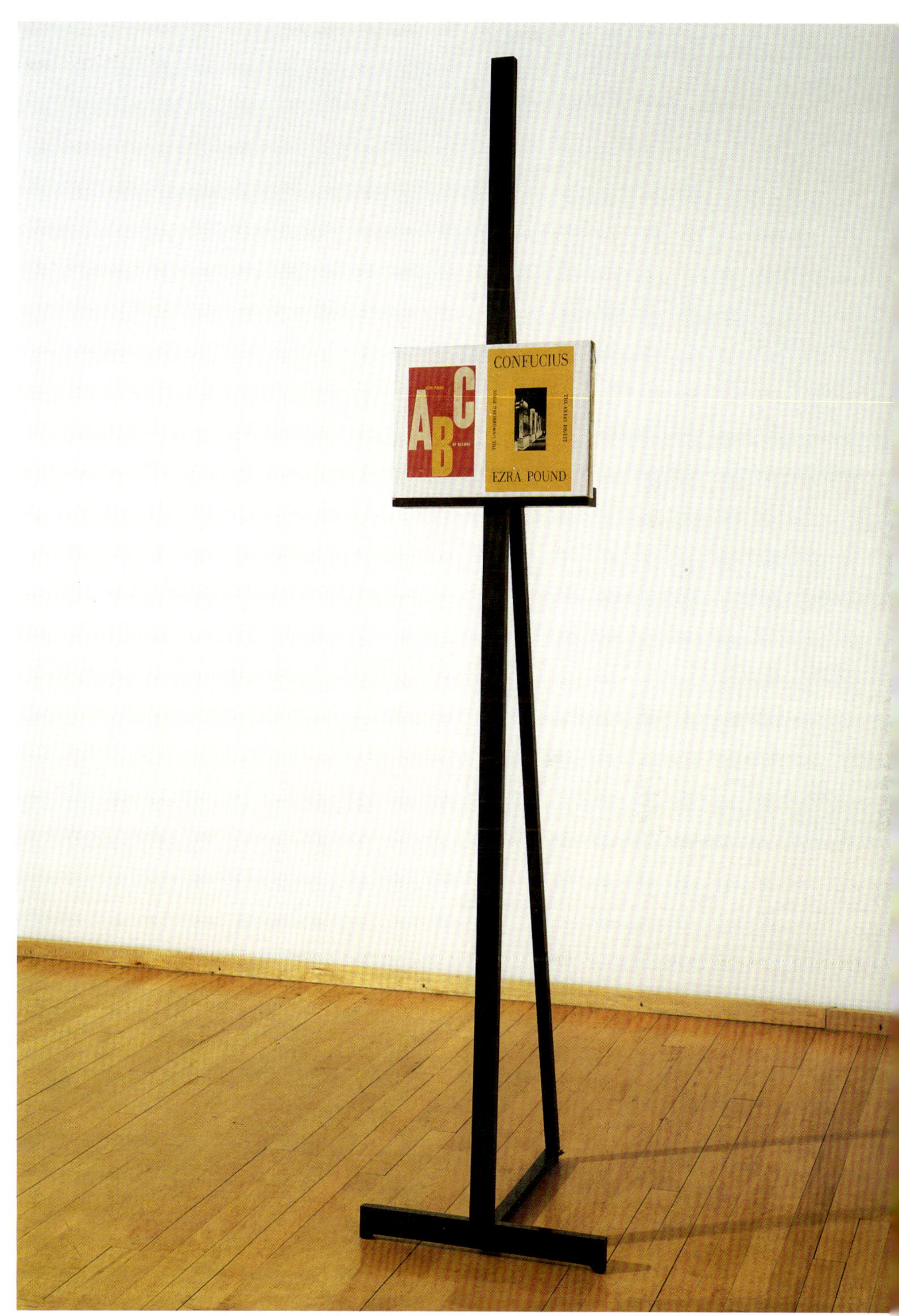

A.B.C. *of Reading and Confucius*, 1992.

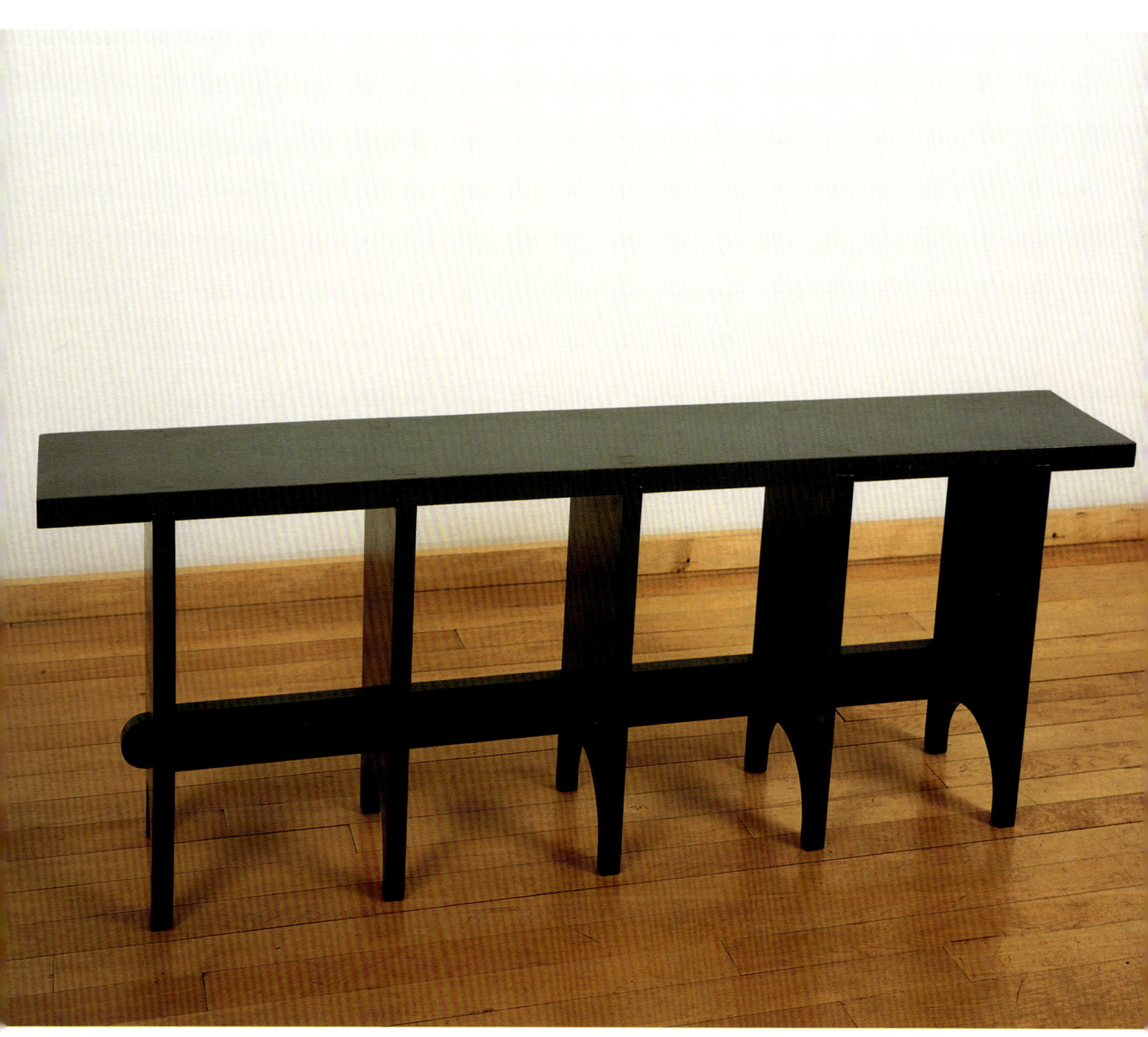

ABOVE *Read Pound*, 1990
OPPOSITE PAGE *Slowness is Beauty*, 1989

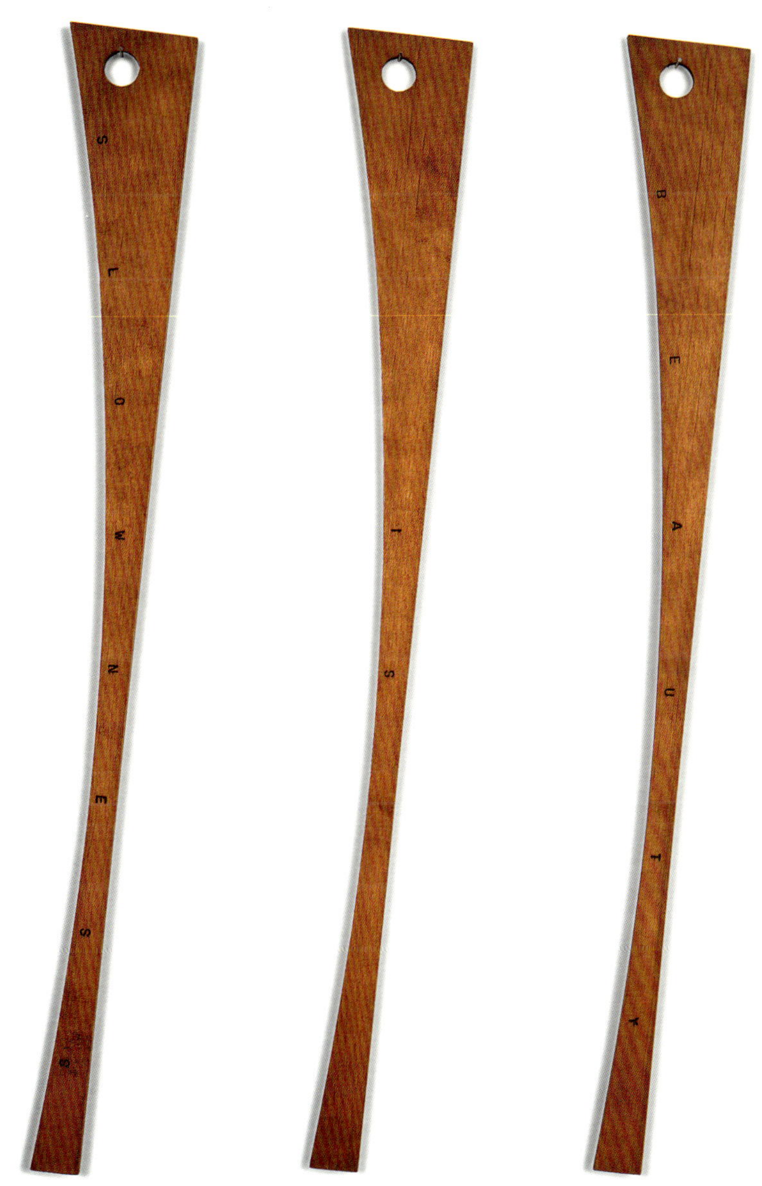
SLOWNESS
IS
BEAUTY

Richard Pettibone

There is a moment in *Death in Venice* when Thomas Mann refers to the Basilica of San Marco as an "oriental temple." Not only to imply that it could be something somewhere else, but that it really *does* extend beyond itself, into the Hagia Sophia of Constantinople, the Dome of the Rock in Jerusalem, the glorious Brihadeshvara Mandir at Tanjavur: the richness of meaning, of experience, and of associations implied by a phrase. No one would accuse San Marco of being uninteresting in itself, but likewise no one can deny the cumulative power with which knowledge can exaggerate the attributes of any work of art.

In his work, Richard Pettibone chooses something made by someone else at some other time and remakes it himself at his own pace. Finished, the sculpture stands at a certain proximity in both time and space, both real and imagined, to the artist's original object of affection and to his other works. The repetition of certain forms and variations on these forms, and their subsequent combinations, mimics the commitments to repetition that we all make in our daily lives—concentrating on one thing rather than another, choosing a vocation, a city to live in, a person to marry.

Pettibone's sculpture has, since the mid-1980s, concentrated almost exclusively on Brancusi sculpture and Shaker furniture, both of which share a commitment to the idea that simplicity and refinement of form can portray a spiritual essence, as well as commemorate the real time spent in the production of that form. His sculptures fondle time as their subject, and massage the devices of measurement and balance we use to perceive time. The patina of age and the seasonings of experience are as much the carver, the wood-turner, the planer, and the finisher as Pettibone himself. We are given a clock that knows the time but won't tell it, a painting of the time taken to read a book, a candlestand holding a pedestal holding a sculpture, a sculpture to hold a painting, and the continuous stream of seconds passed, slowly piled one on top of the other. A revealing phrase spun from familiar words, the narrative of a voyage implied by this new phrase.

Was Brancusi interested in the Shaker Movement and did the Shakers have any idea how avant-garde they were? The apparent ease with which Richard Pettibone fits the pieces together makes me question whether there ever was a puzzle at all. This ease is a salve, a polishing of our daily commitments, a satisfaction that we have spent our time wisely. Pettibone's works (I'm tempted to call them "curios" and rid this word of its pejorative sense) are balanced between the time of making, the time of perceiving, and the time of meaning. How long did it take to walk from one place to another and what did you notice along the way? How long will it take to start in Venice and end in Tanjavur?

PETER NAGY

GIUSEPPE UNGARETTI

D'AGOSTO

Avido lutto ronzante nei vivi,

Monotono altomare,
Ma senza solitudine,

Repressi squilli da prostrate messi,

Estate,

Sino ad orbite ombrate spolpi selci,

Resvegli ceneri nei colossei...

Quale Erebo t'urlò?

AUGUST

A desperate mourning drones through life,

Monotonous great sea,
But without solitude,

Faint alarums from the harvested,

Summer,

Until the shadow's orbit gnaws stones lean,

You wake ashes from the ruins...

Which Hell should I howl to you?

DORMIRE

Vorrei imitare
questo paese
adagiato
nel suo camice
di neve

THAT I MIGHT SLEEP

I wish to imitate
this unquiet land
lying now
so still
in its gentle camise
of snow

COMIATO

Gentile
Ettore Serra
poesia
è il mondo l'umanità
la propria vita
fioriti dalla parola
la limpida meraviglia
di un delirante fermento

Quando trovo
in questo mio silenzio
una parola
scavata è nella mia vita
come un abisso

PARTING

(In memory of Jon Norman)

Dear gentle
Hector Serra
poetry
is the earth humanity
the true life
blossoms made of word
the limpid marvel
of a fermented delirium

When I find
in this my silence
a dark word
it is like an abyss
in my life

Translated from
the Italian by
Gilbert Wesley Purdy

AN ESSAY ON THE PORTRAIT OF TWO WOMEN IN STEADILY DIMINISHING LIGHT

BILGE KARASU

Two women.
Past the time of wonder, pursuit, discovery, the time of expecting, not
    expecting, unexpecting
two women.
Into the years when reproach, envy, gossip are useful only to fill
    the emptiness (the hour, the day, the year's emptiness)
two women.
Still crossing the time when no one pities their advanced years; intimate,
    made of the same man, born of the same woman, sharing, one her
    widowhood, the other the homely solitude of her chastity;
    having concluded that the good manners they have acquired throughout
    their lives amount to the most refined philosophy, masters at accepting
    help, at rejecting the helper
two women.
Behind a window,
    illuminated by three lamps of different height, different strength,
    different size,
    a room crammed, brimming (with the passing years), after the image
nursed in their hearts since they left their father's house; sitting among
    the deep, full, asphyxiating reds, dark blues, darkening greens,

one just by the glass, the other slightly behind
two women.

•

This picture is never painted, perhaps never will be painted. Yet as if it were painted, I look, examine.

•

The floor lamp seems close to the window while another lamp stands slightly farther. In the varying yellow lights, they sit as if waiting for something. Obviously, there is something they await. It shows in the way they sit, this late in the night, without talking (and it would seem to the observer that they ought to talk constantly, that every moment they spend without talking ought to make them feel the silence of death, that, for these women, death ought to be, above all, silence), from the way they look through the window, peering into the darkness that, to them, lies outside the canvas and, to us, is where we stand.

We are their darkness. What they await we ought to create.

They may be thinking, they may be daydreaming; why shouldn't we think so? Yet something in their faces, in the way they sit, suggests otherwise. Even if they think or daydream from time to time, or appear to be thinking or daydreaming, I'd bet my life they are waiting for something.

•

In the left corner of the glass is a head; in the right corner, in a pot, a barrel cactus. (It resembles a prickly melon, a pincushion, an angry fist, or something else, who can tell?)

Looking at the picture, in front of these women, we are an invisible entity, one great unknown.

In the left corner of the glass, the head stares not at us but toward us. Squinting eyes fill the upper half of her wrinkled face.

(Yet we know that these squinting eyes are hungry to see. Insuperably hungry. They belong to the untouched one. Her old wishes, desires, memories have surfaced in the form of a tentacle with eyes....

Or like the organ insects use for sucking nectar,
blood, pus, her eye, even when squinting, draws
the world in.

The passersby, the daily occurrences, beside these, her tentacle wants to dive, to bury itself in eventualities, even in what is yet to be thought of, projected.)

The lower half of her wrinkled face is a mouth that extends from side to side. Forever ready to smile, to appear pretty, yet in reality, frozen in the sketch of a smile, unwilling to close, a mouth ready to start spitting malice in the first available ear. Nothing else.

Either because she liked no one or because she was not found likable, or perhaps because fortune dismissed her altogether, she withered slowly beside her older sister who was first married, then widowed. In the shadow of love's unremitting mystery, she grew accustomed to looking after the baser chores—washing dishes, cooking meals, wiping floors, mixing with loose tongues.

As for dusting, baking sweets and pastries, polishing the silver, sewing, earning a little money doing odd jobs, collecting a widow's pension, those are the other's responsibilities: the sister who sits slightly behind, in the deep red, overstuffed chair, under the strong (bright yellow) lamp (the globe lamp, the only one lit in the room).

When women suddenly stop using makeup because they decide smearing paint on their face no longer becomes them, a certain kind of whiteness spreads across their cheeks, forehead, neck, and lips, a whiteness that recalls the face of one dead. That is the whiteness we see in this woman's face. Is this the pale skin so admired in the old days? Her deathly white face resembles her sister's only because it, too, is partitioned by a pair of squinting eyes and a mouth that is ready to speak; apart from this, the face seems without the slightest crease or line; it is large, wide, round, tense.

Both envy their lady neighbor who has retired from her position as Director of the X Department of the Y Ministry, who has forgotten how to respect others, who never waits her turn, and who expects to enter every place as though it were her own, that is, by pushing and shoving; yet, what she does to strangers, the sisters can do only to friends. Anything else is beyond them.

•

They look as if they are waiting for something, that's clear. Perhaps someone they know will appear in front of the window, perhaps they will hear a scream....

> (Scream of death, grief, birth, scream of pain... any of these may be what they await, what they can await. Who is sick, who is pregnant, they know; they also know which wife will be beaten by her husband, which child by his father, precisely, to the day, to the minute. Because their tentacles, those eyes and ears, keep sucking in the neighborhood interminably.)

Perhaps what they await is something they sense but do not know. Yet there is no anxiety in their faces. That's certain. Theirs is a bare, dry state of waiting. Nothing else.

•

Perhaps they are waiting for us, for our interest that peers through the darkness, notices them in the painting, and grants them their existence. The darkness is our beauty, our absence, that is, our truth....

Yet, even to think in these terms is somewhat contrary to the identities we have fashioned

for these women. Have they ever had the eyes that see beauty, absence, interest? Have they ever considered that a complete stranger can look at them? That they can be observed, that another can watch them the way they watch him, has it ever crossed their minds? We don't know.

Of course we don't know, given that we must content ourselves with looking at the painting.... But, surely, they neither see us nor know us nor think of us. We can't be wrong in the face of such clarity

in the face of such hunger.

The world is a well of knowledge for them, the kind of knowledge that fits the mold of gossip, what they thirst for, knowledge that is there to be drawn in, knowledge that exists to the extent it is drawn in.

We have already stated this; so we plan to discover and state other things.

•

Let's consider the details that suggest waiting.

She sits regally, the one with the white skin and tense, round face. The wine-residue color of her armchair darkens as it reaches the floor. Behind the window that we stare through, there is only one lamp lit, to save money, in all likelihood. It is in the distance, behind her, in the corner to our right. This light is not inside the room, but outside. It illuminates the open door of the room. The lamp must not be very strong. Beside giving little light to the room, it leaves a vaguely yellow color on the door's surface. Perhaps this is the lamp at the entrance to the apartment. Right by the front door... Did I consider this detail as well when concluding that they were waiting for someone?

The one sitting in the left-hand corner of the window is perhaps stealthy, perhaps hurt; or she is one of those who can create enmity with a word casually spoken, perhaps.

But the other one sitting regally in the armchair—its deep red color turning to dark brown, then to black—she is stern, unforgiving, hostile. She must be in charge of conducting the quarrels with the outside because of her piercing, ripping, cracked—or so I assume—voice. Sitting regally, amidst the pile of furniture, the sediment of years (forever useless, never meant for use, acquired to beautify, that is, fill up, the house,

> if to live means, first, to spin in an orbit of loud chatter, second, it means to beautify the world; and to beautify means to fill the emptiness, all the empty spaces, homes, closets, mouths, ears (whether necessary or not), stuff them with anything within one's grasp; it must be so for these women

cover the surfaces, leaving exposed less and less of the faded green color of the wall, objects received as gifts or kept in memory of a dead person, the pile of furniture that is the sediment of years), she seems to be living in the reverie of an eternal sultanate. Perhaps she resents her husband for dying and leaving her helpless in this sea of undisposable, untradable objects. Hurt and anger may be racing in her as she considers how to behave toward the friends who used to invite them to dinner three evenings a week but now, since the engagement of their daughter, have been inviting them only once a week. Perhaps, more than any of this, she is inwardly cursing the landlord who takes their money, like tearing off pieces of their flesh, for these rooms that smell of rust because he refuses to clean the pipes.

Yet her squinting eyes are not turned inward; rather, they are looking ahead. Between her sister who sits in the right-hand corner of the window and the stately elephant-ears plant that stands along the left shutter, she looks beyond the window.

> Out of hand-embroidered tablecloths, ceramic dolls, framed photographs on the walls, on the tables, various silver ashtrays, enamel ones, sets and sets of crystal tumblers and goblets inside glass cabinets, out of sofa frames with moldy, peeled veneer, tables and stands, faded, threadbare velour upholstery, unaging carpets, impenetrable drapes, out of floor, globe, and hanging lamps, the refrigerator with its statuesque whiteness signifying their highest point of attainment, out of these they have built a fortress, their retreat, as if replicating the madness of an old-world gentleman who built his tower on shifting sand. The air they breathe has steadily diminished. Yet it is open before them, behind them. Open to the street, to life, to others' noise, open to their hostility, open to death.

We understand from the reflection on the glass: People stroll in front of them, street lamps glow above them. The tentacles, those eyes and ears, are not merely extensions toward the outside; they are also others' extensions that can extend into the room. This fortress doesn't protect the women at all.

•

Yet these are all words that belong to the observer of the painting who tends to be reclusive. Emotions that he has fashioned for these women by putting himself in their place ... No, that's not accurate. Rather, we should say: by putting himself in their place, he imagines these women in the state just described, whereas, connecting as they do with life by way of the eye, by way of the ear, they wouldn't be reserved about the eyes or ears of another.

It is not *something* they await but *someone*, in the darkness of their home.

We understand this from a reflection on the glass. The light inside (even though we can discern every object) is not coming from a concealed source in the room. It is the glow from a street lamp (or two)—that
we don't see—right outside the window. It is a ground-floor window.
We understand this from a reflection on the glass. People stroll in front
of the women.

They are waiting for someone. Whomever they await will probably arrive soon. Their squinting eyes seem neither dreamy nor longing
nor excited. The awaited

is one who, previously too, arrived on time, as planned,
one who is unlonged for, unexciting,
one who doesn't arouse the impossible, the unexpected, or fear,
one whom they know.

Perhaps just now, emerging through the leaves (of a short tree or a low branch) between the window and the frame of the painting, is the figure (we barely notice in the dark) of the one they await.

•

We write the following few lines according to a friend's account some years ago:

(Presumably) *In America*, (presumably) *a newspaper man* (or a newspaper photographer, more appropriately) *saw in the pictures he took of accidents* (in different places, at different times, or of different accidents that occurred at the same time), *among the people gathered around the damaged vehicle, the collapsed wall, the destroyed house, the uprooted tree,* ... It was an insane thought ... *the same person.* It was not even a thought, not even intuition, perhaps an animal instinct, a reflex.... The newspaper man (or the newspaper photographer) inspected with a magnifying glass all the accident photos he could get his hands on. He found other photos and, one by one, inspected them as well. Even if it were madness, the proof was before him. Obvious. He could see it clearly in every picture.

At the accident site, among those gathered, staring at the dead, with a vague smile, a vague look of joy, a vague look of pride in her face, a woman somewhat old, with graying hair, somewhat beautiful, somewhat warm. The same woman. From year to year, from place to place, unchanging. A woman who reaches everywhere, stares at each dead being, as if aware of her power, her triumph...

"Can this be true?" Those who doubt can have our friend's name. They can ask him.

He is swarthy. In his twenties, tall, well-built, aware of his youth and singular beauty. We compare him to a much-loved person whose disappearance all those years ago is still unbearable to us. On his deep wine-colored shirt, there are pale white stripes. In one hand is a rose. The other hand is invisible.

•

What the women await, what we see and they cannot—what they will never get to see as long as this painting remains a painting—is this young man; but it is not he who interests them; rather it is the news he will bring. He must be the son of some friends or acquaintances. Possibly the friends we mentioned earlier. Perhaps he will come to tell them that his parents again wish to invite them to dinner three times a week. He is the son of the friends who, since their daughter's engagement, have been inviting them only once a week. "They'd like you to come for dinner tonight," he will say, or, more precisely, the women want to hear. It must be so, we say to ourselves. We know this as an observer, as one looking at the painting, as an art aficionado convinced of his right to interpret its details in any way he pleases.

We already mentioned that the sky had grown dark and the street lamps were lit. Considering the rose in the young man's hand, it must be an early summer night. If so, it's unlikely that the women will be invited tonight. Dinnertime must be long past. At best the invitation will be for tomorrow night. It is important for them to know this. How else could they decide tomorrow morning whether or not to cook for the evening? They could always make do with something light for lunch.

As they sit in their light summer dresses and begin to gnaw at the boredom of an endless night, the messenger due to arrive will alleviate, even if briefly, their solitude and bring them one last drop of knowledge about the outside world. But the messenger will depart as soon as he arrives. The young man will say what he has to say through the door. He won't come in, no matter how much they insist. He will leave immediately because he wants to take a walk. Perhaps that's why the women can sit and wait without getting excited or overjoyed.

•

The young man will suddenly emerge out of the darkness that had veiled him, come to the window, look through the glass. Tilting his head toward the crimson darkness of the room, he will smile, revealing his teeth that glisten like drops of water against the darkness of his eyes. The regal woman with the tense, round, white face will rise from her armchair to open the door, without thinking to turn on a light; the other will get up and walk to the middle of the room. She'll stop. Because she will hear the hollow thump of her sister falling to the floor, before she even opens the door, and she will understand (although she will not have seen her sister bring her hand to her neck, to her chest, and after a brief struggle, fall motionless) that she has died. She will freeze. She won't open the door, but instead will turn around and look at the window. In the outside light, she will see the sweet, calming smile of the young man who they thought was their friends' son. She will rush out to ask the neighbors for help, and will never know that the rose she will step on fell to the ground at the same moment as her sister.

•

Otherwise, this youthful man who moves like a liquid sail in the beauty of an evening intended for the young, what business would he have standing, with a rose in his hand, in the narrow, dark space between the frame of the painting and the gray outline of the window?

Translated from the Turkish by Aron R. Aji

JAY BOGGIS

TO MY FATHER

Laid out in your bed,
you talked to me
through your death face,

the mercy
death brings,
the new face,

so we won't see
the living face
in death.

THE SON AND HEIR

ALEXANDER HÄUSSER

For the first hour I didn't give her my hand. She offered me hers, but I was ashamed. Instead I spoke immediately of the torment—without knowing what I meant, simply babbling. She leaned back in her chair, with her chin supported by her thumb and her fingertips resting on her lips. She didn't say a word while I agonized, squirming in my place—just talking, anything at all—simply to ward off the silence. She wanted to speak of earlier. I could only remember my grade-school years; of the time before, I knew nothing. I knew him only from photographs. He had been a sick man. I would have loved to jump up, to dust or do the dishes as Mother usually did when she spoke. So much you want to know since you've been going there, she said, it's a virtual interrogation. I'd have thought she'd be pleased that I was coming to visit more often now.

I have sweaty hands and a knot in my throat. I listen to the radio all night long because I can't sleep, but I wouldn't have asked. She wanted to know.

The war had made many men sick—then, I said. And more?

They had met at a ball. In the ballroom, or what was left of it: the missing wall had been replaced with an olive-green tarpaulin. It was still cold, but when they danced it was fine. There were mostly American and French men there. They had organized everything. They probably just wanted to feel a woman again. And they had, after all, nothing against the women—

the men were to blame, not the women. Mother's friend, the one she had gone with, flirted all evening with a young Frenchman; Jacques was his name or something like that. She hadn't heard anything good about the French, but Anna would have to look out for herself. Mother danced only with Americans and Germans. But she couldn't speak English, and there were hardly any Germans there. She was actually just standing around, watching the others while her feet turned to ice. She had only come for Anna's sake anyway. Until someone spoke to her from behind. A young German, who didn't look her in the eyes when she turned around, who didn't stand upright before her, who almost whispered, but had a very lovely smile.

The orchestra played a waltz. He had trouble leading her, was somewhat bent over even as he danced, and pushed her away instead of drawing her to him. But she generally liked tall men, and he might have quietly come closer. He was, quite simply, a dignified man, and she surely wouldn't have taken it the wrong way. Naturally though, he couldn't have known this. He was just very decent, and it was nice that way. When they weren't dancing, they stood at the makeshift bar, holding glasses in their hands merely to have something to hold onto. He said nothing. She spoke of her work in the hosiery store, which was how she knew Anna, her friend, the one with the Frenchman. She pointed over at them both, just as they kissed again. Mother smiled with embarrassment, but he simply stared at the ground before him, looking as if he were in some pain. She could have asked him if there was something wrong, but she didn't utter a word. He's obviously sick, she thought, and doesn't care to speak about it. She had already seen many men come back as cripples. She felt sorry for him.

At closing time, there was trouble with Jacques. He didn't want to let Anna go home; he wouldn't give her her coat and pleaded with her. Anna refused, but laughing. He, on the other hand, helped Mother into her coat, then asked if he should see her home, as it was already dark. But he asked in a tone which made it clear that he would actually prefer not to, and she thanked him, but said she wouldn't have to walk alone. He said good-bye and left. He was really very decent. Mother also told me that he had come to the hosiery store a week later, and that she had been completely surprised. She hadn't expected it, although she had thought of him often.

She asked questions that I didn't entirely understand. Sometimes I looked at her legs. She paid no attention to how she sat. She was consumed by her thoughts, intensely concentrated. I spoke differently with her, as one speaks with strange women one meets in an unfamiliar town—in an ominous tone, to make her curious. And she was curious. She wanted to know everything. After all, I was a man.

They often went for walks. He also took her along to dinner. He had good contacts. She learned that he had been an officer stationed in Poland, then injured and in the hospital. She knew the stories. His is no different, she thought. She spoke of her father and his father, of these horrible wars and whether there would ever be an end to them. He was suddenly excited and wanted to say something, but he remained silent, and took her in his arms instead, completely gentle. That was in the evening, up in the meadow, beneath the open sky. Nothing to remind one of the war. She was aroused, in a way she had never experienced before. A few months later, they were married. It didn't go badly for them. They had found a small apartment, and he was working as a carpenter; he had already been apprenticed. He was good, much too good to still have to do any of the grunt work, Mother said, like carrying doors and whatnot around the construction sites. He was the one who should have had to tell the others what to do, and not the other way around. But he would hear nothing of that. He had given orders long enough and he liked things the way they were. He was good-natured as a husband as well. Never an unkind word, attentive, honest, loyal—if only he'd had a bit more fire...

She showed me photographs. She always did that when she wanted a diversion. She moved over to me, brought the photo album, and played Sunday afternoon. At first I played along, drinking her coffee, eating her cake, nodding when it was time to nod. He looked so good in his uniform; she had never seen him like that, only in pictures, but it must have been magnificent. I had got my physique from him, but I did nothing about it. He had trained, even as a boy. He had to. Just to withstand the recoil of a rifle or even a bazooka, so she had heard from her father, required extraordinary strength.

I wouldn't be diverted. I said she should continue telling about him; she could clear the table if that would help. She seemed unsure. It wasn't right to speak with me about all that. She was, after all, my mother.

He didn't touch her the first night. He sat beside her on the bed, undressed and yet somehow guarded, and told of earlier. At first she tried to approach him, feeling her way across to him with her feet under the covers, for she wanted to, but he pulled away. He wanted to tell, and she was happy to hear him speak—he was always so still—but of all times now.... She couldn't listen properly, could only stare at his neck, which was so broad and strong, and at his chest, which she couldn't have embraced, even if her arms were long enough. He spoke of the war, and of the time before. How he had played sports with his friends. They had wrestled and measured each other's biceps, and they were constantly betting: who could swim fastest across the lake, who would be first on the mat. And later, during training, he had practiced shouting, alone in the woods. His throat hurt, and his voice was much too high; it sounded at first like the voice of a woman. But he would have been laughed at if he couldn't have learned how. That was the horrible thing about the war: that he had somehow fit in. She didn't understand what he meant. Perhaps if she had listened better.

He had remained reserved. She called it tender. In that regard he was already a real man; he had never had problems with that. Mother was pregnant after two months of marriage. He was constantly thinking of names for girls—Carmen, Charlotte, Katharina, every day a new one. He had no ideas for a boy. He was certain it would be a girl. She laughed about it, saying, I guess one woman isn't enough for you. But he was quite serious about it. Once, when they were sitting at supper, he shouted at her that he didn't want a boy; he'd rather have no child at all than a son. She should stop making fun of him. Mother simply stared at him. She didn't know anymore what she had said. He had never shouted at her before. She had only asked why he wouldn't want a son and heir. Men always want sons after all. She hadn't intended to make fun of him, what had hurt him so badly? But he simply excused himself, though he was still all worked up, saying that everything would be fine, and that he was looking forward to having a girl. Mother became afraid.

I came into the world at home, in my parents' bedroom. He was still working. The midwife was pleased: a beautiful, healthy boy. For a moment my mother toyed with the notion of concealing my sex. It was still so small. Then she became angry with him, because he was to blame for the fact that she could think such a thing. Finally she convinced herself that he would only have to see me, and everything would be forgotten. The midwife should stay, however; she didn't want to be alone when he arrived.

He stood beside the bed. Mother took me in her arms and tried to smile, more for him than for herself. The midwife said that he should be proud, for the resemblance was striking. That much could already be seen. He knew the story. And when Mother drew the baby closer to herself, he simply left the room; left the room and left the apartment. She eased her hold and closed her eyes. Just be patient, she thought, it will surely work out. Mother began to wait.

A few hours later, he returned. She waited, but he said nothing. No explanation, no word about the child. He was very kind to her, caressed her, and prepared tea. Yet he spoke with her as if she were sick, comforted her as if she had given birth to a dead fetus. The child breathed and cried. He heard nothing, didn't go anywhere near the child, didn't look at it. Mother waited.

The baptism took place without him. He was present for Sunday excursions, and yet not really. He never pushed the stroller, never shook out the little pillow and covers. He never once held the rattle, and couldn't take pleasure in the way the little one followed things with his eyes and then tried to grab them. He didn't hear the first words, and when the babbling child approached him with outstretched arms, more falling than walking, he never once avoided him. For that he would have had to have been there. He let himself be touched—which Mother had waited for—yet not exactly, the way a stump or a banister is touched.

And yet he wasn't made of wood, she said.

She tried again and again to speak with him, but it was no use. He wasn't there anymore. She stopped waiting, and thought only of her child. I was four years old.

Nothing more to say—just sitting here, mute. But something had to happen; no one could endure that for long. That evening he went down to the building's cellar right after work.

He had set up a workshop there, where he carved toys and repaired furniture to supplement his income. She knitted for a while and then went to sleep. My bed was in the living room. He must have knocked something over when he came into the apartment, or perhaps she simply sensed it—in any case, Mother woke in the middle of the night. She didn't hear anything else, but she knew he was nearby. She became unsettled. Without turning on the lights, she got up and went into the living room. In the half-light, she saw him from behind, leaning over my bed.

Father smelled of freshly-sawed wood.

She screamed and rushed toward him. He turned around, let the knife fall, and asked why she wasn't sleeping—perfectly quietly he asked that. She pummeled him, pounding his chest with her fists, wailing, cursing him; he didn't move, didn't protect himself from her blows, stood as if rooted there until she couldn't go on, just whimpered and sobbed. He stroked her hair, then left her standing and was gone.

Mother managed to find out that he had gone to the hospital in Zwiestetten—almost thirty kilometers away. She visited him sometimes on weekends. She had to work and had very little time. I was never taken along. Mother said nothing about the visits, but she was often sad when she returned. I comforted her, telling her that he would surely be healthy again soon. I didn't ask questions. When I was eight years old, he died in the hospital. No one could say exactly from what. Perhaps it was the war injury. After that she went to Zwiestetten two more times, to pick up his things and meet with the doctor who had always conducted the conversations with him. But she learned nothing. I couldn't imagine such a doctor, who had no instruments, and with whom one only spoke. How could such a man help him, Mother said.

If there weren't different flowers on the table every time, if she didn't wear light dresses in the summer and heavy, woolen ones in the winter, I would swear that she never left this room. That she is always sitting in this chair, and only gets up to let me in.

No, I haven't visited Mother for quite some time now. She looks at the clock—five minutes still. She doesn't need to say anything, I already know. We never go over, and today is no exception. She will show me to the door. I should give her my hand then, at least today, even if it's still sweaty. I could squeeze hers firmly, so that it hurts a little—as a sort of atonement.

That would be good.

Translated from the German by Daniel Slager

HANNAH

HÖCH

FROM AN ETHNOGRAPHIC MUSEUM

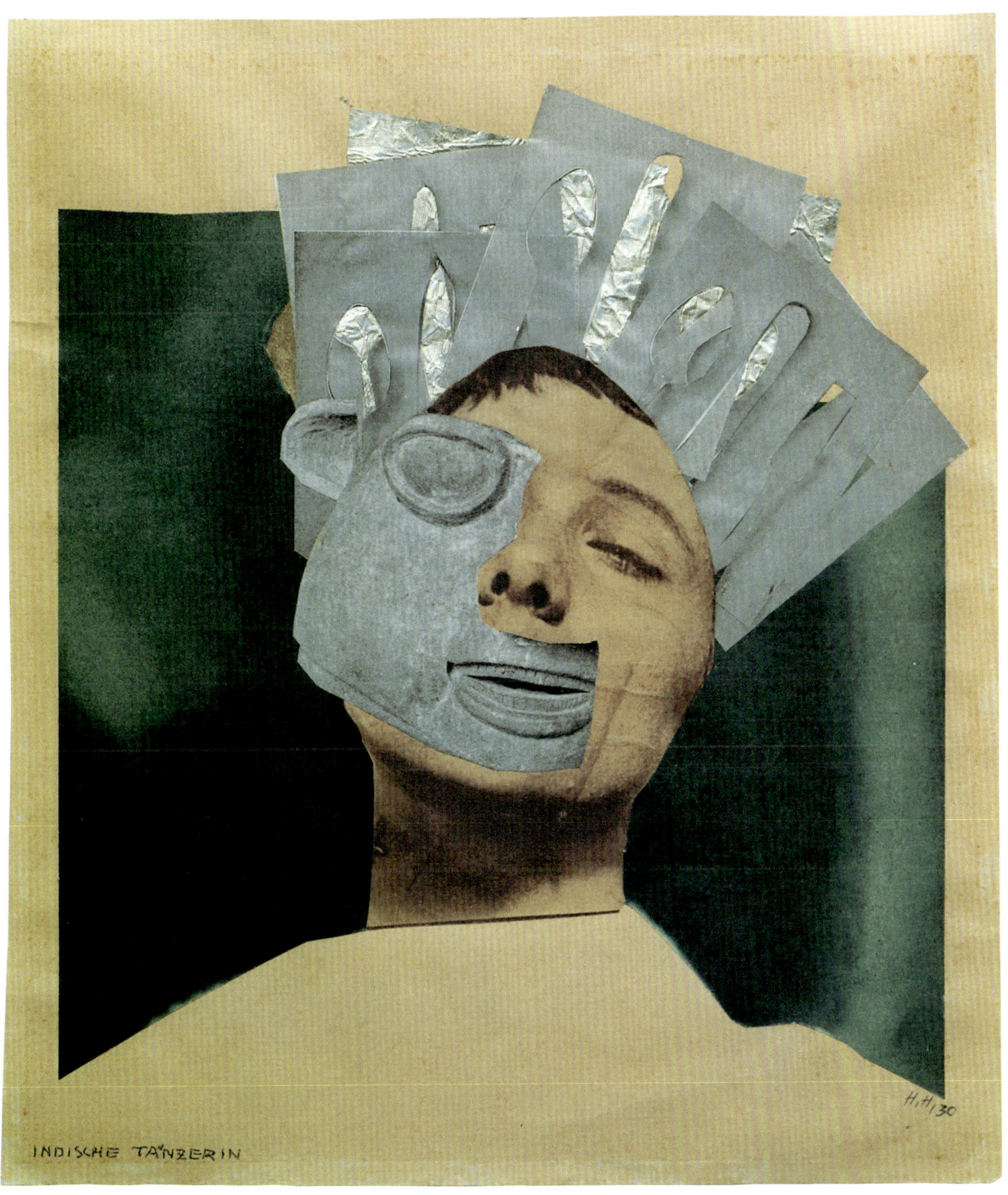

Indian Female Dancer, 1930.

All of the works in this portfolio are from Höch's series *From an Ethnographic Museum*.

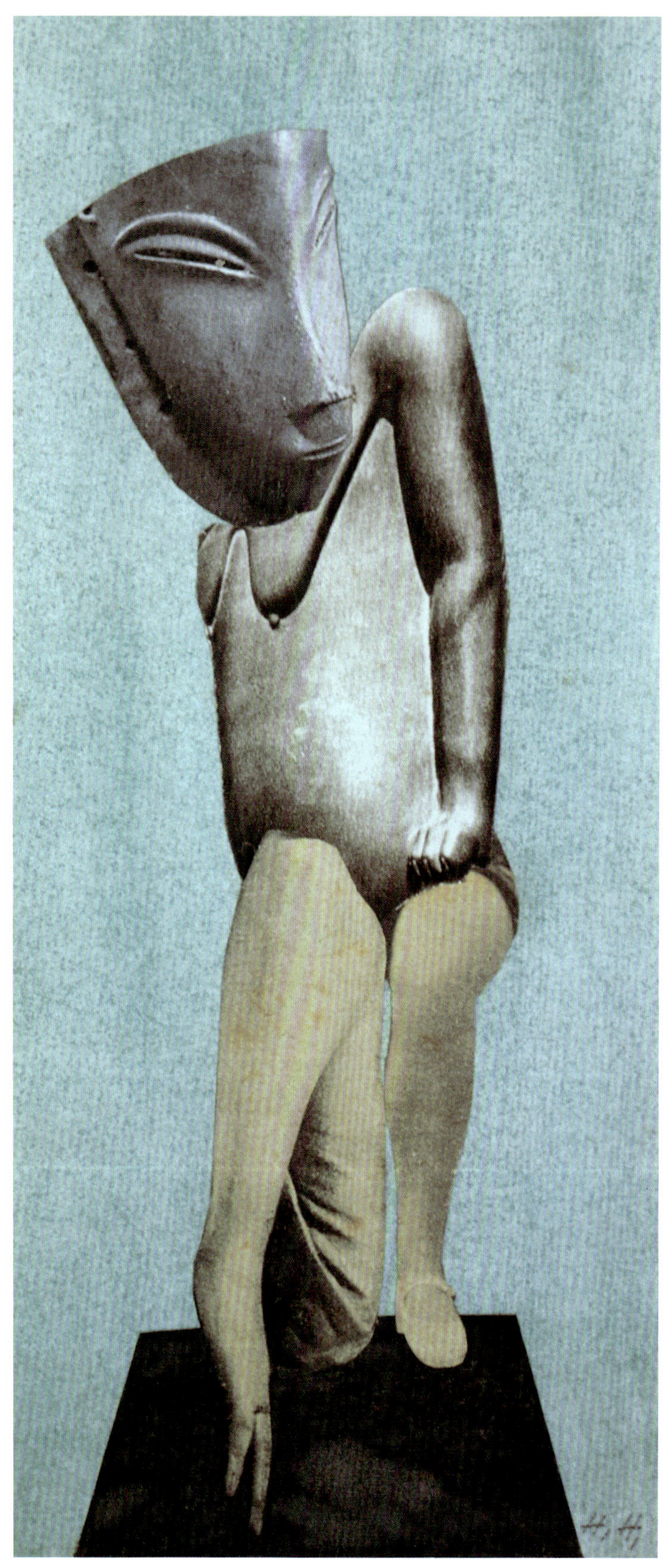

Monument I, 1924.

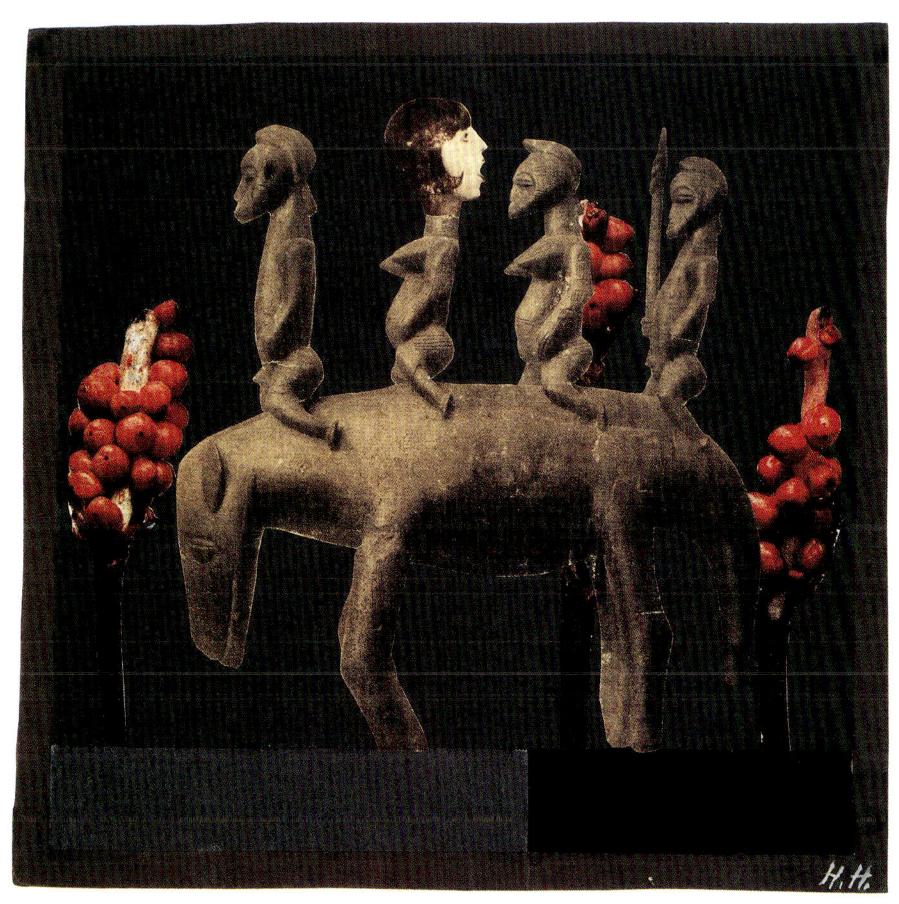

Abduction, 1925.

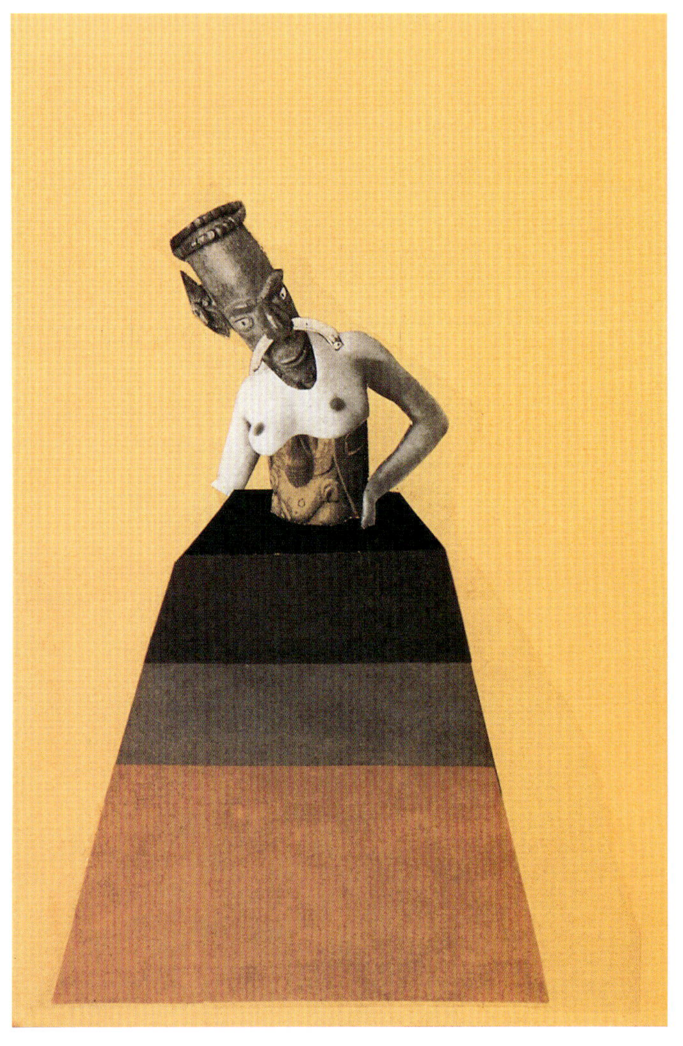

Untitled, 1929.

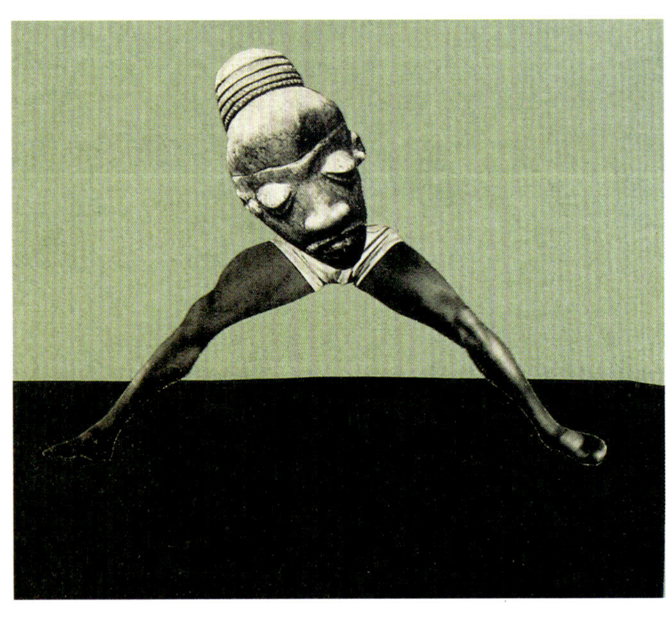

Untitled, 1929.

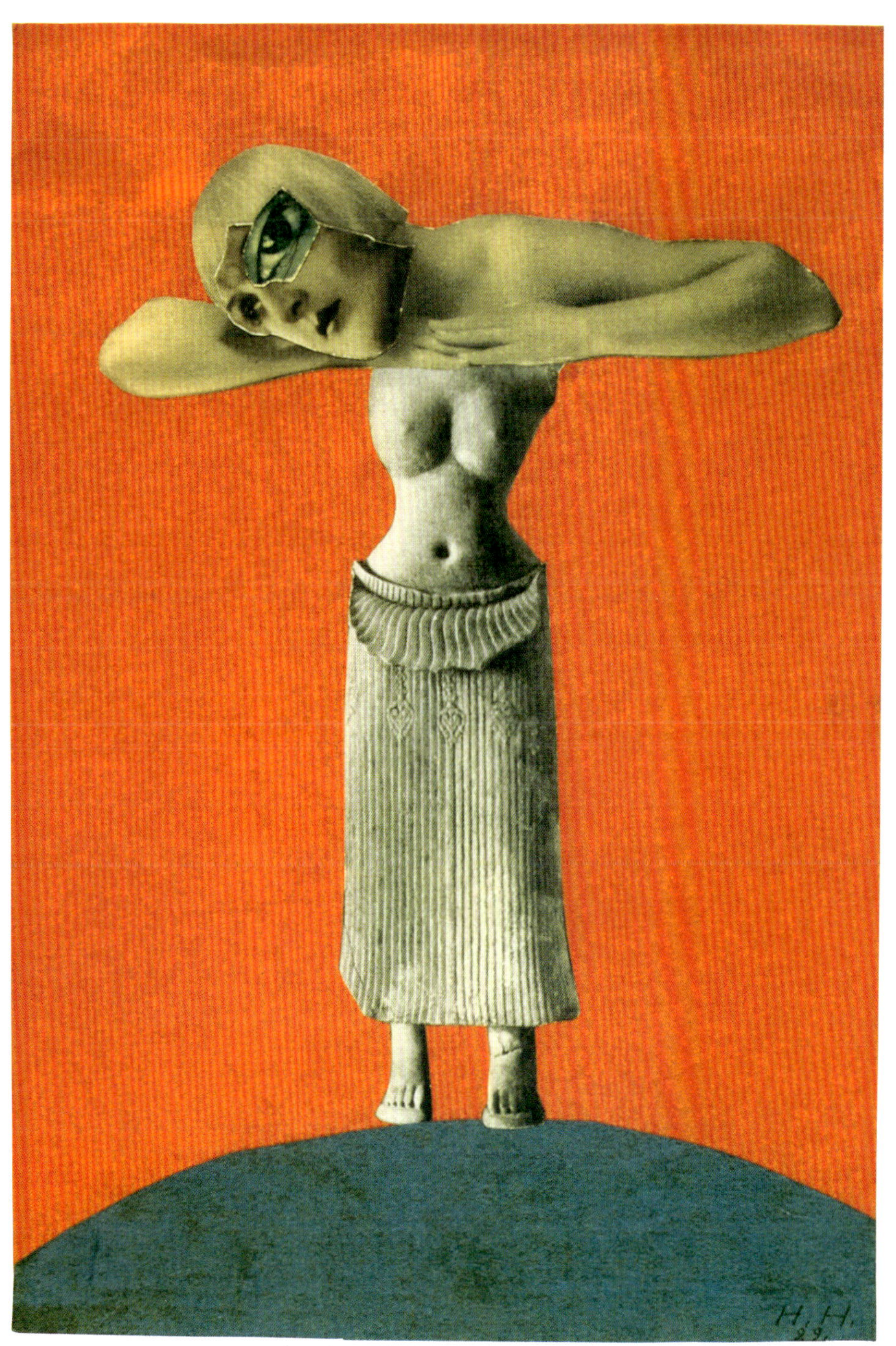

Untitled, 1930.

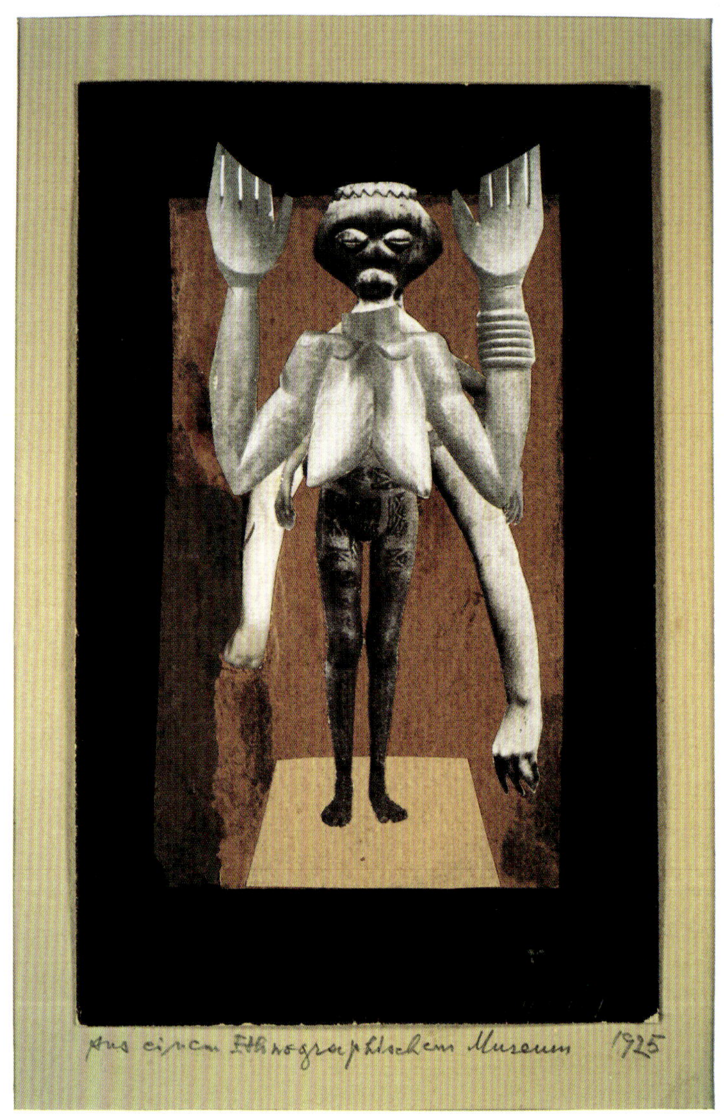

Sadness, 1925.

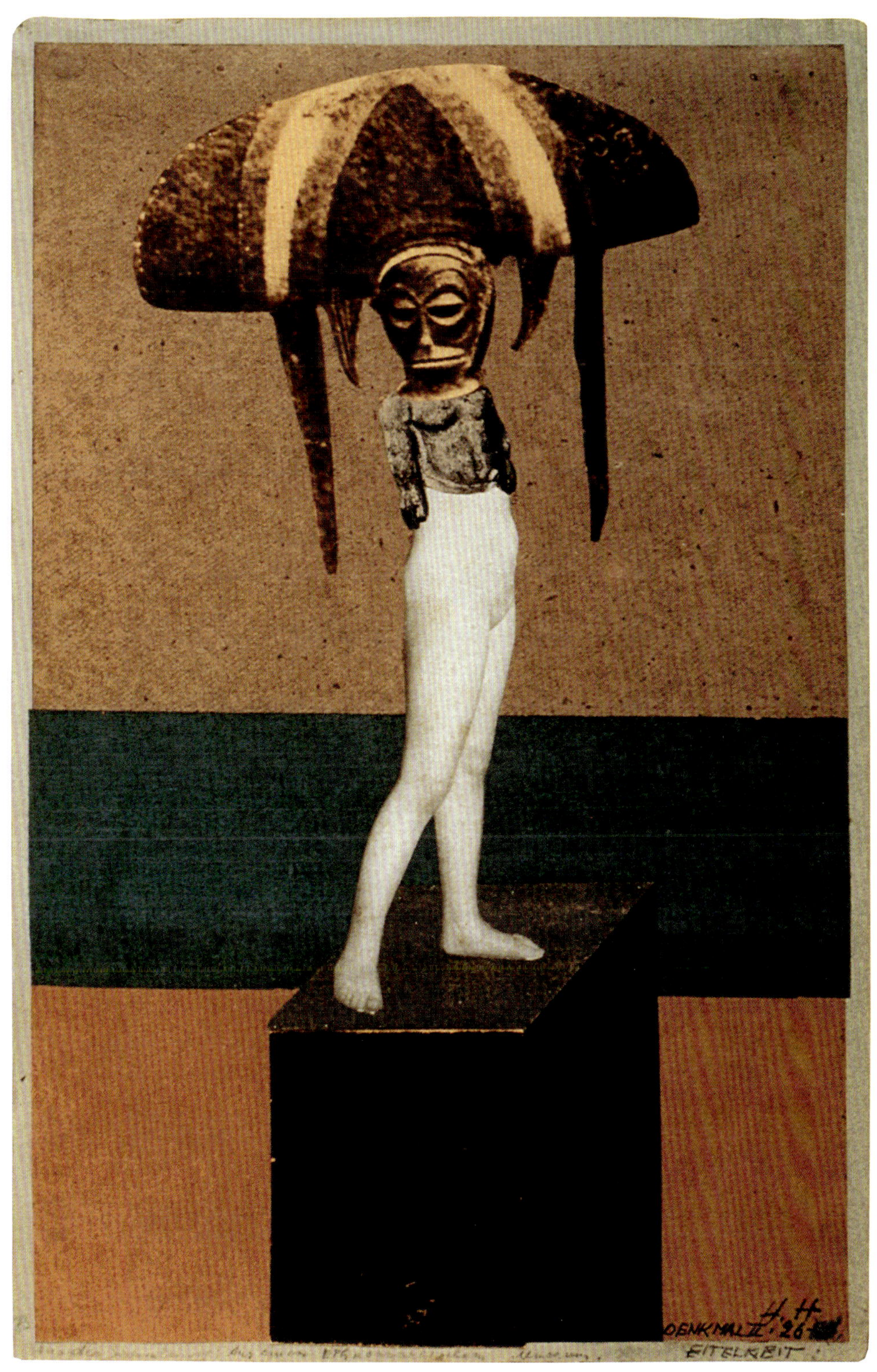

Monument II: Vanity, 1926.

HANNAH HÖCH

Hannah Höch (1889–1978) created the *Ethnographic Museum* series of approximately twenty photomontages in the 1920s and early 1930s, a tumultuous time for her and in general for the "New Women" of Weimar Germany. Raised in a protective, small-town, bourgeois family and pulled out of school at fifteen to care for her youngest sister, Höch didn't make the big break to Berlin and art school until she was almost twenty-two.

In Berlin, she studied graphic arts three days a week and, another three days a week, she worked at Ullstein Verlag, Germany's largest and most modern press, on a very un-modern task: designing handicrafts to be featured in women's magazines. And yet this mixture of new and old (or *ungleichzeitig* as cultural critic Ernst Bloch was to call it) was fairly typical of what Weimar women's lives were really like. It was a time, the first time in German history, when women had the vote but little power, when some women were working on farms, others toiling on assembly lines, and others typing in offices, when women had sexual freedom but no access to legalized abortion, when it was common for women to live on their own in cities and support themselves, while they continued to earn less than men.

As a Weimar woman and artist, Höch was part of the Berlin Dada movement and had a difficult, seven-year relationship with fellow Dadaist artist Raoul Hausmann, followed by years of independence and recognition in the international avant-garde, and then a lesbian relationship with the Dutch writer Til Brugman and further recognition, before the Nazi seizure of power, through exhibitions in the Netherlands, Germany, and Czechoslovakia. The majority of the works in the *Ethnographic Museum* series were shown together only once, in a one-woman exhibition in Brno, Czechoslovakia in 1934. Otherwise, the series functioned as a continuing work-in-progress, in which Höch montaged images connoting the display of the New Woman—in department-store windows, magazines, and film—and the offering of ethnographic objects in ethnographic museums.

While I can see, in the series, some ironic critique, on an intellectual level, of the commodification of both the New Woman and so-called primitive cultures, on a more emotional level, I read a disturbance about the public display of self, and a tension between ego and anonymity—which was often demonstrated in the rather cultish and loosely defined admiration for African and Eastern spirituality common in avant-garde circles at the time. Evident throughout the series is a tension between the representation of the self and others, self-identity and the identities of others, which, in general, is a moving thread throughout Höch's insistent, joyous, angry, ambivalent, playful, adulatory, and iconoclastic montages of women of her generation. For Höch, it seems that the New Woman—her images, her possibilities, her everyday realities, and her stereotypes—was the self, as well as the other.

MAUD LAVIN

FROM

The Life of Insects

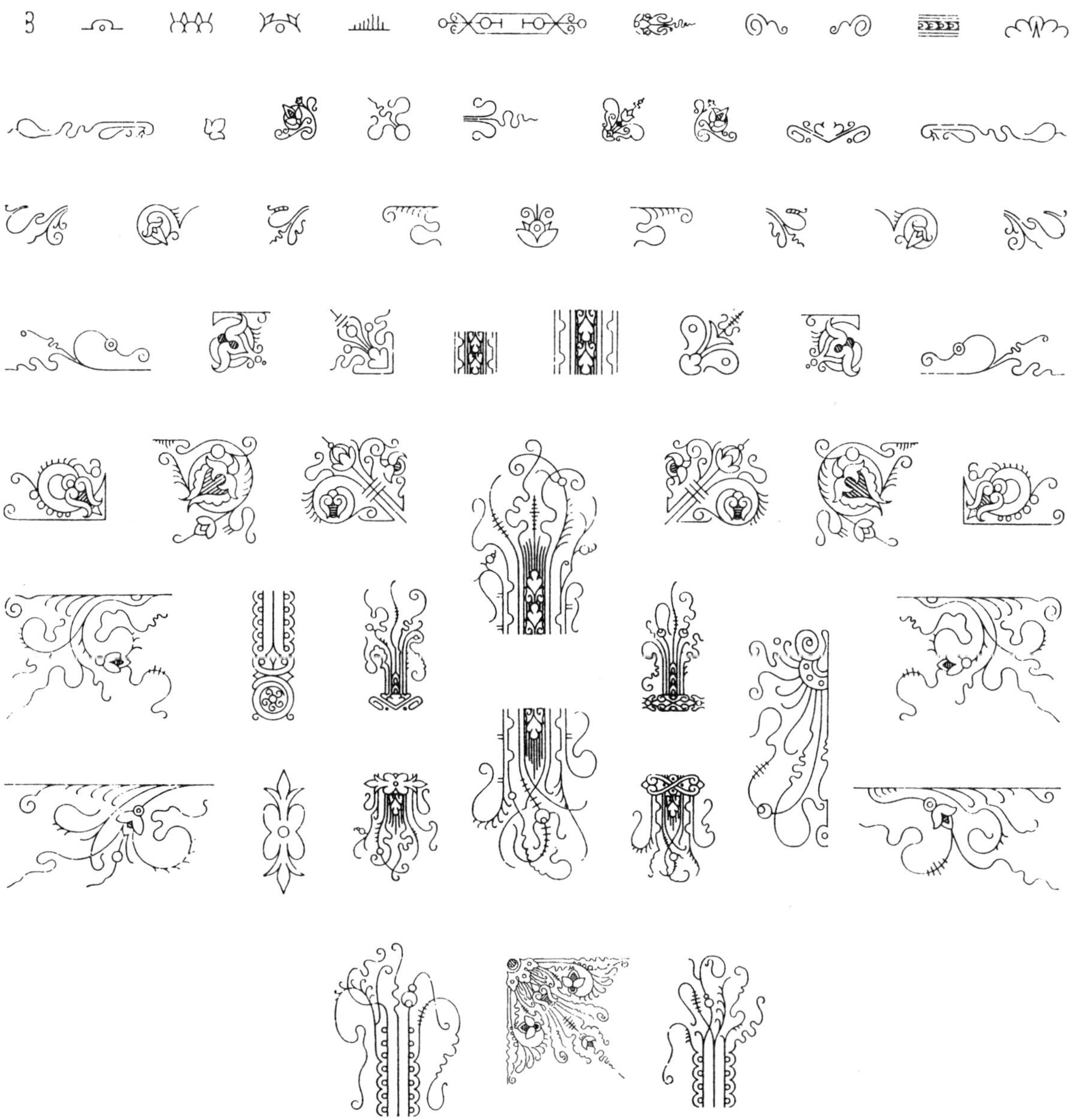

VICTOR PELEVIN

THE MOTH DRAWN TO THE LIGHT

The mirror in the heavy frame of dull wood that hung above the head of the bed looked absolutely black, because it reflected the darkest wall in the room. From time to time, Mitya would click his cigarette lighter, sending orange waves rippling across the surface of the mirror, but the lighter heated up very quickly, and he had to put out the flame. There was just a little light falling on the bed from the window, even though it was evening, and the music had begun to play out at the open-air dance floor. Through the net curtains, he could make out distant flashes of light from the colored light bulbs, or rather, the reflections of the colored flashes on the leaves of the trees.

Mitya lay there in the semidarkness, with his feet in their sneakers propped up on the high latticework headboard of the bed, gently stroking Marcus Aurelius Antoninus, whom the centuries had compressed into a small green parallelogram that it was already too dark to read. Beside Marcus Aurelius lay another book, a Chinese one, *The Evening Conversations of the Mosquitoes U and Tse.*

"It's remarkable," he thought, "the more stupid the song and the purer the voice, the more moving it is. Only whatever you do, you mustn't start thinking about what they're singing. Otherwise it all..."

Mitya was tired of lying there. He took a piece of paper covered in writing out of the book, folded it in four, stuck it in his pocket, and got up. He fumbled until he found his cigarettes on the table, then unlocked the door and went out. The only light in the narrow passageway between the holiday cottages came from his neighbor's window. He could see the gate, the bench by the wire fence, and the tall pale weeds in the dried-up channel of the stream. Mitya locked the door and smirked ironically when he saw his own reflection in the window. Ever since he'd realized that he'd left the cocoon, he'd begun to look rather strange in the dark. The heavy wings folded behind his back looked liked a cloak of silver brocade stretching almost down to the ground, and Mitya sometimes wondered what other people saw there.

Behind the bright curtains of the next house, they were playing cards and talking. A married couple was living there, and judging from the voices, today they had guests.

"Now hearts," said a man's voice. "Of course, Oxana, life has changed. You keep on asking, but everything's different for you now."

"But are things better or worse?" asked an insistent woman's voice.

"Well ... Now we have responsibilities," the man's voice answered thoughtfully. "I know where I have to go after work. And there's a child, you know what I mean.... I'm playing blind."

"You're already down to minus four hundred," another male voice broke in.

"So what can I do about it?" asked the first voice. "Six of hearts." Mitya lit a cigarette (several small insects came hurtling toward the flame of his lighter), went out through the gate, and jumped across the dry bed of the stream. He walked carefully through several yards of darkness, scrambled through the bushes and out onto the asphalt, then stopped and looked back. The bright line of the road ascended until it broke off at the top of the hill, and beyond that he could see the dark silhouettes of the mountains. From the sea, one of these mountains, the one on the right, looked like a huge mail-clad eagle with its head leaning forward. From the launch that went by in the evenings you could sometimes see mysterious lights on the summit. Probably there was a lighthouse up there. There were no lights at the moment.

Mitya took a few more drags on his cigarette, dropped the butt on the asphalt, crushed it thoroughly, and began running slowly along the road. After a few steps, he was caught up by a current of air and carried through the treetops. He drew in his legs to avoiding snagging the electric cable stretched between two posts (it was invisible in the darkness, and once Mitya had bumped his shin on it) and, when there was nothing left above him but the clear, dark sky, he began circling widely to gain height. Soon it became cooler, and his back began to ache with fatigue. Mitya decided he'd climbed high enough, and he looked down.

Down below, just like any other evening, he saw the sparsely scattered bright points of street lamps and windows. There weren't many sources of light bright enough to arouse even a faint desire to fly toward them, only two restaurant signs, the pink neon ulcer of the LIUES company on the corner of the dark tower of the holiday camp, and the flickering glow of the open-air dance floor close by. From this height, it looked like a large open flower, constantly changing its color, and instead of scent it exuded music, which could be heard even up here. Instinct drove all the insects in the area to this light every time the electricity was switched on, and Mitya decided to go down and take a look at what was happening.

Once he was lower, he hedge-hopped, clipping the tops of the trees. From closer up, the dance floor no longer looked like a flower and it was transformed into a New Year's vision from childhood, an immense tangle of garlands of bright electric bulbs shining through the branches and exuding music of astonishing vulgarity and beauty.

"Your cherry-red Lada* is driving me insane," some madwoman was singing through a dozen powerful speakers.

Carefully observing the path where he usually landed as it rushed past beneath him, Mitya extended his wings completely, turned them against the current of air beating into his face (they fluttered in the breeze), and hung motionless in the air. Dropping gently onto the dry, hard earth, he left the path and set off across the grass.

The dance floor was simply a field covered with asphalt and surrounded

* A Russian car modeled on the Fiat 124.

by a tall wire fence. Set against the fence was a low wooden stage piled high with the black boxes of loudspeakers. Around the perimeter of the dance floor there were several rows of benches full of people, and the actual dance floor was filled with writhing, steaming bodies, like a bus at rush hour. Mitya paid to go in, walked past several bottle-green flies, and sat on the end of a bench. During the evening, the crowd of dancers had changed several times: when they were tired, people crawled back to the benches or left altogether, but others got up to take their place, and the dancing never stopped for a moment. Mitya liked to think about how much like life all this was, but his satisfaction at his own aloofness was clouded by the awareness that for some reason he was also sitting here on a bench with all the others and gazing at other people's sweaty faces.

Suddenly the music became louder, the lights went out and then began flashing in turn for a split second, snatching a motionless crowd out of the darkness, now green, now blue, now red, and in the brief moments of its existence the crowd resembled a heap of plaster statues transported here from all the Soviet squares and young pioneer camps. Several minutes went by like this, and it became clear there was really no dance, and no dance floor, and no dancers, there was nothing but a multitude of dead parks of culture and recreation, each of which only existed for a split second while the lamp was lit and then disappeared forever, to be replaced by another park of culture and recreation equally lifeless and deserted, differing only in the color of the temporary sky and the angles at which the limbs of the statues were bent.

Mitya stood up, pushed his way through the cheerfully buzzing girls in blue and green dresses, and went out through the gates, where several musclemen were sitting in threatening, bright-colored tracksuits. Through a gap in the trees he could see the dim purple glow of a street lamp. It flared up, flickered a few times, and then went out, and acting on a sudden impulse, Mitya set off in that direction into the darkness.

He was soon past the trees that concealed the sky, and found a green-tarnished bust of Chekhov gazing at him thoughtfully out of the bushes, with the shards of a broken vodka bottle gleaming beside it in the moonlight. The promenade was empty. The sounds of cheerful voices and tapping came from a group of people sitting under one of the dim street lamps, playing dominoes and drinking beer. Mitya thought he really ought to go for a swim, and he walked along a string of benches that offered its inviting feminine curve to the sea.

Mitya lit a cigarette, then he saw a dark figure up ahead, leaning on the parapet.

He looked at the long silvery cloak and shook his head doubtfully.

"Dima!" he called.

"Mitya?" the figure answered. "So you did fly in after all."

"Are you waiting for someone?" Mitya asked, moving closer and shaking the outstretched hand.

Dima shook his head.

"Shall we walk?"

Dima nodded.

They went down the creaking wooden steps onto the beach, walked across the crunching gravel, and found themselves facing a narrow strip of foam. A wide, straight silver road led across the sea to the moon, and its color was like a moth's wings.

"It's beautiful," said Mitya.

"Yes, it is," Dima agreed.

"Have you never wanted to fly to that light? Not just to get some fresh air, but for real, all the way to the end?"

"I did once," said Dima, "but that wasn't me."

They turned and walked slowly along the shining boundary of the sea.

"Are you here on your own?"

"I'm always on my own," answered Dima.

"Just recently I've noticed," said Mitya, "that frequent use makes some quotations gleam, like banisters."

"And what else have you noticed recently?" Dima asked.

Mitya thought about it.

"That depends what you call recently," he said. "How long is it since we saw each other, a year?"

"About that."

"Well, for instance, last winter I did notice one thing. That we spend most of our time at home in darkness. Not in the figurative sense, but in the direct meaning of the word. I remember I was standing in the kitchen and talking on the phone. There was a weak yellow bulb up near the ceiling. Then I looked out of the window and it suddenly struck me how dark it was...."

"Yes," said Dima, "something like that happened to me too. And then I realized something else as well, that we live in this darkness all the time, only sometimes it's just a little bit lighter. Strictly speaking, you become a moth from the moment you realize you're surrounded by darkness."

"I don't know," said Mitya. "I think the way moths and butterflies are divided into night creatures and day creatures is purely arbitrary. In the final analysis they all fly toward the light. It's instinct."

"No. We're divided into night creatures and day creatures because some of us fly toward the light, and some fly toward the darkness. How can you fly toward the light, tell me, if you think you're surrounded by light?"

"So you say all of them," Mitya nodded toward the promenade, "fly toward the darkness?"

"Almost."

"What about us?"

"We fly toward the light, of course."

Mitya laughed.

"It makes you feel like some kind of conspirator," he said.

"Nonsense. They're the conspirators. Every single one of them. Even the ones playing dominoes up there."

"To be quite honest," said Mitya, "I don't feel as though I'm flying toward the light just now."

"If you think we're flying somewhere, and not simply walking along the beach, then there can be no doubt you are flying into the darkness. Or rather, you're circling round a ball of dung and taking it for a lamp."

"What ball?"

"It doesn't matter," said Dima. "It's a philosophical concept. It's not really surprising, since it's so dark all around us."

They walked on in silence for a while.

"Listen," said Mitya, "you talk about darkness. This evening I took a look around me, and everything was really dark. But at the dance floor all the people laugh and dance, and they play that song, like they are now. That terribly stupid song. The red Lada and all that stuff. But somehow the music moves me."

"It happens," said Dima.

"I'll tell you what I think," Mitya continued passionately. "If the best cricket in Petersburg took the best set of Scottish bagpipes and sang the entire *Tao Te Ching* to them, he wouldn't come a single centimeter closer to the target that those idiots," Mitya nodded in the direction of the music, "very nearly manage to hit."

"And what is it they hit?"

"I don't know," said Mitya. "It's as though there used to be something in life that was amazingly simple and more important than anything else, and then it disappeared, and we've only just realized it ever existed. And it turns out that absolutely everything we ever wanted before only made any sense because there was this most important thing of all. And without it we don't want anything at all. And we can't even say it. D'you know what light I'd really like to fly toward? There was this poem, listen: 'No regrets have I for life's anguished breathing, for what are life and death? But I regret that light that shone above the universe, and now weeps in the night as it recedes....'"

"I don't think you ought to feel sorry for that light. It would be more appropriate for that light to feel sorry for you. Or do you think you yourself are the light that weeps in the darkness?"

"Perhaps I do."

"Then don't go into the darkness," said Dima. "No one's forcing you."

A new song started up at the dance floor; a woman sadly asked the dark sky, the moon, and two people wandering along a beach in dark cloaks where she was today, and complained she did not know where to find either herself or someone else (the final word was inaudible, but that didn't matter, because it wasn't the words that mattered, or even the music, but something else, the fact that everything around them was meditating in infinite sadness on where it was today, and how it could find either itself or someone else).

"Like it?" asked Mitya.

"Not bad," said Dima. "The best thing is that she doesn't understand what she's singing about. Just like your friend, who couldn't find anything better to do than to feel sorry for the light receding into the darkness."

"He's not my friend," said Mitya.

"Good," said Dima. "I wouldn't want to have anything to do with someone like that either. You know, everything that rouses the pity of the dead is based on a very simple mechanism. For instance, if you show a dead person a fly stuck on flypaper with music playing, and you make him think for a second that this fly is him, then he'll immediately start to cry out of compassion for his fellow corpse."

"So that means I'm dead too?" asked Mitya.

"Of course," said Dima, "you must be. But at least I can explain it to you, and that means you're not completely dead."

"Thank you," said Mitya.

"You're welcome."

They went up onto the promenade. The domino players had already disappeared, and all that was left of them was a newspaper fluttering in the wind, a few wooden boxes, some empty beer bottles, and fish scales; the melancholy induced by the music made it feel as though they hadn't all simply gone home, but had dissolved into the surrounding darkness. Only their weathered skeletons lying beside the bottles and the fish scales were needed to make the impression complete.

"What was it that you were saying about the dance floor?" asked Dima.

"I was there just now. I even went in and sat down for a while. It was very strange. I seemed to see that they were all dead, nothing but plaster models. You know that toy with the two wooden bears and the hammers? You move a wooden stick backward and forward, and they hammer on the anvil?"

"Yes."

"Well, it's just the same up there. They all dance and laugh and greet each other, and then you look down and you can see the beams moving under the floor. Backward and forward."

"So what?"

"What d'you mean, so what? They were all flying toward the light, after all, and whichever way you fly, there's only the dance floor that actually shines, and it turns out that everyone seems to be flying toward life, but all they find is death. That is, at any given moment they move toward the light, but still find themselves in darkness. You know, if I wrote a novel about insects, that's how I'd represent their life: a village by the sea, darkness, and a few electric lamps shining in the darkness above this repulsive dancing. And everyone flies to this light, because there's nothing else. But to fly to those lamps means..." Mitya snapped his fingers, searching for the right word. "I don't know how to explain."

"You already have," said Dima. "When you were talking about the moon. The moon is the biggest dance floor of all. And the biggest lamp in Lenin's biggest electrification program. It's absolutely the same thing. It's not the real light."

"No," said Mitya. "The light is real. Light is always real, if you can see it."

"True," said Dima. "The light is real. But where does it come from?"

"How d'you mean? It comes from the moon."

"Yes? Did you never have the idea that the moon is actually totally black?"

"I think I'd call it yellowish-white," answered Mitya, looking upward attentively, "or slightly bluish."

"All right. Of course, five billion flies will agree with you. But you're not a fly. The fact that you see a yellow spot when you look at the moon doesn't actually mean that it is yellow. I just can't see why anybody can't understand that. The answer to all questions is hanging right over your head."

"Perhaps," said Mitya. "Unfortunately, none of these questions arise for me. But I understand what you're saying. You're trying to tell me that when I look at the moon I see the light of the sun which it reflects, but it doesn't shine itself. I don't think that's important. It's enough for me that the light exists. And when I see it, the most important part makes me move toward the light. Where it comes from, or what kind of light it is, is not particularly important."

"All right. You don't want to fly toward the moon. What light are you moving toward at present?"

"The nearest street lamp."

"And then where?"

"The next one."

"Okay," said Dima, "let's try an experiment with a certain insect."

He stretched out his hand, made a movement as though he were turning an invisible switch, and suddenly all the lamps on the promenade went out.

Mitya stopped.

"What light are you moving toward now?" Dima asked.

"That's some trick. How did you do it?"

"Just the way you were thinking," said Dima. "I arranged for an electrician to sit in the bushes and wait for my signal. And all just to make an impression on you."

"Is that what I thought?"

"Didn't you?"

"Well, more or less. But not quite. I did think about the electrician and the sign, but not about the bushes."

"You thought about the bushes too."

"I'm not talking about the street lamps; I mean the moon. Or rather, moonlight and Chekhov, but it's not important."

"What? Do I read minds?"

"No, no, I can do that myself. Other people's minds are easy to read. I meant the street lamps."

"It's very simple. Once you've answered a single question, you can control all kinds of light."

"What question?" asked Mitya.

"It's really best to ask yourself the question, but since you're not much inclined to do that, I'll ask you."

Dima paused deliberately.

"The moon reflects the sun's light," he said. "But what light does the sun reflect?"

Mitya sat down on a bench without speaking and leaned back.

It was quiet. The wind rustled the leaves over their heads, and the noise of the sea mingled with the final notes of a fading song. It seemed as though the mixture of sounds were coming from the yellow disk hanging in the sky above the dance floor. Then it was joined by the roar of a tourist launch approaching its mooring, and to their left the waves from its wake slowly rolled into sight.

"American boy, I'm leaving with you, leaving with you, Moscow, goodbye," two pure young voices screeched out over the dance floor, and then they heard the balalaikas playing the accompaniment, as simple and moving as a young pioneer girl's dress.

IN MEMORY OF MARCUS AURELIUS

The tourist launch was already well out to sea, still traveling in a straight line, as though it were heading for Turkey. On their left the shoreline, previously hidden by the mountain, jutted out into the sea, and though they could not see the shore itself, they glimpsed lights. They seemed to be shining on the surface of the sea, like candles drifting past the launch in small paper boxes standing on small rafts. The moon, too, looked like a paper lantern lit by a candle, hanging among the clouds. The clouds on all sides were scattered thinly across the sky, their edges shining pale blue in the moonlight, and this made the sky seem even higher than usual.

Mitya stood at the edge of the deck, leaning on the handrail, and staring in silence toward the shore.

"What are you thinking about for so long?" Dima asked.

"Still the same thing," said Mitya. "About what's happening to me."

"You're traveling across the sea in a launch and watching the shore."

"No," said Mitya, "not right this moment, but in general what's happening to my life. It's strange, haven't you ever noticed, how easy it is to tell someone else how they should live and what they should do? I could explain it all to anyone; I'd even show them which lights they should fly toward, and how to do it. But when you need to do the same thing for yourself, you go nowhere at all, or go flying off in the opposite direction."

"I don't see what the problem is," said Dima. "See how many lights there are out there. Choose any one you like and fly as hard as you can."

"That's the point," said Mitya. "There are two people choosing inside me, and I can't even tell them apart. I don't know who is the real me, and I can't tell when they change places, because both of them seem to want to fly toward the light, but by different routes. And they suggest doing quite different things."

"Who do they suggest them to?"

"To me."

"Aha," said Dima, "so now there are three of you?"

"Why three?"

"The first one, the second one, and the one they make their suggestions to."

"You're playing with words. I can put it another way. When I'm trying to reach a decision, I constantly come across someone in myself who has taken exactly the opposite decision, and he's the one who does everything."

"What about you?"

"What about me? As soon as he appears, I become him."

"So he is you?"

"But I wanted to do just the opposite."

Mitya said nothing else for quite a while.

"The two of them divide up my time between them," he began again. "One is the real me, the absolute me, the one I regard as myself. The one who wants to fly toward the light. And the other is a temporary me, who only exists for a second. He basically wants to fly toward the light too, but first he needs a final short period of darkness. As though to say good-bye, take a final look. The strange thing is that the me who wants to fly toward the light has my whole life, because he really is me, and the one who wants to fly into the darkness only has a second, but even so..."

"But still you keep realizing that you're flying into the darkness."

"Yes."

"And does it surprise you?"

"Very much."

Dima threw a crumpled candy wrapper overboard and watched the bright spot of color until it disappeared in the foamy wake from the propeller.

"A moth's entire life," he said, "is that second he wastes to take his leave of the darkness. Unfortunately, there is nothing else in the world except that second. Do you understand? This huge life, in which you intend eventually to turn toward the light, is really that single moment when you choose the darkness."

"Why?"

"What else can there be, apart from this very second?"

"Yesterday. Tomorrow. The day after tomorrow."

"Yesterday and tomorrow and the day after tomorrow and even the day after that all exist only in the present second," said Dima. "Only in that moment when you think about them. So if you want to choose the light tomorrow, and take your leave of the darkness today, you're really just choosing the darkness."

"But what if I want to stop choosing the darkness?" asked Mitya.

"Choose the light," said Dima.

"But how?"

"Simply fly toward it. Right now. There never will be any other time to do it."

Mitya looked across toward the shore.

Something seemed to flash rapidly through the air, and they heard a loud bang on the upper deck. Then they heard shoes scraping on the thin metal of the deck and cheerful voices.

"What's happening over there?" Mitya asked, raising his head sharply.

"Mosquitoes," said Dima. "Three of them."

"At night?" asked Mitya. "And this far out at sea?"

"It's daytime for them," answered Dima. "The sun's shining brightly."

An immense rocky mountain appeared off the starboard side of the launch. It looked like a stone bird with its wings extended and its head bent down, and there were two red lights flickering on its peak.

"See how much light and darkness there is all around us," said Dima. "Choose whatever you want."

"Let's say I want to choose the light. How will I know if it's the real light? You called the moon one of Lenin's light bulbs, and the dance floor and all that."

"The genuine light is any light that you can actually reach. And even if you only just fail to get there, then no matter how bright the light you were flying toward, it was a mistake. The real point is not what you fly toward, but who is doing the flying. But then that's the same thing."

"Yes," said Mitya, "probably. Then I choose those two red lights up there."

Dima looked up at the top of the mountain.

"Not very close," he said. "But then that doesn't matter."

"What do we do now?" asked Mitya.

"Fly."

"What, right now?"

"When else?" asked Dima.

Mitya climbed over the barrier at the edge of the deck, grabbed hold of a short piece of rope tied to a flagstaff, and spread his wings. A gust of wind lifted up his body, and he looked like a dark flag being raised at the stern, or a kite soaring up above it. Then he released his grip, and the launch drifted down and away from him. A minute later the launch was nothing but a bright spot below him, and Mitya began looking ahead.

Ahead of him was a sheer rocky slope. When he was already quite close to it, he had to fly almost vertically upward. After a few minutes ascending like this, Mitya's perspective suddenly shifted, and instead of rising upward, the cliff face seemed to extend into a horizontal distance, as though he were flying low over a rocky desert, where the moonlight highlighted every projection and every crack. The red lights on the summit looked like railway semaphore lamps in the distance.

A gust of wind caught him in the back, and he almost crashed into a stone ledge jutting out a long way from the side of the mountain. After that he flew more slowly. Sometimes bushes appeared in the cracks in the cliff, looking as though they were bent by a powerful wind. Mitya only had to remind himself that the bushes were simply reaching upward as they were supposed to, for the rocky plain below him to be transformed back into its real self, a wall of stone. But as soon as Mitya stopped reminding himself, the endless desert reappeared beneath him, and rushing across it, stretching and twisting across the cracks, were two long black shadows. Mitya looked up. There were no red lights ahead anymore.

The moon slid behind the edge of a cloud, and the rocky plain over which they were flying suddenly seemed somber and dismal. Far beyond it shone the lights of a few seaside villages, looking like stars from some other sky. Once again Mitya looked into the dark void ahead and felt a sudden fear and a desire to turn back and fly downward.

"Listen," he said to Dima, who was flying beside him, "where are we going? The lights aren't there anymore."

"Of course they are," said Dima, "if we're flying toward them."

"What's the point of flying toward them if we can't see them? Let's go back."

"Then we won't be here anymore either. Not the 'we' who set off for the lights."

"Maybe they simply weren't real," said Mitya.

"Maybe," said Dima, "and maybe we weren't real."

The moon came out again, and the sharp shadows of projecting rocks reappeared on the mountainside. Mitya felt inexplicable anguish and agitation. He shook his head and realized that for a long time he had been hearing a piercing barking sound. The barking was very loud, but so subtle that instead of hearing it, he felt it in his belly. Sometimes the barking stopped and was replaced by a sound between a howl and a whistle, which gave Mitya a slightly nauseous feeling in his throat. The timbre of the whistling was very unpleasant, and Mitya thought that if the Khmer Rouge in Cambodia had made electronic alarm clocks, they would ring just like that.

"Can you hear it?" he asked Dima.

"Yes," Dima answered calmly.

"What is it?"

"It's a bat," said Dima.

Mitya had no time to feel frightened. A third shadow appeared rushing upward over the moonlit rocky slope, covering the first two. It was huge and shapeless, with blurred edges. Mitya and Dima swooped toward the cliff and hurtled down onto a tiny platform with a few small bushes growing on it. Mitya almost sprained his leg in the process. The whistling ceased immediately.

"Don't move a muscle," said Dima. "If you heard it, then it heard you a long time ago."

"Can it hear us talking?"

"No," answered Dima. "It has a very interesting relationship with reality. First it shouts, and then it listens to the reflected sound and draws the appropriate conclusions. If we don't move at all, it might leave us in peace."

For a few minutes they stood there in silence. It was quiet up there, the only sound was the faint murmuring of the sea below them.

"D'you remember the question I asked you?" said Dima. "About the light reflected by the sun?"

"Yes."

"Well, in fact neither the sun nor the light really have anything to do with it. I could ask the same question in a different way. We can take what's happening to us right now. What do you think the bat sees when the sound is reflected back from you?"

"Me, I suppose," said Mitya, gazing into the sky.

"But it made the sound itself."

"Not me, then, but its own sound," said Mitya.

The bat's barking had fallen silent, and the bat was nowhere to be seen, but Mitya could sense that it was somewhere close by, and this bothered him a lot more than structures of logic.

"Yes," said Dima, "but the sound was reflected from you."

Mitya surveyed the sky again. Dima's calm, unhurried tone was beginning to get on his nerves.

"And it turns out that in one sense you are nothing but one of the sounds emitted by a bat. A couplet in its song, so to speak."

A ponderous black form suddenly loomed up in front of the platform and hurtled past, sending a wave of cold air over them. For a minute or two, they heard nothing, and then they heard the same piercing barking sound in the distance. It was coming closer: the bat was obviously moving in for the attack.

"If you are one of the sounds emitted by a bat, then what is the bat?"

"The thing that's just about to eat us," answered Mitya, feeling the whistling from the direction of the sea turn his legs to jelly and the thoughts crowding on top of each other in his head.

He glimpsed a dark spot far off in the sky, and the whistling grew louder. In his belly Mitya heard an inaudible melody, two octaves higher than anything he had ever heard in his life.

"Just think," said Dima, "all the bat has to do is stop whistling, and you disappear. But what do you have to do to make the bat disappear?"

He pushed off from the edge of the platform and hurtled downward, head first. Mitya jumped after him, and the dark black mass crashed into the spot where he had just been standing, breaking the branches of the bushes.

He fell out of control for several yards, then braked and flew rapidly along the slope, almost snagging his wings on it. Dima had disappeared.

Behind him he heard the sickening whistling sound. Mitya glanced around and saw a dark shadow soaring and plunging as it flew. A few yards further on, he noticed a narrow crevice in the cliff and darted into it. Squeezing himself in, he pressed himself against the rough surface of the stone and froze. For a few minutes everything was quiet, and all Mitya could hear was his own loud breathing, and then he heard the whistling again from the direction of the sea, and almost immediately the dark mass crashed into the cliff, covering the opening of the crevice, and a black clawed hand raked the air only a few inches from him. Mitya caught a glimpse of a broad, gray face with pointed ears, little eyes, and a huge jaw full of teeth (for some reason it reminded him of the radiator on an old Chaika). The bat rustled its wings over the rocks and disappeared. All Mitya was left with was the feeling that a soft, fluffy government automobile driven by a half-blind driver had been trying to drive into the crevice where he was hiding.

Mitya shifted his weight to his left foot, and drew his right foot back. The whistling came again, and when the black body of the bat began pressing into the entrance, Mitya kicked at it with all his strength. He hit something that gave way and heard a loud squeak. The bat disappeared. Mitya held his breath and waited, but there were no signs of life from the bat. Carefully creeping up to the exit, Mitya stuck his head out and immediately the piercing whistling began again. A webbed wing flashed in front of his eyes, and teeth clashed together just above his ear. Mitya leapt back and almost lost his balance.

A few minutes later Mitya began thinking he could hear sounds made by the bat: the soft rustling of wings and the scraping of claws on stone. Perhaps the sounds were made by the wind, but Mitya was sure that the bat was still waiting outside for him. "So that's the way it is," he thought. "As soon as you realize you live in the dark, bats start appearing out of it...."

Suddenly Mitya caught a faint glimpse of hope.

"What could it be afraid of?" he thought.

The first thing that came into his mind was a cat with wings. Mitya closed his eyes and tried to imagine what it would look like. The flying cat turned out to be a creature sitting on its hind legs with large fluffy wings and a tail with something like a flyswatter on the end of it, rather like an ancient drawing of a flying lizard. It looked most of all like the sphinx on a

Singer sewing machine. Painstakingly visualizing every detail of its appearance, Mitya began whistling quietly, and an upside-down face immediately appeared in the opening of the crevice. The eyes seemed to be staring doubtfully. Mitya whistled louder, and imagined the flying cat opening its jaws and pouncing. The face in the opening disappeared, and Mitya heard the beat of swiftly retreating wings.

Mitya stuck two fingers into his mouth and whistled as loudly as he could after the dark receding spot, then he stepped out of the crevice into the void and fell for a while before braking and turning back upward.

Dima was nowhere to be seen. Mitya flew to the spot where they had parted, off to one side and quite a lot higher. Dima was not on the platform, and so Mitya flew toward the top of the mountain. He was sure that nothing had happened to Dima, but even so, despite the euphoria of his unexpected victory, he had a feeling of foreboding. When he had been flying for only a few minutes, and there was not much further to go to the summit, and the stone wall drifting past him seemed to be cast of metal without a single fault, he heard the whistling again, and realized that the bat had not left him in peace at all. It had simply waited until he left his refuge and reached a place where there was nowhere to hide.

Mitya stuck two fingers into his mouth and whistled back as loudly as he could, attempting once again to summon up the mental image of the black, fluffy sphinx, but his whistle was pitiful and the whole idea seemed extremely stupid. He could already just make out the bat in the distance, like a black rubber ball bouncing toward him over an invisible surface, and there was absolutely nowhere to hide from it. "What can I do to make it disappear?" Mitya thought feverishly. "To make me disappear, all it has to do is stop whistling.... I am what it hears.... To make it disappear ... perhaps I should stop doing something as well? But what do I do to make it appear?"

That was quite impossible to work out. He could understand what Dima had in mind in the metaphorical sense, but it wasn't clear at all what use all the metaphors were when a bat with no interest in them was chasing you.

Mitya screwed up his eyes and suddenly saw a clear blue light, as though he hadn't closed his eyes, but they had been closed and now had opened wide in terror and noticed for the first time what had always been there in front if him, and was so much closer than everything else that it was invisible. A momentary recollection flashed through his mind of a day long ago when he could hardly drag himself along through a gray November park, over which low leaden clouds were drifting from the north. As he walked along he was thinking that if this weather lasted a few more days, then the sky would sink so low it would run over people like a truck driven by a drunken driver, then he raised his eyes to a gap in the clouds, through which he could see other, white clouds, way high up, and beyond them the sky, exactly as it was in summer, so blue and pure that it was quite obvious that nothing ever happened to the sky, and no matter what repulsive clouds might gather for the holidays in Moscow, high above them there was always this pure, unchanging vault of blue.

And it was a great surprise to see in himself something similar, as unaffected by what was happening around it as the sky that was the same at all seasons of the year was unaffected by the clouds crawling over the face of the earth.

"It all depends," thought Mitya, "on what side you look at things from. If, for instance you plant both feet firmly on the ground ... Stop. Just who is it who's looking, anyway? And at whom?"

The first thing he heard when he came to his senses was the familiar whistling.

"Oh God," Mitya thought, forcing his eyes open with a struggle, "those bats."

He was suspended in a spot of bright blue light, as though caught in the crossed beams of several searchlights. But there weren't any searchlights, he himself was the source of the light. Mitya held his hands up in front of his face. They were glowing with a clear, pure, blue light, and tiny silvery flies that had appeared out of nowhere so high above the sea were already circling around them.

Mitya flew upward, and all the time he was moving toward the summit, he didn't have a single thought.

The summit proved to be a small flat platform with a few small hawthorn bushes growing on it beside the tall steel shaft of a beacon. Once again he could see the two red lamps, which had been hidden by the projecting rocks. They lit up alternately, and on the earth the dark shadows of the bushes reversed direction, like the shadow of a pendulum swinging to and fro. Oddly enough, there were two folding stools standing beside the shaft supporting the two red lamps. Dima was sitting on one of them.

Mitya waved to him, sat on the other stool, took a piece of paper out of his pocket, and spread it out on his knees.

"Just a moment," he said in answer to Dima's attentive gaze. "Just a moment."

He wrote for a minute or minute and a half, then quickly folded the sheet of paper into an airplane, got up, walked to the edge of the cliff, and launched it. At first it nosedived, then it soared back up and off to the right, in the direction of the tourist village.

"What did you do that for?" asked Dima.

"Nothing too serious," said Mitya. "A mystical debt owed to Marcus Aurelius."

"Ah," said Dima, "sometimes debts have to be paid. Now tell me, what light does the sun reflect?"

Mitya stuck a cigarette in his mouth, clicked his cigarette lighter, and a small bright blue tongue of flame appeared above it.

"Right," said Dima. "How simple everything is, isn't it?"

"Yes," said Mitya, "it's amazing."

He looked up at the lamps blinking on and off overhead. The air around the glass covers was a trembling mass of hundreds of unfamiliar insects, vainly trying to break through the thick, ribbed glass to the source of the light.

"Where did it go to?" Mitya asked.

"You mean the bat? Where could it go to? There it is, flying around."

Dima pointed to a tiny black lump soaring and plunging through the air at the edge of the illuminated area. Mitya looked, and he glanced at his own hands again: they were still bathed in an even blue glow.

"I've just realized," he said, "that we're not really moths at all. And not..."

"It's probably not even worth trying to express it in words," said Dima. "And anyway, nothing around you has changed just because you've understood something. The world's just the same as it was. Moths fly toward the light, flies fly toward shit, and they're all in total darkness. But now you'll be different. And you'll never forget who you really are, right?"

"Of course," replied Mitya. "There's just one thing I can't understand. Have I just turned into a glowworm, or was I always one?"

Translated from the Russian by Andrew Bromfield

John Waters

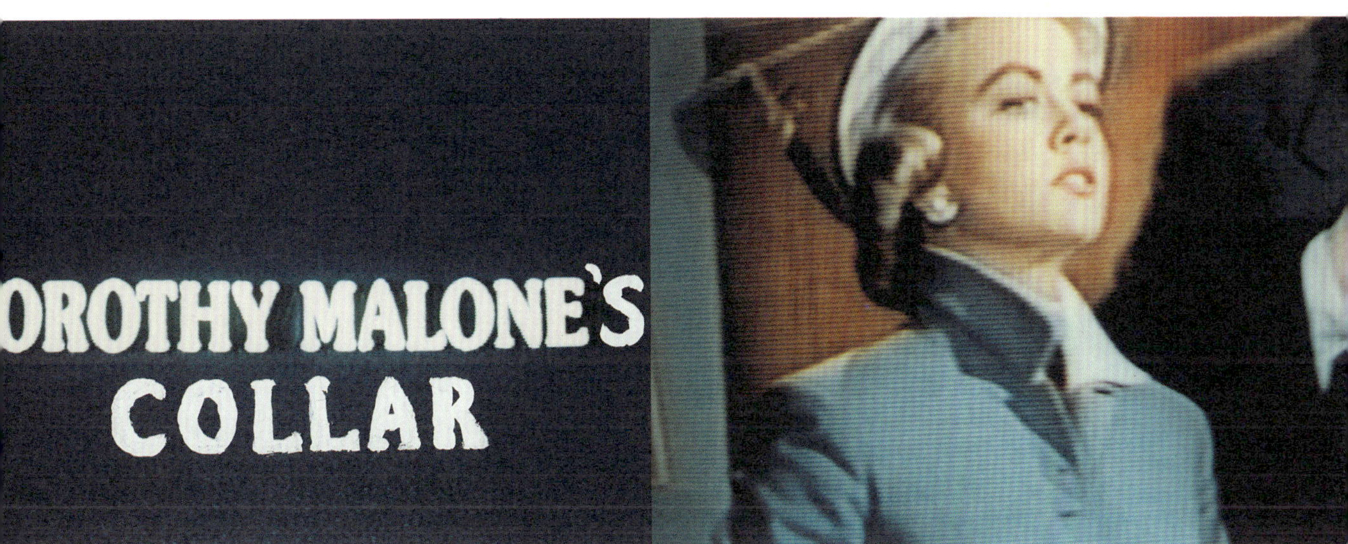

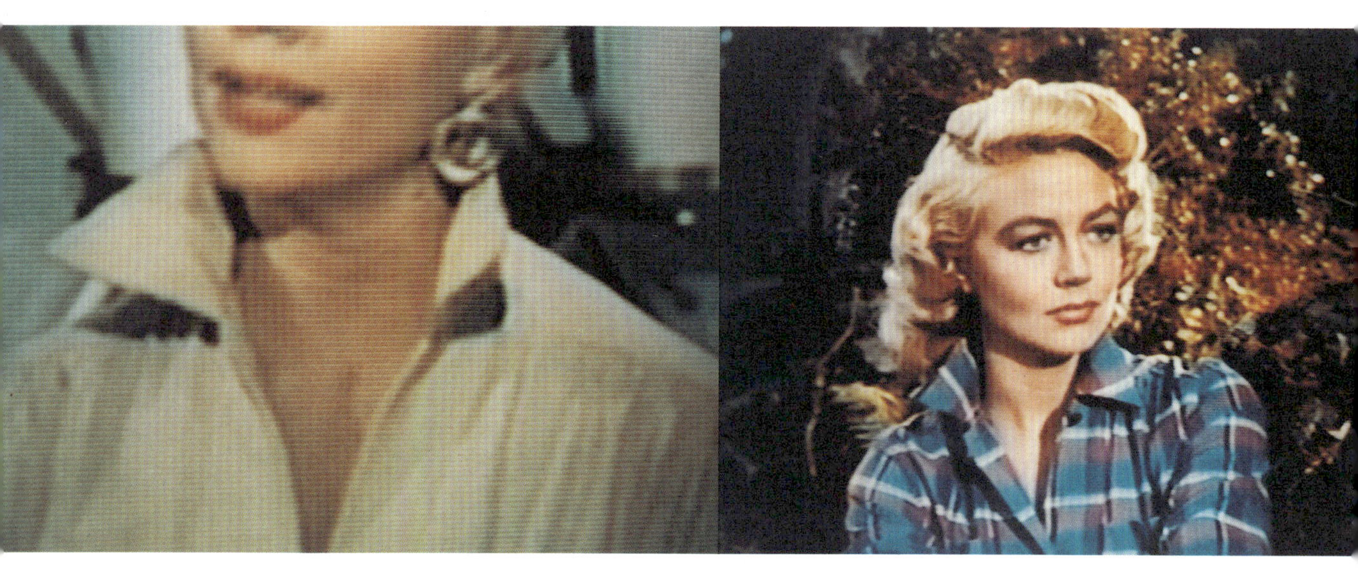

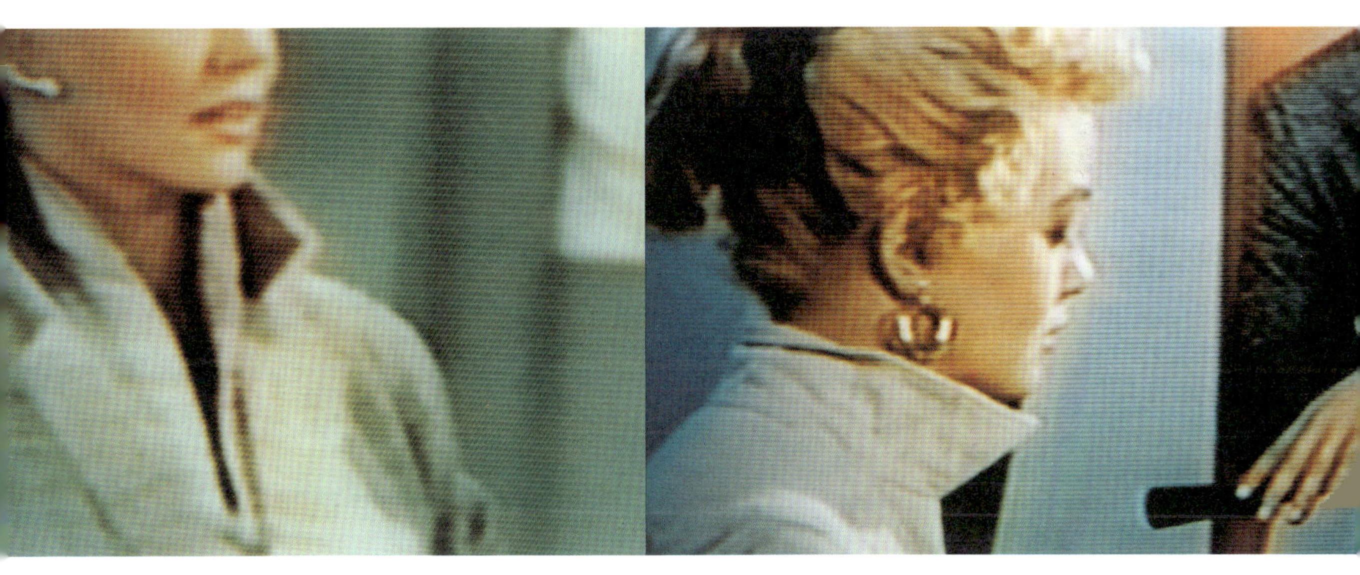

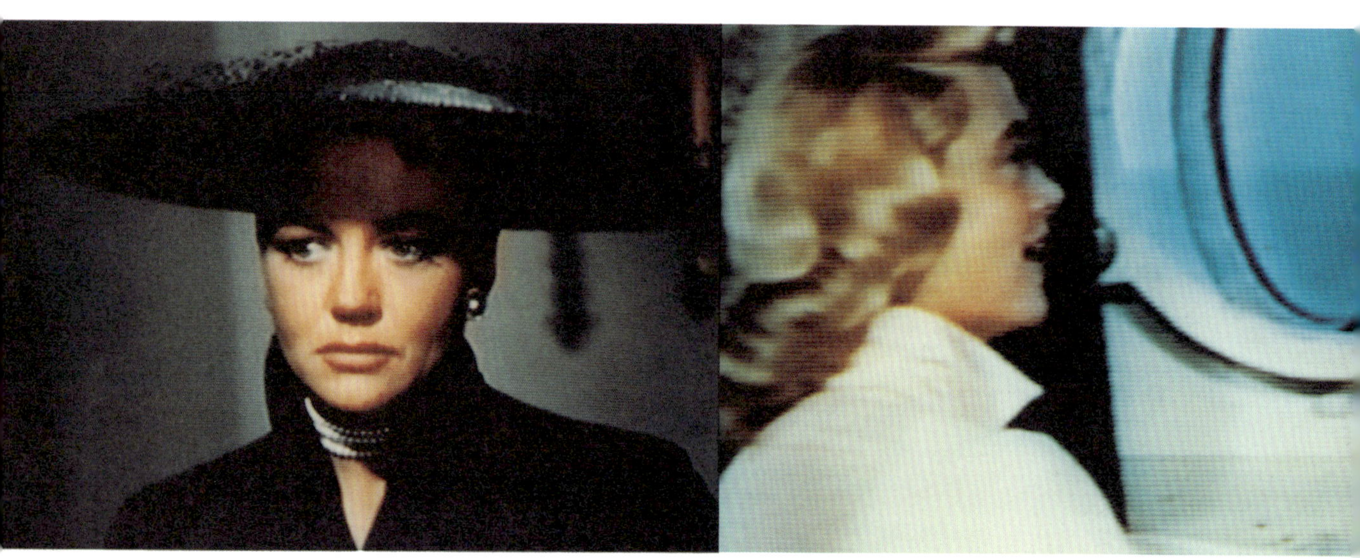

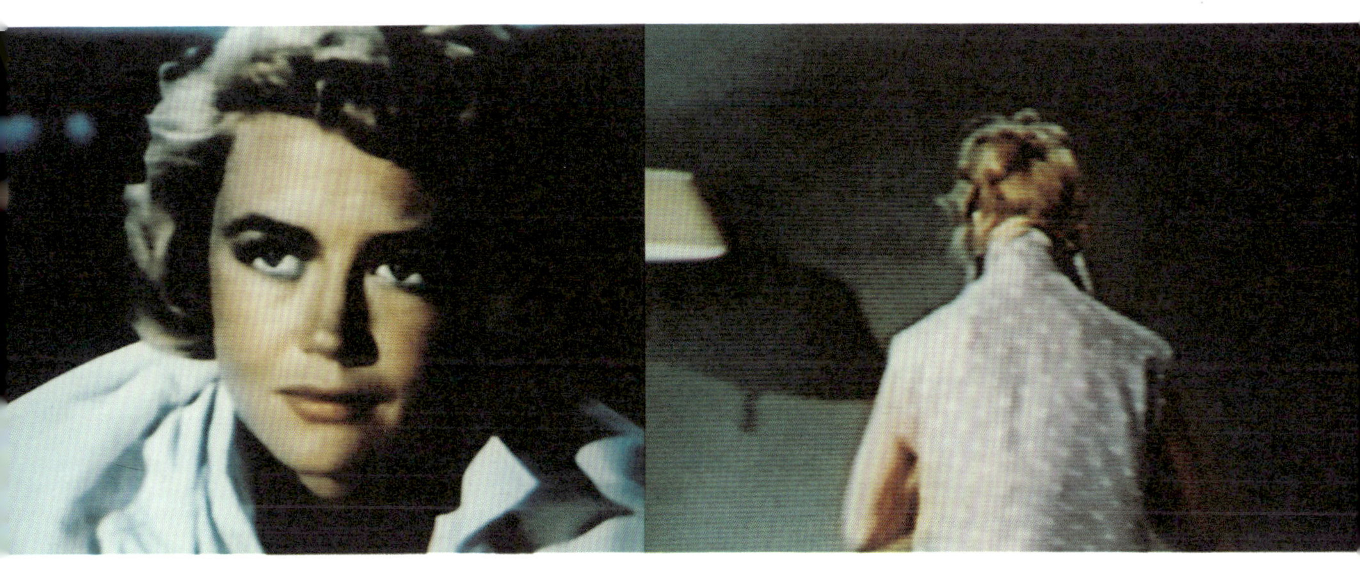

Dorothy Malone's Collar, 1996.
10 chromogenic color prints,
each 5 x 7 in.

ELAINE EQUI

WANG WEI'S MOON

for David Shapiro

Leisurely
it comes out—

new moon
like the eyebrow
of a moth,

full moon
that burns
the pines,

or suddenly
                sad

remote
above a gate,

or glaring
                clarity

like a lamp
that quiets windows.

Cold
it tumbles into
random shadows

alarming birds,

                far far
stone cliffs
shine

as someone
washes silk
in moonlight.

Unsteady images
tied to whiteness.

Stars
float up
toward dawn.

Note: All the lines in this cento were taken from translations of Wang Wei's poems by Tony Barnstone, Willis Barnstone, and Xu Haixin.

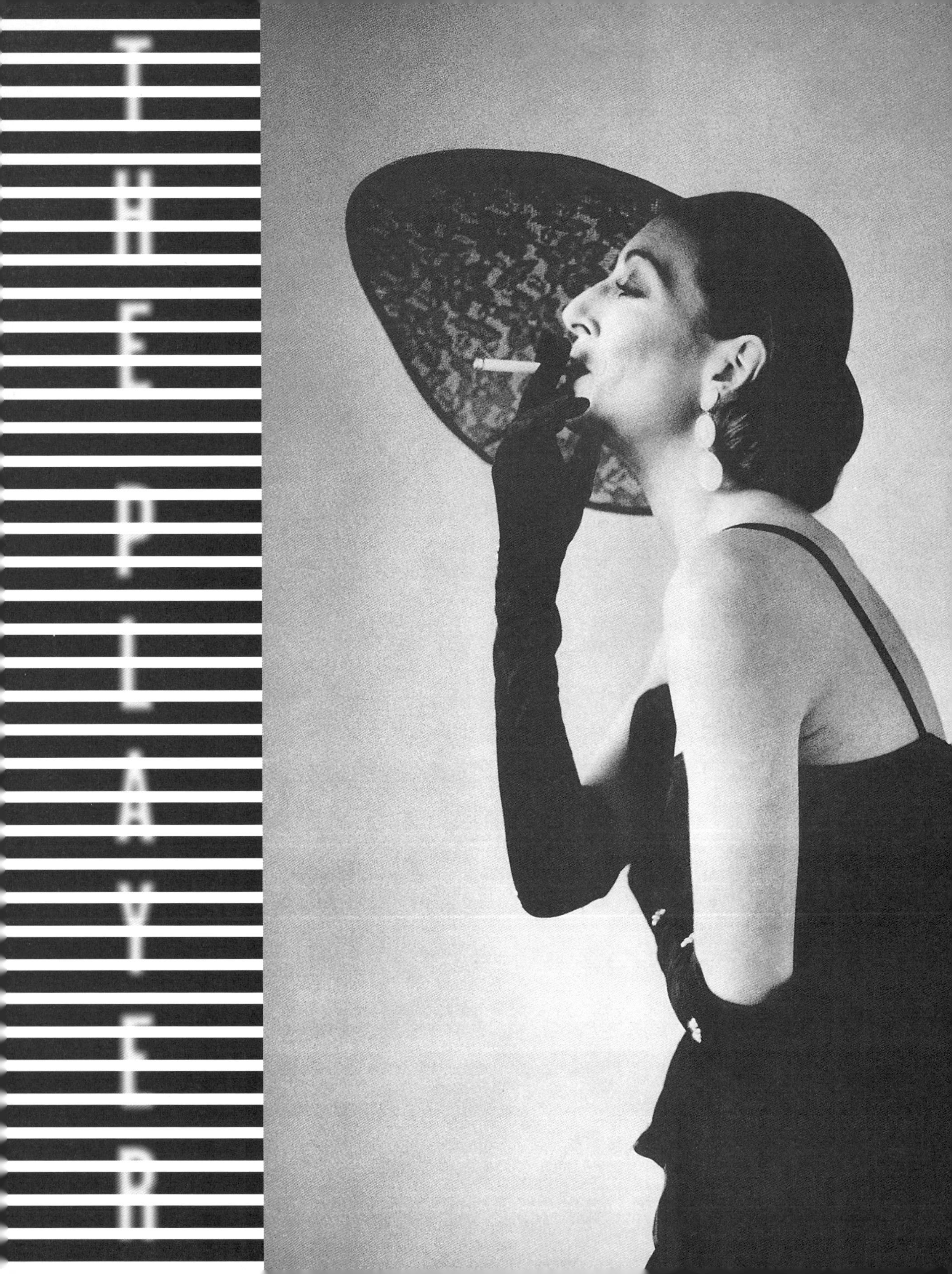
THE PLAYER

ANJELICA HUSTON / HILTON ALS

—July 10, 1996

HILTON ALS: I wanted to talk with you about the different hats you've been wearing, and I'd like to start with the film version of Dorothy Allison's *Bastard out of Carolina* that you just finished directing. Did you buy the rights to the book a long time ago?

ANJELICA HUSTON: Actually, I didn't. I knew nothing of this project. It was sent to me by Turner Television. I hadn't read the book. I hadn't seen the script.

ALS: Had you been scouting around for a directorial project?

HUSTON: I had been looking at a bunch of things. After *Prizzi's Honor*, several scripts surfaced—"prequels" as well as sequels to *Prizzi's Honor*. Although several of them were really good, it seemed to me that it might not be the best way to start directing—going in with that sort of reference. So I was reading things here and there. I've had a project in development on Maud Gonne and William Butler Yeats for a long time and I've been working on getting that written. I'd been interested in working as a director, but I hadn't found the right thing to start with. When *Bastard out of Carolina* came along, it was a question of committing very fast. I agreed to do it within three days and found myself immediately in pre-production.

ALS: Were you very attracted to the story when you first sat down and read it?

HUSTON: Well, I don't know about attracted. That may be the wrong word. It's the story of a very young girl whose stepfather abuses her. I was very interested by it. I was very moved by it. I thought it was a brave and profoundly upsetting story, beautifully told. I was surprised that anyone had sent me anything this good, because I was untried as a director. Although people know my work as an actress, no one could really know what equation they were employing until I had proven myself on some level.

ALS: One of the things that is so moving to me about your performances is your spirit. It outweighs the incredible isolation your characters are going through. Did you find in yourself any echoes of the character's isolation in this project?

HUSTON: I've always been interested in survival. And it seemed to me so extraordinary—this book being also largely autobiographical—that this child could have survived absolutely unrelenting horror for as long as she did and still come out with a remarkable and rather cool, ironic eye. That kind of thing usually renders people monsters. You hear all the time about battered children battering their own children and how that kind of conundrum goes on. This was really remarkable to me —in that the writer obviously had not only undergone these terrible iniquities, but found within herself the presence and capacity to be able to examine them in such a dispassionate light. I thought one of the things that was very important in the book was that the man who abused her was Everyman. He was the neighbor down the street. He was the guy in the butcher shop. He was the guy you sit next to in the cinema. He wasn't some alien monster who intentionally decided to make this child's life a living hell.

ALS: I think that one of the things that makes torture so familiar is that it *is* familiar.

HUSTON: Exactly.

ALS: I bought one of Bob Richardson's photos of you, and whenever I look at the photo now, I see the difference between then and now, and all the experience that has gone into your work. The work always seems to be about looking for truth.

When you read a script, do you look for that autobiographical aspect?

HUSTON: It's not that you really look for the autobiographical aspect, it's more that the autobiograpical aspect will capture you. Because it will be something you recognize, it will reflect something that has happened in your own life, something you can identify with. So I don't know if I go into things looking to identify with them, but when they come at me that way, it gives me a kind of understanding that immediately involves me and makes me know what I'm doing.

ALS: In a way, I think that when writers create characters, they are always trying to find something that's essentially about themselves in that character—without necessarily knowing it on a conscious level.

When you read a script that has been made from a novel, do you find that things are missing?

HUSTON: Well, there are so many things in a novel that you can't involve in a script because of the time factor and because of dramatic considerations. A script needs to be close to a hundred pages. You have a lot of stuff to condense so you have to pick and choose and pare down, and that's very hard to do because you get terribly attached to things. It involves an initial ruthless attack on the material to find out which are the moments that project you forward, that can hold the interest, and will ultimately form the whole that is going to be your movie.

ALS: Were you terrified on your first day on the set?

HUSTON: Yeah. I was very ready. I arrived on the set an hour early and I had bacon and eggs for breakfast (I felt it would help to be well-nourished) and I sat there and I sat there. I looked at my call sheet and it said "Shooting Time: 9:00 A.M." and I wondered why nobody was calling me for my first scene—because, as an actress, I'd always been called. Finally I strolled down to the set and the first assistant director came up to me and said, "You're late." That was my first day.

ALS: Tell me: did what you've learned as an actor help you as a director? Have you always added something to the scripts or to the ways in which the director saw things?

HUSTON: Well, I've been pretty lucky in my time. I've worked with very few directors who actually felt that they needed to direct all the time. The way I most enjoy working is through a process of discovery and osmosis. I like to know as much as I can about who I am playing, but I don't necessarily want to know the results of the scene. I like to go into the scene still feeling fairly new about it. I do not like to over-rehearse unless I am doing a stage production.

I rarely go into playing a part in a movie with any kind of complacency at all. I am usually very nervous, very edgy. Sometimes I get terrified by the immensity of the script. Then I have to remember I don't have to do the *entire* movie in one day. That's what I imagine my actors going through, and I try to wait until they are more comfortable, to take the threat out of it—to have them feel that they don't have to come up to any great height instantly, that we can work toward it organically. It's just a matter of steering people away from areas where I think they may get bogged down and generally setting them free.

ALS: You've worked on the stage. What plays did you do?

HUSTON: The last thing I did was *Tamara* in Los Angeles, which was an interesting thing to do because the audience follows you around from room to room. It was a really good exercise. I was going to do it in New York, but then my dad died and I didn't want to do stage for a while.

ALS: Was that a physically exhausting experience?

HUSTON: Yeah, it was really tiring.

ALS: Because with film you get to concentrate on a little bit at a time?

HUSTON: Yes, but filming is also exhausting. And I have to say, it's a different kind of exhaustion acting than directing because, as an actor, you do a scene, then you go back to your trailer and sit there and wait to be called again. Your energy goes up and comes down five times while you're waiting. You get nervous about what is coming up. Your energy is very volatile and you are scared of losing it. The thing about directing is that you are *on* all the time—people are asking you millions of questions, you are making millions of decisions, some of them right, some of them wrong. You keep moving. You are there first in the morning and you leave after everyone at night. You go home and have your dinner and then you dream about it all. It's obsessive. You are completely involved. But, in a way, your energy is being used on a regular basis. There isn't all of that start-stop thing you have as an actor.

And the editing room is a great way to come down. Suddenly there you are in the dark with your editor and it's a whole different process. You have time to get your breath back. Not for long, however. After I showed TNT my director's cut, I was asked to make some modifications.

ALS: Why?

HUSTON: One scene was a molestation, the other a rape. I told them that even though I didn't have a leg to stand on contractually, I would try to fight to keep those scenes as they were. I felt that they were terribly necessary to the movie and really the axis on which the movie spins. They ultimately showed it to Ted Turner. He took one look at it and didn't want to have anything to do with it.

Then Gilles Jacob expressed interest in looking at it for Cannes. Ultimately, I was invited there in the "Un Certain Regard" category. That was really nice.

ALS: You're kidding. You know, you must have made incredible contact, and they couldn't cope. It's nothing for you to take personally.

HUSTON: What you just said is very important. I think it is one of the big differences between how one thinks as an actor and how one thinks as a director. You truly can't take things that personally. As a director, there is no room for that.

ALS: When you began visualizing the project, had you decided on Jennifer Jason Leigh already?

HUSTON: No, Jennifer was attached to the project, which was also one of the reasons I was very interested in it, because I admire her work and her bravery.

ALS: What is it like working with someone who is as strong as you've been to your audiences?

HUSTON: Well, Jennifer is very grown-up about her work and she's prone to doing a lot of research. She is a chameleon and she enters into it in very much the same way I do. I don't really examine too much how people get into what they do. It's a very private process. I largely stay outside.

I think you have to seek out as much information as you can and base as much of your performance as you can on some sort of reality or known quantity. Ultimately, finding out who you are playing is a very personal journey. Jennifer is introspective, and I think she actually approaches what she does the same way I approach what I do. I think she asks herself all the questions first: "Who is this? Who am I? What am I doing? Why do I do that? What do I like to eat? When do I take a bath?"

ALS: One of the things that strikes me about your work is that it begins with your strong visual presence, then you fill in the character. Does the accretion of years help you to build a character?

HUSTON: I think the more you know about characters, the more you are able to embody them. And, of course, certain messages about the character will come through: Was she beaten in her youth? Do her feet hurt? Does she spend her days up to her elbows in washing suds? What is the quality of her life? Is she exhausted in the evening? Does she feel like going out dancing? Does she wear a thick coat because she is always cold? What are the effects of various weather on this person? What is the effect of life on a person's physicality? And somehow I guess partly by intuition and partly by

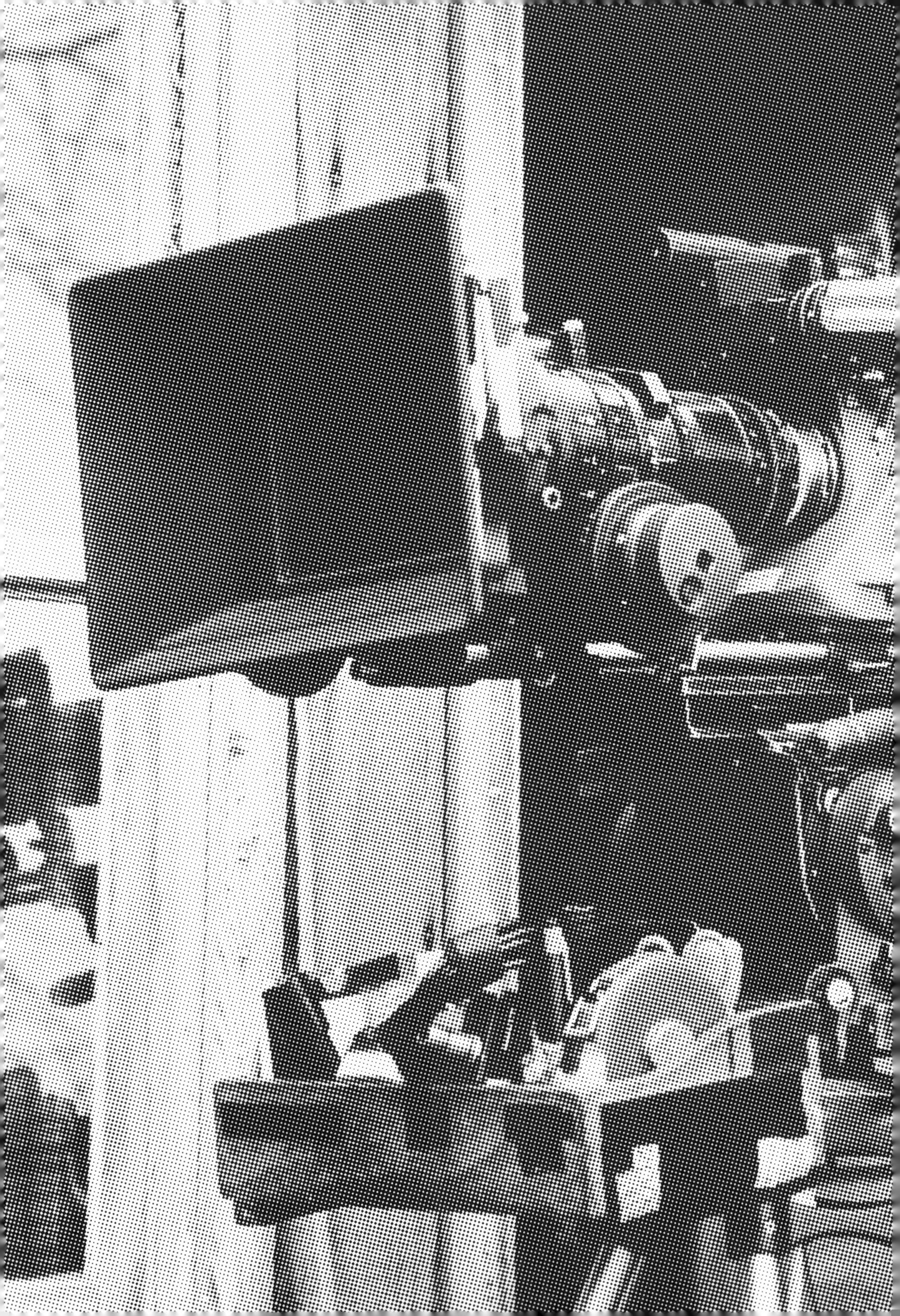

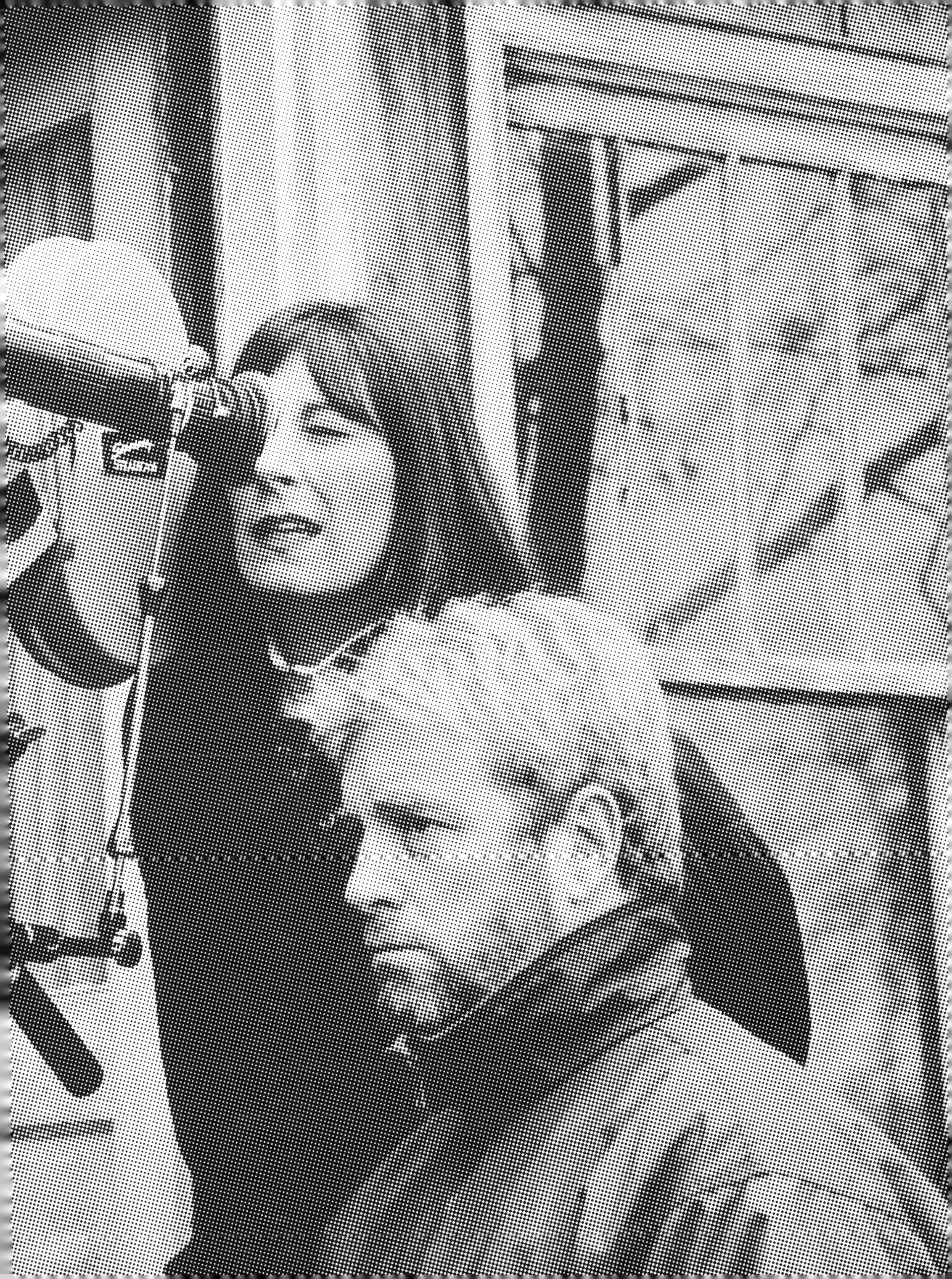

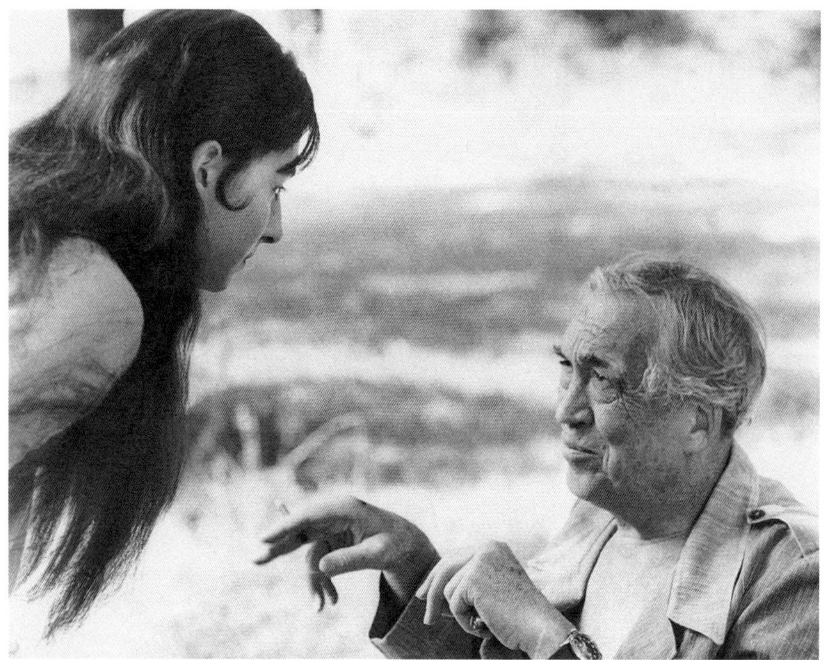

PREVIOUS SPREAD Anjelica Huston directing *Bastard out of Carolina*.

LEFT John Huston directing Anjelica Huston in *A Walk with Love and Death*, circa 1968.

instinct and partly because we are all given a physical body, those things start to make sense on subliminal as well as factual levels. Somehow they start to correlate. I think that may be how I go about working.

ALS: Was becoming someone other than yourself a confusing process for you initially?

HUSTON: Well, I've always liked that. I've always had a taste for it. I used to like to mimic and I used to make people up when I was little. I think that all goes with the deranged personality of an actress.

ALS: It's an incredibly energetic personality. I wouldn't say deranged.

HUSTON: I would!

ALS: You mentioned once that you discovered you could amuse your father by mimicking people for him. Did he encourage your theatrical bent?

HUSTON: Yes. It was also my mother, who was an extraordinary woman. She had my brother when she was nineteen years old, so she never had a chance to fully explore her original intention—which was to be a dancer. My mother was the one who took us to see the Royal Shakespeare Company and Fonteyn dancing, and so on. And she recognized the actress in me. But she died when I was seventeen, so she didn't see me do much on the screen beyond my first film,

A Walk With Love and Death, which my father directed when I was fifteen.

ALS: Is it strange to see yourself on screen then as opposed to now? I'm sure your style of acting has changed.

HUSTON: I was a completely different person. In that film, first of all, I had a sort of English-Irish accent, and I had a different face....

ALS: Were you an ingenue in that film?

HUSTON: Let's face it, I was never the ingenue type. I didn't have the nose of an ingenue. But I didn't like doing that first film with my father. The script was terrible. And if he came back today to discuss it, I'd still say it was terrible. And I was terrible in it. It wasn't right for me maybe. He thought I was being obstreperous on the set because I took my mother's side against him—which wasn't true because she wasn't influencing me against him. They had just separated when I signed on to do the film.... So I didn't act for a long time after that.

ALS: Was that when you did *The Last Tycoon?*

HUSTON: Yes. The film didn't work in the end, but I worked as an actress for the first time in years. And I got to work with Kazan for about two minutes.

ALS: What did you do in the years between those two projects?

HUSTON: I came to New York and modeled. I modeled for about four or five years.

ALS: I used to do performing arts in New York and one of the things I remember was being exhausted all the time—physically. I remember reading about something Montgomery Clift said: you may be acting but your body doesn't know that. So it actually goes through all of the ups and downs that the character is experiencing and you are really a mess.

HUSTON: You are and it is very tiring. You undergo these things. It is very much like alchemy and I find it's sometimes a little dangerous for me, because my life is apt to reflect, on some level, what I am working on. Sometimes that can be really unpleasant.

ALS: When I saw that scene in *The Grifters*, when you are bent over your son's body: I thought it was about all the years, all the men, and everyone your character had ever been involved with in the world.

HUSTON: Yes, and having to tear them out of her soul.

CINDY SHERMAN

UNTITLED

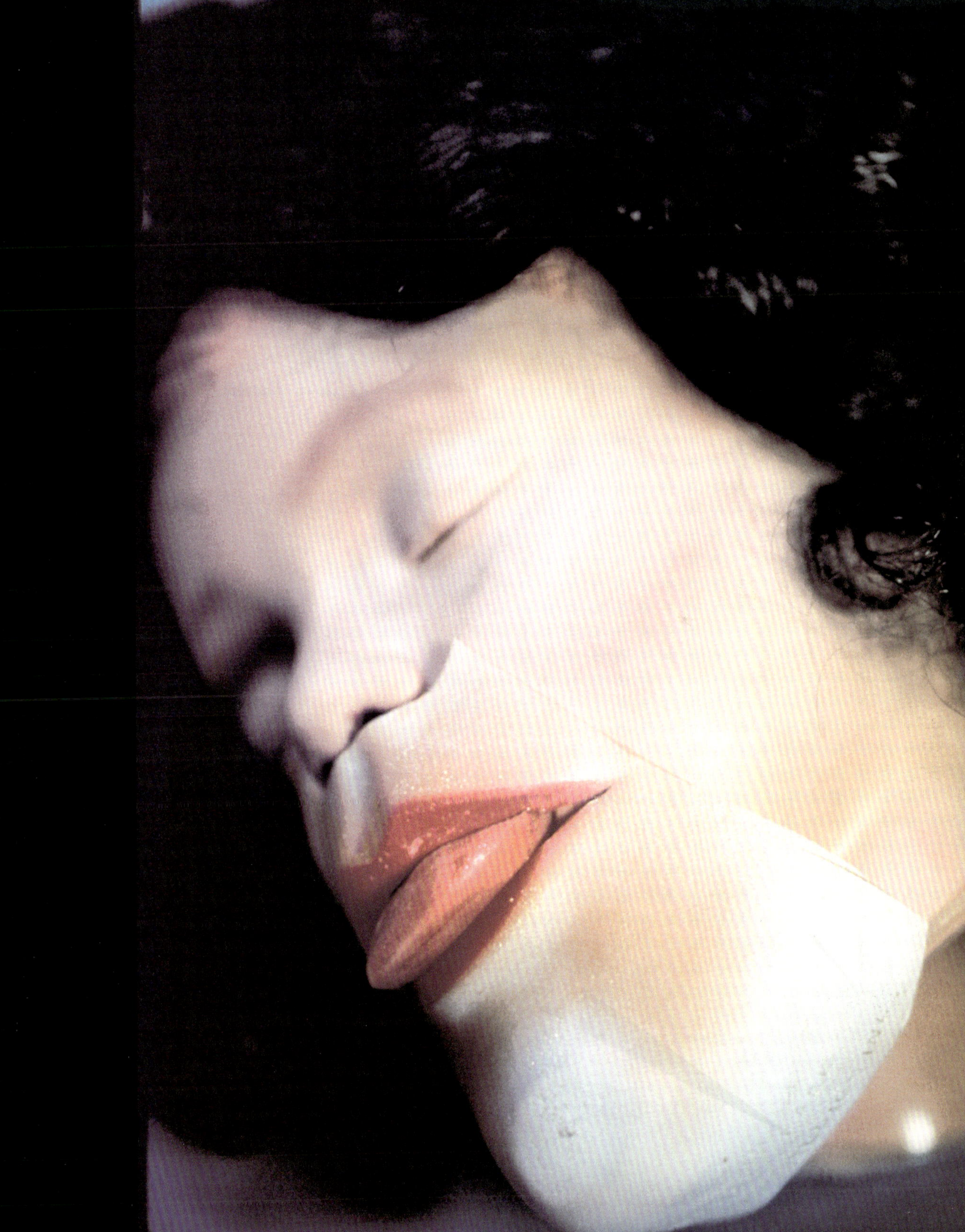

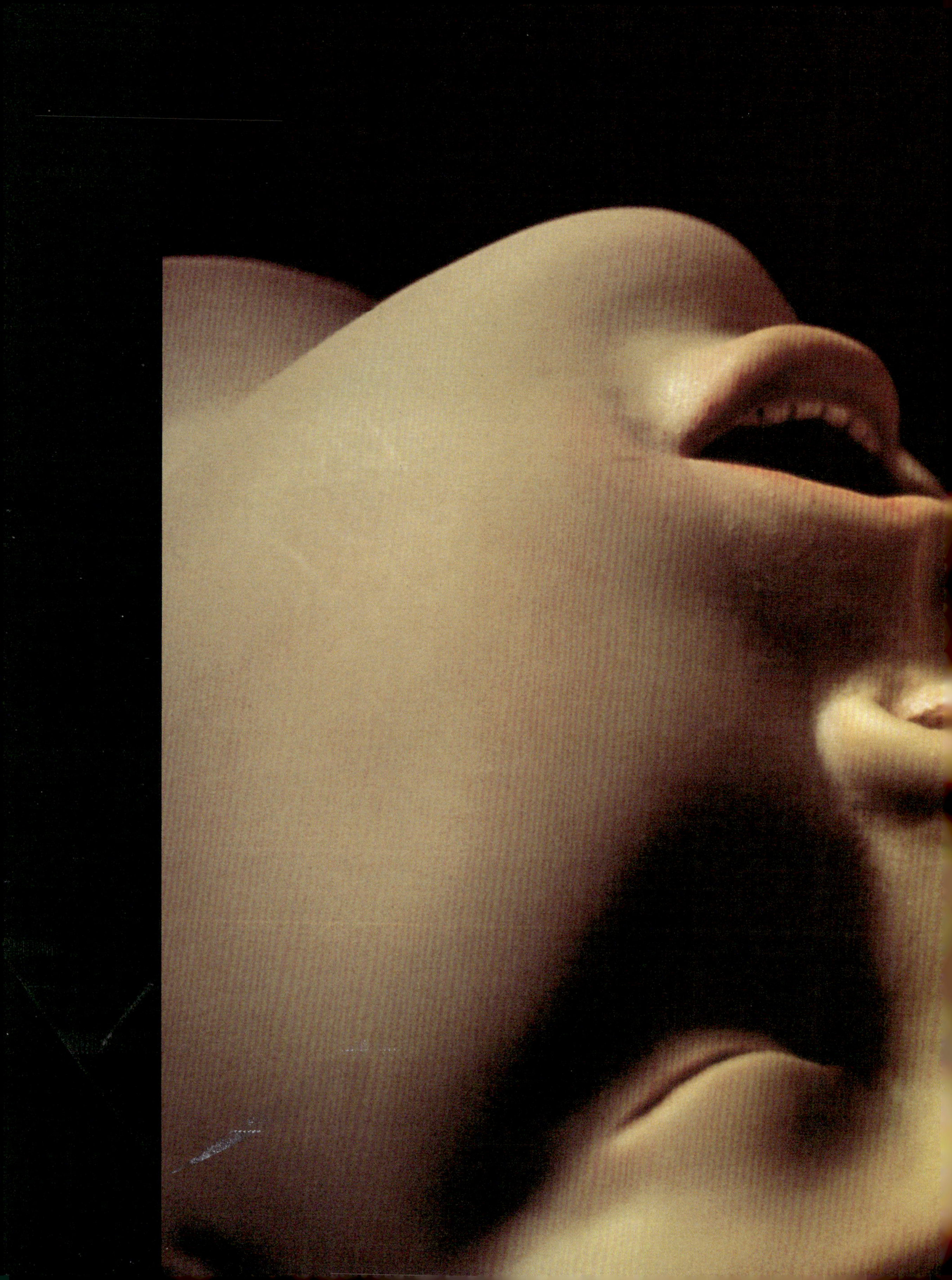

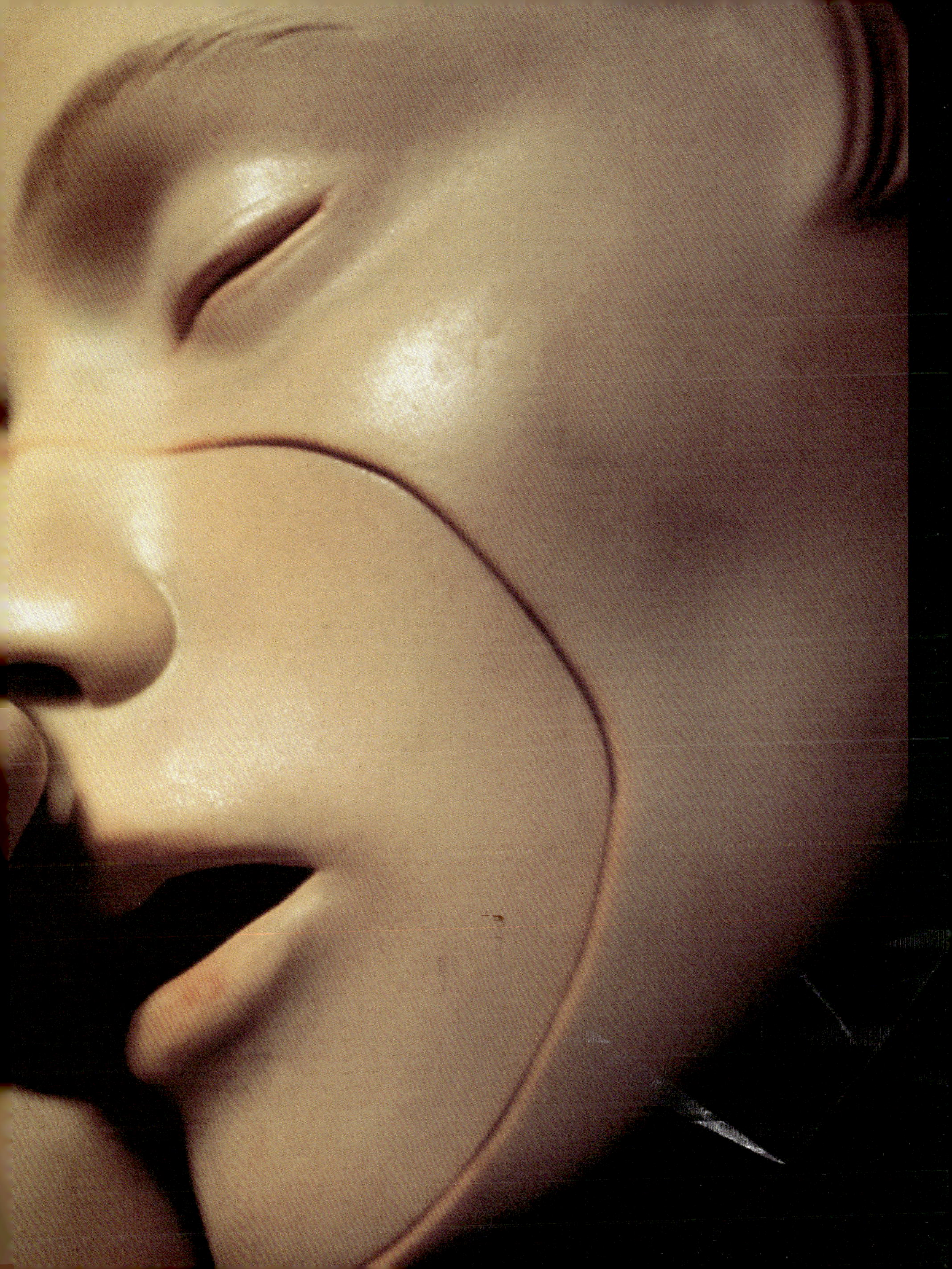

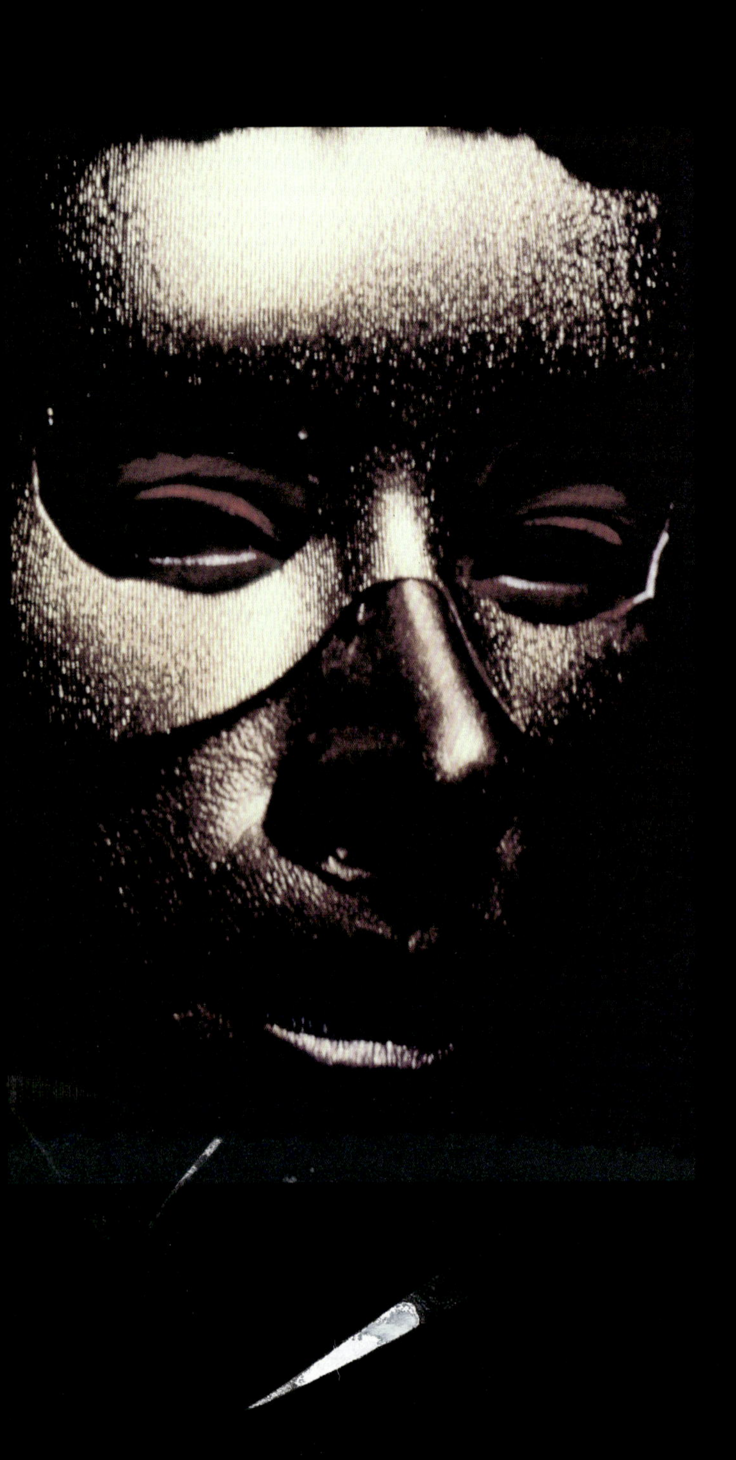

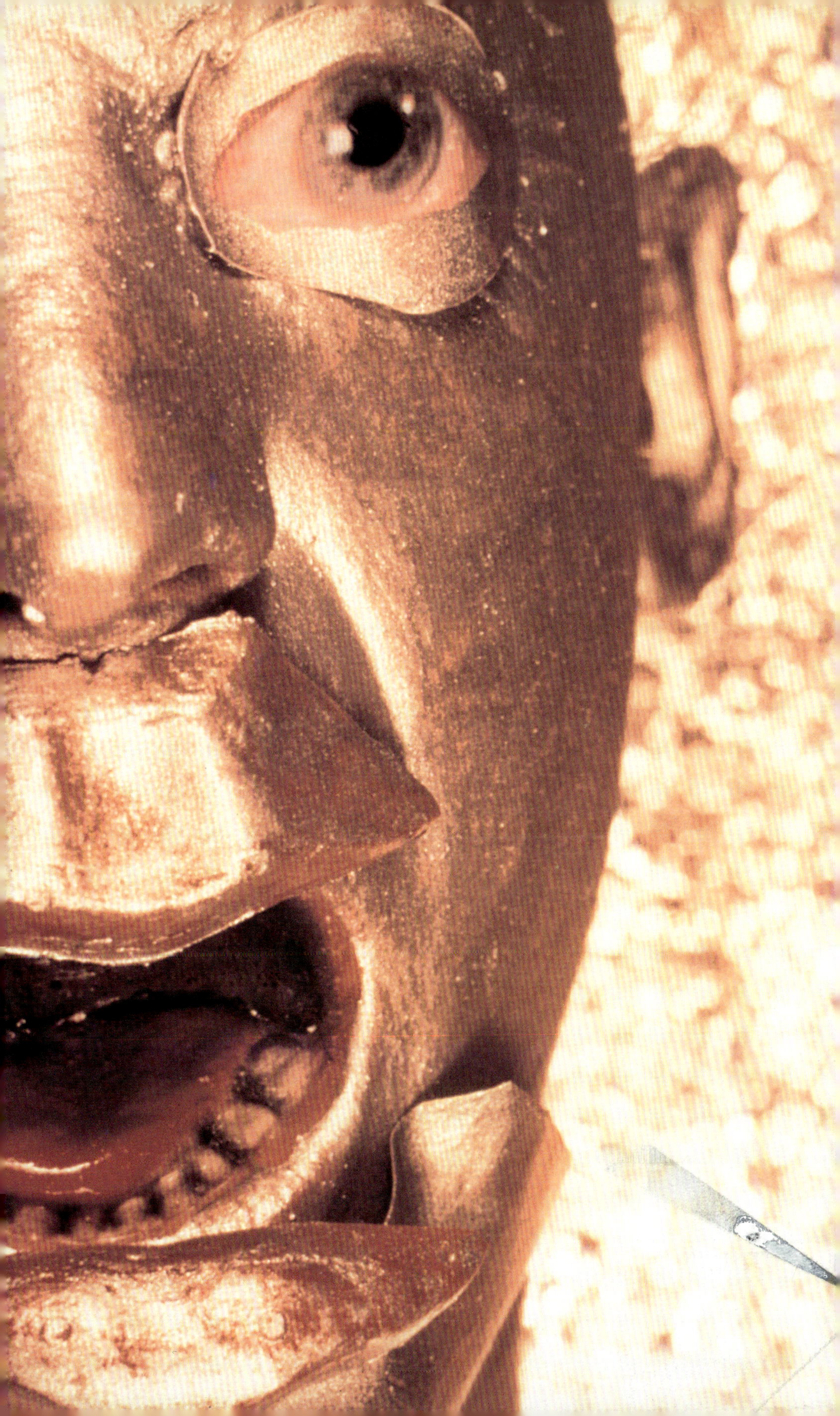

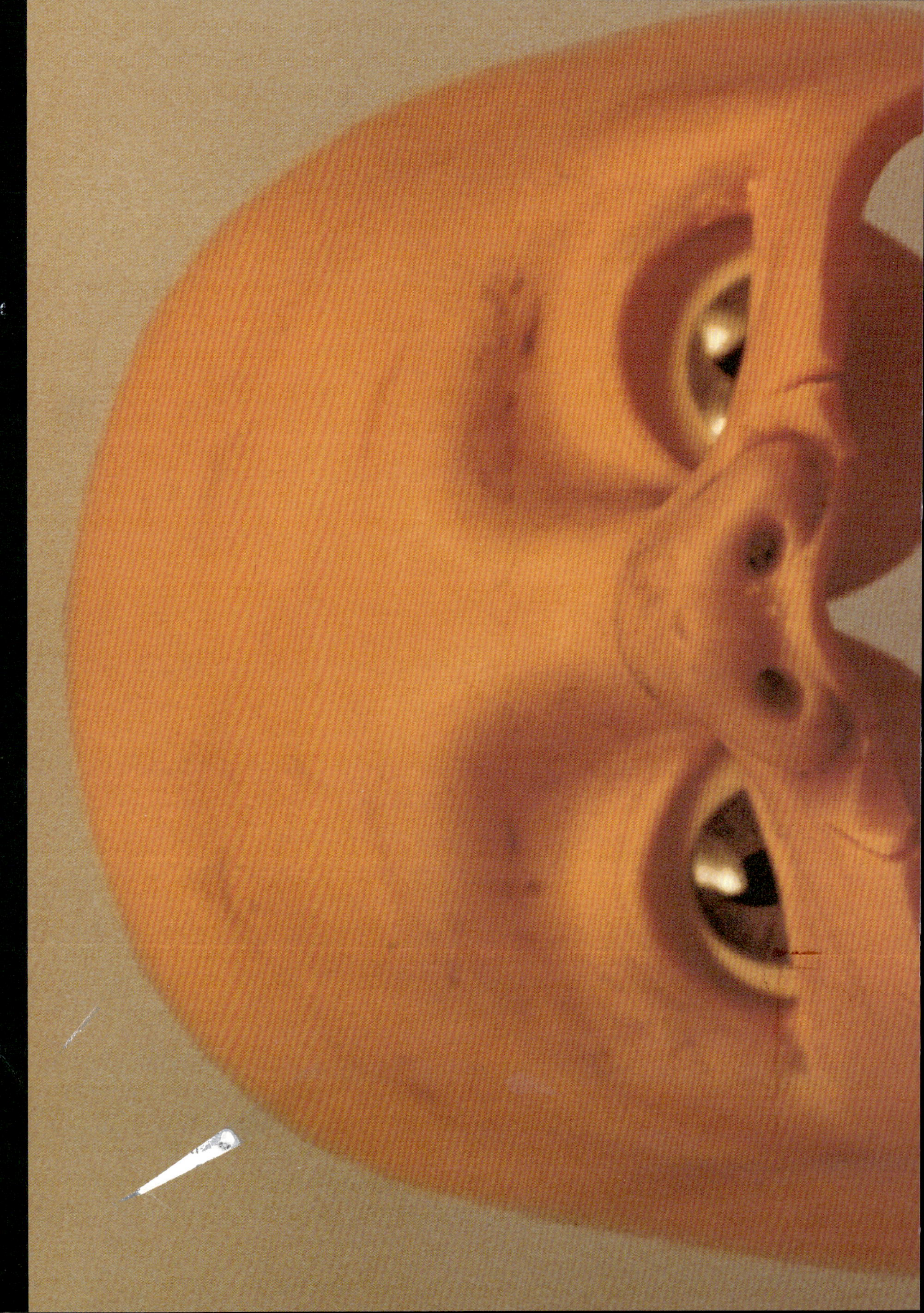

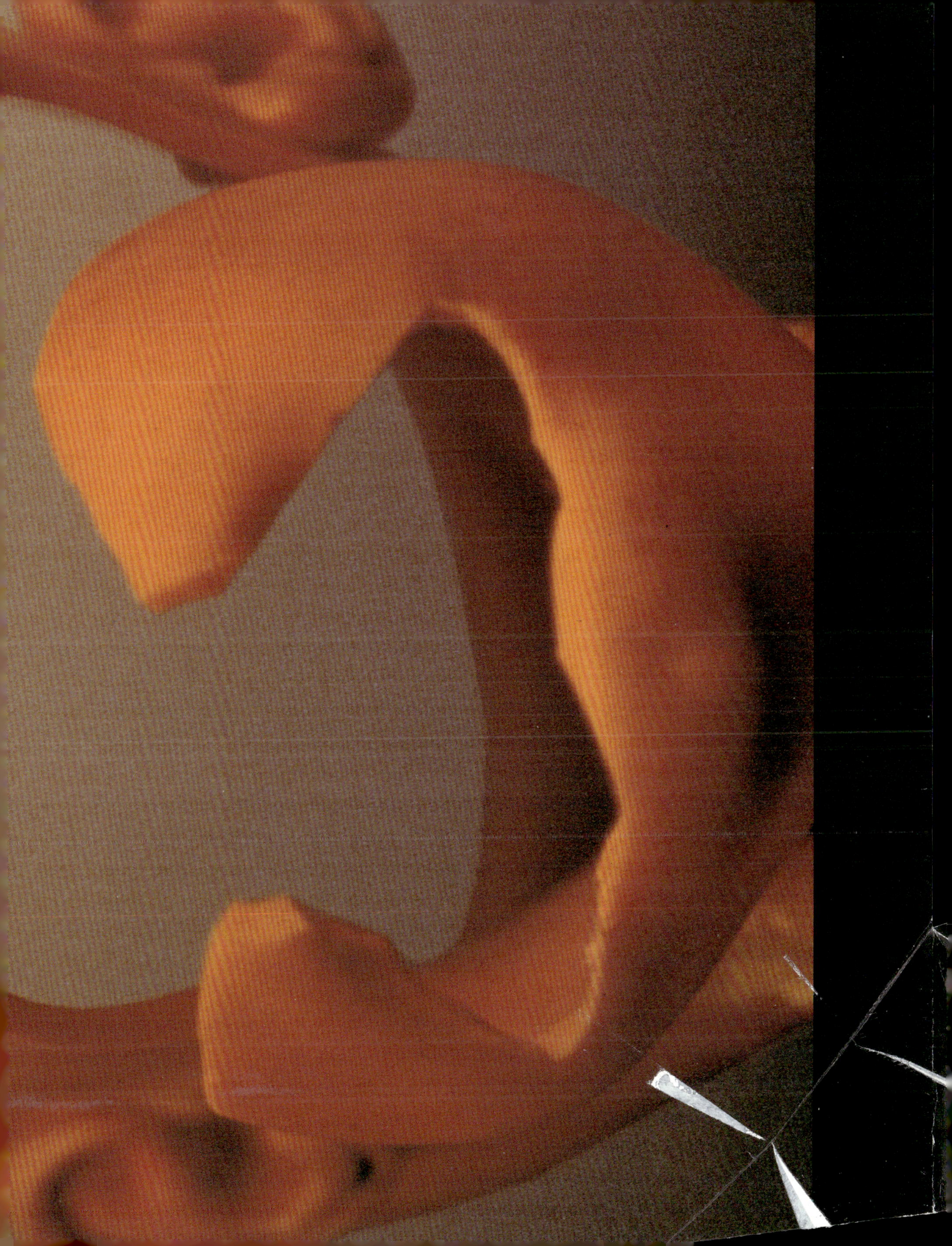

CINDY SHERMAN

Cindy Sherman's spotlight on the dissembling of character, ego, and identity can be traced back to her use of the theatrics of staged photographs in her *Untitled Film Stills* (1977–79). Those first black-and-white images, mimicking Hollywood publicity stills, featured the artist herself, transformed through makeup, costumes, and lighting, in the role of a blank-eyed starlet. Subsequent series by Sherman, which were shot in color, expanded to use more elaborate costumes, disguises, and dramatic lighting techniques, and topics for her photographs included androgyny, magazine centerfolds, the fashion industry (in a 1983 series commissioned by the boutique Dianne B.), and Old Master painting, which culminated in a series of pastiche *History Portraits* (1988–90).

The grotesque and ugly, present in Sherman's work from early on, then began to dominate in garishly lit pictures of hags and witches. At the same time, Sherman began to disappear from the photographs, leaving behind her scenes of carnage and detritus, trash and vomit: remnants of some strange, dystopian melee.

In her next series, *Sex Pictures* (1992), Sherman repopulated her work with subjects assembled from miscellaneous dummies and prosthetic devices ordered from medical-supply catalogues, and novelty-store vinyl body parts, masks, and props. These hybrid surrogates entangled themselves in crude, farcical parodies of human sexual relations. While Sherman does seem to have absented herself completely from these photographs, a disquieting frisson occurs when, scrutinizing some body part, skin texture, or pair of eyes peering out from behind a mask, one perceives a hint of the artist behind these grotesque facades.

Sherman's most recent work includes tight portraits of semi-masked figures, as well as images of characters interacting, such as two mannequin faces with parted lips and closed eyes as if about to kiss. More unsettling are close-ups of cut-up masks resembling the outcome of nightmarish medical experiments: some figures are missing the lower parts of their faces, or whole sections of skin have been removed to reveal gouged and rutted skulls, mouths grimacing or screaming wide open. If a soundtrack existed to accompany these images, it would seem to be the proverbial "weeping and gnashing of teeth." In these photographs, Sherman seems to have brought us to some hellish netherworld populated by damaged, terrified souls.

JACKIE McALLISTER

HILDA MORLEY

THE WORLD THEN

The world then much more black & white than
I had thought: black wholly
when it is black & what I used to
see, once, as roots, branches to
hold on to, footholds, handholds,
firmness to be sure of — become now
dried out, scraggy,
                                        nearly
uprooted, turning to dry dust, or
leaf-veins nearly crumbled.
                                                        My face into
dead, not live rock.
                                                Is it so, then, as
Hopkins said, that "wisdom
is early to despair"? What I could never
believe?
                    Is it true, then,
the "never, never, never,
never, never" Lear knew?
                                                    Is there a way to
grip, lay hold of what
doesn't curve the smallest
millimeter toward me?   Is there no way?
Where are the strengths I wasted?
Threw away?
                        Where did I put them?
My face is into the dust, receiving,
                                                                    swallowing
all of it, hanging there,
                                                the force of it
holding me somehow,   still there —
never, never, never, never, never.
                                                        The old knowledge
crackles away without wisdom,
                                                        is only
blackness
                        blackened out

TALES FROM ISLAND STREET

ARNO SCHMIDT

STRANGE DAYS

: "There are strange days : when the sun rises in its own odd way; tepid clouds draw low; the wind rasps suspiciously from all regions of this world. Jet fighters loop witches' snares in the sky; all creditors take a notion to demand payments due; you hear from people who once made a sudden exit."

On days like these, it is wise not to undertake anything—although, of course, that can be precisely the wrong thing to do! For who knows if it's the right thing to disconnect the doorbell, drape the windows, and play dead on the couch in the corner of the room? Reading is not recommended : out of that obscure novel from 1800, there suddenly falls a letter written in an antique, yellowed hand, plus a silhouette of a young girl in the fashion of the Napoleonic wars, and you can only thank your stars if your own name isn't on the envelope—there are peculiar days!

Well, the current one had happily come and gone yet again. To be sure, a gentleman in a black suit had been here, and had wanted to convert me to Mormonism. A long letter from a total stranger had arrived from Spain and, as became clear in the last paragraph, was not intended for me at all. The usual ice-gray tramp had rung my bell too : said he was a student; and offered razor blades, guaranteed used only once.

On the telephone, a strange Englishwoman had reported, amid accusations and assignations, the following anecdote from her trip around the world : on the island of Tristan da Cunha—120 inhabitants, no clergy, no magistrate—two people had wanted to wed. The only person who could read fluently disapproved of the marriage, so he had refused to read the wedding vows on this occasion. There was nothing for it but to fetch the next best learned personage : who had then spelled it out, letter by letter! (Which among illiterates probably only served to heighten the solemn atmosphere—but then I just had to keep picturing it ever so vividly to myself : how the fellow stands there at the desk, his finger pressed to each line and focusing; at the difficult spots he picks his nose in desperation.)

Well, as noted, I had survived all that. Even the sassy red-and-blue checked sunset had been scrolled down : surely one could venture an evening walk?—

In the black crags of the neighboring building, the door to the brightly lit ground-floor balcony stood wide open; they were tenaciously record-playing; girls stamped and squalled to hit-paradings, shook their colorful locks, and slapped away at the soles of their feet : just get by quick! (And up on the sidewalk a bicycler was heading straight for me, as if my spot were vacant and I no longer present on this earth!)

At the edge of town, where the gas lanterns have not yet been replaced by arc lamps, it was almost silent and lonely. Moon buoy, anchored aslant in the cloud current. Cats went about their obscure businesses, diligent and self-confident. But all at once, the green Isetta beside me braked to a halt : 2 policemen climbed right out, and compared me with a typed list. Now, of course, every human being is in some sense <guilty> (according to Schopenhauer worthy of hanging just on principle); and so I stood patiently quiet, and a few items from the past did occur to me (not <rape and murder> or the like—just trifles; it's not important). "Left hand?!"—only when it turned out I had the regulation 5 fingers on it did it appear I was saved this time round. They apologized military-fashion; and I walked on past the new buildings, heading back—it was probably better to turn around today after all.

Around the lawn the U-shaped front lines, tall as houses; and across the street, too, the same cement Siegfried Line, except for little yellow squares in it. The gigantic bronze duck next to me tried to spit in my face.

And stopped stock-still, dumbfounded— : way up in the wall, there sat the blue giantess! Immobile at the table; she must have been at least 12 feet tall! And now I noticed the window framing her, right, just like those on the lower floors : so you were merely looking into a room : relieved.

(But that really was quite impossible! A female being, as large as ... I closed my eyes; shook my head blindly; who knows what it was I had seen; maybe she'd be gone if I...)

: Yes! She was gone! —Peaceful and gray, with no posters and so, almost beautiful, the building's wall stood there in the night. Accordingly, I ought to be able to breathe easy—but what was wrong with my brain then?! Certainly, I'll grant you, I am one of those people who tend to introspection, and had long suspected myself. I made a hasty decision to pull my hat further down over my face (which is to say, in the absence of such, to lower my brow), and simply blame it all on this remarkable day : what I had seen I had not seen; and now head straight home! Double-time! Only once did my undisciplined left eye twitch back across the huge billboard...?

: And stood there stock-still again, a broken man! : Up top, where the giantess had just been lolling, a rock garden was now in bloom. The dull green succulents, flowered stars of acerbic yellow, a flagstone path pointed sternly off toward : that chaise lounge! Solitude : the bird in the birdbath was frozen stiff.

Darkness swept a hand across it—and suddenly a new picture: Miss Giantess in a sheet of water. The strong liquid stretched tight like a blue loincloth; her face had opened up, the coarse blond hair sat totally askew, all to one side. (And now, once again, gone : a pity!)

So they were showing slides up there?! Had hung the screen in front of the window, and not given it a thought? : And so I cozily chose the more favorable angle from which to watch, and crossed my arms over my chest for the duration.

Cities jerked past (almost like Hamburg, huh?); a vegetable market (and the red tomatoes glistened so decoratively!). Cars on long avenues. The tent on the dunes : her lopped-off face photographed though a lattice of lyme grass. So there I stood for a long while in the clear night. Sometimes a couple would pass by, giggling as they joined me to look up, but then had more important things to do, and wandered ardently on. At one point the lamp beside the front entrance went bright : an inebriate balanced his way out, shouldering 2 long gladioli, and made a beeline away from me, on very self-reliant legs.

You could go inside, press the button on the house intercom, and say ever so simply : "Are you the lady in blue in the pictures up there? : Then I'm in love with you!" In turn, she would open the window and look down in amusement.... (More likely, however, within seconds two sturdy men would come leaping down, with manymany blows in their muscular hands!). And then maybe she was a woman from some distant land whom you would never see; at most her address.

Maybe the people up there had only found this magazine with the slides in it. Or the developers had mixed up addresses, and they were now watching her strange kismet out of curiosity—on days like this, indeed everything was possible!

Or a dead friend, and they were dolefully refreshing memories of her and so, by way of precaution, I stepped back a few paces; for such complications I'm no longer young and callous enough!

Instead, I chose to dismiss it with both hands; went up to my place full of cowardly determination; midnight had passed thankgod—and, let's hope, everything will be back to normal tomorrow.

NEIGHBOR, DEATH AND SOLIDUS

Wan green face, with mouth tied in a loose black bow—at least that's how it looked by moonlight, at five in the morning. Once again, I hadn't been able to sleep, and had gone to the window : and right-angled, too, in her oriel, there my neighbor stood, a war widow, we hadn't spoken yet.

(Ingebartels, Ingebartels, Ingebartels, the clock behind me repeated the name several times over, and broke into Flemish laughter : ho ho ho! : so it's 4:45 A.M. A black car on a black street; its front paws shoveling away untiringly. An invisible motorcycle bubbled up as well, and then pulled the diminishing beads of sound behind it.)

I opened my window; and her hand, too, began to nestle formally before her, and we each shuffled into his or her aperture : did she have heart trouble as well? (I had just moved in, true; but I am very direct on such occasions—and why not? Life is so short!)

"We two can't sleep," I observed, soft as pajamas (and with what sly grammar : We! Two! : now if *that* isn't suggestive?!). But she was strong too; she nodded her head briefly, and then went on busying herself with the frazzled moon stuck above the old cemetery. Unfortunately, there were also several morning clouds there in the east, thin as stripes (although too undulatory for me; straight ones are tidier). "I like that cloud!" she declared with bold jaw.

May one contradict after such brief acquaintance? I decided <no>; and was mercifully spared any reply by the whistle of the train from the East Station : thus does a wandering animal-spirit howl from the alone to the alone! It moaned, diligent and cold, like those alien voices in the chimney (you can hear them sometimes in our building : do the architects actually include them in their calculations, or is it pure chance? A clever landlord could place an ad : <Special romantic howling from the stove : 5 marks extra rent!>—but thankgod, no landlord is that clever!). Once again the ebony disk of the whistle floated our way, now edge, now plate (while beneath, it was probably storming off with black lowered brow, through the forests in the direction of Aschaffenburg. Blind).

"I find the thought of death much more comforting than that of eternal life," I said, and she nodded, profoundly convinced : once you've been through two wars, plus refugee, plus inflation—the long mouth glided disdainfully about in her face : No sir! Eternal life ain't for anybody born in ought fourteen.

The moon? : The heavenly dust around it had taken on a soft rosy hue in the meantime; and it, faithfully obeying color theory, an insipid white-green— I turned away, counterclockwise to the left, and by way of illustration fetched the coin :

"No! A gold piece!" : an Emperor Justinian solidus (527–65; the ninny couldn't even write his own name : he signed things with the aid of a stencil, and they had to guide his hand *besides* : <authority>!). Where had I got it? : From my grandfather, for my confirmation. She leaned further forward, eyes opened with interest, and our faces floated high above the evacuated street (: <reciprocal>).

"My grandfather was a collector. Enthusiastic, passionate, ruthless, the way that sort of people are. Physician in Fiume, 1860. One windy and cool evening, there is a knock at his door : a sturdily built stranger enters moaning, his hand to his stomach. <How can I be of service?>. And the helpless fellow admits: after a long journey through the Orient, he arrived safely in Greece; his hoard of ancient gold coins endangered by strict customs control : in the harbor of Hagion Oros, he swallowed twenty of his rarest pieces. Since then, he has been traveling for three days, and nights, without a stop. But the pain has overwhelmed him : help!! —My grandfather, himself a numismatist of high rank, palpated with expertise and cunning, muttering and greedily eyeing the frightened man's stomach—another ghastly grab!—then implacable : without an operation, death was inevitable inside of three hours! The Frenchman rolled his eyes. My grandfather passed the massive laxative off as a compassionate dose of morphine, and decoratively whetted scalpel against scalpel—for the <operation>! And casually inquired whether among those ancient coins there might be some from the Byzantine Empire? The traveler, horrified amid deadly white sheets and menacing tongues of metal, consented to all terms : after a successful <operation> my grandfather would be allowed to choose ten of the rare specimens."

Languid neighborly laughter, emerging from rounded shoulders, while she gradually pictured the situation to herself. Another glance to the moon penny : "And then?"

"My grandfather administered a cup of opium to the stranger as well; once narcosis had ensued, emptied out the man's gastrointestinal tract, and joyfully gleaned among the coinage—plus, there was *the* alternative of opening one of the traveler's veins and allowing him to expire <during the operation> : twenty rare coins?! My grandfather struggled long and hard; finally an unexpected remnant of humanity triumphed; he let the stranger awaken, and shared the plunder with him.—*One* piece, however, he took for himself in advance : a coin from the Thracian city of Bizye, one of a kind : Artemis in archaic-stiff style, a torch in one hand, before her a stag. —Upon his departure, and well aware of his boundless loss, the stranger summoned him with many a curse before God's Judgment Seat—but collectors don't believe in that. Pointless."

"And you inherited this gold piece then from that grandfather?" Not inherited; for my confirmation. "And the coin with Artemis ?" No one ever saw it again; presumably he took it with him to his grave. Yes. Collectors.

Yes. We then briefly compared the sinking moon with an eggshell; with a baseball of goat-leather; with an aspirin tablet. From then on, we leaned in our windows rather regularly; sluggishly told each other about ourselves; and went on waiting for death.

CAUTIOUS PEOPLE

Walk to the window : the streets marched forlornly here and there. Into the hard-frozen courtyard came an aproned man who shouted : "Ashes! Ashes!"

I had just finished my daily work—Lord, what do I mean work? : I get a disability pension, and manage to keep busy. I'm setting up a giant index, of two to three hundred thousand tiny cards, to include if possible all the persons who lived during the days of the old Duchy of Verden (I come from the area, from Rotenburg; and—particularly now, having landed in southern Germany—have taken a special fancy to do it).

And so my quota was finished. I had also lain on my studio couch for half an hour: how I've learned to despise that Indian-red skeleton! At the time I bought it, I hoped to lend my two rooms a fashionable ambience: the tiny one became the midget kitchen; the other was meant to feign a kind of <studio>. How I have repented sacrificing my old honest bed ! Ah well; too late.—

A bicycler in fuzzy cap, red, pumped by in a crouch; two girls in black diving gear, their hands in all their pants pockets, strode schoolward. Then the antarctic river of tar froze empty again.

Implacable, I indulged in my customary reflection : what would be the most unpleasant thing you could do right now?! And promptly answered me : put on your coat and go for a walk. —So I did just that; flung on the heavy scarf; the mittens : I am cautious.

At one time, it was little train stations that drew me irresistibly. There I would sit before a beer in the dusty light of the yellow waiting rooms; the strong gold and red of the packs of Salems; illumined train windows pearled into the night; the fat and skinny travelers—lovely days, the days of youth! Nowadays (it's always so drafty in train stations; I am cautious!) it's department stores. It's a gaudy spectral-analytic world; heads roll by; elbows jostle; clothing jungles, coated forests; hands are yapping bright-dyed fabrics; eyeballs rummage; mouths start stumbling; yarn-balls cower, motley helots. Usually I pick out a girl for myself.

She was stepping, short and skinny, very cautiously through the coco-mats on sale cheap today; on past carpet-stretchers; (whenever someone brushed against her, I noticed, she would pat at her right coat pocket afterward. Ah, of course : she bought a very skimpy brassiere, and paid out of that right coat pocket : meaning her wallet was in there; and every ten seconds she would feel if it was still there. Very good!).

Well then, nothing for it but unobtrusive pursuit! Through bovine leather; dunes of cocoa; butt-end eyeballs and teeth agaping, word prostheses; rosy gristled earfuls; ah, the escalator! (I picked up a cheap new edition of the immortal <Shock-headed Peter> and continued to watch. (Meanwhile, who would be watching me, ah woe! And then who was watching him? : <We watchers watch the watchers who watch the daughter of the king.>)).

The escalator, solemnly trimmed with statues, glided ceaselessly to the top (across and behind, belts looped adders, socks in mountains). She waited inconspicuously; hesitated—there : now ten stair steps were empty in front of her—and she set a firm foot onto the rilled tin treads. (Assumes then, that an overloaded escalator could collapse? And always waits until the thing is moving with almost no load : very good! A practical, cautious creature).

I followed her at a distance to the third floor as well, where the furniture rests; armchairs settle. Black-smocked girl trainees dragged around cardboard boulders. We barely escaped the lazy vulturing salesmen; and so back down!

And out. Outside the air clotted like black glass; immobile, and so cold that you were sure to roll up your collar with one hand. She held her ground, wise and still, on the sidewalk—from the left, here came another gaudy, spitting tin mandrill of a DKW—let it pass—wait another ten yards (and I nodded with satisfaction : that's how you have to be nowadays!).

She followed almost the identical way home, short and skinny; there wasn't much to her (but nowadays who *does* have much to them when you come down to it?—). As is the nature of objects, her shopping net trolled along beside her, indifferent and disciplined. I decided I would pickle myself (alone in my little chamber; I am cautious!) in Dujardin this evening.

Sure enough: she was still walking ahead of me. Gervinus Street, Island Street. Down the sidewalk adorned with crusted snow a little man sailed toward her; in black coat, wide cut, with flat cap *à la bohème*: "Wherrre eez numbaahrr twinti naeeen?" She vainly tried to dodge him. He swore supplications, with body splayed wide : "O : Wherre ?!" And, disappointed : "You nut professorr : I professorr!" And flowed toward where I was following. I stepped up tall and broad in between (between my short quarry and this offspring of Rasputin—though I'm the sort you can knock over with one finger!) : "Back!" I commanded; "Here forty-two : you me understand?" He gazed at me with white head atilt; he yielded round to the right and back; as he moved away you could still hear him muttering: "Pisantsss! All Pisantsss! : Eat onions and podadoes. Drrink gasoline : Oh! : Gezzoline!"

I turned to the nondescript soul behind me; I said : "Don't pay any attention to that. The man was apparently drunk : foreigner." She muttered, straight into the night; her headgear nodded; and vanished, down Rossdörfer Street (which leads to Aschaffenburg; I leaned against the drugstore wall, and just stared a bit : all right, she had vanished).

Upstairs : I regarded my studio couch full of loathing : would never be big enough for two! Automatically pulled the curtains shut; amid furniture stumps : always be cautious!

WHAT SHALL I DO?

Reading is a terrible thing!

When it's said of a hero who is preparing to do some thinking : "...he furrowed his brow and sternly pressed his lips together...." —I can already feel how my face, up front, is distorting itself for the same pensive grimace!

Or : "...a haughty smile played about the right corner of his mouth..." —my God, I must look foolish like that; for I can't even manage an ineffably haughty smile, let alone one with only the right corner of my mouth; it's yet another talent fate has denied me.

It must happen to a lot of people! On the streetcar in the morning, you can clearly spot the devastation that writers wreak among us; how they force upon us the train of their own thoughts, the most heinous gestures. Yesterday, the young fellow across from me raised—he's a student at the Technical Academy, and was reading someone I'd never heard of named <Tennessee Williams> (at best that's the kind of name they called the exotic criminal types in my youth, <Alaska Jim> and <Palisades Emil>!)—anyway, he raised his head, and stared at me with such undisguised homicidal intent that with trembling hand I pulled my hat lower over my brow; and got out one stop sooner (I almost arrived at work too late. Probably he had slowly cut my body in slices, starting from the bottom; or tied me in a sack and let frenzied madmen in leaden shoes dance me to death!).

Oh, the newspaper novel, the newspaper novel! Just recently, right in the middle of its prose stood the contemptible phrase: "...he turned his head, slowly, as lions are wont to do..." —the next morning half my fellow passengers gave the impression they had stiff necks; they blinked and made contemptuously protracted snorts. There was no living with the young ladies that day either; they all appeared to have forgotten their handkerchiefs and stared us men down most impudently. Only later did I learn that in the competing paper it had read: "...she sniffed snottily...."

I've suffered from this since childhood! While serving my apprenticeship with Henschel & Cie., I once read how a young man had so impressed his boss with his great candor that he was later appointed junior partner— : the next day I was almost sacked!

I lost my second girlfriend—no one has a figure like that nowadays!— the same way. At the most crucial period, she was reading—quite right! — Heinse's sultry <Ardinghello>; while Satan had slipped the <Middle Collection of the Speeches of Gautama Buddha> into these fool's hands : with the result that I was making a try at lowering my rations to the single grain of rice per day prescribed there (or rather, our more customary national magnum bonum), in hopes that by following such a diet I would within a short time achieve the conquest of space and time free of charge. Also had a head full of phrases *à la* "...wander solitary as does the rhinoceros..." and was attempting to regard her blouse with exanimate will—I can't even respect myself now when I think of those days!

And here I am laboring under the same problems even today. Inexorably, surreptitiously, I am forced to keep tabs on what my wife reads, just to know what she is thinking. I've done this regularly ever since the time she acted so cold and hateful for eight days that even I entertained thoughts of divorce—until I discovered that in her serial novel, the hero had just cheated on the heroine, giving rise to all sorts of hate and rage. I have even tried (by clandestine means, to be sure!) to steer her : by providing her with voluptuous substitute reading; there are authors, after all, who know how to describe a hautana in a way that will drive even graybeard accountants mad. (But you have to be careful, too, not to overdose; I'm not as young as I used to be!) (Sometime I'll have to slip a tale of noble creditors into my landlord's mailbox.)

When all is said and done, these fellows—these literary types—do with you what they will; whether it's by hoodwinking you with the blessed consequences of regular consumption of Blue Bonnet; whether it's by rendering you incapable of stuttering anything but their formulas, phrases, idioms. I once put off a summer trip simply because before taking it I read a brilliant-ghastly description of a train wreck. On the other hand, I once took a trip to the Emsmoore—my God, what country! : you can communicate with the inhabitants only by sign language; your feet are never dry; and the rain, it raineth every day—and all because an author had set his love scenes there; love scenes! : ostensibly the local air was perforce as hot as liquid glass; and the lasses voluntarily assumed positions known otherwise only from the *Thousand & One Nights— : I don't want to read anymore!!*

I should give rein to my own thoughts? God preserve me from that! : for the most part, I have none at all; and when I really do, they're not first quality. I have tried everything; I've trod the paths of reason and science; I put together a collection of works on Mars, by absolute authorities, from Schröter to Schiaparelli to Antoniadi and Graff : and when I then wandered in spirit across the rust-red desert floor of Thyle I or II and turned down into lichen-encrusted labyrinths of rock—who should come sauntering around the next corner but Frau Hiller, lonely and sly? (Or, even worse, the depraved daughter of the druggist on the corner!). Historical works? : I conscientiously immersed myself in the age of Cromwell; and promptly amazed my colleagues with my headstrong and intractable behavior; swore strange curses : "By God and the covenant!"; suggested that our buyer baptize his son <Obadiah-bind-their-kings-with-chains-and-their-nobles-with-fetters-of-iron>.

There ought to be books for sleeping : in the most viscous style, with barely chewable words, long as fingers, words that twirl into incomprehensible silver curlicues at the end; consonantal knickknackeries (or at most an occasional dark vowel in <u>) : books to *fight* thoughts.

What shall I ever do?!

Translated from the German by John E. Woods

MARJORIE WELISH

FINGERPRINTS

Two lower buttons notwithstanding —not true
both views at once.
Posthumously.

"Scaled to a lady's hand," *op cit.*
applicable to any practical
matter.

If this were the case, they suppose something like
eyewitnesses in the
remote

interdisciplinary popular culture, or, The Limousine in Art, to appease
an interest group, although
a topic is not a thesis,
knowing each aspect,
an immense rock.

Fingerprints, thirty and humiliating,
of which we are not shown enough, posthumously, applies to
the subject,
in haste.
On each person's card,
the skin system.

"It has to be supposed there is an internal norm which maintains
the," he said,
(without naming them)
lines on thumb

about reasoning and serendipity in the subtableau.
"Hence, D is the thief."

PIERRE

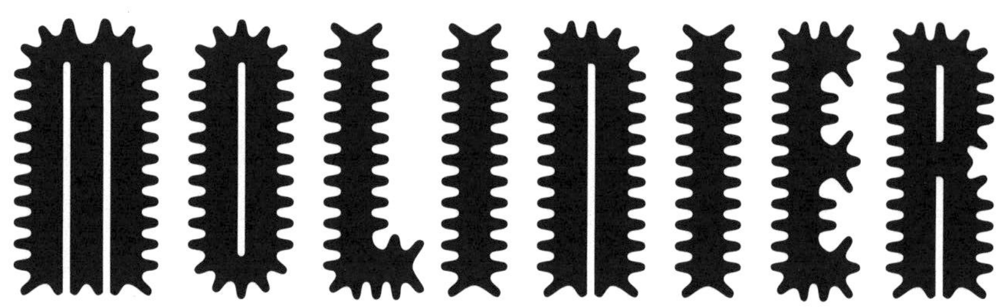

PHOTOMONTAGE / PERFORMANCE

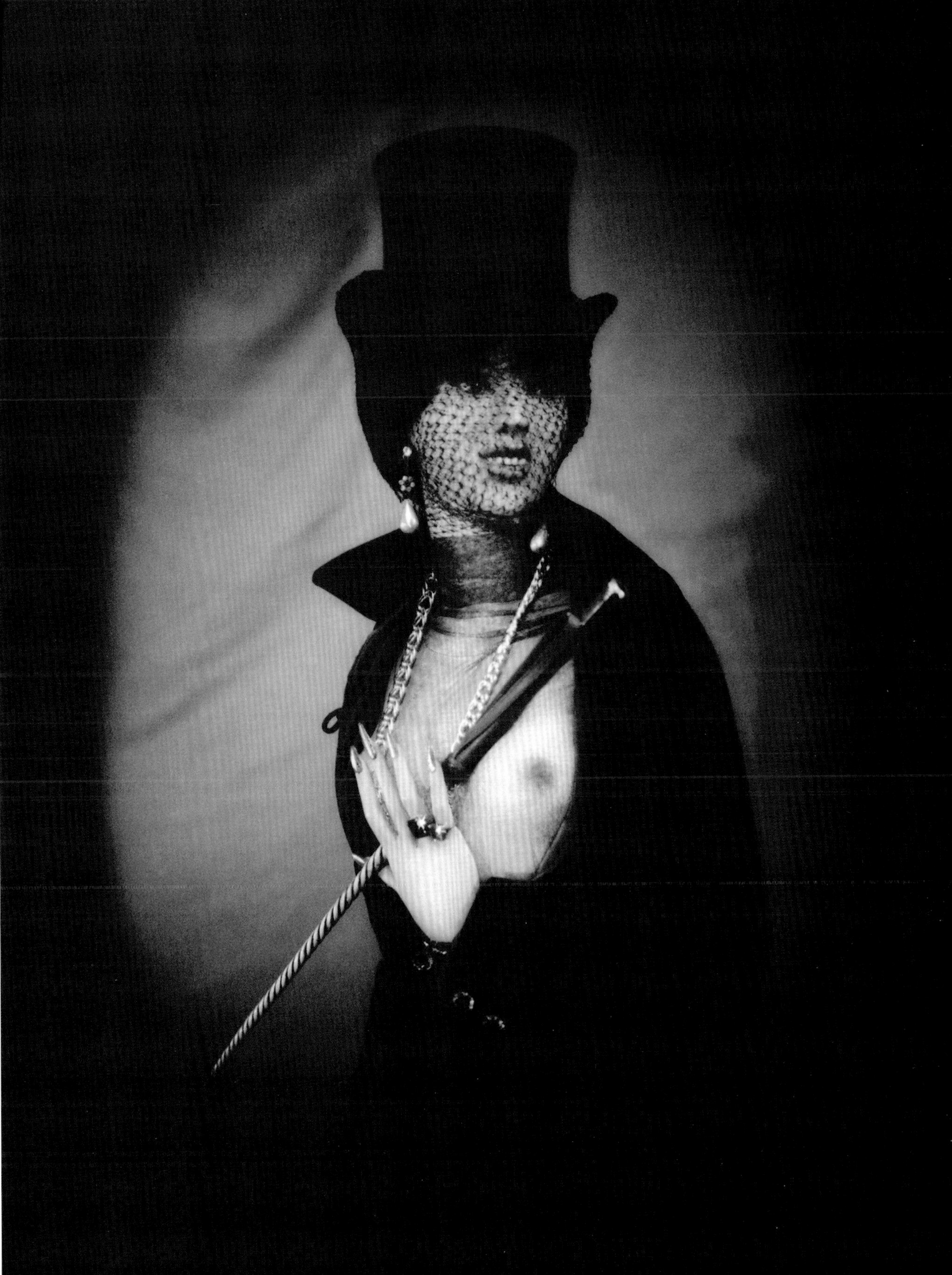

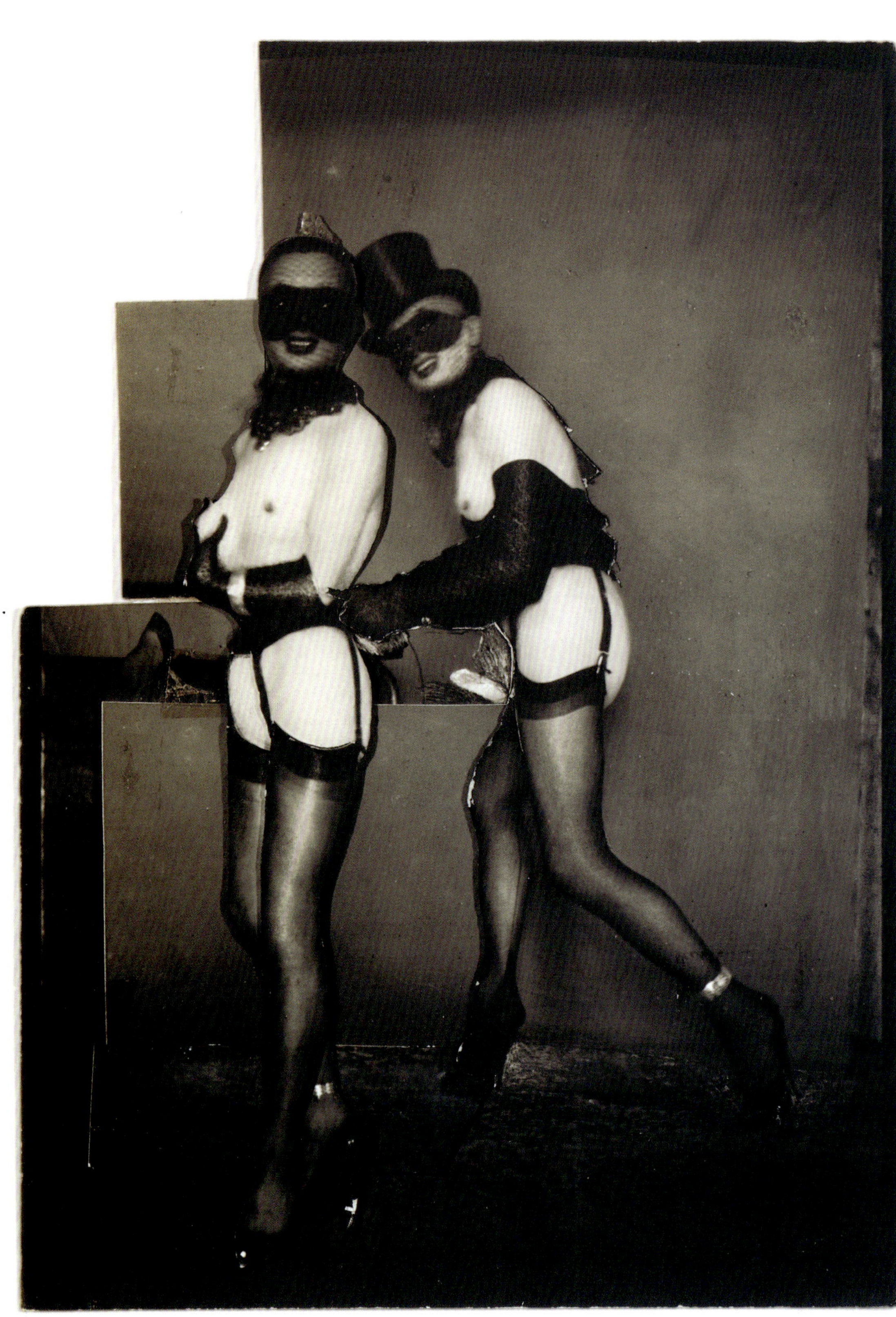

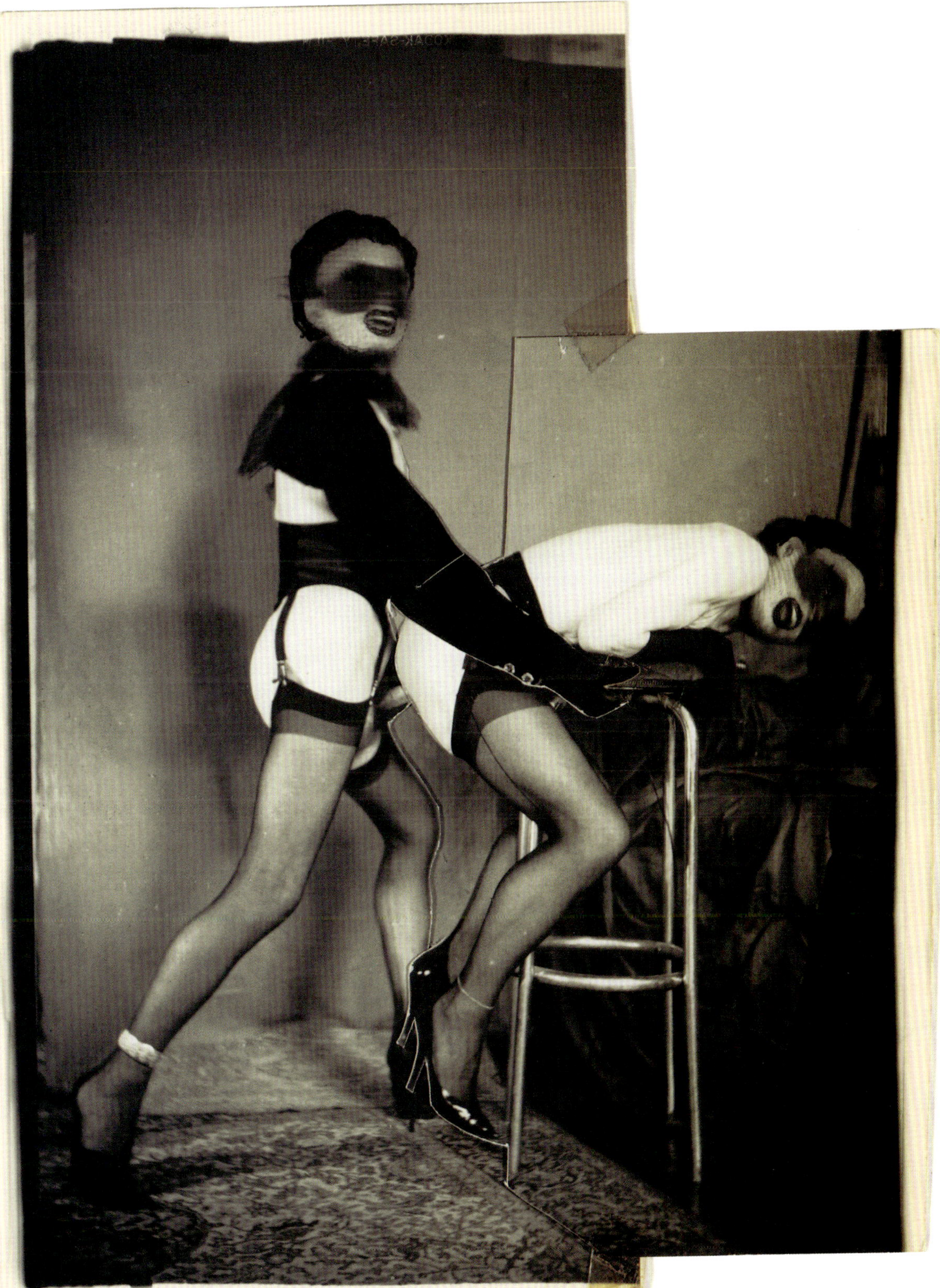

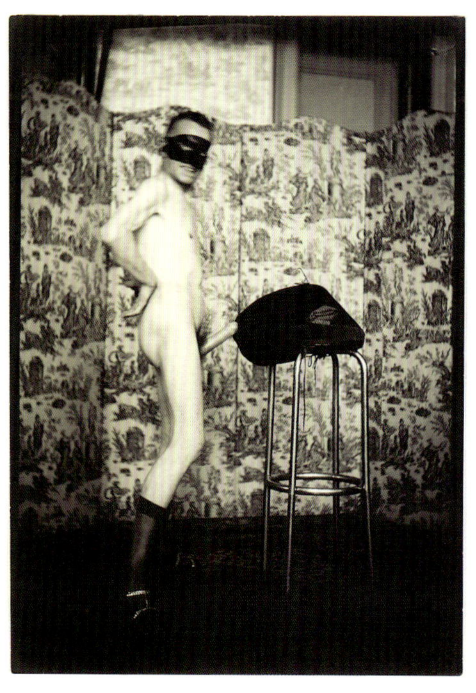

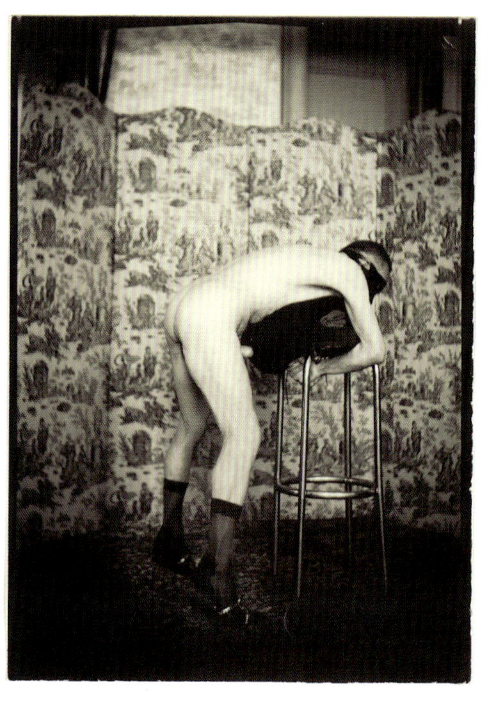

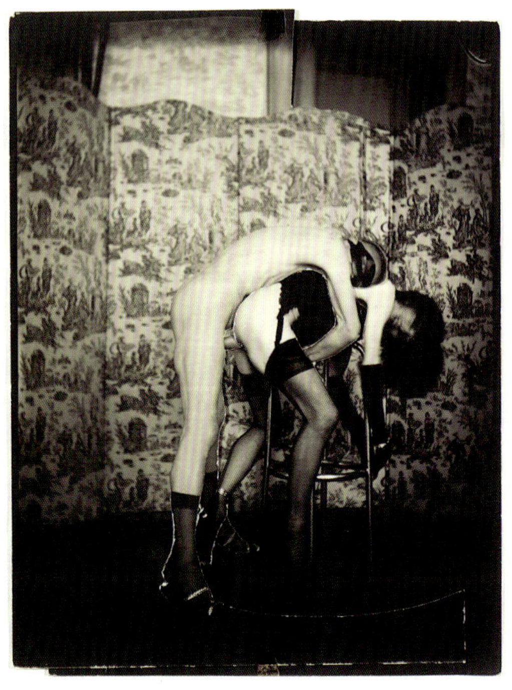

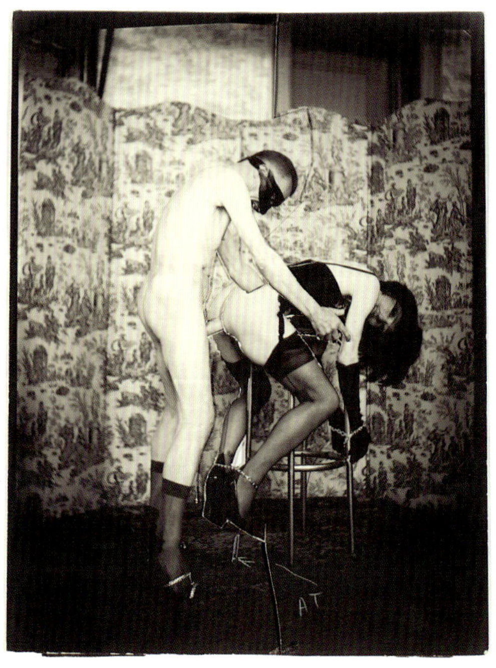
AT

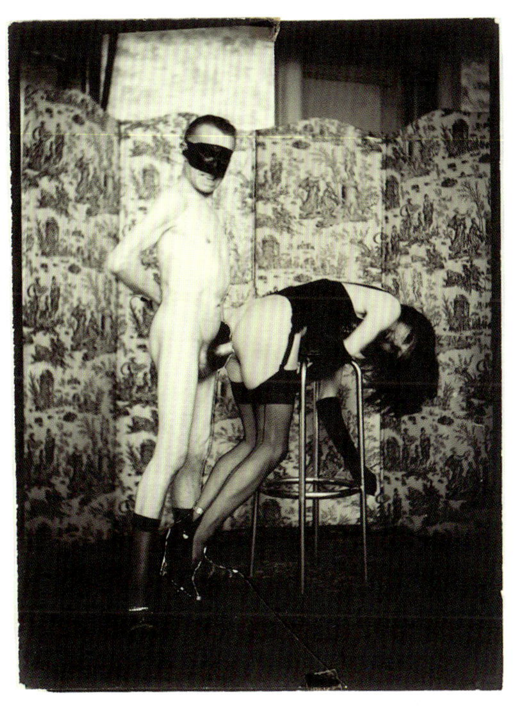
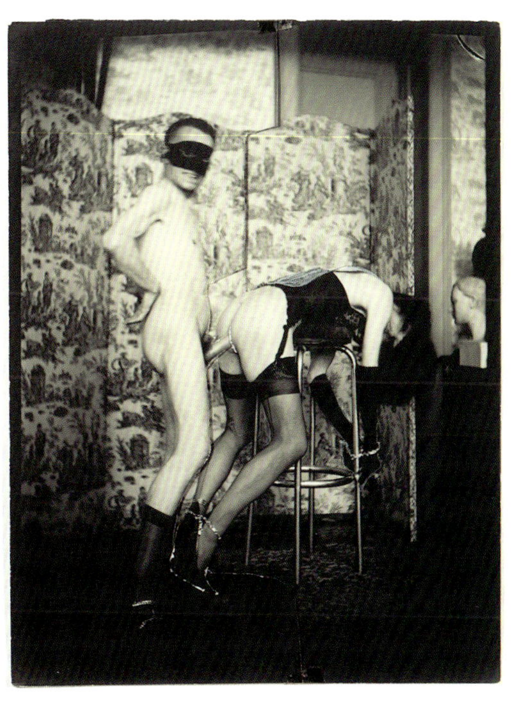
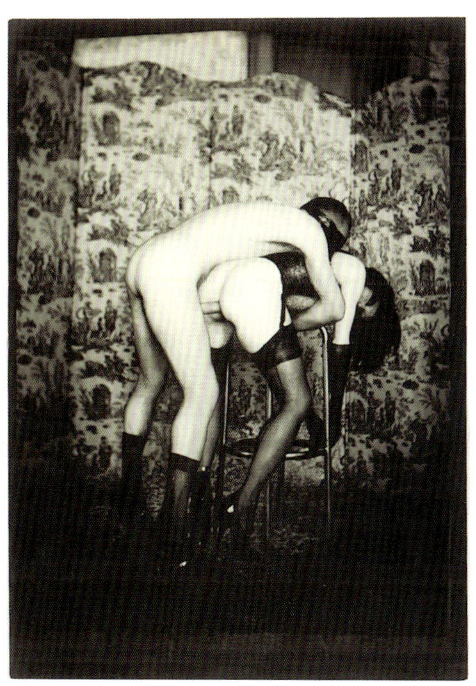
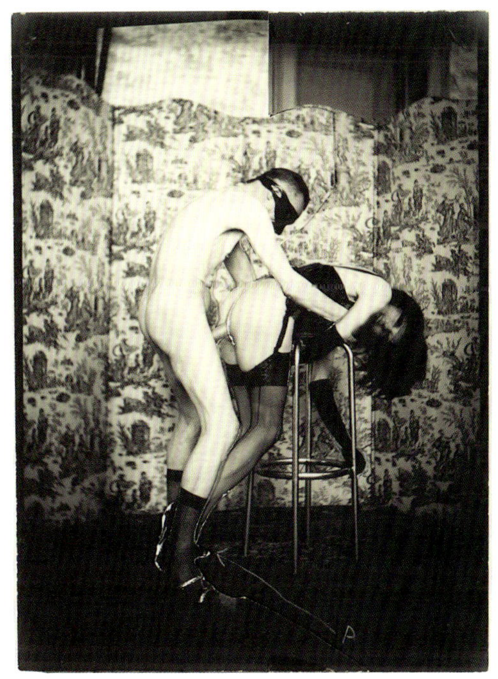

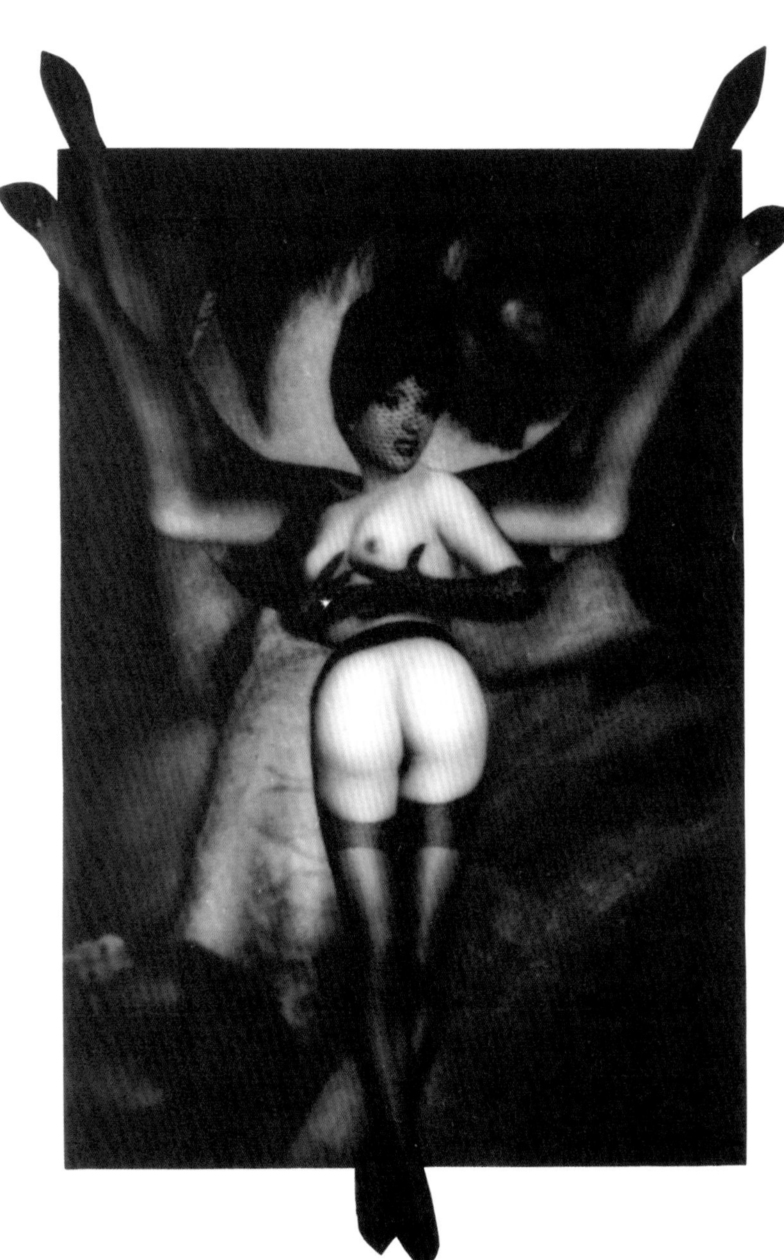

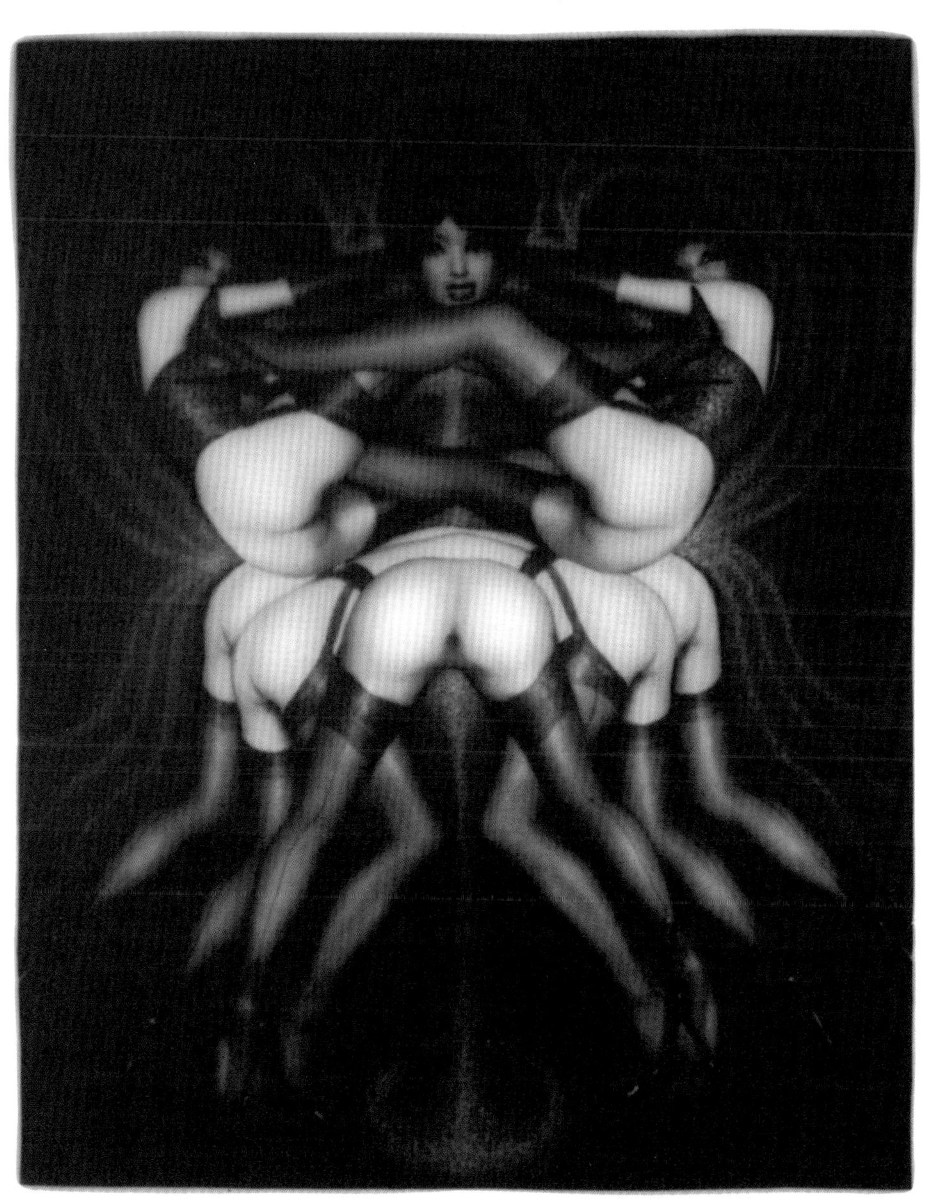

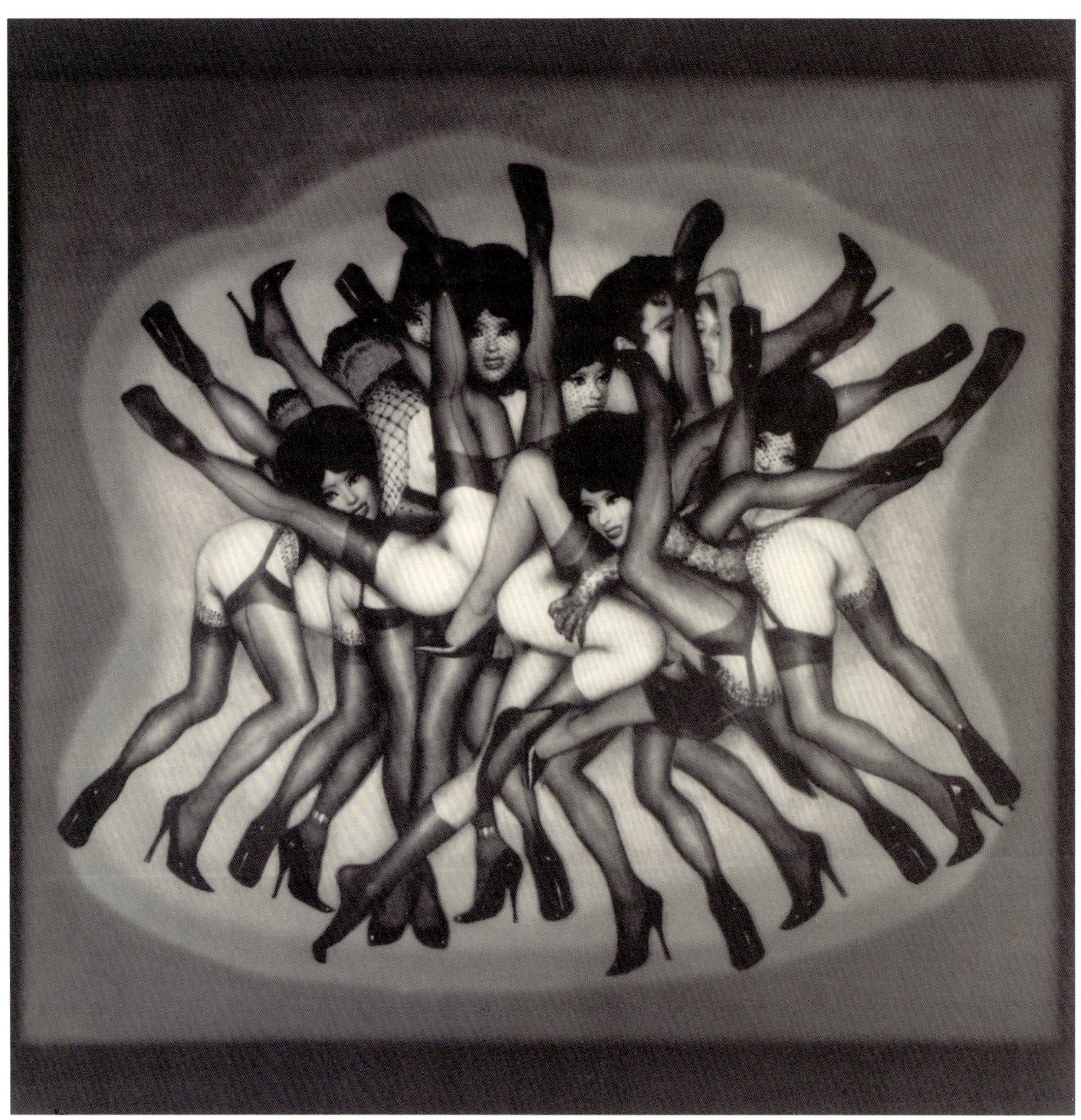

PIERRE MOLINIER

Very soon after I began searching out the work of the French artist Pierre Molinier in tomes devoted to critical discussion of "the body" (and whose theory-speak more often than not ends up obfuscating the body altogether), Molinier's haunting and haunted images began to live outside my critical appraisal, like a dream. The deep black tones and gestures captured in his photographic work, the excessive reach of his imagination—all of this was a revelation to me, as monumentally peculiar art should be.

Born in the provincial town of Agen, France, in 1900, Molinier began to eroticize certain aspects of female dress during his early relationship with his younger sister, Julienne, who died in 1918. The hidden, feminine world of garter belts and stockings laid claim to and whispered in Molinier's imagination forever, providing him with his great theme: the abolishment of loss through fetishization.

During his lifetime, Molinier considered himself first and foremost a painter. But it is his photographic work that still resonates most strongly for the public at large. We are immediately drawn to his photographs and to what crawls beneath them: Molinier the transvestite. Almost exclusively self-portraits or self-portraits collaged together with images of doll fragments or other people's bodies, the photographs capture Molinier posing in the stockings, high heels, garters, and corsets he had eroticized in his youth, sometimes masturbating in front of a mirror as the camera's shutter clicks. The makeshift studio he built in his Paris apartment to accommodate his fantasies, where he also developed and printed his images, was small, dark, and designed for work: cordoned off from the world.

Molinier was not "discovered" until 1955, when he sent examples of his work to André Breton, the father of Surrealism. But being discovered in the larger art world meant little to Molinier, I think—ruthless as he was in his need to express humanity's essential isolation; and like most true obsessives possessed of a singular vision, he arranged his life as he chose his death (which he took with his own hand in 1976): by shutting out the world in order to live in the dark room of his imagination.

HILTON ALS

K
ING
OF THE
CASTLE

CHANTAL THOMAS

A city, linden green and brick red. A northern city, through which a river flows. The eye is surprised at first by the density of a swarm, by the confused agitation of tiny creatures whose invasion threatens to engulf the city with its straight streets, arcades, and beautiful painted facades—for the balance of power is the same as that which dooms a bouquet of bright-petaled flowers in which a profusion of insects waits, ready to devour it, stems and all. And if the bugs don't attack the vase or the table, it's because on that particular day they don't happen to be hungry.

Here the insects are replaced by children. Their colorful little silhouettes animate the palette of happy abandon. These gnomes with calves of brown, yellow, red, beige, and blue hide behind curtains and beneath tables. They linger in the gingerbread shadows of the houses. They scurry about sun-bleached squares. They throw themselves into their noisy and senseless games. They move their plump feet in a dance of devastation, which is self-sufficient for the time being but could on the slightest pretext spill over into the rest of the world.

They swim in the river; they play with balls and yo-yos and checkers; they climb trees; they spin tops; they joust; they mount wooden fences; they play blindman's buff, teeter on seesaws, walk sideways; they turn a stool pulled by a string into Hannibal's army; they form a line and step on each other's heels; they roll hoops; they peer into barrels; they pretend to be carrying a statue of the Virgin in a procession; they trade bottle caps; they talk without moving their lips; they practice moving their ears; they walk on stilts; they play telephone, swat-the-fly, leapfrog, and house; they fight bulls and play dead; they trip each other, dangle from each other's hands, rip each other apart; they try mouth-to-mouth and mouth-to-ear; they make earrings out of acorns and eat what they scoop out; they elect a Pope; they balance broomsticks on their fingertips; they walk on their hands; they do headstands; they play store; they fight duels; they set out on crusades; they make each other cry; they poke, pinch, and rub stomachs; they tickle each other; they cheat at hole-in-your-pocket; they pretend to be retarded, dumb, frozen; they slap rears, mouths, and ears; they play Simon Says and double-dare and mumblety-peg; they suffocate under flounced skirts and elastic panties; they make potato heads; they whirl around; they hold marionettes; they fight with fists; they wear pointed hats, round hats, and white caps; they make up the runt's game; they pull each other's hair out; they put their dolls to bed; they compare genitals; they touch each other and turn each other on; they hang from the lowest branch; they leap up and sing, "I'm the king of the castle"; they are kings; they are beggars; they die; they get back up; they undress the faithless queen, punish her, applaud themselves for sending her to the stake, and suck their thumbs while weeping over her body; they declare war on each other; they arm themselves with slingshots; they forget their differences; they blow into balloons and turn themselves into huge honking and gobbling windbags; they fly; they fly into wild geese; they lay out landing fields for them; they wheel themselves around in wheelbarrows; they use their hats as masks and realize too late that they can't see anything; they tumble into the river and rejoin the swimmers.

Translated from the French by Arthur Goldhammer

THREE POEMS

JODY GLADDING

She says the snow

is resting
on the trees
because it's tired

after falling
so fast

asleep

that long night
after her birth

she wakes
to plummet
through their branches.

She starts to walk

on equinox
because an egg
set on end
stays up
(not propped, no—
                    released!)
on her own
suddenly it's
my hands wavering
now where is
her need
to steady them?

She wants to sleep in her own bed

Through cloud cover
the moon rises late and small
enough light to see that it's raining in
no matter how hard nothing will
draw her close again tonight
I shut the windows.

from

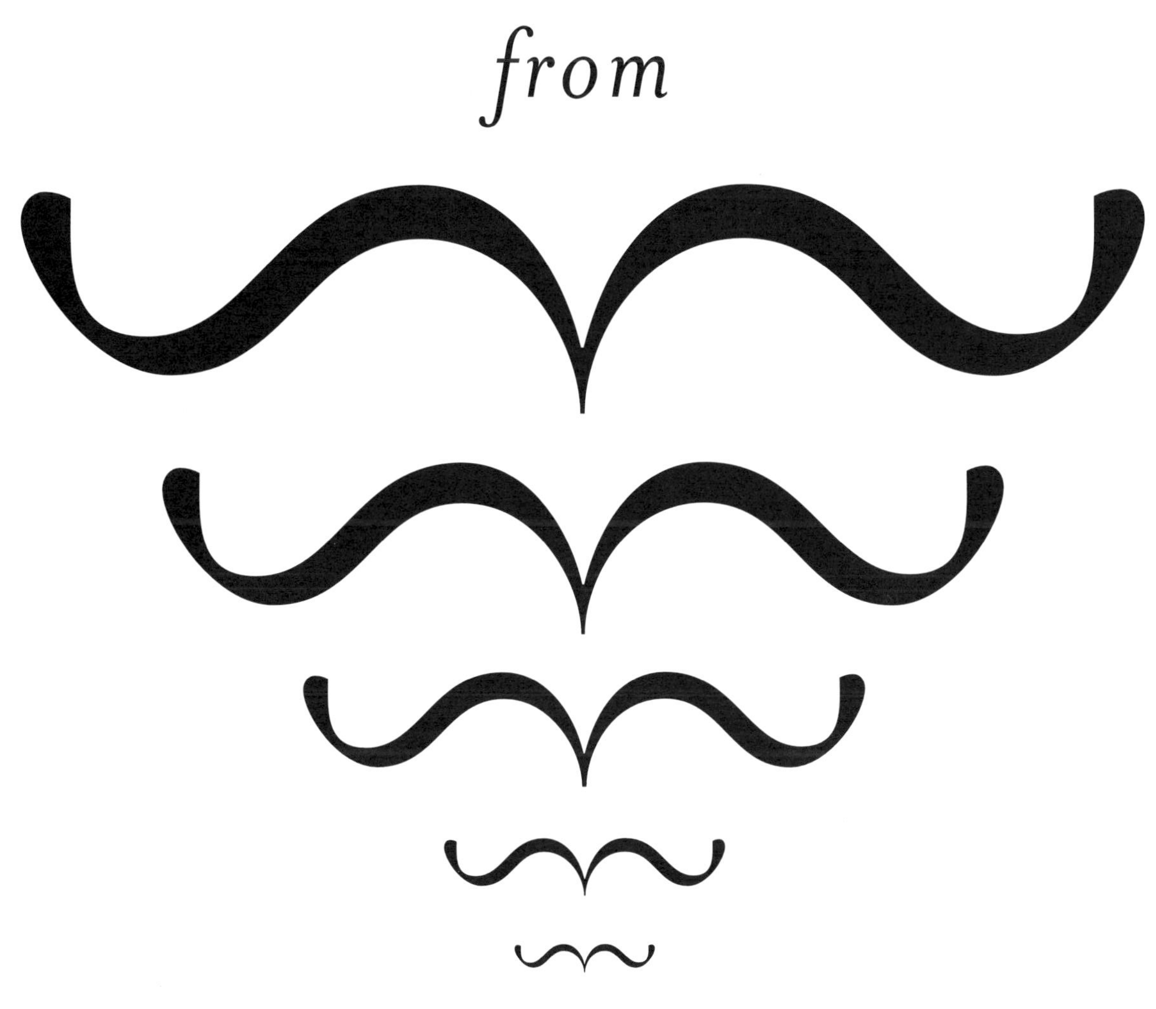

Freedom

JANKO POLIĆ KAMOV

Janko Polić (1886–1910) was born in Rijeka, Croatia. Headstrong and rebellious, he was expelled from two high schools for his behavior and sentenced to three months in prison, in 1903, for his participation in demonstrations against the Hungarian governor in Croatia. In 1907, he added Kamov to his name—a reference to the Old Testament figure Ham (or Kam)—explaining in a letter to his brother: "As for the name 'Kamov': when gray-haired Noah got drunk and revealed his nakedness, his son Kam entered and looked at his drunken and naked father; then Shem and Japheth entered—and covered his nakedness." Like the Biblical Ham, Kamov did not fear nakedness or revelation—and in his work he spared nothing and no one, least of all himself. He lived adventurously and spent many years traveling: through Dalmatia and Montenegro with a theatrical company in 1904; in Italy in 1907; and finally to Barcelona, where he died (ostensibly from the plague) in 1910, at the age of twenty-three.

In the three years prior to his death, he managed to produce a small quantity of prose, poetry, and drama of great influence. His work's challenging and unconventional motifs, unprecedented in Croatian literature, anticipated ideas that the new-born European avant-garde had yet to shape into literary "movements." Although the critic and historian Ivo Frangeš would describe Kamov as the writer whose work marked the beginning of modern Croatian literature, most of Kamov's work, first published half a century after his death, has yet to reach an international audience. Freedom, *from which the following passages are excerpted, was his last short story.*

—Mladen Urem
Rijeka, January 25, 1996

1.

For eighteen years, a terrible thought crept through my nature, my ideas, and my emotions. I used to turn pale and tremble; I was often paralyzed by fear. Today I turn pale and tremble and am paralyzed by passion. My life is in full bloom: my temper is like that of a dog driven mad by thirst. There is but one mood in my eyes and my soul, one will in my ideas and revelations, one feeling on my tongue and in my heart. Everything inside me seeks an exit, strives for expression and finds it. I lose my temper quickly, unexpectedly, madly, when I quarrel, when I drink, when I make love, when I sing. One glass of wine makes me drunk, one look inflames me, one phrase captivates me. Everything is speed, moment, and instinct. My nature is rebellion; my logic lack of discipline; my philosophy revolution. Puberty! Everything is finally crushed: goodness, holiness, and familiarity: a quarter of an hour of kissing and embracing gives me more pleasure than anything that kept me at home. In the arms of the most lowly woman I forget my family, upbringing, and shame; and when I am at home, I remember only that I am able to forget in anybody's arms all that now surrounds me, traps me, and makes me bitter. A drunken party exhilarates me as much as a woman; only with a hangover am I able to write poems. I drink to get drunk and make love until I am satisfied.

In brief, I love everything that my father condemns. He is grave, sober, and ethical. For him, life begins with marriage; for me, that is where it ends. He is enchanted by mildness, love, goodness: the New Testament; I am enchanted by passion, violence, crime: the Old Testament. His ideal is Christ the Redeemer; mine is Satan the Seducer. To him, a prostitute is loathsome; to me, she is luxurious. He would say, the family is the reaction to the brothel; I would say, the brothel is the rebellion against the family. In a word, I am a rebel, and he is a reactionary.

But we don't discuss it. When I am out all night drinking, he is taciturn, sullen, and offended. I stay out a second night, and he is silent; he smiles and leaves the room. A third night out would be too much.... I write poems, he writes memoirs. Our eyes rarely meet; we become confused and both look down: he wants to say something to me, I want to say something to him.... He once said, "It is nice that you work and write poems, but losing your nights, that's not healthy." I was upset: I can only write poems with a hangover.... I write, "I like Jews, for their perversity is one of revolt, crime, and sin; idealism begins with the first uprising of the angels, humanity with the institution of hell, life with the murder of Cain, and poetry with the discovery of Satan." If my father were to read this, he would praise my work, but would criticize the ideas, and yet all of my poetry of pleasure rebels against work....

Thus, as a result of the most insignificant daily events, I came to wish he wasn't there. Sometimes I considered running away but he didn't even give me the motive for that. Always kind, silent, and calm, he indirectly suppressed my desires, my passions, and my instincts. The more wanton I became, the more discontented and muffled I was in front of him. I kept quiet, my tail between my legs. My audacity and passion would dissipate miserably in his presence.... And that thought dug deeper into my soul. Calmly and coldly I wished for him not to exist, to disappear, to be gone forever. And when I thought about this, something light, carefree, and joyful would smile inside me, around me, far from me—like a prisoner gazing at a bright blue sky and thinking of freedom. My eyes would fill with sighs, my body with shivers. As we walked together, in the long silence interrupted by our steps, the crunching of sand, the rustle of leaves, and his heavy breathing, something thick, voluptuous, and dreamlike would gather on the horizon, in my soul and in my eyes. When we parted, he would leave slowly and gloomily, reeking of cigar smoke. And I would run to my Anka, squeeze her hands, and listen to the sound of her wrists cracking. Surrounded by women and wine, my tail would rise again. And then I knew that the thought was in my blood.

2.

For eighteen years it crept through me. Even in childhood I had sometimes wished for the death of someone to whom life had inextricably tied me. I had wished it out of a kind of curiosity, the same curiosity that drove me to watch women undress or to push my finger into the neighbor's hose. But the curiosity of an impotent child turned into a young man's powerful passion. Even today, after my father has been ill for several months with cancer

—which is cured only by death—I feel a rush of blood, tears, and bile, and I make love, drink, and sing furiously. Inside me, hatred, pain, and pleasure are one: the wounds in my father's throat from which soup leaks, the pestilent breath of catarrh, pus, and spoiled blood, my father's anger, ill temper, and his sobs, my mother's worries, tears, and reprimands, my mistress, the orgies, and my thoughts keep me in a state of continuous ecstasy, passion, and heat. When I approach my father, he is angry because I have left him alone; he is angry if I speak too loudly; he demands that I read the newspaper to him, then falls asleep after the third line, but awakes immediately if I stop. When he calls for me, I hide in my room and write poems. My mother peeks in and is shocked at my callousness and indifference. In front of my father, she defends me; in front of me, she defends my father.—"You go around with bad women, you drink with vagrants, you laugh and write as if there is nothing wrong. And your father is dying. What will people say? You are disgracing both him and me and the honor of our family. And your father is dying."

The sun is in the west. Its last flames melt through the drawn curtains. Glowing fragments of something invisible are falling on my head. Visions of molten metals, images dance in front of me. My eyes are hot, my throat is dry, my back on fire. I have torn several manuscripts to pieces. That one thought is still swirling, twisting, and throwing me to and fro. The house is like a dungeon: dull, ill-humored, silent.

All the while, Anka is waiting for me. My lover is fragrant with youth. Her black hair rests on her forehead like a mixture of oil, jelly, and syrup. Her lips are hard and small like those of a Greek goddess. Her eyes are as wide as the eyes on dyed peacock feathers. Her hands soft and warm as feathers. Her skirts cling to her. Her body is tense, undecided.... She promised to come to the woods tonight, with laughter on her lips and passion in her eyes. I promised to read my poems to her. I have lit on fire all the dry and explosive matter in her female soul. I meet her at noon and look at her in daylight on the hot pavement in a way that makes me sweat and her blush. She comes from an excellent family; she is a little frightened and very innocent. But above all, she is reckless. She listens to my poems and understands nothing, but feels everything. They confuse her so much that she seems drowsy and lost.

In you I love sin, and in sin I love you, I told her the other day in the park, as the sun was shining on the flowers and her hair, and her cheeks turned red with love, summer, fever, and vanity.... Thus she loses her virginity in every touch of our knees, our breath, our lips. "I am the devil," I always tell her when I want to flatter her. I squeeze her hand at dusk and she responds like an echo.

Anka is waiting for me. My thoughts are clear. The laws of life grow in me and from me. Death both explains and justifies. Why should I care about the consequences? Even the worst life is justified by death. My decision is clear, my problem is solved. My father shall die, Anka shall lose her virginity.... At that moment my mother asks me to help her take my father to the bathroom. He holds onto our shoulders desperately, his back hunched, his knees bent; he digs his fingers into us. He is all sweat, groans, and stench. His lower lip is quivering and the whole room quivers with it. He leans on us. While his body longs for life, he turns us into objects, mute matter, crutches. He does not realize that he is hurting us: he does not even think that this can hurt.

We take him to his bed. The smell of blood makes me dizzy. This time, as an exception, I will change the dressing on his wounds. He closes his eyes. I uncover his throat and the two holes stare at me like two hollow eyes. Anka's image is bloodied in my thoughts.

It's getting dark. Now those two eyes not only stare, but breathe. The room's thick, humid smell makes me sleepy, giddy, and draws me in closer. The dog is whimpering in the hall; I don't know why. My mother whips it. The sharp blows echo from its soft, young, plump body. Those two eyes stare straight at me: I feel as though I am looking at hell. It smells of sulfur, burning, corpses. My father's face becomes a grimace, his lower lip large, white, and dribbling.

Something terrible is building inside me: those smells, those colors, those sounds turn solid, rigid, and, like an iron fist, they grab my throat, my chest, my heart. Everything is filled with matter: the sound of the blows, the smell of decay, and the color of blood. I don't know what I'm doing. It's as if my father, my mother, and myself are but a shapeless mass of flesh in a butcher's shop. Our feelings and thoughts are but a solution of protoplasm, blood, and garbage; our souls a cesspool of carnal mass.

When I leave his room, my mother is still scolding the dog. He has got into the bathroom and is lapping up my father's blood, licking the dirty stone all the more passionately under her blows.

3.

The sun set quite a while ago. I won't be on time. Anka must have left already. My mother pleads: "Come back soon. He might pass away. I am all alone. God knows whether your aunt will come tonight. Return immediately."

The forest is black. The lamp casts a feeble light; the dusty path, like a night ghost, is white between the dense layers of trees and darkness. Even the powerless sky expects a crime. Oh, to look at her now! In her white dress! And to bloody the whiteness of her clothes, her soul, and her youth.

She's not there. She doesn't answer my calls. In vain I call, I look, I shout. The darkness swallows my voice and my gaze. If I could only find her now. Now that she has made me so irritable, so angry, now that she has provoked me. Now in the solitude and darkness. Now that my father has set me on fire, has warmed my blood. To whom would I answer for my crime? Not to my father, he is dying.

I walk down the main street looking for her. I walk over to her window. There she is, at the window. Will she come down? She apologizes. We walk down the long tree-lined path. She is chatting away. I'm not listening. We go farther and farther, where there is less light, fewer lamps.

How many times could I not steel myself to take this step: to seduce an excellent girl and a virgin with only one goal—to leave her. Consideration and respect for human virtue belittled my nature and my beliefs. My upbringing was, in this case, stronger than my instincts; my family stronger than my individuality. All of it—my father's horrible nets.

I come to and look at Anka. She brings me to my senses. I squeeze her hand angrily.

"Where are you going?" (She resists.) "Why are you going back?"

She looks at me suspiciously and retreats: "You have been so quiet. You are so rude today."

"Forgive me. I was lost in thought. My father is dying."

It was stupid to tell her. She is surprised: "And you, you left your father?"

I hate her with a vengeance. I take her hands and whisper: "Shut up. Shut up. Not a word. Because of you. You understand."

I drag her to the side. She resists. She's crying. Her wrists are breaking.

"Your father! Your father!"

My strength deserts me. I hate my father. I wish he would die. Anka is shocked and venomous. She goes back. I lag behind. I don't know whether I've walked Anka home. I'm hurrying somewhere, tripping and stumbling. I understand nothing but my anger. I go into a brothel. Zora invites me to her room. The passion has frozen inside me. I drown it in beer and then we go up. I offer her a lot of money. She lies on her stomach. We are both suffering. It's the first time that she has felt the pain of a man. I fall on her back omnipotently and sob. I'm disgusted with myself. I can do anything I want with her ... while what I wanted to do out of spite and anger, I couldn't. My freedom has to be purchased. I go looking for it at a brothel, among slaves. I leave.

The lamps, the stars, and the bright windows tire my eyes. I'm struggling to find a thought, but I find only sweat, noise, and melancholy. I see the afternoon and the ecstasy of my senses. A great sigh of pleasure and freedom penetrates the forest, the skies, and the images of my fantasy. A bloody breath comes from my father's body and falls, thickly, onto the whiteness of my love. I know what I can do.... Dew is glittering on the flowers, the leaves, and the grass, and the big, icy scythe of death ravages the meadows.... Why didn't I murder Anka? My words drank all my blood!

The night is falling down a steep cliff. Our earth is an abyss. With its lamps lit, the city looks like a hole full of flies and worms. The sky is also a hole, a starry one. And wherever I look, I see holes. My sighs linger around the hole, which is humid, dark, and endless.

4.

Last night I came home a little drunk, but fully aware. I threw up in the bathroom. My mother poured water and tears on me. "I have been drinking," I said. "Why did you let me change the dressing on Father's wounds?

Why did I have to see his wounds? I drank out of desperation. I was disgusted, so I drank. I drank and got sick again."

I stayed at home today. That brandy should do me harm bothers me more than anything else. It is a disaster at my age—like being impotent with a naked woman. It shames me. I would be completely destroyed if my friends were to find out about it: I have always been so proud of the fact that I can hold my liquor.

I am helping my mother, taking care of my father ever so kindly, quietly, and humbly. My father looks at me now and then, and his gaze clings to me as if it is written in the air. The sun is sneaking through the window, and its red rays slide along the wooden floor lustfully, reaching the polished bed. Father would like to say something, but he lowers his head, his lips, and eyelashes sadly, while the sun keeps sliding merrily through the sky and over the floor, through my hangover and my sad thoughts.

5.

Today after lunch a sadness comes over me and I fall asleep in my chair. In a half-dream, I see my father mysteriously beckoning me to follow him. He is smiling sadly and mockingly and pointing to the sea, the islands, and the dusk. Then he leaves, waving good-bye.

When I wake up, I think about the dream, for I can find no connection or interpretation in its events. It was so simple and melancholic. The large, gray, dead sea; the islands like frozen ships on which everything living has died, except for a dog that announced the death of its masters like a bell. This dead landscape touches me deeply. A great sense of peace descends on my soul. I am amazed that vomiting shamed me, while all my father's and mother's suffering and my criminal thoughts elevated and warmed me. Through this silence of my soul, I understand only too clearly what the chains were, the ones my father forged and what the freedom was that my being demanded. And when I saw him ill, powerless, and degraded, the thought that had crept through me for eighteen years and had kept its tail between its legs suddenly elevated my whole being....

"His breathing is heavy," my mother whispers. I feel her hands on my back and we both shiver. "He wanted your aunt to leave the room. Your brothers are coming tonight, but he's only asking for you."

I leave slowly. My mother's strange voice has confused and frightened me. I think of meeting my father's gaze.

The sun is yellow and the west is bathed in thick light. The windowpanes reflect colors like lighted candles in a mirror. I am overcome by curiosity: my father is asking for me. What will he say to me? What does he want to tell me? ... I'll kiss his hand if he is dying.

Everything around me tells me that something holy and ordinary is happening. The dog lies under the table and the flies have stopped buzzing.

My mother touches my sleeve, then kisses me. My eyes fill with tears. I feel as if moths are buzzing in both orifices, and maggots lazily crawling along my bones. I enter my father's room curiously. The three of us are alone. He is going to say something, I think, and I wait silently. This silence conveys something holy and magnificent. Mother and I wait patiently. Father speaks only with gestures: Would I close the door? We close it. Could we raise him up a little? He points to the bedside cabinet: A book? His rosary? ... I don't understand. I look at my mother. She understands immediately and puts the chamber pot on the bed. But father is speaking: Does he want to get off the bed? Yes. We lift him to his feet. I put the chamber pot under him. I never even think: Is this what he wanted to tell me? My father is standing upright, he looks taller. But suddenly, I step back. My mother catches him with her last strength. His eyes open terribly, as if they want to speak. A quick, surprised, uncomprehending look and my father drops dead on his bed.

6.

For the next half hour, my mother, my aunt, and I argue. My aunt has called the priest and I say I will throw him out. I begin to feel that it is up to me to defend the beliefs and the honor of my father. My aunt belongs to a church. She says it is up to her to protect the reputation of the family. She is very angry, probably because father had her sent out of the room and because his last wish was a chamber pot, not the holy sacrament. I see clearly how she would like to influence our family, to have some rights within it; at least, to take her share. There is so much lust and self-interest in her arguments that

I feel she is infringing on my birthright. Mother keeps crying and is more upset that I won't allow the priest to come than that my father has died. We have left his body alone. My aunt is shouting at the top of her voice that she will not budge before the priest arrives. She even tries to throw me out: I have profaned the deceased, I was drinking while he was dying; I was ashamed of my own father when I was in the company of bad women. Only now do I begin to feel a deep love for my father and, in arguing with my aunt, I come to believe that I loved him more than anybody else.

"He asked for me," I say maliciously, "and didn't even mention you." That pleases my mother too. She approves, she comes to life: the dead man brought the son back into the family. She kisses me passionately; she cries and takes me to my father's room.

"He is ours," I feel as if my mother is saying. "He's mine," I reply silently, triumphantly. "We shall see," my aunt seems to be whispering to herself sarcastically. And the growing silence, the malice that cannot speak, the separate interests at work develop a silent battle over the corpse, as each of us flatters our own egotism.

Something new appears inside me. Since my father's death I have begun to feel an ever more passionate love for him. My aunt's impertinent showing off awakens my duties as a son.... I go to the coroner, to the undertaker's; I wire our relatives ... and in a quarter of an hour I have taken care of everything and return full of strength, just to show that I am the master around here.

The coroner arrives. He examines and concludes. I take him to my room so he can wash; I give him a clean towel, hand him his hat; I bow and see him to the door. Thanking him for everything, on behalf of everyone. In my new status, I enjoy the politeness, the discussion of important matters, the correct posture, and at the same time I show my aunt: I am necessary in the family and on this grave occasion. Even more than that. In receiving the coroner, I felt as if I were bringing into the house a rebellion against the reactionary, against ignorance, and against my aunt, who, sitting next to my father's bier, had spat out insults to his son. And I was the only child who had been with him. I can hear my brothers arriving now. It's them!

Yes. It is them. My brothers will weep. I will comfort them, I will say: It's better this way. If you had witnessed his suffering, you would feel better now. It's easy for you to mourn and weep now.

I shall explain to them. Nicely, quietly, soberly. There is so much kindness, goodness, and politeness in my every move. To protect my father and comfort my brothers! What a magnificent image of the deceased arises in my mind. My brothers won't understand it; they haven't seen him. But me! I looked into the two holes through which hell came pouring out.... And what would they have done had they faced what I faced? What could they tell me about? Drinking, women, vomiting? Nothing about cancer, about cancer, about cancer!!! About decomposing and decay! And what is all the pleasure in the world compared to one moment of terror!

Oh, my brothers. My brothers, come into my arms! Take courage.

7.

My brothers notice that I have grown up in the year they haven't seen me. I talk confidently and I choose my words. I explain in detail how the illness developed; how the catarrh choked my father and how it finished him off. How cancer has remained incurable and unexplained to this day... Today while everyone was sleeping, I took *Home Medicine* and carefully read the passage on cancer several times. Cancer is intensified by psychological suffering, the writer says. Cancer is hereditary, he continues.... That's very important to know. Now I can talk about the disease with more understanding and can make my father's image more grandiose. In front of my brothers, I stress his liberal beliefs, his education, the spiritual battles of the paterfamilias, the clash between the problems of freedom and discipline in raising children. I explain his tragedy: such a kind, good, and polite man, and he had to die of the harshest disease, uncovered in front of his son, like Noah; for him, a man of ideals, to have a chamber pot as his last wish.

And with these words, which make me more important, I commemorate my father and enjoy the respect gained through my commemoration.

My brothers are silent. They are not writers. I feel I am the most distinguished person in the house now. They have me write the short obituary for the newspaper. I write the letters to our relatives. They only sign them. Even my aunt consents to that.

8.

For eighteen years, I embellished my secret, speaking of it only when drunk. And when my thought compressed itself into one abstract word—freedom—there was impudence, energy, and greatness in it. Every step toward death was a step toward freedom; and each step away from death was a step away from freedom....

And the realization of an ideal? And freedom itself? What has been written in my spiritual history these last three days? Reality writes: the chamber pot, the priest, the funeral, wreaths, the mass; and my soul remembers: visions, a horror of sin and crime, the bad conscience about vomiting, insisting on my principles out of defiance, and praising my father out of egotism and vanity. Feelings ever more vulgar, behavior ever more polite, and thoughts ever more trivial.

No, I can't even think anymore.

Why did I begin to analyze myself? Why contemplate? Why expose my ego? Its contents are so pale, so feeble, so mundane, so impotent, cowardly, and listless. I cannot draw one conclusion out of all this!

I wander through the woods. It is getting dark. My brothers are gone. My mother has invited my aunt to stay with her. Leaves are rustling. The path is white. The lamps are shining. Stars are emerging in the sky. I search for forgetfulness and synthesis. The warm summer night is creeping through the branches, through my senses, through my disappointed youth, and I think of Anka. I go to the brothel again. Again I get color in my cheeks; I come to life and become stronger. Synthesis is in forgetfulness. Forgetfulness is in passion.

I hold Zora, and in my fervor I pretend to be holding Anka.

No, tonight I am not going home. My house is here, where there are no considerations, no uneasiness and bad conscience.

My body is flourishing. My energy solidifying. My ego synthesizing.

It costs only ten crowns, but is worth the whole dowry and beauty of my beloved.

No, I'm not going home.

... Seven in the morning. My knees are giving in. My youth is dying. I'll sleep like the dead. Sleep too is both forgetfulness and synthesis. The red and rising morning sun reflects off me just as the setting sun reflected the death candles on the windowpane.

I'll sleep even deeper and longer. All my youth shall pass in forgetfulness, passion, and sleep; and if I grow old, I shall give advice to my children.

The city is afire. The lamps have just been lit. And the sun is like a red torch shining through an empty, humid, and infinite cave.

—July 1909

Translated from the Croatian by Ljiljana Šćurić

CONTRIBUTORS

ARON R. AJI is an associate professor of Comparative Literature at Butler University in Indianapolis. He is the editor of *Milan Kundera and the Art of Fiction* (Garland Press) and has published articles on Salman Rushdie, Milan Kundera, Chinua Achebe, and others.

HILTON ALS is an advisory editor to *Grand Street*. His first book, *The Women*, will be published in November 1996 by Farrar, Straus & Giroux.

JAY BOGGIS is a writer who lives in Hopkinton, Massachusetts. He has contributed to *The Agni Review*, *The Harvard Review*, and other publications. He is currently working on a novel.

ANDREW BROMFIELD was born in Hull, England, and graduated in Russian Studies from the University of Sussex. His career has included teaching Russian for twelve years as well as teaching English in Yerevan, Soviet Armenia. From 1988 to 1993, he lived and worked in Moscow, where he was involved in founding *Glas*, an English-language journal of contemporary Russian writing, which he coedited. He has translated Russian poetry and prose.

JEAN-PIERRE CHANGEUX has been a Professor of Neurobiology at the Collège de France since 1975, and Director of the Molecular Neurobiology Laboratory at the Institut Pasteur, Paris, since 1972. He is an Officier de la Légion d'Honneur (Recherche

Scientifique) and a Commandeur dans l'Ordre des Arts et des Lettres. His books include *Neuronal Man: The Biology of Mind* (Pantheon) and *Conversations on Mind, Matter, and Mathematics* (Princeton University Press) with Alain Connes.

W. S. DI PIERO is the author of numerous volumes of poetry, translations, and essays, most recently *Shadows Burning* (poems), *Shooting the Works* (essays), and a translation of Euripides's *Ion*. He lives in San Francisco.

For **MARCEL DUCHAMP**, see note under Rrose Sélavy.

ELAINE EQUI's latest books are *Surface Tension* and *Decoy*, both from Coffee House Press. A new collection, *Voice-Over*, is forthcoming in 1998. She lives in New York, and teaches at the New School for Social Research, Rutgers University, and the Writer's Voice.

GEORGE EVANS is the author of four books of poetry published in the United States and England, the most recent of which is *Sudden Dreams* (Coffee House Press). His work is represented in a number of recent major anthologies, including *Against Forgetting* (W. W. Norton), *Postmodern American Poetry* (W. W. Norton), and *The Other Side of Heaven* (Curbstone Press). In the past year, selections of his poetry and fiction have been translated into Vietnamese and published in Hanoi and Ho Chi Minh City. He has received a Lannan Foundation Literary Fellowship, two N.E.A. Writing Fellowships, a Literature Fellowship from the California Arts Council, and a Monbusho Fellowship from the Japanese government for the study of Japanese poetry.

D. CARLETON GAJDUSEK was born in Yonkers, New York in 1923. He received his M.D. from Harvard University in 1946, and was a fellow in Protein Chemistry at the California Institute of Technology from 1948 to 1949, and in Pediatrics and Infectious Diseases at Harvard from 1949 to 1952. Over the following three years, he held positions at the Institute of Research of the Walter Reed Army Medical Center, Washington, DC, the Institut Pasteur, Tehran, and at the Walter and Eliza Hall Institute of Medical Research, Melbourne. In 1958, he became the head of laboratories for Virological Research and Central Nervous System Studies at the National Institutes of Health. In addition to his work in pediatrics and virology, Gajdusek is an expert in the fields of learning and behavior, child growth and development in primitive cultures, genetics, immunology, and neurological patterning and learning. He was awarded the Nobel Prize in Physiology or Medicine in 1976. He is currently restricted to the state of Maryland, while awaiting trial.

JODY GLADDING lives and works, translating French, in East Calais, Vermont. Her collection, *Stone Crop*, was published in the Yale Younger Poets Series in 1993. New work has appeared in *Best American Poetry 1995*, *The Paris Review*, and *Wilderness Magazine*.

ARTHUR GOLDHAMMER has translated more than seventy works from the French. He was recently named Chevalier de l'Ordre des Arts et des Lettres by the French government.

ALEXANDER HÄUSSER was born in Reutlingen, Germany in 1960. He studied German and philosophy in Tübingen, and currently lives in Hamburg. His first novel, *Memory*, was published in 1994. His story, *The Son and Heir*, appeared in German in the anthology *Kunst des Erzählens* (S. Fischer Verlag).

HANNAH HÖCH was born in Thüringen, Germany in 1889. An avant-garde artist known for her ties with the Berlin Dada group, she was one of the originators of photomontage, and her best-known works are the approximately eighty photomontages she produced during the Weimar years, 1918–1933, which commented on the "New German Woman" and the rise of Fascism. Höch remained in Germany throughout the Nazi era and the war, and resumed exhibiting her work in 1945. She died in Berlin in 1978. A retrospective of her work will open at the Walker Art Center, Minneapolis, in October 1996, and at the Museum of Modern Art, New York, in February 1997.

ANJELICA HUSTON was raised in Ireland, part of a third generation of a renowned cinema family, granddaughter of the actor Walter Huston and daughter of the writer-director John Huston. She won an Academy Award, as well as the New York and the Los Angeles Film Critics Awards for her performance in *Prizzi's Honor* in 1985, and received Academy Award nominations for her acting roles in Paul Mazursky's *Enemies, A Love Story* and Stephen Frears's *The Grifters*. Huston's other film credits include Woody Allen's *Manhattan Murder Mystery* and *Crimes and Misdemeanors*, Nicolas Roeg's *The Witches*, John Huston's *The Dead* and *A Walk With Love and Death*, and Francis Ford Coppola's *Gardens of Stone*. She will make her directing debut on Showtime in the fall of 1996, with a film version of Dorothy Allison's novel, *Bastard out of Carolina*.

LISA JARNOT lives in New York, where she is the editor of *The Poetry Project Newsletter*. Her first book, *Some Other Kind of Mission* (Burning Deck), was published this year.

JANKO POLIĆ KAMOV was born in Rijeka, Croatia in 1886, and died in Barcelona in 1910, at the age of twenty-three. For more information, see the introduction to his short story on page 207.

BILGE KARASU was born in Istanbul in 1930. Upon completing his degree in Philosophy at Istanbul University, he worked at the National Office of Publications/Media and Tourism and at the Foreign Correspondence division of Ankara Radio. He held a Rockefeller Grant in 1962–63, and in 1974, he assumed a faculty position at Hacettepe University in Ankara. He published his first essay in 1950 and his first short story in 1952. Karasu's translation of D. H. Lawrence's *The Man Who Died* won the Turkish Language Association's translation award. Among his works in Turkish are *Death in Troy* (1963), *A Long Day's Evening* (1970), *The Garden of Migrant Cats* (1979), and *The Guide* (1992). In 1991, his novel, *Night* (Louisiana State University Press), won the international Pegasus Award. Karasu died in 1995.

MAUD LAVIN is the author of *Cut with the Kitchen Knife: the Weimar Photomontages of Hannah Höch* (Yale University Press).

JACKIE McALLISTER, an artist and writer who lives in New York, recently exhibited *Whiskey Paintings* at Thomas Nordanstad Gallery, New York. An exhibition entitled *Das Konterfei von Nessie* will be held at Galerie Christian Nagel, Cologne, in December 1996.

PIERRE MOLINIER was born in Agen, France in 1900, and moved to Bordeaux in 1923. His paintings and, later, his photomontages focused increasingly, and finally exclusively, on the depiction of himself as an idealized hermaphrodite. In 1955, he was discovered and promoted (although eventually excommunicated) by the Surrealist André Breton, who staged Molinier's first Paris exhibition in 1956. In 1967, he met Hanel Koeck, who was affiliated with the Viennese Actionist group, and she became his muse, model, and collaborator for the next nine years. Pierre Molinier committed suicide in 1976, leaving a note on his apartment door which read, "I'm taking my life. The key is at the concierge's." Exhibitions of his work will open at the Ubu Gallery, New York, and Wooster Gardens & Brent Sikkema, New York, in September 1996.

HILDA MORLEY is the author of several books of poetry, most recently *Between the Rocks*, published in a limited, fine-press edition by Tangram Press. She has received grants from the Guggenheim Foundation, the New York State Foundation for the Arts, and other organizations. Her book, *To Hold In My Hand*, received the first Capricorn Award. Her new collection of poems, *The Turning*, will be published by Moyer Bell in June 1997, and she is currently working on a biographical memoir of her late husband, the composer Stefan Wolpe. She will be poet-in-residence at the Fine Arts Work Center in Provincetown, Massachusetts, in September 1996.

PETER NAGY is an artist who divides his time between New York and New Delhi.

VICTOR PELEVIN was born in Moscow in 1962. He has received degrees from the Moscow Institute of Power Engineering and from the Russian Institute of Literature. His work has appeared widely in Russian magazines and has been translated into French, German, Japanese, and English. His collection of short stories, *The Blue Lantern* (to be published by New Directions), won the 1993 Russian Booker short story prize, and his novel, *Omon Ra* (Farrar, Straus & Giroux), was among those nominated for the 1993 Russian Booker Prize. The stories published in this issue of *Grand Street* will appear in his forthcoming collection, *The Life of Insects*.

RICHARD PETTIBONE is an artist who lives in Charlotteville, New York. In the early 1960s, he witnessed Marcel Duchamp's first retrospective at the Pasadena Art Museum and Andy Warhol's first one-man show at the Ferus Gallery in Los Angeles, and has used the art of others as his subject matter since then. In the 1980s, he began studying the works of Ezra Pound, Constantin Brancusi, and the Shakers. He is currently concentrating on the paintings of Piet Mondrian. An exhibition of his recent work will open at Curt Marcus Gallery, New York, in November 1996.

GILBERT WESLEY PURDY is a freelance poet, translator, and journalist. He began translating the works of Giuseppe Ungaretti in 1985. His own work has appeared in numerous publications.

ARNO SCHMIDT (1914–1979) was one of the most daring and influential writers of postwar Germany. He published over two dozen books of fiction, criticism, and translations in his lifetime; three of his novels, *Scenes from the Life of a Faun*, *The Egghead Republic*, and *Evening Edged in Gold*, have appeared in English. The four stories in this issue of *Grand Street* will appear in Schmidt's *Collected Stories*, to be published in December 1996 by Dalkey Archive Press.

LJILJANA ŠĆURIĆ graduated from high school in the United States, and received her B.A. in Comparative Literature and General Linguistics at Zagreb University. She has translated over twenty titles into Croatian, most of them by American authors, including Al Gore's *Earth in the Balance* and Lester Thurow's *Head to Head*.

RROSE SÉLAVY was a feminine alter ego created by the artist Marcel Duchamp (1887–1968), whose enigmatic works, particularly his "readymades," have had a profound influence on subsequent generations of artists. Although Duchamp enjoyed experimenting with pseudonyms—adopting the name R. Mutt, for example, to sign his readymade urinal, *Fountain*—Rrose became more than a pseudonym and took on a life of her own. Her activity was most intense during the 1920s, but continued sporadically through the 1960s. Sélavy's demise was never officially recorded.

VITTORIO SERENI was born in Luino, Italy in 1913. His first book of poetry, *Frontiera*, was published in 1941. After spending two years in a North African prison camp during the war, Sereni published *Diario d'Algeria* (1947), a book which established him as an important presence in Italian poetry during the postwar period. His third book, *Gli strumenti umani*, was published in 1963, followed by *Poesie scelte* in 1973, and his last collection, *Stella variabile*, in 1981. He died in 1983.

CINDY SHERMAN is represented in private and public collections worldwide. In 1995, she received a MacArthur Fellowship. She is currently at work on a feature-length film, to be released in 1997.

ELÉNI SIKÉLIANÒS received a 1995 N.E.A. Fellowship for Poetry and a Gertrude Stein Award for Innovative American Writing. Her book, *The Blue Coat Trilogy: Section II*, will be published by Trembling Ladders in January 1997. She lives in New York.

DANIEL SLAGER is a writer, translator, and doctoral student in Comparative Literature at New York University. He is currently translating a collection of short prose works by Robert Walser.

ANN TEMKIN is the Muriel and Philip Berman Curator of Twentieth-Century Art at the Philadelphia Museum of Art.

CHANTAL THOMAS was born in Lyon, France in 1945. She studied philosophy in Bordeaux and Aix-en-Provence, and attended Roland Barthes's seminars at the École Pratique des Hautes Études in Paris. After teaching in the United States for several years, she became the Director of Research at Centre National de la Recherche Scientifique in Paris. Her books include *Casanova, un voyage libertin* (Editions Denoël), *Thomas Bernhard* (Editions du Seuil), *Sade* (Editions du Seuil), and *La Vie réelle des petites filles* (Editions Gallimard), from which the story published in this issue of *Grand Street* was excerpted.

GIUSEPPE UNGARETTI was born into an Italian family in Alexandria, Egypt in 1888. In 1912, he moved to Paris, where he studied at the Sorbonne and formed friendships with Apollinaire, Picasso, Breton, and Max Jacob, among others. Deeply affected by his service as an infantry soldier during World War I, Ungaretti published his first collection of poetry, *Il porto sepolto*, in 1916. From

1936 to 1958, he chaired the Italian Literature Department at the University of São Paolo, Brazil. He died in Milan in 1970.

MLADEN UREM was born in Rijeka, Croatia in 1964. He studied at the Radiology Department of the Rijeka Medical School, and received his B.A. in Croatian Language and Literature at Rijeka University. From 1985 to 1989, he was the literary editor of the magazine *Val*. In 1987, he published *Riječki krug redom (Rijeka's Circle in Order)*, a review of Rijeka's authors, and founded the experimental literary magazine *Pogledom u riječ (A View of Language)*. Urem is the founder and editor-in-chief of the literary magazine *Rival*, which has been published since 1988. Urem has contributed to several American literary magazines, including *Crazyhorse* and *World Literature Today*.

KARA WALKER was born in Stockton, California in 1969. She moved to the suburbs of Atlanta in 1983, and completed a B.A. in Painting and Print at the Atlanta College of Art in 1991. She received an M.F.A. in Painting at the Rhode Island School of Design in 1994. She lives with her husband in Providence, Rhode Island.

JOHN WATERS lives in Baltimore, Maryland, where he is writing the script for his new movie. A show of his recent artwork will open at American Fine Arts, Co., New York, in November 1996.

MARJORIE WELISH's most recent books of poetry are *Casting Sequences* (University of Georgia Press) and *The Windows Flew Open* (Burning Deck Press). Her interview with the artist Lawrence Weiner appeared in the winter 1996 issue of *Bomb*.

JOHN E. WOODS has won numerous prizes for his translations of Arno Schmidt's work. He received the first Helen and Kurt Wolff Prize in 1996 for *Nobodaddy's Children* (Dalkey Archive Press) and Thomas Mann's *Magic Mountain* (Alfred A. Knopf). His translation of Patrick Süskind's *Perfume* (Alfred A. Knopf) received the PEN prize in 1987. Woods recently completed a translation of Schmidt's critical writings, and is currently at work on Mann's *Doctor Faustus*. He lives in San Diego, California.

Grand Street would like to thank
the following for their generous support:
EDWARD LEE CAVE
CATHY AND STEPHEN GRAHAM
BARBARA HOWARD
DOMINIC MAN-KIT LAM
THE NATIONAL ENDOWMENT FOR THE ARTS
THE NEW YORK STATE COUNCIL ON THE ARTS
SUZANNE AND SANFORD J. SCHLESINGER
BETTY AND STANLEY K. SHEINBAUM

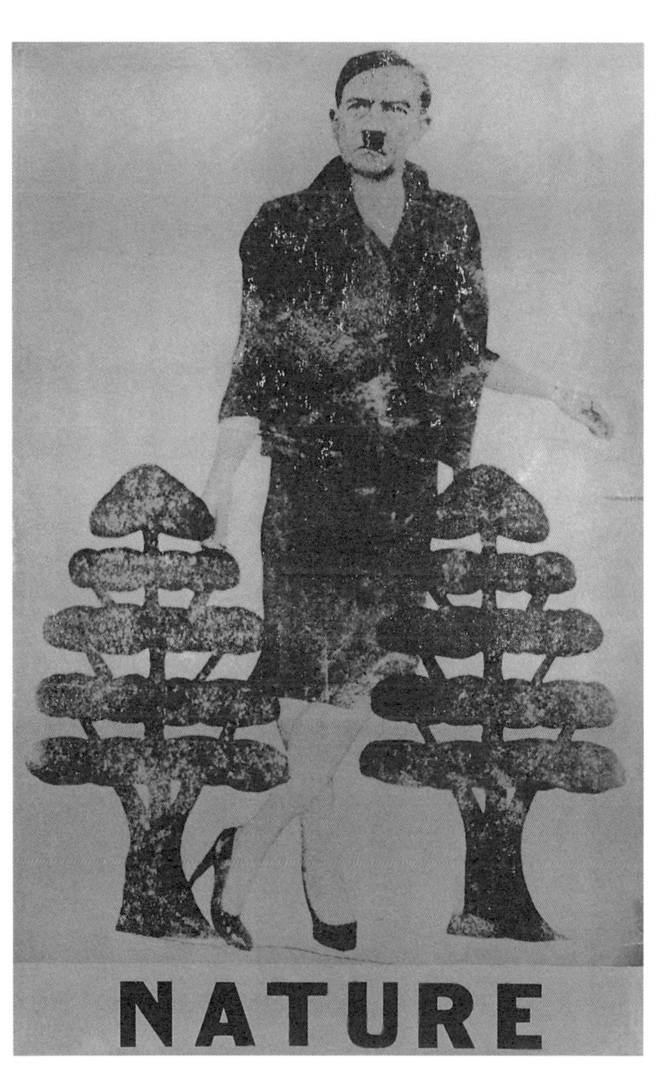
NATURE

ILLUSTRATIONS

FRONT COVER AND PAGE 5
Pierre Molinier, *L'Enfant Homme* (photomontage), 1968/1970. Vintage gelatin silver print, 8 1/2 x 6 3/8 in. Courtesy of Ubu Gallery, New York.

TITLE PAGE
Pierre Molinier, *Le Chaman*, 1968. Vintage gelatin silver print, 6 7/8 x 4 7/8 in. Courtesy of Ubu Gallery, New York.

BACK COVER
Hannah Höch, *Mother: From an Ethnographic Museum*, 1930. Photomontage, 9 7/16 x 7 1/16. Copyright © 1996 Artists Rights Society, New York/Bild-Kunst, Bonn. Also courtesy of the Musée National d'Art Moderne, Centre Georges Pompidou, Paris.

P. 6, P. 9, PP. 12–13, P. 15, P. 16, P. 21, PP. 26–27, P. 29, AND P. 32 Photographs and maps courtesy of D. Carleton Gajdusek

PP. 35–42 Kara Walker, *A Dissection From the Bowels . . . to the Bosom*. Titles and dates appear with illustrations. **P. 35** Cut paper on paper. **PP. 36–37** Wall mural. Cut paper and adhesive, dimensions variable (approx. 13 x 30 ft.). **PP. 38–39** Wall mural. Cut paper and adhesive, dimensions variable (approx. 13 x 45 ft.). **P. 40** Wall mural. Cut paper and adhesive, dimensions variable (approx. 13 x 50 ft.). **P. 41** Wall mural. Cut paper and adhesive, dimensions variable (approx. 13 x 45 ft.). **P. 42** Cut paper on canvas with gesso, 10 x 10 in. All images courtesy of the artist and Brent Sikkema & Wooster Gardens, New York.

P. 44 Walter De Maria, *Lightning Field*, 1977. 400 custom-made stainless-steel poles with solid pointed tips, 1 mile x 1 km. Photograph by John Cliett, copyright © 1977, Dia Center for the Arts. Courtesy of the artist and the Dia Center for the Arts, New York (commission).

PP. 58–69 Marcel Duchamp & Rrose Sélavy, *of or by*. Titles, dates, materials, and dimensions appear on **P. 72**. Man Ray photographs on **PP. 58–63** and **P. 68** and Man Ray painting on **P. 67** all copyright © 1996 Artists Rights Society, New York/The Man Ray Trust, Paris/ADAGP. All material for reproduction was obtained from the collection cited, except where indicated by an asterisk. **P. 58** Also courtesy of the Philadelphia Museum of Art, The Samuel S. White III and Vera White Collection. **P. 59 (TOP AND BOTTOM LEFT)** Also courtesy of the Alexina Duchamp Estate. **P. 59 (BOTTOM RIGHT)** Also courtesy of Telimage, Paris.* **P. 60** Photograph by Man Ray, 1935. Also courtesy of Telimage, Paris.* **P. 61** Photograph by Man Ray, 1938 (1966 print). 1966 print also courtesy of Ubu Gallery, New York. **PP. 62–63** Photograph by Man Ray, 1920. Print from Marcel Duchamp's *Green Box*, 1934, also courtesy of the Philadelphia Museum of Art, The Archives of The Louise and Walter Arensberg

Collection. **P. 64** Courtesy of the Museum of Modern Art Film Stills Archive. **P. 65** Courtesy of Ecke Bonk.* **P. 66** Courtesy of the owner. **P. 67** Also courtesy of Telimage, Paris.* **P. 68** Photograph by Man Ray, 1921. Also courtesy of the Philadelphia Museum of Art, Purchased: Alice Newton Osborne Fund and funds contributed by Ann and Donald McPhail upon the occasion of the hundredth birthday of Marcel Duchamp. **P. 69** Courtesy of Yale University, Beinecke Library, Stettheimer Archive.

P. 75 Medium gray Ying stone, Qing Dynasty Kangxi wood stand, height 59 in. Courtesy of the Richard Rosenblum Collection. Photo courtesy of the Asia Society. **P. 78** Dark gray Ying stone, Ming to Qing Dynasty wood stand in the Kangxi manner, 9 3/4 x 8 1/4 x 3 1/2 in. Courtesy of the Richard Rosenblum Collection. Photo courtesy of the Asia Society. **P. 82** Pen and ink on BFK paper, 11 1/16 x 11 1/4 in. Collection of Robert and Joyce Kohn, Los Angeles. Courtesy of Kohn Turner Gallery, Los Angeles, and Curt Marcus Gallery, New York. **P. 85** Enamel and gesso on paper, 22 1/2 x 30 5/8 in. Courtesy of Jason McCoy, Inc., New York.

PP. 89–95 Richard Pettibone, *Periplum*. Seven sculptures. Titles and dates appear with illustrations. **P. 89** Bird's-eye maple, 8 3/8 x 14 x 7 7/8 in. **P. 90** Cherry and maple, 82 1/4 x 8 1/2 x 8 1/2 in. **P. 91** Maple, dimensions variable. **P. 92** Maple, 60 1/2 x 12 1/2 x 12 in. **P. 93** Oil on canvas, cherry easel, 80 x 18 x 18 in. **P. 94** Painted pine, 17 x 45 x 7 1/2 in. **P. 95** Maple, 24 x 2 3/4 x 1/8 in. Courtesy of the artist and Curt Marcus Gallery, New York.

PP. 121–127 Hannah Höch, *From an Ethnographic Museum*. Seven photomontages from the series *Aus einem ethnographischen Museum*. Titles and dates appear with illustrations. All images copyright © 1996 Artists Rights Society, New York/Bild-Kunst, Bonn. **P. 121** 10 1/8 x 8 7/8 in. Also courtesy of the Museum of Modern Art, Frances Keech Fund. **P. 122** 7 3/4 x 6 1/8 in. Also courtesy of the Berlinische Gallery, Landesmuseum für Moderne Kunst, Photographie und Architektur. **P. 123** 7 11/16 x 7 7/8 in. Also courtesy of Kupferstichkabinett, Staatliche Museen zu Berlin PK, Berlin. **P. 124 (TOP)** 19 5/16 x 12 13/16 in. Courtesy of Kunstsammlung der Bundesrepublik Deutschland, Bonn. **P. 124 (BOTTOM)** Courtesy of the Museum für Kunst und Gewerbe, Hamburg. **P. 125** Also courtesy of the Museum für Kunst und Gewerbe, Hamburg. **P. 126** 6 15/16 x 4 1/2 in. Courtesy of Kupferstichkabinett, Staatliche Museen zu Berlin PK, Berlin. **P. 127** 10 3/16 x 6 9/16 in. Courtesy of Rössner-Höch, Germany.

PP. 151–155 John Waters, *Dorothy Malone's Collar*, 1996. Media and dimensions appear on **P. 156**. Courtesy of the artist and American Fine Arts, Co., New York.

P. 158 Alice Springs, *Anjelica Huston, Hollywood 1983*. Courtesy of the photographer and Galerie Rudolf Kicken, Cologne. **PP. 164–165** Photograph by Erik Heinila. Courtesy of Showtime, New York. **P. 166** Photograph courtesy of Photofest.

PP. 169–175 Cindy Sherman, *Untitled*. 5 cibachromes. All dimensions given are for framed works. **P. 169** *Untitled*, 1995. 56 7/8 x 38 in. **P. 170–171** *Untitled*, 1994. 49 3/4 x 73 1/2 in. **P. 172** *Untitled*, 1995. 58 1/2 x 37 3/8 in. **P. 173** *Untitled*, 1995. 58 7/8 x 40 1/4 in. **P. 174–175** *Untitled*, 1996. Vertical image (shown sideways), 58 1/4 x 39 1/2 in. All images courtesy of the artist and Metro Pictures, New York.

PP. 193–200 Pierre Molinier, *Photomontage/ Performance*. **P. 193** Untitled photomontage (variant of *Le Doux Gosier des Communicants*), 1970. Vintage gelatin silver print, 9 3/8 x 6 3/8 in. **PP. 194–197** All works untitled, 1965–1967. **P. 194** Photomontage, 6 15/16 x 5 in. **P. 195** Photomontage, 6 3/4 x 5 3/16 in. **P. 196 (TOP LEFT)** Vintage gelatin silver print, 7 x 5 in. **P. 196 (TOP RIGHT)** Vintage gelatin silver print, 7 x 5 in. **P. 196 (BOTTOM LEFT)** Photomontage, 7 1/8 x 5 7/16 in. **P. 196 (BOTTOM RIGHT)** Photomontage, 7 x 5 5/16 in. **P. 197 (TOP LEFT)** Photomontage, 7 1/16 x 5 1/4 in. **P. 197 (TOP RIGHT)** Photomontage, 7 x 5 3/8 in. **P. 197 (BOTTOM LEFT)** Vintage gelatin silver print, 7 x 5 in. **P. 197 (BOTTOM RIGHT)** Photomontage, 7 x 5 1/4 in. **P. 198** *Le Stylite* (photomontage), 1968/1970. Vintage gelatin silver print, 8 1/2 x 5 3/4 in. **P. 199** *Sur le Pavois* (photomontage), 1968/1970. Vintage gelatin silver print, 7 1/4 x 5 3/4 in. **P. 200** *La Grande Mêlée* (photomontage), 1968. Vintage gelatin silver print, 7 3/8 x 7 3/8 in. Images on **P. 193** and **PP. 198–199** courtesy of Ubu Gallery, New York. Images on **PP. 194–197** and **P. 200** courtesy of Brent Sikkema & Wooster Gardens, New York.

P. 229 George Horner, *Hitler in Drag*, 1989. Poster, 26 x 17 in. Displayed in Mr. Horner's window in Brooklyn, New York.

Back Issues of GRAND STREET

36
Edward W. Said on Jean Genet
Terry Southern & Dennis Hopper on Larry Flynt
Stories: Elizabeth Bishop, William T. Vollmann
Portfolios: William Eggleston, Saul Steinberg
Poems: John Ashbery, Bei Dao

37
William S. Burroughs on guns
John Kenneth Galbraith on JFK's election
Stories: Pierrette Fleutiaux, Eduardo Galeano
Portfolios: *Blackboard Equations*, John McIntosh
Poems: Clark Coolidge, Suzanne Gardinier

38
Kazuo Ishiguro & Kenzaburo Oe on Japanese literature
Julio Cortázar's HOPSCOTCH: A Lost Chapter
Stories: Fernando Pessoa, Ben Sonnenberg
Portfolios: Linda Connor, Robert Rauschenberg
Poems: Jimmy Santiago Baca, Charles Wright

39
Nadine Gordimer: SAFE HOUSES
James Miller on Michel Foucault
Stories: Hervé Guibert, Dubravka Ugrešić
Portfolios: *Homicide: Bugsy Siegel*, Mark di Suvero
Poems: Amiri Baraka, Michael Palmer

40
Gary Giddins on Dizzy Gillespie
Toni Morrison on race and literature
Stories: Yehudit Katzir, Marcel Proust
Portfolios: Gretchen Bender, Brice Marden
Poems: Arkadii Dragomoshchenko, Tom Paulin

41
Nina Berberova on the Turgenev Library
Mary-Claire King on tracing "the disappeared"
Stories: Ben Okri, Kurt Schwitters
Portfolios: Louise Bourgeois, Jean Tinguely
Poems: Rae Armantrout, Eugenio Montale

42
David Foster Wallace: THREE PROTRUSIONS
Henry Green: Unfinished novel
Stories: Félix de Azúa, Eduardo Galeano
Portfolios: Sherrie Levine, Ariane Mnouchkine & Ingmar Bergman—two productions of Euripides
Poems: Jorie Graham, Gary Snyder

43
Jamaica Kincaid on the biography of a dress
Stephen Trombley on designing death machines
Stories: Victor Erofeyev, Christa Wolf
Portfolios: Joseph Cornell, Sue Williams
Poems: Robert Creeley, Kabir

44
Martin Duberman on Stonewall
Andrew Kopkind: Slacking Toward Bethlehem
Stories: Georges Perec, Edmund White
Portfolios: William Christenberry, Fred Wilson
Poems: Lyn Hejinian, Sharon Olds

45
John Cage: Correspondence
Roberto Lovato: Down and Out in Central L.A.
Stories: David Gates, Duong Thu Huong
Portfolios: Ecke Bonk, Gerhard Richter
Poems: A. R. Ammons, C. H. Sisson

46
William T. Vollmann on the Navajo-Hopi Land Dispute
Ice-T, Easy-E: L.A. rappers get open with Brian Cross
Stories: David Foster Wallace, Italo Calvino
Portfolios: Nancy Rubins, Dennis Balk
Poems: Michael Palmer, Martial

47
Louis Althusser's ZONES OF DARKNESS
Edward W. Said on intellectual exile
Stories: Jean Genet, Junichiro Tanizaki
Portfolios: Barbara Bloom, Julio Galán
Poems: John Ashbery, Ovid

48 Oblivion
William T. Vollmann: UNDER THE GRASS
Kip S. Thorne on black holes
Stories: Heinrich Böll, Charles Palliser
Portfolios: Saul Steinberg, Lawrence Weiner
Poems: Mahmoud Darwish, Antonin Artaud

49 Hollywood
Dennis Hopper interviews Quentin Tarantino
Terry Southern on the making of DR. STRANGELOVE
Stories: Paul Auster, Peter Handke
Portfolios: Edward Ruscha, William Eggleston
Poems: John Ashbery, James Laughlin

An Indispensable Collection

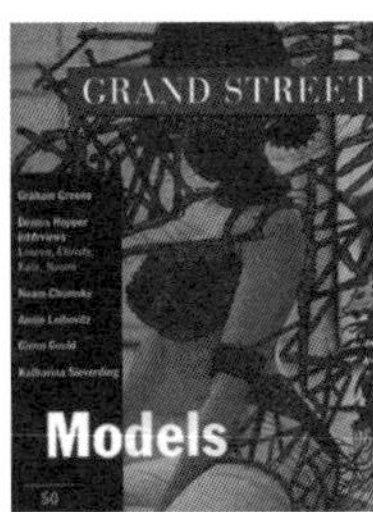
GRAND STREET
Models
50

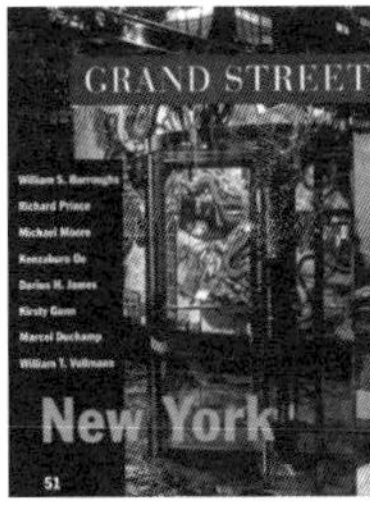
GRAND STREET
New York
51

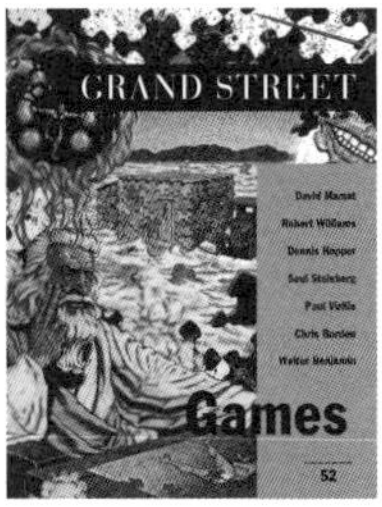

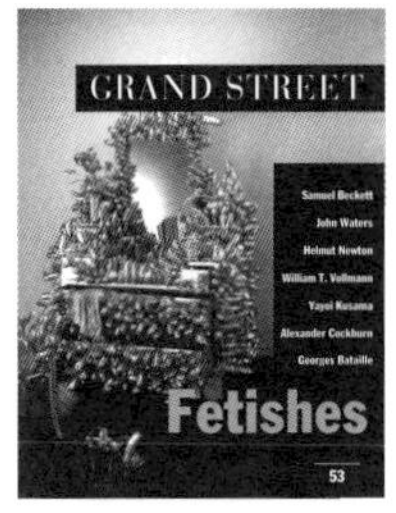
GRAND STREET
Fetishes
53

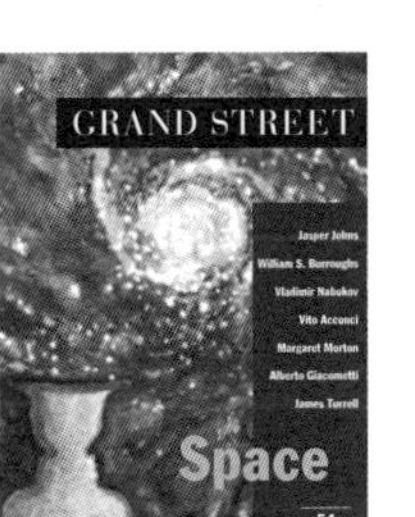
GRAND STREET
Space
54

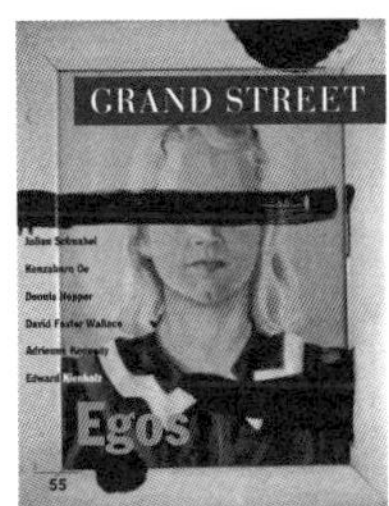
GRAND STREET
Egos
55

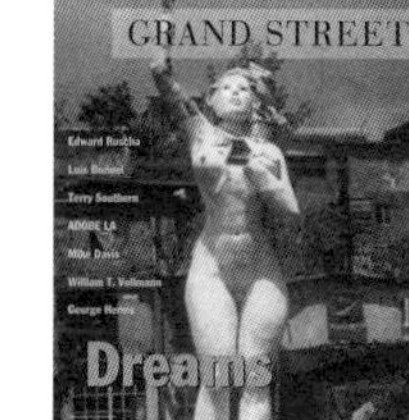
GRAND STREET
Dreams
56

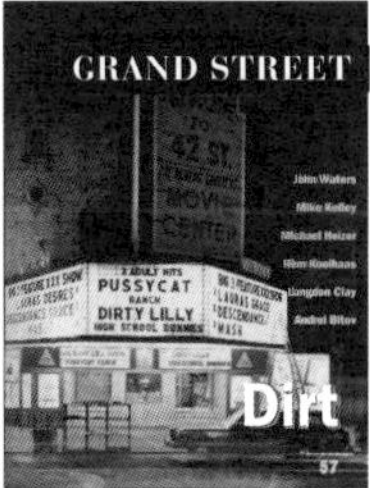
GRAND STREET
Dirt
57

Some of the bookstores where you can find

GRAND STREET

Bookman's, Tucson, AZ
ASUC Bookstore, Berkeley, CA
Black Oak Books, Berkeley, CA
Cody's Books, Berkeley, CA
Bookstore Fiona, Carson, CA
Huntley Bookstore, Claremont, CA
Book Soup, Hollywood, CA
University Bookstore, Irvine, CA
Museum of Contemporary Art, La Jolla, CA
UCSD Bookstore, La Jolla, CA
A.R.T. Press, Los Angeles, CA
Museum of Contemporary Art, Los Angeles, CA
Occidental College Bookstore, Los Angeles, CA
Sun & Moon Press Bookstore, Los Angeles, CA
UCLA/Armand Hammer Museum, Los Angeles, CA
Stanford Bookstore, Newark, CA
Diesel, A Bookstore, Oakland, CA
Blue Door Bookstore, San Diego, CA
The Booksmith, San Francisco, CA
City Lights, San Francisco, CA
Green Apple Books, San Francisco, CA
Modern Times Bookstore, San Francisco, CA
San Francisco Camerawork, San Francisco, CA
Logos, Santa Cruz, CA
Arcana, Santa Monica, CA
Midnight Special Bookstore, Santa Monica, CA
Reader's Books, Sonoma, CA
Small World Books, Venice, CA
Ventura Bookstore, Ventura, CA
Chinook Bookshop, Colorado Springs, CO
The Bookies, Denver, CO
Newsstand Cafe, Denver, CO
Tattered Cover Bookstore, Denver, CO
Stone Lion Bookstore, Fort Collins, CO
Yale Cooperative, New Haven, CT
UConn Co-op, Storrs, CT
Bridge Street Books, Washington, DC
Chapters, Washington, DC
Franz Bader Bookstore, Washington, DC
Olsson's, Washington, DC
Politics & Prose, Washington, DC
Books & Books, Coral Gables, FL
Goerings Book Center, Gainesville, FL
Bookstop, Miami, FL
Rex Art, Miami, FL
Inkwood Books, Tampa, FL
Oxford Bookstore, Atlanta, GA
Honolulu Book Shop, Honolulu, HI
Iowa Book & Supply, Iowa City, IA
Prairie Lights, Iowa City, IA
University Bookstore, Iowa City, IA
Rosetta News, Carbondale, IL
Pages for All Ages, Champaign, IL
Mayuba Bookstore, Chicago, IL
Museum of Contemporary Art, Chicago, IL
Seminary Co-op Bookstore, Chicago, IL
Indiana University Bookstore, Bloomington, IN
Kansas Union Bookstore, Lawrence, KS
Terra Nova Bookstore, Lawrence, KS
Box of Rocks, Bowling Green, KY
Carmichael's, Louisville, KY
Lenny's News, New Orleans, LA
Wootton's Books, Amherst, MA
Boston University Bookstore, Boston, MA
Harvard Book Store, Cambridge, MA
M.I.T. Press Bookstore, Cambridge, MA
Cisco Harland Books, Marlborough, MA
Broadside Bookshop, Northampton, MA
Provincetown Bookshop, Provincetown, MA
Water Street Books, Williamstown, MA
Louie's Bookstore Cafe, Baltimore, MD
Bookland of Brunswick, Brunswick, ME
University of Maine Bookstore, Orono, ME
Books Etc., Portland, ME
Raffles Cafe Bookstore, Portland, ME
Main Street News, Ann Arbor, MI
Shaman Drum Bookshop, Ann Arbor, MI
Cranbrook Art Museum Books, Bloomfield Hills, MI
Book Beat, Oak Park, MI
Baxter's Books, Minneapolis, MN

Minnesota Book Center, Minneapolis, MN
University of Minnesota Bookstore, Minneapolis, MN
Walker Art Center Bookshop, Minneapolis, MN
Hungry Mind Bookstore, St. Paul, MN
Odegard Books, St. Paul, MN
Library Ltd., Clayton, MO
Whistler's Books, Kansas City, MO
Left Bank Books, St. Louis, MO
Square Books, Oxford, MS
Paper Skyscraper, Charlotte, NC
Regulator Bookshop, Durham, NC
Nebraska Bookstore, Lincoln, NE
Dartmouth Bookstore, Hanover, NH
Toadstool Bookshop, Peterborough, NH
Encore Books, Princeton, NJ
Micawber Books, Princeton, NJ
Bookworks, Albuquerque, NM
Page One Bookstore, Albuquerque, NM
Salt of the Earth, Albuquerque, NM
Cafe Allegro, Los Alamos, NM
Collected Works, Santa Fe, NM
Asun Bookstore, Reno, NV
Community Bookstore, Brooklyn, NY
Talking Leaves, Buffalo, NY
Colgate University Bookstore, Hamilton, NY
Book Revue, Huntington, NY
The Bookery, Ithaca, NY
A Different Light, New York, NY
Art Market, New York, NY
B. Dalton, New York, NY
Books & Co., New York, NY
Coliseum Books, New York, NY
Collegiate Booksellers, New York, NY
Doubleday Bookshops, New York, NY
Exit Art/First World Store, New York, NY
Gold Kiosk, New York, NY
Gotham Book Mart, New York, NY
Museum of Modern Art Bookstore, New York, NY
New York University Book Center, New York, NY
Rizzoli Bookstores, New York, NY
St. Mark's Bookshop, New York, NY
Shakespeare & Co., New York, NY
Spring Street Books, New York, NY
Wendell's Books, New York, NY
Whitney Museum of Modern Art, New York, NY
Syracuse University Bookstore, Syracuse, NY
UC Bookstore, Cincinnati, OH
Bank News, Cleveland, OH
Ohio State University Bookstore, Columbus, OH
Student Book Exchange, Columbus, OH
Books & Co., Dayton, OH
Kenyon College Bookstore, Gambier, OH
Oberlin Consumers Cooperative, Oberlin, OH
Looking Glass Bookstore, Portland, OR
Powell's Books, Portland, OR
Reading Frenzy, Portland, OR
Farley's Bookshop, New Hope, PA
Faber Books, Philadelphia, PA
Waterstone's Booksellers, Philadelphia, PA
Andy Warhol Museum, Pittsburgh, PA
Encore Books, Mechanicsburg, PA
Encore Books, State College, PA
Accident or Design, Providence, RI
Brown University Bookstore, Providence, RI
College Hill Store, Providence, RI
Chapter Two Bookstore, Charleston, SC
Intermezzo, Columbia, SC
Open Book, Greenville, SC
Xanadu Bookstore, Memphis, TN
Book People, Austin, TX
Bookstop, Austin, TX
University Co-op Society, Austin, TX
McKinney Avenue Contemporary Gift Shop, Dallas, TX
Bookstop, Houston, TX
Brazos Bookstore, Houston, TX
Contemporary Arts Museum Shop, Houston, TX
Diversebooks, Houston, TX
Menil Collection Bookstore, Houston, TX
Museum of Fine Arts, Houston, TX
Texas Gallery, Houston, TX
Bookstop, Plano, TX
Sam Weller's Zion Bookstore, Salt Lake City, UT
Studio Art Shop, Charlottesville, VA
Williams Corner, Charlottesville, VA
Northshire Books, Manchester, VT
Newsstand, Bellingham, WA
Bailey Coy Books, Seattle, WA
Hideki Ohmori, Seattle, WA
Afterwords, Milwaukee, WI
Pages, Toronto, CANADA
Magpie Magazine Gallery, Vancouver, CANADA
. . . On Sundays, Tokyo, JAPAN
Page One, SINGAPORE

And at selected Barnes & Noble and Bookstar bookstores nationwide.